Praise for MAAME

'Lively, funny, poignant . . . Prepare to fall in love with Maddie. I did!'
BONNIE GARMUS, *Sunday Times* bestselling author of *Lessons in Chemistry*

'Utterly charming and deeply moving . . . Maddie's journey will resonate with anyone who's had to grow up – or who's still trying to'
CELESTE NG, *New York Times* bestselling author of *Our Missing Hearts*

'Honest, warm, heart-breaking and heart-healing. It felt truly modern, yet somehow timeless. I adored it'
NIKKI MAY, author of *Wahala*

'A poignant coming-of-age tale about finding strength, hope and courage . . . Maame's quiet confidence is true to life and liberating'
LIZZIE DAMILOLA BLACKBURN, author of *Yinka, Where is Your Huzband?*

'Meeting Maame feels like falling in love for the first time: warm, joyous, a little bit heartbreaking and, most of all, unforgettable'
XOCHITL GONZALEZ *New York Times* bestselling author of *Olga Dies Dreaming*

'I loved every page of this beautiful, heartwarming, empowering book. An exceptional debut from an incredibly exciting new talent'
BETH O'LEARY, *Sunday Times Bestselling* author of *The Flatshare*

MAAME

JESSICA GEORGE

HODDER &
STOUGHTON

First published in Great Britain in 2023 by Hodder & Stoughton
An Hachette UK company

1

A CIP catalogue record for this title is available from the British Library

Hardback ISBN 978 1 52939 557 0
Trade Paperback ISBN 978 1 52939 558 7
eBook ISBN 978 1 52939 559 4

Typeset in Sabon MT by Hewer Text UK Ltd, Edinburgh
Printed and bound in Great Britain by Clays Ltd, Elcograf S.p.A.

Hodder & Stoughton policy is to use papers that are natural, renewable
and recyclable products and made from wood grown in sustainable
forests. The logging and manufacturing processes are expected to
conform to the environmental regulations of the country of origin.

Hodder & Stoughton Ltd
Carmelite House
50 Victoria Embankment
London EC4Y 0DZ

www.hodder.co.uk

For Dad

MAAME

(Ma-meh)

Chapter One

In African culture— Wait, no, I don't want to be presumptuous or in any way nationalistic enough to assume certain Ghanaian customs run true in other African countries. I might in fact just be speaking of what passes as practice in *my* family, but regardless of who the mores belong to, I was raised to keep family matters private. So if my dad has his own bedroom or my mum goes abroad for inexplicable lengths of time, it's common knowledge within our household that we keep that business, and all matters like it, to ourselves. 'They just won't understand, you know? We're Ghanaian, so we do things differently.'

Growing up, school dynamics, books and shows on TV told me that best friends tell each other everything. It was almost the sole requirement, but I had to bend this rule, knowing that the pieces of information I withheld meant I could never truly qualify as anyone's best friend, not when no one really *knew* me.

Even now, none of my friends – helpfully, I don't have many – know that every weekday I start the morning the same way. I wake up five minutes before my alarm and wait for it to go off at 6 a.m. I blink away any sticky traces of the night and tread silently downstairs, past my dad's bedroom – now relocated to the ground floor – and into the kitchen. I close the door to restrict travelling noise and pour myself a bowl of cornflakes, eating a spoonful at a time as I move around the kitchen.

It's a small, functional area with a gas stove (in desperate need of cleaning, but I assign that task to tomorrow evening), an oven with a missing grill door, a tall fridge, a smaller freezer filled with various unidentified let-me-not-waste-this food pieces (sorting through assigned to Saturday afternoon) and a washing machine that dances out from under the countertop when it's on, but when empty is just light enough to push back with the weight of my body. Said countertops are a white-speckled dark grey with a dull sheen that I think is meant to trick you into believing it's marble.

I take a container of lunch from the batch I made on Sunday for myself, then cook pasta for Dad's lunch and leave it covered in the microwave. The rice I make for his dinner goes on a shelf in the cold oven. I cut up oranges for both our snacks – *Should I save the strawberries for tomorrow?* I tap my nails on the kitchen counter, considering the expiry date. *Nah, go for it* – and leave Dad's in a covered bowl, packing mine into another container.

None of my friends know it's when I'm out of the shower that I hear Dad's carer Dawoud come in. Today he's on the phone, likely to his wife in Yemen where he's from – he told me about her once. She's supposedly very beautiful.

Dawoud is a bit of a giant, well over six feet and only a little round in the middle, with grey hair on his head and several strands escaping from his ears. A smoker in his sixties, he has a loud but hoarse voice. My dad's fifty-seven, has never smoked and stopped drinking years ago. Age is a terrifyingly inconsistent beast.

I cream my skin and pull out my Tuesday dress, navy, short-sleeved, loose-fitted and below my knees, because no one in the office wears jeans. I tune in to a prayer channel Mum likes to randomly quiz me on, whilst pulling on black tights and inserting two gold studs that were passed down to me into my ears. I set a reminder to call Doctor Appong, my dad's GP for the last three years, at lunch for Dad's swollen feet, and look through my emails to find that we don't qualify for a council tax reduction.

Downstairs, Dawoud is in the kitchen making toast, and tomorrow will be porridge because the two meals alternate on weekdays. I walk into the living room and tell Dad, 'I'll make you pancakes on Saturday.'

'Oh, goody,' he says smiling, but he won't remember the pancakes until I feed them to him on Saturday morning. That's how his Parkinson's works. He can remember constant, repetitive things, like mine and Dawoud's presence, but short-term details won't sit in his brain for very long. They literally go through one ear, settle long enough for him to reply, then go out the other. Some days his medication will assist, but other days I think the meds are too busy tackling his swollen joints or his shaking hands, his high-blood pressure or his difficulty speaking, to lend a hand.

I have a picture of my parents taken in September 1984 and in it Dad is tall and handsome with an Afro and a silver chunky bracelet he still wears to this day. Whenever I look at that photo, I think of my last day at college, eight years ago. My year were having a party thrown in a bar, our equivalent of a prom, I guess. I didn't end up going even though I was asked. By Connor . . . no, Charlie, the quiet guy in my maths class that I had no idea even liked me. I did say yes; I bought a dress, but then I had to cancel on the day.

Poor Charlie. An hour before I texted him to say I couldn't make it, my dad received his diagnosis: Parkinson's disease.

We'd all been quick to blame the ageing process for his 'clumsiness' or short-term memory. I mean, we've all put our keys down and then declared them missing two minutes later, so who were we to judge? But then one evening, Dad got lost.

I was back from school and the only one at home when he called the landline.

'Madeleine? Maddie,' he said. 'I think . . . I don't know where I am.'

It wasn't what he said that made me grip the phone tighter; we live in London: easy to get lost, but easy to find your way back. No, it was the fear in Dad's voice that got to me. Over the course of my life, Dad had shown himself to be many things, but *afraid* was never one of them.

I made him pass the phone to a nearby woman, who explained that he was only ten minutes down the road.

'Are you sure?' I asked her.

'We're definitely on Spar Lane,' she said. 'I live here.'

I knew then that Dad hadn't simply fallen asleep on the bus or mistaken an unfamiliar street for a shortcut, but that he genuinely didn't know how to find his way home using the route he'd been taking for six years.

I jogged to Spar Lane and there he stood, in front of the gate of someone's house, looking left and right, left and right. *Trying.* I reached him and jokingly threw my hands in the air. 'You walk down here every day!'

He nodded but didn't smile, and as we walked home, the frown stuck between his brows deepened until we passed where he bought newspapers on Sundays and his shoulders sank with relief.

I now mark that day as The Beginning.

Scientific studies have shown that genetic factors can play
a part in developing Parkinson's disease as a result of
faulty genes.

Most cases of Parkinson's aren't hereditary however a
medical study recently revealed that patients suffering
from early-onset Parkinson's disease are more likely to
have inherited it.

Parkinson's disease can be triggered through a complex
combination of genetic susceptibility and exposure to
environmental factors such as toxins and trauma.
Genetics cause up to 15% of all Parkinson's.

Hereditary Parkinson's continues to be rare. The majority
of Parkinson's cases are 'idiopathic'. Idiopathic means
there is no known cause.

I suppose now is as good a time as any to let you know that
I have an older brother, James. He lives in Putney, so it's just
Dad and me here in Croydon. My mum spends most of her
time in Ghana, running a hostel that my grandfather left to
her and my uncle when he died. She'll come back home for
a year, then return to Ghana for a year, rinse and repeat. It
wasn't always a year-long thing, she used to only go for a
couple of months at a time, but excuses would sprout up
like inconspicuous mushrooms: 'It's so expensive and long
a flight, it doesn't make economic sense to stay here for

such a short time' or 'British weather doesn't agree with my arthritis' or 'My brother is no good; he's not business-minded like me.'

A year after Grandad passed, I overheard talk of upheaving us all to Accra, but Mum said no. 'My degree from Ghana helped me not one bit here and Maddie is an A* student. That cannot go to waste. She will do better than us if here, and so you, their father, must stay.' Thus her yo-yo travelling began.

My brother James pretty much left when Mum did. She was the iron fist of the household and Dad didn't know what to do with us when she was gone, so he did very little. James also didn't know what to do with himself, so he spent most evenings and weekends at various friends' houses. I barely saw him. He went to a different school than me and then straight to somebody else's house; he had decided early on that his friends were his family.

Mum hated that; she'd shout on the landline, punctuated by the automated voice reminding us how much we had left on our blue calling card. 'Stay home, James! Stop eating at other people's houses when your father has put food in the fridge. Their parents will think you have no mother!'

James, at fifteen, would shout back, 'I don't!'

I'd lie to friends and tell them Mum was only gone for a month or two, three tops, because I knew they wouldn't get it. They'd ask, 'What about you?' But I was fine. I was raised to be independent, to wash my own clothes, to shop for food and cook my own meals, to do my homework on time, to iron my uniform and assemble my school lunch. I didn't need to be looked after. I was proud to be so trusted – I didn't know any better.

Then they'd ask, 'What about your dad?' And he was fine too because my parents aren't the same as yours and their marriage isn't conventional. They do things their own way. I thought back then that it worked. I ignored James when he said that it didn't.

Dad's sitting in his armchair by the window facing the TV. He always looks thinner in the mornings, his loose cheeks a little heavier (the medication ate a lot of his fat in the early stages), but doesn't everything look different in the morning compared to how it did the night before? He's still handsome in my eyes; we keep his hair, hardly any of which is grey, cut short, and his face looks brighter after its morning wash.

If I had more time, I'd sit with him for a bit. I like our living room in the mornings. The floors can get quite cold as they're light wood (easier for spotting and cleaning up any mess), but I've timed the heaters to come on when Dad's helped out of bed. The walls are painted a peach-orange and we've got mismatched shawls and blankets covering the cracks in our tan faux-leather furniture. Whenever Mum returns from Ghana, she gets the sofa coverings to match the armchair's coverings, but I forget to wash and dry the sets at the same time.

'I'm leaving now, Dad,' I say, loud enough for him to hear. 'See you in the evening, okay?'

His eyes don't focus on me and they're not quite set on the TV either, but when he hears the word 'okay', his eyes widen and he replies, 'Okay,' and smiles again.

I turn to leave and throw, 'Love you,' over my shoulder.

My hand is on the door handle when I hear him shakily say, 'I love you, too.'

I turn back to him and the words 'You do?' are out of my mouth before I can stop them.

Dad frowns like he doesn't understand my question; his eyes are trying to find mine whilst he struggles to turn his neck. Then Dawoud bursts into the room with breakfast.

I step out of his way. 'Bye, Dawoud.'

'Bye Madeline-y!' he calls after me.

I'm replaying Dad's words inside my head whilst looking for my keys. I know my dad loves me . . . it's just been a while since he's said the actual words. A very long while.

Outside the house, I notice that a fox has gotten into the neighbour's bin and has ripped through the bag, trailing food and rubbish across the pavement. This is what David Attenborough was warning us about when we decided to encroach further on their habitat. But we didn't listen.

'Been there,' I say in solidarity.

I'll write next door a note explaining the trick is to put a few loose bricks on the wheelie bins at night, and post it through their letter box after work. They only moved in a few weeks ago and I don't know them yet, so I won't sign it.

I try to see what I can decipher about my new neighbours by their garbage. I see that they don't make an effort to recycle, so sadly they themselves are trash. It's a shame, because one of them was playing music last night, which I could hear through our thin walls, and their taste in 90s R&B is pretty good.

The 250 bus is rounding the corner when I get to the bus stop and it's already filled with schoolchildren getting off in three stops. Per usual, I stand and watch fifteen more shove their way on in front of me, jamming the closing doors. I take a picture of a girl's backpack caught between the doors and send it to Nia.

Maddie
Were we ever this annoying?

Nia
Lol, yeah. Driver of the 156 used to hate us
Remember that day he saw all of us waiting and just shook his head and drove off?
Not our fault we were loud. We were hyper from those neon KA drinks and fizzy strawberry laces

I smile at Nia's quick response, because it's 1 a.m. where she is. She's always been a night owl and I picture her with her ombre locs piled on top of her head, listening to music on her bed with the back of her legs flat against the wall.

I look up at the bus and the girls squashed tight at the front, giggling together. I had a lot of friends at school, all through to college, even, but when they moved out of London for university and I stayed put to look after Dad, we drifted apart. I realised then that our friendships were not based on loyalty or love but convenience and proximity. I went from a close group of seven to one. Nia.

Nia's been my best friend for almost ten years now, but she's currently doing a Business degree in Utah. She took a few gap years to work when we all went to university and so she's only now in her final year. She'll be back home in the summer – hopefully, for good.

I wait four minutes for the next bus and arrive at Thornton Heath station nine minutes before my train. I stand two feet to the left of the third bench so I'll be one of the first to board. On the way home, I'll stand on the right side of the live departure boards at Waterloo station, waiting for the 17:53 train. Monday to Friday, always the same.

My train arrives and it's busy as always with no seats available, but I rarely hunt for one. I look for an empty corner, settle in with my bag between my legs, fold my book in half and read.

When we arrive at Balham, it gets really full and I do what has fast become a habit of mine. I peer over my page and people-watch. Playing my favourite game, I mentally ask: who here loves their job? Could it be the blonde woman in the brightly patterned summer dress? Who here hates their job but can disguise that feeling for the required amount of time? The man in a navy suit with short braids and massive headphones? Who couldn't care less, so long as they're paid? The suited and booted city slicker, sighing impatiently when the train stops at a red light, standing far too close to the woman in front?

Whilst we're overground at Clapham Junction, I take my phone out and turn my data on.

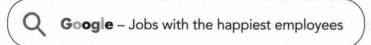

Number one on the list is . . . teaching.

That's got to be a lie. Considering I was a student not too long ago, I'm qualified to say, with a respectable level of certainty, that they're some of the worst treated people out there.

2. Nursing

3. Charity sector

4. Events management

On a list of jobs that have the unhappiest employees:

1. Customer service

2. Hospitality

3. Administration

When Waterloo station approaches, I brace myself for another day at a job Google itself has deemed deserving of a bronze medal in the race to unhappiness.

There's always a rush to get off the train; no one wants to be last, but surely it can't have anything to do with an irrepressible desire to get to work that eleven seconds earlier.

As soon as I'm separated from the mass of people, a message from Mum comes through. Just seeing her name flash reminds me of last night's phone call.

'Maddie, can you transfer me some more money, please?'

'Hello, Mum. How are you?'

She laughs and it tinkles effervescently. 'Hello, darling. I am blessed. Now, I've found someone with better conversion rates than last time, so let me give you the address. Do you have pen and paper?'

'I don't have any spare cash this month.'

'Why? Have you been recklessly spending?'

'No.'

Pause. 'What's wrong, Maame? You don't sound right. Tell your mother.'

Mum alternates between calling me one of three things: my name and all its variations included, a term of endearment, or Maame. Maame has many meanings in Twi, but in my case, it means woman. I've been called Maame ever since I can remember and I loved being referred to as a woman when I was still a girl. I loved being viewed as a grown-up before I'd even gotten my period. But now I—

'Maddie?' And I can hear the impatience coating the edge of her syllables like ever-present shadows.

'I'm not feeling very well.' The sun stays out late now, so I've shut the curtains in my room. I'm sat in a corner of my bed with my knees to my chest and I think about how to best describe how low I've felt without being able to list any defining reasons for it. When I feel my time to explain is running out, I say, 'I'm just sad and, I think, anxious.'

'About what?'

'Just everything I'm doing at home and at work. I feel heavy and hopeless and tired and like I'm not really living—'

Mum sighs. 'Maddie, please.' She stretches each word to emphasise the weariness behind her begging. 'You like to complain about this too much. You're not doing a lot, really, are you? You should see how the children here live. Don't you relax when you come home from work and on the weekends? It's because you don't ever go out.'

My eyes begin to water.

'I have said you need to go outside more because you'll never find a husband sitting at home,' she continues. 'Your father doesn't need company during all the sun's hours. That's why you're sad all the time – you have no fun.'

I almost tell her that fun doesn't equate to happiness; at the very least, it *lends* you happiness and I want to know how to keep it. I've Googled **How to be happy**; I've taken walks in the park and written long gratitude lists; I'm consuming more fruits and vegetables and going to bed early; I've given out compliments and practised mindful breathing. I *have* tried to fix myself.

'I think maybe I should go to the GP and—'

'No. We don't rely on the GP for things like that,' Mum says. 'They'll just give you drugs; they work on some kind of commission with it.'

'I highly doubt that's true.'

'I know more than you do about how the world is working, Maddie,' she says. 'They'll give you drugs for ailments that do not exist and then you will get sicker. It's not necessary. With God, there is no illness He cannot cure, that's why we rely on Him for all things.'

I quietly ask, 'Then why doesn't He give you money?'

'He blesses me through you, my daughter,' she says with finality.

I hug myself a little tighter.

'Have you been praying and reading your Bible?' Mum asks. 'You know you always get like this when you stop, when you give the devil a chance. Have you been tuning into that prayer channel I told you about – the five a.m. one?'

After we hang up, I start making dinner for Dad. Tears pour until I can taste salt. 'Something is genuinely wrong with you,' I whisper, cutting peppers. 'You're so messed up. Chemically imbalanced, maybe – you should google that. You can't be sad for no reason; it's not a human's natural state. In life, you're meant to be happy or content, only experiencing *moments* of sadness, so if sadness is your natural state, what does that say about you?' I put the knife down and slap my palm against my forehead. 'Just fucking stop it.' Surely, if I hit my head hard enough, I can fix my brain.

I wipe my eyes and keep cutting the peppers.

Chapter Two

I could take a more direct line into the West End, but morning walks featured extensively on all the 'How to Be Happy' articles I read – something about daylight exposure. Besides, it only takes twenty minutes to walk along the River Thames, which today shimmers near-blue in the sunlight. I plug in my earphones and listen to a band a colleague introduced the office to by plugging her speaker in on the one Friday afternoon senior management were away. A band whose songs make me think of summers that don't belong to me; of new Converses and cold drinks, short dresses and barbeques, and fleeting bursts of perennial freedom.

I work at the Covent Garden Theatre, more commonly known as the CGT. Named somewhat uninspiringly after its location, it's a giant, haphazardly geometrical, Brutalist concrete building reached by crossing Waterloo Bridge. I enter through the backstage reception, which means I have to be buzzed in, but I've tried the other four entrances and got lost each time. The staff themselves describe the building as a maze, and rumour has it that the reason no map of the theatre exists is because no one knows where everything is.

I walk past the stage doors and dressing rooms and once in the lift press for the third floor. Walking through my department's double doors, I see the 'kitchen' area (quotes intended as it's simply a flat surface with a kettle and shelves heavy with various teabags, mugs and plastic cups) hasn't been cleared. That'll be my job then.

The day before, I used the petty cash to buy the office enough prosecco and snacks to celebrate Freya in Marketing's birthday; it wasn't one of Dawoud's nights to give Dad his dinner and put him to bed so I couldn't stay, and since my boss had a day of external meetings, I actually got to leave on time. I see now that the party extended throughout the office, with cups left on one side of the room and opened packets of crisps on the other.

As a department, we're seated in a U shape, our desks attached to three walls, leaving the fourth for the Director's office. It's a nice enough space, with an unassuming atmosphere, maroon carpet and cream walls, but the best thing about it is that one side (the one I face) is made entirely of windows that give an incredible view of the Covent Garden Piazza.

I greet Zoe who works on our brochures and Frederica who assists the online team, then clear up while my computer loads.

I work as a PA for Katherine Fellingham, Director of Marketing & Publicity at the CGT, and my day mainly consists of rearranging her diary to avoid all the clashes she's added in overnight, managing her expenses, making her cups of Earl Grey tea, then cleaning her mugs in the bathroom sink. Yes, it is the job I signed up for, but that's always been my problem. I struggle to remain in office jobs for more than nine months at a time because there's no joy in it and you cannot convince me otherwise. I can't comprehend living to work, but then I'm afraid of working just to live.

I'm paid twenty-four thousand pounds per annum before tax, don't unnecessarily spend, and have a savings account with a little over four thousand pounds in it that I barely touch because I never know when Mum will need it. I scroll through job websites on a daily basis hoping the perfect position will announce itself, but I'm not even sure what field it would be in and whether my experience at this point would stretch much beyond menial office work.

'Good morning, Maddie.'

I turn in my seat as Katherine approaches her desk, which is situated behind its own door. She's wearing her circular glasses today and recently cut her brown hair into a bob. Teamed with her 5' 2" height and wind-painted cheeks, she looks younger than her forty-seven years.

'Morning, Katherine. How was your weekend?'

'Lovely, thanks. David and I caught the penultimate performance of *Closer Still* at the Lyceum – have you seen it?'

'No, not yet.' I never will; the remaining tickets, last time I checked, cost somewhere in the three-figure bracket. 'Would you recommend it?'

'Oh, definitely.' She unbuttons her blazer and crosses her ankles at the brogues. 'It was brilliant – you really have to try to catch the final show on Thursday.'

Claire, the general manager, walks in and asks, 'Is this *Closer Still*?' Her dark ponytail swings like a pendulum even when she stops and she has her work shoes in her hands, ready to swap out her trainers. 'Incredible, wasn't it?'

I leave them to their conversation and return to my emails – mostly people asking for Katherine's time. The simple answer is she doesn't have any and they know this, but they also know that Katherine suffers famously from FOMO (fear of missing out). On a senior level where she is one of only two women, she feels she can't turn any meeting down, so she instructs me to find the time, even if it's during her lunch hour.

A couple of weeks ago, she was diagnosed with depression. She told those working directly under her, then told me herself after she'd accidentally copied me into an email to HR explaining why she'd need time off. Despite a month's leave being granted, she returned to work the following week and took to smiling in front of us and crying in the toilets, returning with red eyes and puffy cheeks.

No one did anything about it. Claire even pulled me aside and told me not to mention it to anyone because if even one of the eleven (out of thirteen) male directors found out that 'Katherine couldn't cope', they'd think her too weak for her position.

'Does that really matter?' I asked. 'I mean, what they'll think of her? Katherine's not well.'

'Of course it matters,' Claire said. She barely reined in an eye roll before replacing it with folded arms. 'Even though she does more and works harder than any of them, they'll replace her with yet another man if they find out she's depressed. She and I have seen it happen twice already. Why don't you make her a cup of tea?' she suggested. 'Katherine will be fine in an hour.'

Claire was wrong.

'Morning, Maddie.' Ellie's next to arrive. She too rushes in, but likely because she woke up late; her blond hair is scraped back, she's missed a button on her corduroy dungarees and her Converse lace has come undone. She sits and lets out a breath of air.

'Morning, Ellie.'

Ellie's my line manager, even though she started after me and is only a year older. We were friendlier at first, joked around a bit more, but that dried up like the arse of a prune on a date and time I still can't stick a definitive pin in. Sometimes I lie in bed at night and briefly wonder what it was I did to her, even though it doesn't bother me enough during the day. For some reason, at night, when you're meant to be sleeping, your brain wants answers to everything.

I think Ellie just prefers the other members of the team because she knows they're staying, whereas I walk the corridors with an invisible sign around my neck announcing I'm soon to hand in my notice. I must reek of un-fulfilment at work, which is funny, because I started with bright eyes and worn trainers and now the two have reversed.

I came upon this job through Access All Areas, a social enterprise dedicated to getting more under-represented young people into London's creative industries. They informed me the Director of Marketing at the Covent Garden Theatre was looking for a PA and admin assistant. I'd never considered working for a theatre because I never went to the theatre. You were either a cinema or theatre person, and that depended largely on your budget and upbringing. However, I needed a job and met seventy per cent of the experience required. I did as much research as I could and was excited to read that they'd had a few changes in senior management in order to focus on 'reflecting diversity' in both their shows and staff.

I'd gone for an interview and whilst the panel were all white, at least they were all women, and on my way in and out, I saw people like me. We were still the minority, but compared to my previous jobs, it was a sizable difference. Weeks in, I realised they were mainly front of house, serving staff. The departments I interacted with were stiflingly white, to the point where in every meeting I took minutes for, I was the only Black person in the room.

You have no idea (or maybe you do?) how this can make you feel. It's mentally exhausting trying to figure out if I'm taking that comment on my hair or lunch too seriously. It's isolating when no one I know here is reading the Black authors I am or watching the same TV shows. (You should have seen their blank faces when we were talking nineties/noughties TV, specifically *Friends* and *Frasier*, and I happened to mention *My Wife & Kids*.)

When you're in a job you don't love but need, it must help to have someone close by to share light moments with. I do have Avi (you'll meet her later on . . . prepare yourself) who works on the floor below me, but honestly, we don't have that much in common and I only see her for about thirty minutes every week. So for the remaining thirty-seven hours my silence is punctuated only by work requests and conversations I'm not invited to.

I'd wanted to leave CGT before my probation period was up seven months ago, which spat in the face of my parents and grandparents' work ethic. My mum said it was a privilege I had the opportunity to jump from job to, albeit low-paying, job. I knew I had my degree in English Literature to thank for that, but it's the least being forty thousand pounds in debt could do.

'Why are you never happy, Maddie?' Mum said. 'I wanted you to be a lawyer, doctor or a vet, any of which would be more exciting, but you chose this. And all you have to do is sit in front of a computer all day, no? You're hardly on your feet. Your generation just don't know.'

I get where she's coming from because she doesn't see jobs as something to be enjoyed but rather endured in order to pay bills – the completion of which should spark some semblance of joy. For Mum, work-related happiness is directly proportional to how much you earn. Still, that doesn't change the fact that although I didn't think I'd be rich I expected to be happy and the failure to do so has left me gasping for air most of the day.

Maybe the reason Mum struggles to understand me is because she preaches her experience; no one told her she could do anything she wanted. My parents were Black immigrants in eighties London; they didn't have time for hobbies or the ability to seek job-fulfilment opportunities.

I should remember to view things through a similar lens, to remember my dad needs me to have a stable job that allows me to help out with bills and get home in time to feed him dinner and put him to bed four evenings a week.

If only logic and reason overruled emotion.

After lunch, I head downstairs to meet Avi. I always split my lunch hour in two: twenty minutes for food and forty minutes of daydream-fuelled walking. Usually I'm by myself, but today Avi's coming with me since she'll have to walk over the bridge to meet her boyfriend.

'How is Jake?' I ask as we set off. We pick my favourite route, which is a little longer but means we pass a road of flower shops, bakeries and pubs before reaching the bridge.

'He's fine,' she says. 'He told me last night that he wanted to try anal, so we did.'

Avi Jeeto, ladies and gentleman. Avi's half English, half Indian, has a dark bob that curls at its ends and is a serial oversharer. She used to have my job before she moved departments and we became friends during the handover period. I think she's great, but unfortunately for me, so do many others. She's been working at CGT for five years and has managed to accumulate a mass of friends so our social-ising is limited to these occasional lunchtime chats.

The sun is out so I have to shield my face with a hand when I look at her. And also because eye contact doesn't feel appropriate for a conversation like this. 'I don't know how to process this information.'

She pulls out her sunglasses. 'That's what I said.'

'You just announced it so suddenly.'

'Again, what I said.'

'It's a lot to take in.'

Avi tilts her head back and laughs.

I decide the best course of action is silence. It works and the next thing Avi says is, 'Still can't get over your hair, by the way.'

'You don't like it?'

She shrugs and slides behind me to let a pair of joggers pass. 'I'm used to you with braids in – it's just different now.'

I gave braided twists a rest for the first time in three years when it started wreaking havoc on my hair's edges; last week, I went to a salon specialising in type four hair and had my hair treated and blow-dried so that I now brush it into a low bun for work.

'I bet you got so many compliments in the office though,' Avi says.

We share a smile. 'Of course,' I say. 'Not a word before.'

We get onto Waterloo Bridge teeming with cyclists, shop-pers and workers on their lunch break. I look over the bridge and there's a tour boat gliding underneath us.

'Are you moving out soon by any chance?' Avi asks. 'I have a friend with a room she needs to fill and you're the only person I know still living at home.'

Great, I can now add Avi to my list.

List of people who think I'm a loser for still living at my parents' house:

Nia (even though she technically lives
at home for three months of the year)
Shu (best friend no.2)
Mum
*Boy at bus stop who snorted after eavesdropping
on my* private *conversation*
Me
Avi

'Is it *that* weird that I still live at home?

'It's not that it's weird; it just doesn't make sense,' Avi says. 'You can afford to move out and it's not like you're saving for a mortgage on this salary, so why live at home?'

Avi doesn't know about Dad, so I shrug.

'You didn't even move out for uni,' she continues. 'Don't you want a bit more . . .' She shimmies with her shoulders. 'Freedom? Nights out. Friends over. Men.'

'I'm just not boy crazy at the moment,' I defend. 'There's plenty of time for that.'

'The time is now, Maddie,' and she pounds a fist into her open palm. 'You're twenty-five. You're meant to be getting as much dick as possible!'

'Avi!' I look apologetically at the mother shepherding her toddlers away from us.

'Relax,' Avi says, tilting her head to the sun. 'It's called being in your twenties, which you only get to do for ten years in your entire life, and guess what? You're already halfway through.'

Oh God. I am halfway through. Five years of my twenties have disappeared into the ether and I live at home, have no boyfriend or obvious career path and I'm still a virgin.

'Where's the room?' I ask. 'Just out of curiosity.'

'Crouch End.'

'North London? That's too far.'

'No it's not. You can get the Northern Line to Waterloo.' She looks at me. 'You meant from where you live now?' She rolls her eyes. 'I'm going to give her your number. She'll send you pictures of the place later.'

'Fine.'

'Well?' she asks. 'Aren't you going to ask me how anal went?'

I blink. 'You know, Avi, finishing that conversation didn't even cross my mind.'

She tilts her head in disbelief. 'Really? I'd want to know.'

'You and I are very different people.'

She doesn't let this fact deter her. 'It was uncomfortable at first but wasn't the worst. You know when something's just not meant to be stuck somewhere?'

'Oh, look, there's Jake.' *Thank God.* I give him a frantic wave before recalling how and *where* he spent last night, dropping both my hand and gaze. 'I'll leave you two to it.'

I turn back the way I came when Avi hollers, 'Are you going to tonight's show? We're all going for a drink before if you wanna join.'

'No,' I shout back. 'I have plans tonight.'

When I walk back into the office, Katherine is stalking my desk despite the fact I have five minutes left of my lunch hour. Her cheeks are red and patchy and she exhales when she sees me. 'Oh, there you are, Maddie. Finally back, then?

That's fine,' she says. 'Can you print me a few things, oh, and pop downstairs and grab me a coffee? I needed one half an hour ago but couldn't find you.'

Whilst in line at the in-house coffee shop I check my phone for any new job alerts. I scroll through two pages to find nothing non-PA-related I'm qualified for but three that I'll apply to anyway.

It wasn't a complete lie – what I told Avi. I do have plans tonight, just not of the sociable kind.

Back at home that evening, I heat up the rice I made a pot of but bake the fish fresh. I add some salad to the plate and a glass of water to the tray and take it into the living room. I sit on the chair to the right of Dad's and we watch TV as I feed him.

This part of Dad, of Parkinson's, happened slowly at first and then escalated so quickly I almost don't remember witnessing the signs. He'd drop his plate and I'd call him clumsy; he'd spill water down his front and he'd pat himself dry. Then his cutlery kept slipping through his fingers when he ate, until it was impossible for him to hold it steady at all. He began skipping meals just to avoid the truth all together.

Dad eats well today, which makes me happy. I used to panic and hear imaginary thunder when he didn't clear his plate or if he fell asleep long before it was time for bed, convinced it was an early sign of something else. The more I read on Parkinson's, the more I discovered just how unwieldy and elusive it was; a sprawling tree of disease with each branch detailing a possible symptom or consequence. I'd lie awake wondering if he'd die in his sleep and how it would be my fault for not calling a doctor and saving him when I could. I'd creep down at maybe two or three in the morning and listen outside his bedroom door for sounds of his snoring, only returning to bed when I heard it.

I'm more aware now. Sometimes he's just not up to it and what matters most is that he eats something before taking his medication, even if only a slice of toast. Each tri-daily dose of tablets is separated into a packet and I pop out the one for Tuesday evening. I place one tablet after another into his mouth and hold the glass of water to his lips. He has to swallow twice and chase with more water. He always closes his eyes for a bit after.

I take his tray back to the kitchen and start washing up.

When it's time for bed, I hook my arm into his, bend my knees and help Dad out of his chair. Slowly, we shuffle to his bedroom.

I brush his teeth using a cup as a sink, replace his top with a pyjama shirt, change his catheter bag but keep his tracksuit bottoms on.

I put Dad to bed four times a week, so I have the routine down, but I must do something wrong this time because when I lift his legs into bed, a sting rips my back open, it's like *pulling* a thread loose of its stitched pattern. I drop Dad's feet onto the bed's metal railing.

'Sorry, Dad.' I haven't hurt him; his evening meds make him too drowsy, but my back is screaming and I need to bite my lip to keep them closed.

I pull his duvet up to his neck, kiss his forehead, then turn off the light.

When I leave his room, I remain bent forward, slowly pulling myself up to ease the tight ache until I'm standing upright.

Fuck.

ZF: Anyone else got really bad lower back pain? I'm only 24 and I wanna know if it's anything serious.

MT: Lol back pain at 24? What the fuck happened to you?

KS: For your information **MT**, the number of young people experiencing back pain is rising so it's not funny. **ZF**, try having a hot bath or placing an ice pack over the painful area?

TP: Have you tried yoga? I'm a yoga instructor and you can find a number of useful stretches on my website here . . .

CC: It's all linked to the Government, but no one ever believes me. From a young age we're told office jobs are the goal. Then you sit at a desk hunched over 9–5, 5 days a week for most of your younger years until it's too late to do anything else but get a 'helpful' chair

LG: Why would the government want a nation suffering from back pain?

CC: So we don't take over

I call James that evening, but typically he doesn't answer and instead calls back hours later. I have to turn the light on as he switches on the video camera. I can see he's in his car.

'Hey, Mads!' He's got plaits in his hair now and they're long enough to lie down instead of stick up. When he smiles, his gold tooth glints. Growing up, James and I were always told that we had great smiles – smiles that show perfect teeth and soften our faces. It's one of the few things we both inherited from Dad. 'Dad asleep?' James asks.

'Yes, which is why I called,' I tell him. 'I could use some help with that. My back hurts from lifting Dad from his seat and into bed. Can you do one of my nights each week maybe?'

James scratches what I know to be a phantom itch on the back of his head. 'Ah, I can't really come all the way from Putney just to put Dad to bed, Mads,' he says. 'And you know my work schedule is unreliable. It's not fair to promise you a day and then not come because I gotta be somewhere else last minute.'

James's friend hit the Rap & Grime music scene hard and made it big (I'm talking MOBO and BRIT Awards), so he's part of that team – chauffeur at times, social media manager, tour companion. Mum jokes he's a glorified hype man, only there to boost an ego. I think he's hoping to one day join the music scene himself.

'Right.'

'Anything else I can help with, though?' he asks.

'The council tax bill has come in.'

He sighs and scratches the beard growing on his neck. 'Sorry, Mads. I'm a bit short on extra money, but remind me next month, yeah?'

'Sure . . . but you've been saying that for a couple of months now.'

'I know, I know,' he replies, looking away. 'Things are just a little tight, at the moment. You know I just got back from Japan.'

Do you hear yourself? That's what I want to ask, but instead I mouth: *Must be nice.* Then say, 'Shouldn't the flight have been paid for since it's your job?'

'Yeah, it was, but I spent too much. I wish I was good with money like you.'

'I don't really have much choice.' I keep my tone light, but I'm not happy. Not so much at the empty money promises, but because I'm reminded that he can get away with it. If he says he has no money, short of stealing from his wallet, I have to accept that. He knows I'll pay the council tax because I'm living here and can't just sit back as bills pile up.

'I know that,' he says, 'but I live on my own. My rent's not cheap like yours. Mum has you payin' only four-fifty. Mine's over a grand cos it's Putney. Just use a bit of your savings and hit me up next month to replace it. You all right, though, yeah?' he asks. 'You heard Mum's comin' back soon?'

'Yes, she told me last week,' I say. 'She hasn't booked her flight yet.'

'Let me know when she does. I'm not tryna be around too much when she's here.'

Shouldn't be too difficult. 'Okay.'

He laughs but doesn't mean it. 'I forgot you're on her side.'

'I don't take either of your sides. I'm neutral. Like—'

'Yeah, Spain. I know, I know.'

I smile. 'Switzerland.'

'Close enough, no?' he asks. 'But yeah, you know I don't like the way she moves or acts with Dad. Your husband is here sick so what are you doin' in Ghana all the time? She leaves you to deal with everything.'

Something you two have in common.

'She's running Grandad's hostel,' I say. 'You know Uncle doesn't help much, so it's only her, really.'

James presses his lips together and shakes his head.

'What?' I ask.

'Nothin',' he says. 'You just don't know Mum like I do, Mads. When I went to Ghana to check up on things, she was movin' a bit mad.' I look away from the camera. 'Yeah,' James says, 'I can tell you don't wanna hear it and that's why I don't say nothin'. Anyway, listen, I gotta go, but I'll come to the house soon, yeah? Bye, Mads.'

'Bye, James. Love you.'

'Love you too, sis.'

I put my phone down and turn off the light.

James says he knows Mum better than I do, but I'm the one who saw her phone messages the last time she was here; messages about missing and loving each other to and from an unsaved number beginning in +233.

Maybe that's what James saw in Ghana. I'm glad I had the excuse of looking after Dad to avoid that trip. It's easy to throw a phone back onto a bedside table and pretend as if nothing's changed – maybe harder if you see it with your own eyes.

I think of what Mum may be doing right now. If she's alone. Betraying Dad seems a cruel act on her behalf, but although I've never been one of those children to saint their parents, I can't think too badly of her. She's still the mum who let me climb into her bed and skip a day of school when I had the scariest of nightmares; the mum who would come into my room and pray for me every hour when my period pains left me bed-bound; the mum who would brag to anyone listening about having the well-behaved, responsible, A-grade gift from God.

It's fine. Really.

Just another secret to keep.

Chapter Three

I spend Sunday morning cleaning Dad's room; it takes me twice as long due to my residual back pain. It's now less of an ache and more of a constant pinching; I called the GP for an appointment but the soonest available was Tuesday afternoon, so I take paracetamol in the meantime.

I mop his wooden floor and change his bedding. I wipe down the room windows, tackle the toilet and rinse out the bucket Dawoud uses to wipe Dad with when his legs are too weak to make it upstairs to the bathroom. Months ago, I put in a request with the council to have one built downstairs, but we're still waiting to hear back.

I head off to church a couple of hours later and Shu calls me on the way. Which is unusual because Shu only accepts text messages and considers spontaneous phone calls a personal attack.

I met Shu at Birkbeck University. She walked into our lecture (English Literature, which she eventually dropped for International Business) late and rather than stand and find her friends, she took the empty seat next to me. Her black hair was longer then, but she still has the same high cheekbones and gap in her front teeth, the same fondness for oversized jumpers, and she still can't leave the house without three layered necklaces on.

'Hey, I'm Shu – you got a spare pen?' was her opening gambit.

'Maddie,' I said, handing her one.

She looked in her bag, then back at me. 'Got any spare paper, too?'

I soon became the girl she sat next to in lectures when she forgot her laptop. I was easy to find because I always sat at the front of the middle block, right at the edge so I could be the first to avoid the conversational mass when it was over.

'Why you always in a rush to leave?' Shu once asked.

'I try to avoid being swallowed by the crowd.'

'Where do you go?'

'If I haven't got another lecture, I go home.'

'That's sad.'

'I don't disagree.'

'You live in London?' she asked. 'You sound kinda posh.'

'Thornton Heath. You?'

'Hackney – know the area?'

'Not well, but it's nice to properly meet you . . . Shu?'

'Yeah, short for Meixiang-Shu.'

After multiple well-meaning attempts on my part, she looked me dead in the eye and said, 'I appreciate the effort, but your pronunciation is shit – just call me Shu.'

Shu and I used to be much closer, but now she has a steady girlfriend – Lydia – and a new high-powered City job that demands more hours than she's technically contracted for. And with Dad needing Maddie-imposed round-the-clock care these days, I don't see her much.

'Glad I got you before church,' Shu says. 'I'm about to view another place.'

'Oh, yeah.' I use a finger to block my other ear as I walk down Tottenham Court Road. 'How's the flat-hunt going?'

Shu moved out of her parents' place as soon as she turned eighteen, *literally*. Shu was born at 3.57 p.m. and at that

31

exact time on 25 July she stood up in her room, grabbed her bags, said, 'Fuck this place,' and walked out. Shu can be a little dramatic, but she left for good reason. When she came out to her parents, they *said* they loved and accepted her, but things weren't the same between them again. That's as much as Shu would tell me. Now her tenancy's coming up at her flat in Hornsey and she doesn't want to renew. She can afford a place on her own but she'd rather save for a mortgage deposit and last I checked, Lydia wasn't ready to take the co-resident plunge.

'I've got two more tonight.'

'What about the Camden flat you liked?' I ask.

'I had to turn it down. The girl I'd be sharing with was too pretty.'

A man with a worryingly lifelike parrot on his shoulder edges past me, but it's central London on the weekend, so I don't bat an eyelid. 'You'll have to walk me through that reasoning, Shu.'

'She won't admit it, but Lydia's got a . . . what's the British way to say it? My gran would say "sticky eye".'

'Wandering eye?'

'Yeah, maybe. Anyway, I don't want to feel insecure in my own home when my girlfriend's round,' she says. 'If only you were ready to move out, then we could find a nice two-bed place and have a good time from the start. You know to take your shoes off when you come in and I already know why your hair's a hundred times shorter after you wash it.'

I stop in the street. 'Are you saying I'm not threateningly pretty?'

'When you make an effort, yeah, but I got nothing to worry about cos you're so innocent. When Lyd was

32

looking at your chest, you told her where you got your jumper from.'

'I thought she liked the button design.'

'She did not.'

'Maybe she did.'

Shu sighs which means she's rolling her eyes. 'Are you ready to move out or what?'

I pause outside the church building. A warm, jealous pang hits my chest as I briefly think about what it would be like being responsible for only myself, for spending my time however I want. I immediately feel guilty and shake my head; it's not Dad's fault he needs me.

'I like being at home. I don't think that'll change any time soon,' I say.

Shu knows Dad has Parkinson's but she's unaware of how serious it is. She regularly asks how Dad is and I always respond 'Fine' and she hears the silent '. . . you know, considering', but she doesn't ask for specifics. Not because she doesn't care, but because she's just as private as I am – maybe more so. I think she asks herself, if the roles were reversed, would she want someone asking all the time? The answer is no.

Shu sighs again. 'Fine, fair. Enjoy church.'

'Thanks. Love you.'

She laughs and it's a burst of energy. 'You always gotta say it,' she says. 'Why can't you end a conversation without saying it?'

'Just say you love me too and hang up.'

'Yeah, you too.'

When Mum's here, I join her at a small Pentecostal church in Croydon. There the pastor can easily make eye contact with any person from the pulpit and everyone knows too much about each other. When Mum's in Ghana, I go to a church in central London. I found out about it because Shu goes here, not weekly, but 'when I can, innit'.

I liked that they called themselves a contemporary Christian church and that hundreds attend each sermon, guaranteeing anonymity. I attended one Sunday, alone because I preferred mornings whilst Shu preferred the evenings, and liked it enough to keep returning. The sermons are taught by different preachers, so you never know who you're going to get, and they're all relatively young. They speak about Christianity in the era of social media and increasing peer pressure; they speak about being the love in a world often shown to be full of hate; they find ways to make the Bible relatable and I don't leave feeling like I'm not *enough* of a Christian to call myself one. Each session is ninety minutes long and they encourage you to stick around after and meet people – if you like. I prefer to get home to Dad.

I take a seat on the ground floor at the end of a row and settle in.

I can hear Dad talking as I let myself in from church and I think maybe Dawoud has come even though he's not due, but when I step into the living room, there's no one but Dad there.

His eyes are wide and he's speaking in Twi. I can't grasp what he's saying because it's too broken. I hope he's speaking to me, but, no, he's staring into the corner, a blank patch on our living-room wall, and talking to someone who is not there.

'Dad?'

He doesn't stop talking and staring.

'Dad? Who are you talking to?'

The corners of his mouth pull down. He blinks and slowly extends his arm, as far as he can, to point at the empty space. 'My . . . my sis . . . ter,' he says.

'Auntie Mabel? Is she here?'

'No. No. Re . . . Rebecca.'

I swallow. My Aunt Rebecca died in Ghana when I was three years old.

'No, Dad,' I say softly. 'She's not here.' I wave into the space and repeat myself, but he continues to frown and point at the blank wall.

He leans his head back and still staring says quietly, 'My sister, Rebecca.'

I go over to him and gently shake his arm. 'Dad?'

He blinks and finally looks at me. He looks at the wall and then to me again. He closes his eyes and a tear runs down his cheek.

I hold his hand. 'Sorry, Dad,' I say quietly. 'I . . . I'm sorry.' I dab his cheek with my coat sleeve and then kiss his forehead. I sit there, cradling his shaking right hand with both of mine until he falls asleep.

I leave the room and pull my phone from my pocket. My hands are shaking as I call Doctor Appong's direct line. I tell him about the hallucination and he assures me it isn't rare for the medication Dad's on, but for my peace of mind, he'll come by tomorrow to check on him.

'Not today?'

'I'm not in the office today, I'm afraid.'

'Right! Sorry, it's Sunday. I forgot again. I'm sorry. It's just . . .' I pinch the bridge of my nose to block the fresh tears. 'Will tomorrow be too late?'

'Maddie, everything is fine.' His tone is patient, reassuring, with confidence bolstered by decades of medical practice. Or it could be pity. I still remember the frown on his face the day he came to see Dad and asked where Mum was. I told him it was just me at the moment and that's when he gave me his direct line. When he left I swore I could see him shaking his head as he walked away. 'You say he's not displaying any other symptoms?'

'No, he's a bit tired though.'

'That's normal. You don't need to worry. You can call me again if something else happens, but he should be okay, all right?'

I nod, then remember to say, 'Yes, thank you.'

Doctor Appong was right. When Dad wakes up, he doesn't seem to remember anything and he's as fine as he was the day before. The memory clings to me however, through the afternoon, through dinner and up until the night. I called James, but he didn't pick up, then I sent a WhatsApp to Mum, but she hasn't replied.

I lay awake in bed thinking about before Dad was ill. It's been eight years, so it takes me a while to remember. To remember I used to leave Dad to his weekends because that's how he preferred it, and I would spend Saturdays and Sundays with school friends I don't see anymore.

Dad and I never spent that much time together, nowhere near as much as we do now. With Mum in Ghana every other year and James adopting himself into other families, I grew up alone. Dad left me to it because he knew he could. I was the well-behaved one.

But if I'd realised how much that pressure would build inside me, the slow descent into a dull existence, days blemished with concern for my dad and whether I'm look-ing after him properly – well, I would have stayed out late some nights, lost my virginity at sixteen instead of still having it, developed a fondness for alcohol, sat at bars, smoked weed, danced at clubs, and turned strangers into friends.

The truth is, it took a while for me to get comfortable around Dad, without Mum there as a buffer. He worked as a security guard for a private school in Wandsworth, which meant he was home in the evenings, but he would sit at his desk reading a newspaper or watching TV and I'd be in my room. That was normal for us. We aren't a sit-down-and-have-dinner-together kind of family, except for some Christmases.

Last Christmas, Mum stayed in Ghana and James went away with friends, so it was just Dad and me. We watched *The Grinch* in comfortable silence. Dad suffers from diabetes, too, but I unwrapped a chocolate and popped it into his mouth. Mum called us in the evening and James the following day. I thought I would mind that we weren't all together for Christmas, but really, it just felt like any other day.

Mum doesn't call until Tuesday when I'm sat on a bench at the South Bank, facing the river.

'Darling, did you go to church on Sunday?' Mum asks. 'What was the message?'

'There were a few,' I answer. 'Queen Vashti was about people-pleasing, Mordecai about surrounding yourself with people who are loyal and honest, and Esther about having faith in the scariest of times.'

'Good. I like the sound of that,' she says, satisfied. 'Remember to meditate on the scriptures of Esther. It's a great passage. So . . .'

'Have you met someone yet?' I mouth the familiar words along with her. A conversation with my mum rarely passes without this question. 'Since last week?' I roll my eyes. 'No, I haven't.'

'Did you not talk to anyone new at church?'

'No.'

'Why not?' she asks. 'You tell me it's mostly women at your work, but are there no men at your church?'

'I don't go to church to meet men, Mum.'

'Maybe that is the problem,' she says. 'Where else do you expect to find God-fearing men if not at church? You know your cousin Glory, here in Ghana?'

'No.'

'Well, she's just gotten married. She's twenty-four, I think. Younger than you.'

'Lucky her.'

'Luck has nothing to do with it, Maame.'

'Fine. Mum, why didn't you call me back on Sunday?'

'I got your message but knew it wasn't serious when I didn't hear from you again,' she says. 'Is your father okay now?'

'Yes. Doctor Appong came by yesterday to check on him,' I answer. 'He said there was nothing to worry about, but it was still scary.'

'It shouldn't be. What did you just learn about Esther and faith?' She doesn't even wait for me to answer. 'To *have* faith – that's what you should take away from Esther,' Mum says. 'These things will happen with his numerous medication, so no need to work yourself up. All right?'

There's no use in saying anything other than, 'All right.'

'Good. What did you get up to on Saturday?'

'Not much,' I answer. 'Cleaned the house, then sat in the living room with Dad and read for a bit.'

'On a Saturday night?'

'Would you rather I was out getting drunk?'

'Of course not! Don't say things like that. Only loose women get drunk. Are you a loose woman?'

'No, Mum.'

'Exactly. But are you not tired of your four walls?' she asks. 'You're a good girl, Maddie, but staying home all the time to look after your father, it will make you resentful. You don't have to watch him twenty-four-seven; you can leave for a few hours here and there. Like you said, you are tired of everything you do at home, so go outside, otherwise you'll never meet someone to marry.'

I don't say anything.

'When you're older, you'll wish you did more. You will,' she continues. 'I know more than you, Maddie. Anyway, I called to say that I've booked my ticket and will be home next week. Your uncle wants more time with the hostel – bit late to help out now, but anyway. I'll be back to stay for a year, possibly more. So now you can move out and live your life a bit.'

I put my lunch down beside me. 'Move out?'

'Yes, whilst I'm watching your father, at least. Surely you're thinking about it, eh? Are you going straight home tonight?'

I get a small kick out of answering, 'Actually, no. I'm going to a play.'

'On a date?'

I deflate. 'No, for work.'

There's a couple seconds of silence before she says, 'There will be men in the audience. Maybe you'll sit next to one.'

When she ends the call, I stare out to the river.

Mum actually *wants* me to move out? I never considered she'd want to be home alone and responsible for Dad. I guess me finding a husband and having children before I'm thirty takes precedence.

My parents aren't together, but they are. 'We are still married,' Mum said when James had asked, 'but we are apart. Divorce is not really a thing for us.' I'd wanted to know if the 'us' referred to our religion, culture or just them, but I kept my mouth shut. I knew not to ask too many questions. Which is odd when I think about it now; I knew to keep family matters private from outsiders but never considered the secrets we were possibly keeping from one another. 'It's not something to spread around, okay?' Mum quickly added. 'Family business.'

Could I finally move out? My refusal to leave hung on the fact that Dad needed someone more constant than Dawoud's visits, but Mum will be here. I'd have to return when she eventually left again, but while I have the chance . . .

Maybe I could get out more. Meet people. Meet *someone*. Finally have an answer to Mum's perpetual question. What could it hurt to go on a date, knowing I wouldn't have to rush back home after? To invite a man into my house, introduce him to my friends and be introduced to his. What could it hurt to maybe even fall in love?

I download the RentARoom app before returning to the office.

Katherine is once again prowling my desk, but this time she has her fists balled at her side and her shoulders under her ears as if trying to contain what's threatening to escape.

'Have you seen the state of my diary?' she explodes at the sight of me. She's red in the face, spittle clinging to her bottom lip and her high-strung voice wobbles at every other syllable. *Shit.* She usually reserves her tears for whatever

40

toilet stall is available at the time, but it doesn't look like she can help herself. Suddenly I think: *This is a long time coming.*

I don't know how to handle this and no one in the room rushes to my side, so I'm shaking when I wake my computer up and switch onto her diary. It's full of accepted invitations and clashes that weren't there an hour ago.

'I didn't accept these meetings,' I tell her.

'I did!' she says. 'They've been sitting in my inbox and now there's clashes all over the place and I can't have any clashes!' She presses her palms to her eyes. 'I can't – I *cannot* do this!'

I'm facing her, but I can feel the entire office watching. My heart is pounding and my eyes are stinging when I quietly say, 'This isn't my fault.'

Katherine's hands drop from her eyes and she stares at me, her pupils flickering from side to side. 'Look at my diary, Maddie! This is your *job*!'

'Okay,' Claire says, finally getting up from her seat. 'Katherine, why don't you leave Maddie to sort out your diary – I'm sure it won't take her very long.' She speaks as if reasoning with a toddler and ushers Katherine back into her office. 'Whilst she's doing that, I'll make you a cup of tea, how's that sound?'

'Yes, thank you, Claire,' Katherine says between laboured breaths. 'That's very kind.'

I turn back to my computer, feeling everyone's eyes still stuck to me.

I don't cry until enough time has passed for me to inconspicuously use the bathroom. There I ruminate on whether Katherine has a favourite cubicle to cry in, and if I'm currently sat in it.

41

At least I'm not in the office all day. I leave at three in the afternoon to make the GP appointment for my back. Even though I'll return in the evening for a play, my shoulders drop once I'm outside the building and waiting for my train.

I lie on my boobs, shifting uncomfortably, in the overly bright office of General Practitioner Shazia Rana. She's not a conversationalist, so the silence, whilst she slowly dons a pair of gloves, makes my ears ring. I wonder if I should mention I have highly sensitive nipples which means I can never sleep on my front and whether that's something I should be worried about.

Doctor Rana walks up to the table and asks me to lift my jumper so she can feel for anything obvious on my back. This is quite difficult to do when lying on your belly, but I give it my best shot. I remember too late how tight the neck hole of this jumper is and, to stop my legs flailing from the effort, decide to just lie there with half my face obscured by polyester masquerading as cotton.

She presses my back with cold gloved fingers and goose-bumps prickle the surface of my skin. 'How are you today, Maddie?'

Her voice is very gentle, perhaps because she's concentrating on the task at hand, but I actually stop to think about her question. The truthful answer is: not great. My back still hurts and my four nights a week aren't helping; I hope I never see my dad hallucinate again; I don't want to work another day for my boss; my mum's returning from Ghana soon; I'm still crying at night and that might be the only thing that puts me to sleep.

However, I can't say any of this because sometimes asking how someone is serves solely as a passing pleasantry and the only acceptable answer is some variation of 'Fine, thanks. You?' But maybe – what if she really does want to know how I am?

'Well, I'm—'

'I'm just going to press a little harder,' Doctor Rana says.

I blink and nod. 'Yes, okay. Thank you.'

Probably for the best.

'Well, there's nothing that gives me cause for concern which is good,' Dr Rana says, returning to her desk. 'You say you hurt your back lifting heavy boxes at work?'

I lift my head and lie, 'Yes.'

'But it says on your file you're a personal assistant.'

'Oh, erm, I was just helping the stage crew out. They were short-staffed.'

'But it's not part of your role?'

Role. 'Not exactly.'

'Best to avoid then.' She turns back to her computer screen and says, 'I'll write you a prescription and combined with avoiding any further strenuous activity, you should be fine.'

I press my lips together and nod. 'Right.'

Tonight's play, the one I missed watching with Avi, is loosely based on the Salem witch trials; an accused witch must prove she's pregnant to avoid being burnt alive. I'm here because staff often get complimentary tickets and Katherine wants us all to attend when we can so we're always up to date with CGT's plays. Since we're given the time and date, I can rarely make it because performances don't always land on Dawoud's nights.

I try to focus on reading the play's outline, but I'm still thinking about my afternoon – Katherine's meltdown and

43

how I really don't want to return to work tomorrow, and Doctor Rana (*What if you had said more? Why did you lie about* how *you injured yourself?*). Sitting alone in a foyer swarming with people waiting to enter the theatre doesn't help.

With my Tuesday dress still in the wash, I'm reasonably dressed in grey pinstripe trousers, a white jumper and a large cardigan, but to give you a sense of the remaining audience, CGT is located within walking proximity of a coffee shop brazenly charging six pounds for a small latte and a restaurant masquerading as a pub called *Gentri-Pied*. So patrons and audience members – primarily of a certain age and demographic – tend to dress in suits, ties, dresses and heels.

To explain away my lack of the aforementioned dress-code, I keep my work lanyard around my neck.

I'm glad to find my seat just before the lights dim and the show starts.

During the interval, I use the bathroom, then head to the second floor to see the exhibition. It's free for anyone visiting and is made up of podiums showcasing our costume department's best designs from previous plays.

I slip into the milling crowd and bend over, reading the placard for a floor-length, gold-yellow dress made of feathered layers, alongside a matching molten-gold halo crown with each spike covered in shimmering crystals. It's stunning and I wow audibly.

'I'll have to let Sophie know you're a fan.'

I turn to my right where a white man in a suit and dress shoes is looking at me. My pulse quickens because there's no mistaking he's talking to me. He's handsome, with a long face, dark hair and dimples that stretch down to his jaw when he smiles.

'I'm sorry?'

'My friend Sophie helped design this collection,' he says.

'Really?' I look back at the bright dresses and glittering crystals. My mind blanks briefly. 'That's impressive.'

'That's what we tell her,' he replies. 'Did you manage to see this show when it was on?'

'No, I missed it' – my night to help Dad to bed – 'but I heard it was highly theatrical, you know, top hats and jazz hands. The literal definition of a show.' *Are you talking too much? I feel like you're talking too much!*

He rubs his chin with a hand and his silver watch hits the light as much as the yellow dress' headpiece does. 'It really was, if not too ostentatious. I'm Ben, by the way.' He holds out his hand.

Oh fuck. I've been keeping my hands locked so I wouldn't default to wild, nerve-fuelled gestures. I unclasp and take his gently. 'Maddie,' I say.

'Short for Madeleine?'

'Yes.'

'A beautiful classic.'

Oh fuck. Is that . . . a line? I think it is. Just be cool and say something interesting.

'I used to hate it.'

'Why?'

Yes, Maddie – why indeed? Why did I say that, to this stranger called Ben? Especially since I don't fully understand why I used to hate my name; something vague about how I don't quite match it. I am simply not the person you'd expect if you'd only heard the name Madeleine Wright.

45

'I'd look in the mirror and never felt like it fit,' I answer.

'I get that,' he says. 'I used to hate being called Benjamin, still do. I grew up with friends named Jared, Brick and Colson. I felt incredibly ordinary.'

I smile and say, 'Oh, the trials and tribulations of Benjamin . . .?'

'Featherstone.' I raise an eyebrow and he laughs. 'Fair enough,' he says. 'Do you have a less pretentious surname?'

'Wright,' I answer. 'Madeleine Wright.' I press my lips together and nod. 'Circumspect parents,' I add. The bell rings for the play's second half. 'Oh, I have to get back.'

'You're here for the show? I came last night – that's a shame.'

'It is? Is the second half not very good?'

'I meant, with my luck I would have been sitting right beside you and now I've missed out.'

Marry me?

I nod and smile. 'Yes, that is a shame.'

He considers me. 'Or maybe not,' he finally says. 'Perhaps I could take your number?'

I miss so much of the play's second act because all I can think about is Ben. He asked for my number and I gave it to him. He said he looked forward to talking to me again. WHAT DOES THAT EVEN MEAN? I'd google it, but phones out during a theatre performance are prohibited.

'How do you plead?' an actor onstage asks.

'Not guilty!' the witch proclaims.

'Burn the truth from her!' a jury member screams.

I think he's in his late-twenties. Ben Featherstone. What if he does ask me out on a date? I can't go. What if it's my day with Dad? What happens if it's not and the date goes well? Eventually Ben would want to see where I lived. He'd expect me to live alone or with flatmates, like most people in their twenties. Maybe I shouldn't have given him my number, but it just slipped out. Did I shout them at him or relay the numbers in a nonchalant fashion? Why am I so bad at this?

Lack of practice.

My first and last boyfriend (unless you count being married to Jeremiah Stephens for the duration of lunch break in year three, which I don't, because he promptly divorced me and was married to Kerry Jennings by Golden Time) was a boy in my year when I was seventeen. Eight years I've been out of the game, and it was hardly what you'd call a relationship anyway. We only held hands and kissed (no tongue) near the bus stop after school for nearly three months. He grabbed my boob a grand total of four times – and it was always the left one. We broke up weeks before our last day of college because he wanted to be single for Freshers' Week of university. I haven't had another boyfriend since.

'How long must I proclaim my innocence?' the witch cries. 'Drown me and I sink, then I'm innocent but dead. Drown me and I survive, you burn me at the stake!'

What if Ben calls and expects an actual conversation? I hate talking on the phone. My eloquence only reveals itself when I can take the time to think about what I want to say, write it down and edit it a few times before hitting *send*.

Even at the obnoxious, egotistical age of seventeen, my 'boyfriend' and I didn't have much to say to each other. Our phone calls were so awkward, just gaps of silence and, intermittently, breathing. I shudder at the memory.

47

Members of the audience gasp.

'How can that be?' an actor declares, and I realise I've missed something crucial in the play.

I try to pay attention.

I really hope Ben sends a text instead of calling.

Chapter Four

Ben doesn't call or text, and I endlessly alternate between relief and disappointment, until an actual piece of life-altering news occurs.

I think I may have found the perfect flat.

With my current salary and atypical lack of a social life, I'm hoping to rent a room in London for a maximum of eight hundred pounds a month with bills included, so I spend my free evenings and entire weekend at viewings until I meet Jo Bowen (whose name is actually Joseph because her mother believes free speech can't exist if any words remain gender-assigned. Jo has a sister called James who goes by Jamie and a brother called Elizabeth who goes by Eli). Jo has a room available in a three-bedroom flat in Wandsworth located a ten-minute walk from two stations.

Hi Maddie,
Yes, the room is still available! You'll be living with me and another flatmate called Cam, who moved in last week. She works as a primary school teacher's assistant and I work in the charity sector. Are you free to view the room and meet us Sunday afternoon? x

The ground-floor maisonette is an old build and the land-lady, Winnie (Jo's mum, and possibly short for Winston?), bought this house in the seventies. The kitchen has white panel cupboards, an old-fashioned oven and linoleum floors; the fridge is the most modern fixture. The corridor is long but narrow, Cam's room is next to the kitchen, and the living room is bright and colourful, with a red sofa in the middle and a teal armchair with a tartan blanket draped over it in the corner. A painted tapestry of a rural village hangs on the wall and two tall bookcases are slotted into opposite corners. Like the kitchen, it has enough room for three people, and there's even a small garden out the back. Upstairs, Jo shows me a separate toilet and bathroom. I picture myself in the tub, lights off, candles lit, bubbles, music, Shloer in a wine glass and bath bombs that change the colour of the water pink.

Then we walk into what would be my room. It's bigger than the box room I currently reside in at home, and I briefly consider what I'd do with the space if it were given to me.

The room comes with a double bed, a large wardrobe, wide windows and a small desk and chair. The rent is more than I hoped to pay, but this is the best flat – and residents – I've found by far.

Before Jo, I'd spent an entire day wishing the opportunity to move out had been presented to me earlier. Only a day before my search began, Shu messaged to say Lydia had agreed to them living together and they were now looking for a place for just the two of them. Since then I'd met shared-bathroom-nightmare Carrie, who'd left two used tampons floating in the toilet; four-in-the-house-and-there-fore-four-sets-of-crusting-washing-up-left-in-the-sink Jennifer, and who could forget are-you-single-because-this-is-an-*open*-kind-of-house Tim? I'd of course met some

50

regular people too, but not surprisingly their rooms were snapped up before I'd even caught the train home.

Usually I'd stand in the corner whilst I was essentially interviewed by the prospective flatmates, but Jo offers me a cup of tea and a seat on her squashy sofa and when Cam is off the phone we all talk about work, books and social lives (theirs far more distinct than mine).

Jo has wavy dark-blond hair and bright blue eyes that make me think she could cry on cue, whilst Cam is the opposite. She has short brunette hair (which I think used to be longer because she often reaches up to pull it into a ponytail before realising she can't), brown eyes, a slim face, very . . . unobjectionable. Ryan Fellows in secondary school once called me plain-looking. He was surprised by my offended reaction. He said it was a compliment, that there was nothing odd about my face, that I still looked nice without any make-up on. Looking at Cam, I understand what he was getting at.

'I'm still new around here,' says Cam, 'but it's a great area. The commute is easy and there's shops and bars everywhere.'

'My two previous flatmates moved out to move in with their partners,' adds Jo.

Cam rolls her eyes and says, 'Social convention strikes again.'

'You wouldn't move in with a partner?' I ask her.

'Oh, I would,' she says, 'but I like to indulge in hypocrisy every now and again.'

Cam leaves shortly after to meet a friend for dinner and it's just Jo and me. I suddenly remember what Shu said about threateningly pretty flatmates. As Jo speaks about the decline of our government and whether Eton College is

51

worth all the praise if this is what it keeps churning out, I consider her. She has big, pale blue eyes, round cheeks and an easy smile, with a needle-thin gap in her front teeth. She has on a giant blue jumper, grey leggings, pink socks, and her feet swing inches from the floor.

Am I threatened by her? *No.*

Not because she isn't pretty – it's because . . . well, why should I be threatened when I don't have a Lydia, a partner to protect? Why should I feel threatened when I don't see myself having someone to shelter against the harsh vicissitudes that is other female beauty?

I think of Ben who has yet to call or text.

'I think that's enough about me,' Jo says. 'Cam, even though she moved in only last week, is great, as you saw. She can be a little sarcastic, but aren't we all? She's not much of a girly girl, but I kind of like that. I can throw enough glitter around for the three of us. Are you very girly?'

'Oh.' I frown. 'I'm not actually sure.'

Jo tilts her head and I wonder if I've failed the interview. She smiles. 'Still finding out who you are?' she asks.

I consider her question. 'I think I'm just starting to learn, actually.'

On my way home, Jo messages to say that after a phone call with Cam, they've decided the room is mine if I want it.

And I do – the only problem is, they need someone ASAP.

My options are to miss out on the room or start paying rent in a week's time. Although it's a great flat, this isn't a decision to take lightly. I really have to consider whether—

I send Jo the deposit straight from my savings account.

It's not my day to give Dad his dinner and medication, but I text Dawoud that I will tonight, though if he can still come to put Dad to bed that would be great. Even with the prescription painkillers, my back still pinches slightly when I reach down.

I make lasagne from scratch, taking out the cooked beef mince I made yesterday and layering the pasta with it, alternating with yogurt-based white sauce. I plate up a piece and add the usual side salad. 'Time for dinner, Dad!' I gently kick the door open since my hands are full. 'I made lasagne.'

'Oh, goody,' Dad says. He smiles widely but isn't looking directly at me.

I feed him small bites and we watch a football match. I say, 'Mum's back on Thursday. Hopefully she'll cook all your favourites.'

I feed him another forkful and take a deep breath.

'So I'm going to be moving out soon.'

He continues to chew his food and watch the TV.

'I'm going to be leaving home, Dad,' I say. 'To live somewhere else? Is that *okay*?'

Then I feel mean, as if I'm tricking him with the word 'okay'.

He says, 'Hmmm,' but chews a little slower.

I lower the fork I was going to offer him. My heart gently beats. 'Can I?' I ask quietly. 'Can I go, Dad?'

He stops chewing and frowns. He's trying to speak, but as usual right before his meds, his brain won't allow him to form the words that must be on the tip of his tongue.

'It's a flat in Wandsworth,' I say, offering him more food. My eyes are suddenly stinging and my voice is a touch deeper. 'Remember our first house in Battersea? Well, it's walking distance from there.'

I give him some salad and a player on the TV scores a goal.

'I'm not leaving until Mum's back, but you'll hardly notice I'm gone!'

His face is blank.

'I'll be coming to see you lots, to check up on you, *okay*?'

He nods.

There's something about a penalty, but I have no idea who it's been awarded to.

I stare at Dad, and he's closed his eyes, so I put his tray down. I place my hand gently on top of his. I pat it softly then reach for his evening medicine packet.

Chapter Five

'Maddie, can we speak for a moment?'

I've only stepped through the office doors and almost walk straight into Ellie. It's obvious she's been standing there waiting for me.

'Sure.'

I walk to my desk, but Ellie tightens her messy bun, adjusts her glasses and says, 'No. Erm, in a meeting room.'

I frown. 'Is something wrong?'

'We can talk more when we're in there.'

There's a sudden pit in my stomach I can't attach to anything tangible. Naturally, I think of everything I've done wrong in my life up until this point.

'Can I put my things down?' I ask.

Ellie looks at Claire, who's just joined us, ponytail forever-swinging. 'It's all right if you want to bring them with you,' Claire says.

I follow them to the meeting room two doors down in silence and take a seat. My heart beats erratically and I'm beginning to sweat.

Claire closes the door and attempts to smile. The two of them take seats opposite me. Claire speaks first. 'An incident arose yesterday when you were off.'

'Yes,' I start. 'I . . .' My voice wavers and I cough. I booked the day off to spend with Dad, but I don't want to tell them that. 'I'd booked the day off in advance.'

'We know. That's not the problem,' Claire says. 'Yesterday morning, Katherine had an external appointment in her diary. She made it to the supposed location – two hours away.'

I look at both Claire and Ellie in turn; I can't even guess where this is going.

'It turns out the date of the meeting had changed,' Claire continues, 'but you didn't amend her diary. Katherine returned to the office, in the afternoon, very . . . out of sorts and we all know how temperamental and delicate she is at the moment.'

I sigh, relieved. There *has* been a mistake, after all. 'I didn't put anything into her diary for yesterday morning,' I explain. 'And I made sure her day made sense before the weekend. I wasn't told before then that any timings had changed. Did she accept an amended invitation that went directly to her or something?'

Claire looks away. 'Maddie, needless to say, Katherine no longer feels you're suited for the role as her PA.'

I blink and shake my head. 'You're firing me?'

Claire leans in and I can smell the citrus in her perfume. 'No, *we're* not, but Katherine does feel the two of you are no longer compatible and has decided she needs some-one . . . more equipped. Someone who would spot some-thing like this coming.'

What, a psychic?

'Someone who can anticipate her thoughts, rather than wait to be told. To know when she might need a coffee instead of a tea. Someone who can ensure her workspace is clutter-free at all times. Unlocking her office door before she arrives. We all know Katherine is fragile and struggling a bit, so it's really about taking care of the little things she doesn't want to think about, just to alleviate the pressure. She needs—'

'A carer?'

Claire and Ellie simultaneously blush.

'We just think you're more suited to an independent role and that's admirable!' Claire says.

My supposed line manager Ellie just sits there, hunched forward with her hands in her lap, looking everywhere but at me.

I catch my reflection in the window, release the tension in my forehead. 'I'm being fired?'

'As it's a sudden termination in contract, we'll pay you for the weeks in the month you have worked, including today,' Claire says, 'and I can promise you, Maddie, should you need a letter of recommendation, I will write you a stellar one.'

'We all know Katherine's been struggling for a while now,' Ellie finally says. She clears her throat. 'You shouldn't take it personally.'

I press my lips together and briefly consider spitting in her eye but decide that would be disgusting and maybe assault. Plus, lucky for her, my mouth is completely dry.

'You don't have to leave right this minute,' Claire says. 'You can stay in here for a while, if you'd like,' but she leans back into her chair, presentation over. Any questions?

I again look at them each in turn and the word *fake* springs to mind. It wasn't long ago Katherine was scream-ing at me because of calendar clashes *she'd* caused. As soon as Katherine had gone to her next meeting, they both came rushing to my side, telling me how unacceptable it was, how out of line Katherine had been and was I all right? Are you sure you're all right, Maddie? I'd felt like they were on my side, and it had made that afternoon disappear quicker. Little did I know, they didn't give a shit.

'I think I'll leave now.'

They each sigh with relief.

'*Fuck*. I've just been fired.'

No one pays any attention to the woman with wide eyes standing under a bridge, talking to herself.

I look back in the direction of the theatre, at the doors I was, to all intents and purposes, kicked out of. I look out at the stream of pedestrians around me; everyone is just going about their day.

Having nothing to do on a weekday has never happened to me before. Whenever I take days off, it's not to rest but to get other things done: doctor appointments, washing my hair, immigration office visits when we realised Dad's visa had expired. Even yesterday saw me cleaning the house and sorting through bills whenever Dad slept.

God, I can't tell Mum I've been fired. There exists no greater shame in her mind than forced unemployment. She'd think it was my fault because there's always a reason someone is fired. What reason do I give her? A missed invite in Katherine's calendar that I didn't even accept? She'd never believe me.

Understandably. Because aren't you supposed to get fired for atrocities like sleeping with the married boss, embezzling money or, you know, murder? All that had died in that office was my will to live; all I did was . . . I'm still not clear on what I did or didn't do, but I know it didn't warrant immediate dismissal. I still had my mid-morning snack in my bag. Had I even taken my jacket off since I shrugged it on this morning?

I shuffle on the spot before heading back into the train station. I sit and wait for the 9:33 train. I have never gotten on the 9:33 train. At least the carriages will be empty.

Q **Google** – What to do when you've been fired

Shit! You've been fired! Here's what you need to do next
1. Rejoice – you're free from the repressing, grinding perpetual cog of capitalism
2. Search for a new job – you may want to return to the repressing, grinding perpetual cog of capitalism, and that's okay. It's never too early or too soon to dust off the old CV and start looking for new jobs. The sooner, the better.
3. Make a claim to the employment tribunal (p.s. it is a faff and it's unlikely you'll win the case) and/or submit a grievance – if you have been unjustly fired, this is the best way to stick it to the man who did the firing.
4. Start budgeting – because, let's face it, you're broke now, or at least will be once you realise your next pay cheque won't come until after interviews, job acceptance and a full month of employment.

I try a different search result.

Q **Google** – What to do after you've been fired

• Ask for a written and signed statement explaining your termination

- Seek unemployment benefits
- Have faith in yourself and your future

I place a damp hand on my forehead to cool it down.

A text message rolls down my phone screen from an unsaved number.

> Hi Maddie. It's Ben from the other night. How have you been?

Ben. Of course *this* is when he'd decide to text me. Then I remember the flat I've just paid the deposit and first month's rent for. I can't deal with all of this right now. I switch off my phone and take a deep breath.

'*Fuck*,' I exhale.

The man in a suit sitting two seats from me with grease on his tie looks up from his before-10 a.m. burger and says, 'Same.'

Chapter Six

Let's just pause here and take a second to look at my life as it currently stands.

The Life of Maddie
Unemployed
Contractually obligated to pay £850 rent
a month for new flat
Mum's coming home tomorrow
Savings have taken a hit due to deposit, first month's rent
and now no incoming pay cheque
I'm single and Mum's coming home tomorrow

I decide to start with the first and most pressing issue. I open my CV and type 'PA jobs' into Google. But . . . do I *have* to be a PA? *What else are you qualified for?* I have a First in English Literature, thank you very much – that's got to do something for me. Maybe it's time to give the publishing industry another try. I applied to so many editorial roles before CGT because . . . well, I like books, but got rejected from them all with no explanation as to why. Maybe with CGT experience under my belt, I'll have more of a chance.

Q **Google** – Editorial assistant jobs

Search pages upon search pages reveal themselves to me and not just in editorial but roles in marketing, sales and audio. There are so many to apply to. I can't believe it. Maybe me getting fired was a blessing in disguise because it looks like hiring season in the publishing industry is— Twenty-three thousand pounds a year?! I thought I was supposed to be making *more* money as I got older. That was the deal, right?

The doorbell goes and I toss my laptop aside to answer it. 'Auntie Mabel!'

'Baaba, I didn't think you would be home,' she says. 'I expected Dawoud.'

Whoops. 'I've got the day off work today,' I tell her, repeating what I told Dad. 'Holiday day.'

'I see. Then how are you, Baaba? Is your father in?'

Auntie Mabel is the only member of the family to call James and me exclusively by our Ghanaian name days. I was born on a Thursday, so my middle name is Baaba, whilst James was born on a Monday, so his middle name is Jojo.

'I'm fine, thank you,' I answer, taking the heavy bag, currently releasing auspicious smells, from her shoulder. 'And yes he is.'

When my auntie asks if Dad is in, what she really means is, is he awake?

I open the door wide so, with the help of her cane, she can slowly climb in. 'How are you, Auntie?'

'Fine, by the grace of God,' she says. 'You already know about my back and my foot. Living room?'

I nod, then say, 'Yes' because when I was eight years old I learned the hard way how rude it is in our culture to address your elders non-verbally, even for the shortest of responses. I never saw that slap on my temple coming, but I've never forgotten it. Her name was – wait for it – Aunt Patience. She had short eyebrows and rough palms. I don't think she was even family; she was married to one of mum's 'cousins' or something.

I love my Auntie Mabel, however. She's blunt and feisty but in a way that doesn't offend me. She's younger than Dad but looks just like him, which must be why I can see bits of me in her. We have the same full lips and strong jaw.

Today she has on her customary black cotton head wrap, tracksuit bottoms, trainers and a jumper before her coat, and as always my attention is first drawn to the marks on her cheeks. 'Not scars, Baaba. Tribal marks.'

She lives in North London and has her own list of health problems, not limited to sore joints, so she only comes by once or twice a month. But her monthly appearance serves us better than James's. She brings Dad home-made pepper soup, which I put straight on the stove, and she sits with her brother for hours talking in Twi.

Dad understands more of his language than English (maybe because he's been speaking it since he was old enough to) and, these days, even finds it easier to communicate in. I can understand what's being said, even when interchanged between Twi and Fante, but I wish I could speak the language. My parents spoke it all the time at home, but James and I only got as far as understanding it, always responding in English. We'd be prompted to do otherwise, but we could never grasp it and I didn't consider it important in my more adaptable, formative years; all my friends spoke English, and I still understood what my parents were saying regardless, so why bother? I never thought a day would come when I felt left out.

If I hadn't made it clear before, let me do that now. Dad doesn't get a lot of visitors. He never had many friends; used to be a bit of a recluse, a hermit. Mum often jokes he's where I get my solitary nature from. She made it seem as if it's one of Dad's faults, that he lacks social graces. I, however, see it for what it really is: he's an introvert.

The world is filled with two different kinds of people: those who need to be surrounded by others and those who do not. Dad and I are simply the latter, James and Mum the former. Whenever Auntie Mabel comes round, I wonder what became of Dad's few friends. I've never asked and now he won't remember.

There used to be a man Dad would laugh, watch football and drink beer with. A man I called Uncle (he wasn't blood-related) . . . Richard? Albert? Caleb? I sometimes think about what happened to him. It's possible Uncle X saw Dad's health deteriorating and couldn't handle it. It happens. When people are ill to the point of no return to full health, to the person they used to be, some don't have the stomach to stick around. We don't appreciate being reminded of our own body's weaknesses, our lack of control and inevitable mortality. Or maybe moving from Battersea to Croydon put distance between them, a distance Uncle X couldn't be bothered to continually cross.

Now Dad doesn't have any friends who aren't family. Which isn't entirely the case for me, but not too far off.

If I were Dad, which of my friends would I see monthly? Who would come to visit me with a home-cooked meal? *Would James even?*

I hang around for a few minutes, then excuse myself, leaving Dad with his little sister.

So that's now Dad and my auntie I've lied to. I don't want to tell Dad I've been fired. I don't want anyone to know I've been fired, and unless I tell them, no one will ever find out.

I briefly close my eyes.

Okay, maybe I can say I chose to leave because I'm a woman of principle and I wasn't going to take another day of tyranny under the—

I sigh and pick up when Avi calls. News about me being fired yesterday has spread around the office, and when I tell her what happened, Avi shoulders a steaming mass of indignation on my behalf.

'Senior members of staff can't keep getting away with this!' she whispers. 'It's like we're disposable! You should complain to HR.'

'You know, Google said something similar. You think it's worth doing?'

'What have you got to lose?' she asks, and I think she might be right. 'The office is *so* weird now,' Avi tells me. 'I walked in this morning and it was just a creepy atmosphere. Katherine's still crying in the toilets, but then smiling like a maniac at everyone like she didn't fire you for no reason.' Avi pauses to lower her voice. 'Listen . . . everyone's on your side by the way,' she says, 'but obviously we don't want to say anything in case, you know, we get fired too.'

After the phone call, I open my laptop. Emboldened, I write an email to HR explaining the unfairness of the situation. I write of 'the bureaucratic-soaked injustice perpetrated by senior members of staff who, aided by HR, seek to further harden the hierarchical blocks of which constitute the theatre's current foundation'. I end with a thinly veiled (okay, *empty*) threat to sue, but with an after note stating I will still be expecting a decent reference should a future employer ask for one.

Auntie Mabel stays for a few hours and calls me down when she's on her way out.

'How is Jojo?' she asks. 'The big, strong boy.'

I inwardly roll my eyes. James is hardly a *boy* at twenty-eight. It's obvious who her favourite is, but I don't mind because Auntie Mabel is James's favourite too; she would cook a lot for us when Mum first started travelling to Ghana.

'He's fine, Auntie,' I answer.

'Good, good. Your mother's back tomorrow?' she asks when we're in the corridor. She leans heavily on her cane, but I know better than to offer a seat – 'It's my brother's house, Baaba – I know I can have a seat and I will sit when I want to be seated.' Auntie Mabel's the youngest of four children (Aunt Rebecca was the oldest, followed by Uncle Freddie, who rarely leaves Ghana, then Dad) and in her early fifties, but she's had joint problems for the last two decades. She managed to keep finding ways to overrule them, but I remember when she had to concede and how she slung biblical curses at the cane when she'd first had to use it.

'Yes,' I answer. 'I'll be moving out now that she'll be back.'

I watch my auntie intently because I have such respect and love for her that if she told me to stay, I wouldn't want to disappoint. I would stay.

'Well . . .' She frowns, but then sighs. 'It is time. It's never been right: you being here, the only one responsible for your father,' she says, and inwardly, I sigh with relief. 'You're too young and need to live your British life. You know, in Ghana, it is the children's responsibility to be the primary persons of care for an ill father *but only* if his wife has passed.' She sniffs and stamps her cane. 'When she is back, your mother can step in and do her duty. Hmm. I must go now. I'm travelling to Ghana next week to visit Freddie, so I will see you another time.'

I help her down the step. 'Bye, Auntie. Love you.'

'You as well, Baaba.'

When I bring Dad dinner, I notice his finger and toenails are freshly trimmed and Auntie Mabel's put on a new pair of thick sock boots for his swollen feet.

I push the stool back to the corner as she must have been sat on it when she tended to his nails. The last time I was in Ghana, ten years ago now, I couldn't understand how the women in my family did it: hunched over bowls when pounding yam, stooping for water, sweeping with short-handled brooms. If I sit improperly at my desk for four hours, my back screams all the way home.

It's a reminder: the women in my family have spines of steel.

Chapter Seven

I hear Mum before I see her.

'Forty-five pounds for a cab?' she says. 'You're a thief. God will not bless you.'

I take a deep breath and open the door.

'My baby!'

She wears black trousers and a loose white top. Her hair used to be longer but she must have cut it recently and her growing Afro is forming tight coils. Her skin is flawless as always; spots struggle to break the surface because her diet in Ghana is different from mine here. She eats only yam, rice, soup, chicken and vegetables. She drinks litres of water to keep up with the sun. Mum's naturally lighter than James and I are, but she always returns from Ghana darker. She spends a lot of time outside, rushing between hostel rooms, cleaning the compound and negotiating with contractors. Her tan is a reminder of the fact that she is more active, more alive, when in Ghana.

'Oh, I've missed my baby so much!' When she hugs me, I rest my head on her shoulder; she's shorter than me by a couple of inches, but she has strength in her body so the hug still feels like it's mine. She smells of cocoa butter and faint perfume.

'How are you, Mum?' I ask when she lets go.

'I'm blessed, my dear. My bags, please.' I bring them in and she asks, 'How's work?'

I focus on heaving her suitcase over the threshold. 'Fine. Using up a few holiday days. You've cut your hair?'

Mum runs a hand through her coils. 'Yes, it was so damaged and shorter is more manageable for the heat.' She walks into the living room and loudly says, 'Fiifi' – Dad's Ghanaian name – 'how are you doing?'

I watch Dad closely, but he simply smiles at Mum. 'Fine,' he says.

Mum pats his arm. 'Always happy to see me, hmm? You're well?' Dad slowly nods and she says, 'Good, good. Anyway.' She walks into the kitchen next and I already wish she would stop and sit down. Her energy makes me restless. I remember it's not my house and that my daily routine will have to change in order to accommodate her presence.

'Has your father eaten?' Mum asks, opening the fridge.

'It's not his dinner time yet.'

'I am hungry – have you prepared anything?'

'There's lasagne in the fridge.'

She inspects the container. 'I hope it's seasoned well.'

She gets two plates down from the cupboard above the sink. I don't usually eat for another hour still, but she's already spooning out two portions. I go into the living room. 'Hey, Dad, you *okay*?'

He smiles. 'Yes, I'm okay.' His face and demeanour hasn't changed since this morning; at first, I wonder if he really realises Mum is back. Then, as I eat in the kitchen, balancing my plate in one hand, fork in the other, and Mum tells me about running the hostel in Ghana, I wonder if my dad's brain has made him think that Mum never actually left.

James
Is Mum back now?

Maddie
Yep

James
You still moving out?

Maddie
Yes

James
It's about time but are we sure we wanna leave Dad with Mum?

Maddie
You can always move in for a bit. My room will be empty.

James
Lol that room is a shoebox Mads. And no one can look after Dad like you. You're his favourite

Chapter Eight

Unbelievable. I was hoping to open my emails and find a job interview offer but instead I'm greeted with a single-line response from HR at CGT.

From: HR@thetheatre.com
To: mad.wright@gmail.com
Subject: RE: Injustice I tell you!

Thank you for your email, Maddie. We will consider this matter further in due course.
Sincerely,
The HR team

My bedroom door handle rattles and Mum lets herself in. I close my laptop and frown at her. 'Do come in,' I say.

Mum shrugs. 'It's my house,' she says.

'Technically, it's Dad's. His name is on the mortgage.'

She swipes at me. 'Did I not bear his heavy children, hmm? You were the heaviest, you know. James wasn't allowed to carry you in case he hurt himself. Come help me in the garden.'

'. . . And you shouldn't be cooking him lunch and dinner every day,' Mum says. 'That's why the carer is here; I don't know how many times I must tell you that.'

Mum squints in the sun as I hand her a peg and she throws a clean sheet over the garden dryer line. This is nice, hanging up the washing; a nice, normal mother-and-daughter activity. All that's missing are sun hats, lemonade and enjoyable conversation.

'You'll wear yourself out,' she continues. 'No wonder you were sounding so miserable on the phone as of late. You've been doing too much. Your father isn't well and he needs professionals looking after him, not a twenty-three-year-old.'

'I'm twenty-five, Mum.'

'Yes, of course.' She raises her eyebrows. 'It's because you're not married, so my brain thinks you must be younger.'

Wow.

'How has your father been doing anyway? I try to talk to him, but he doesn't understand me, I think.'

'He's better,' I answer truthfully. 'You were right about that.'

She stops to look at me as if I've stated the obvious. 'I am never wrong,' she says. 'All is well. Maybe now you can feel comfortable living your life in your new flat. Do you have a boyfriend yet?'

I remember Ben's text and how I've yet to reply. The longer I leave it, the more I feel it's too late. 'No, Mum, I don't.'

She drops her arms from the line. 'That's weird, isn't it?' she says, looking at me. 'You know, you're so pretty. I know all mothers say that about their daughters, but many mothers are lying. You actually are beautiful, so I don't understand it. Twenty-five and no boyfriend, ever.' She narrows her eyes. 'You're not into girls, are you?'

'No, Mum, I'm not.'

72

'Huh, very weird then.' She pushes her mouth down, hitching up the sleeves of her tunic. 'When do you plan to get married?' Before I can answer, she says, 'You don't have long. I know you think you do because you're twenty-five, but it is only men who can make babies whenever. For us women, there is a clock.' She makes a grabbing motion with her hand, so I give her another clothes peg. 'Time is running low because you'll have to meet the man,' she continues, 'date, then wait for him to propose, be engaged, then marriage before you even think of children, especially if you're going to have more than one. You want more than one?'

'Maybe.'

She sighs. 'How can you not know, Maame? How can you not think of these things?'

'I do, but children are worth *really* thinking about,' I say. 'Looking after children properly . . . it's hard.'

'I know that, I am a mother.' *There's more to being a mother than giving birth* . . . 'You need not think too hard, because for women, babies are natural. It is men who need the help. You'll be fine once you start to have them.' I want to say: I'd like to be more than a 'fine' mother, but it doesn't come out in time. 'Also, you have me to guide you, if you are scared.'

I don't say anything about this.

'Are you looking in the right places?' Mum asks. 'Like I have said, church is a good place. You want to make sure you get the right partner; you have to pray about it, pray that God sends you the right man. Look at what happened to me and your father. I don't want that for you, my only daughter.' Seconds later, she adds, 'Who will you marry? Will he be Black?'

'Mum, I don't know. I don't have a crystal ball.'

She whips her head round at this. 'I should hope not. Crystal balls are witchcraft. Anyway, I don't mind if he is white – with the time it is taking you, we can't afford to eliminate too many prospects. No, so long as he is God-fearing, that is number one, and financially stable, number two. Although, someone from our own culture will be easier for you.'

'You just said you don't mind.'

'I still have a preference,' she says. 'Dating a Black, if not Ghanaian, man will be easier because there is less to explain. Do you understand this?'

I'm about to say I do but—

'That way it's not always "why do you do this" and "why do you think that". They will already know because they have lived it. When someone doesn't understand you, how you are, why you are, you will find yourself fighting losing battles every day. They will seem small at first, but you will spend your life watching them grow, in size and importance. Listen to me, Maame. Your mother is very wise in these things.'

I can't help but agree with parts of her statement because I know she's speaking from experience. Dad, although also Ghanaian, wasn't the best husband and James and I grasped that early on. This still dramatically calls into question Mum's *it would be easier if he were* . . . manifesto, but I do see where she's coming from. Dad's foibles are a him thing, not a Ghanaian thing. When well, he was very private, unlearned in effective communication, and was unwilling to spend money, opting instead to save for emergencies – not unlike myself, I realise.

Marriage and fatherhood to him were more an act of duty than anything else, so he had succeeded so long as there was a roof over our heads and enough food in our fridge. The problem for my parents was that Mum needed more. We'd watch her try, especially with home-cooked food and spontaneous hugs, but it was almost as if Dad didn't enjoy being touched. I thought maybe just in front of his children, but one day I asked myself, what if it extends beyond that?

If they were two people I was casually observing, I'd have come to the quick conclusion that they just weren't a match. But because they're *my* parents, I laboured under the delusion that I'd be happier if my parents were together rather than apart, and I'd alternate between who was letting the other down. It used to be Dad, then Mum started to leave and he got ill, so it was Mum letting him down, but by then it was too late for him to ask for all that she'd previously tried to give. Her heart was no longer in it.

James would tell me this moment directly coincided with Dad's diagnosis, but I'd (silently) argue that it happened long before then, before Dad was ill, before Grandad died and left Mum the commitment.

All I know is, their marriage has taught me many things but sadly it's mainly taught me what to avoid.

'Okay, Mum.'

She sniffs, unimpressed. 'I bet you talk to your friends about boys but not your own mother.'

I hand her another peg. 'You once said friends and mothers aren't the same.'

'Of course they're not.'

I roll my eyes when she can't see. 'Some mothers and daughters are best friends,' I point out.

'Those mothers don't know what they're doing.'

'Mum!'

'It's true!' She kisses her teeth to reinforce this. 'We are not age-mates, Maddie. We are not peers. There is a reason mother is one word and friend is another. You should tell your friends some things and your mother everything.'

'Everything proves difficult to fit into every other year.'

She doesn't flinch. 'Then maybe you should spend more time in Ghana.'

'Never mind.'

'Why not?' She hangs up the last of Dad's bed sheets. 'Why don't you ever want to come home?'

'I am home, Mum.'

'You were born here, it's true, but your blood and DNA is in Ghanaian soil. It's been a decade since your last visit. Tell me why you don't love your mother country.'

'It's not that I dislike it. I just don't feel like I belong there.'

'How can you feel like you don't belong in a country where everyone is like you?' she asks.

I already know I can't explain it in a way Mum will find acceptable. To her, if my reasoning isn't logical, then it is false. I can't explain how I didn't like the red grounds of our compound whilst others skipped across it. I didn't like that the last time I was there my cousins made fun of my accent and called me a princess behind my back. I didn't like that the girls had been carrying heavy bowls and buckets, evidently from birth, and when I offered to help, my arms were compared to the legs of a chicken. I wasn't fast enough for *trotros*; I didn't eat enough, my Western diet was failing me and that's why my bum and hips had grown but not my boobs, not like theirs had.

I was used to British rain and struggled under the orange Ghanaian sun; I couldn't balance anything on my head; I couldn't sweep the floors because I failed to fit the African broom end into my palm and use the force necessary to have bound-together sticks work effectively.

76

I look at Mum, how she tilts her head to the sun, and consider whether my reluctance to return to Ghana is comparative to her reluctance in being here.

'I don't speak Twi or any other dialects,' I finally say.

'Whose fault is that?'

I sigh. 'It's fine. I couldn't go anyway. If both you and I aren't here, what about Dad?'

She mimics my sigh. 'Maddie, you can leave him for a week or two. He has the carer and your older brother.' She turns to look at me. 'You are burdened with guilt, but if your father understood what was happening around him, he would beg you to go, to live your life. He and I came to this country so our children would advance; we did not come to hold you back.' She rubs my cheek with her thumb. 'When you see what life is like outside of this house, you will understand and you will wish you had lived sooner.'

Later that night, I lie in bed, chewing my lip and staring at Ben's unanswered text.

Maddie

Hi Ben. Sorry it's taken me ages to get back to you. Family stuff

Hi Ben! OMG how have I only just seen your message? How weird!

Hi Ben. I thought I'd replied but didn't press send!

Hi Ben

Ben

I wondered if you'd text back

Chapter Nine

You've now met my mother so are at least part way to under-standing why I can't tell her I'm unemployed. Even if I did manage to convince her I was fired through no fault of my own, she'd tell me to sue for unfair dismissal. As if we have the funds to take on the conglomerate beast that is the CGT.

No, it's best I keep that to myself.

However, I do tell her I'm searching for a new job, 'a new *challenge*', so when I do get one, my wanting to leave won't have dropped out of thin air.

Instead of going to work, I go to the British Library and spend all day there. I've never been unemployed so don't know what else to do. When I was in university, I worked part-time as a bookseller, then worked as a receptionist for various companies before getting the job at CGT, never a break in between. I only left a job in order to start a new one because I should always be doing something to further myself. Mum once said if I ever struggled finding a job related to my field of study, then I should go into retail for the meantime because at least you learn customer service skills and, no matter the job, you always need good customer service skills.

Little did she know people in retail tend to hate customers.

I find a corner desk, open my laptop and apply to any and all jobs in publishing. I've done as many as are available before it's even noon. I can't leave for another four hours at least, not until the work day is over.

And yes, I *could* tell Mum the reason I'm not going to work is because I have so much holiday saved up due to the fact that I'm such a relentless hard worker, however, then I'd have to be at home.

Every time Mum returns, I realise how much I've gotten used to being alone. Now I have to wait outside the bathroom door, fight for kitchen space, have my meals judged, my social life criticised and privacy invaded. Being at the library for the majority of the day serves to avoid that.

After my first day here, when I managed to apply to all the jobs available within two hours, I developed a better routine. I read a book, apply for jobs, then write. Don't roll your eyes, please. I know it seems almost everyone wants to write something, but I used to write a lot at school. I didn't take it further because Mum said a Creative Writing degree wouldn't give me as many options as an English Literature one (and was I sure I didn't want to be sensible and study Law instead?), so I left it alone. Now I have free time to fill. Besides, signing up to all the publishing newsletters for job opportunities means I also hear of any writing events they're doing. Carrow Books are offering a fiction development programme for underrepresented writers with a deadline weeks away.

Samples will be read by associated literary agents and five selected writers will be offered the opportunity to develop their manuscript through assignments and workshops led by industry professionals. Each writer will also be offered one-on-one mentorship with a literary agent for up to six months.

All I need is a one-thousand word sample of a work in progress. A thousand words is doable and it's not like I haven't got *any* book ideas.

The life and lies of Sherlock Holmes' wife
An adult romance – England's first Black queen
University murder mystery
1960's female gang taking over London

See? I just haven't written anything substantial yet. I've got bullet points and notes and even a spider diagram for the murder mystery, but that's about it. It's like I get two hundred words in and don't know where to go from there.

What's an easy thing to write about?

I open a blank document and write about leaving Dad. How I feel guilty and sad but excited to start living my own life, to find out who I am and maybe even someone to be with. I write about my life finally starting at age twenty-five, when my peers already have partners they want to marry and stable jobs with a clear trajectory. It reads like a diary entry and I hit a block after nine hundred and seventy-one words. I won't send this one in; it's too stream-of-consciousness-heavy and probably doesn't make sense to anyone but me. I'm saving it on my laptop with my other incomplete works when an email pops up in the corner of my screen.

From: Maisie.Foster@orangetreepublishing.com
To: mad.wright@gmail.com
Subject: PA & Editorial Assistant Non-Fiction Books

Dear Maddie,
Thank you for your application for the role of PA to the Publishing Director and Editorial Assistant, Non-Fiction

Books. We were delighted to receive it and would like to invite you for an interview.

Yes! Finally. An interview, and for a job where I'll get to read all day! But Orange Tree Publishing? I've not heard of them; my desperation led me to apply for any and all publishing jobs available.

A quick Google search tells me they're a small press that don't print as many books a year as their giant brothers and sisters. They've lost out on a lot of bidding wars, unable to compete with bigger purses, and a year ago an article was published stating OTP were likely to be bought by Carrow Books just to keep themselves in print. *Yikes.* They're hiring though, so things must be looking up for them. Also, smaller presses might be tighter-knit? It would be nice to be part of a team instead of working for just one person.

I respond to Maisie choosing tomorrow's interview offer. Okay, today is a successful day. I was starting to panic. My tenancy has officially started and I'm moving out tomorrow. Not sooner because Mum wants us to have a family dinner before I leave and James isn't back from Birmingham until this evening. I was a little surprised at this considering, as noted earlier, we're not a dinner-around-the-table kind of family, but she says she's cooking my favourites and James is bringing a cake.

Despite postponing my move for James's benefit, he doesn't manage to make it to dinner. Unavoidable work stuff, apparently; I stopped asking what was so 'unavoidable' a long time ago. At least Mum is partially true to her word and makes jollof rice, roasted chicken and carrot salad before spending most of the evening in her room threatening the hostel's 'crook contractors' with 'British lawyers'.

So it's just Dad and me in the living room on Wednesday evening.

'Fitting,' I say quietly as I feed Dad his dinner. I'm less worried about leaving him now that Mum's got Dawoud to increase his working days and has managed to argue that due to her health and age, Dawoud will have to come every night to put Dad to bed.

'You should have asked for these things,' Mum said. 'Then you wouldn't have been complaining to me all the time.' She had a point, despite its blunt delivery, but the only reason I didn't ask is because I didn't know it was an option. He's my dad and it's only me here, so of course I'd have to play a part. I couldn't comprehend someone looking after him more than a member of his own family did.

Still, I'm happier with the idea of Dawoud taking care of Dad because I've had doubts about Mum's reliability. Sometimes I'd come home from 'work' when it was her night to feed him, and she'd get home later than his 6:30 p.m. dinner time. But Dawoud is always early and likes to sit and talk to (or, rather, at) Dad. I don't know where Mum goes; she says she's visiting various aunties but none of the names sound familiar. 'You have a lot of aunties,' Mum said. 'I don't expect you to remember each one.'

When Dad's eaten and taken his medication for the night, I reheat my food and join him in front of the TV.

'My last day at home,' I say quietly, but Dad's already falling asleep.

Chapter Ten

I don't have much to pack because I wear different variations of the same clothes every week.

It's strange to see the sink without my toothbrush or the banister without my towel, or to see my life in only two suitcases.

Mum's still asleep when I drag them to the door. I go into the living room and kiss Dad on the forehead. I told him again last night that I was moving out today, but maybe it won't register until he doesn't see me tomorrow morning.

'I'll see you soon, *okay*?'

He smiles and tries to nod, but it's early and his medication needs a little longer.

The Uber is here and my heart starts to pound. *Are you doing the right thing? Should you really be leaving home?*

It's fine. Remember, Dawoud's upped his hours.

Mum comes down in her dressing gown to kiss and hug me at the door. We close our eyes and she prays that I'll be safe in the new house; she'll be coming round next week to sprinkle holy water into its corners. I'll have to time her visit for when both Cam and Jo are out.

Her phone vibrates. 'Be safe, my dear,' she says before taking the call upstairs with the bedroom door closed.

I look up at the stairs, then turn away, closing the front door behind me.

I've been added to the house group chat, where Jo told me she left my key under the mat. I'm here alone until my interview at OTP this afternoon, but I have two messages waiting for me as soon as I'm connected to the Wi-Fi.

Jo
We want to go out for dinner tonight to celebrate you moving in! xxx

Cam
So don't cook anything

Maddie
Sounds good!

Before unpacking, I venture around the flat. The utensil drawer gets stuck if pulled out too far. There are blank spaces in the food cupboards and an empty shelf in the fridge. I put the leftovers Mum packed into containers for me in there and the bright orange and red stands out among the yellow cheese, white bread and pale pink wine.

I sit in the living room and look around, but nothing has changed since my first visit. I unlock the back door and step out into the garden. The gate opens up to the other side of the residential square. The garden furniture extends to a picnic table, three mismatched chairs and a mini barbeque in the corner. There's a small tree beside it and weeds stick out from cracks in the ground. Our neighbours on the left have a garden obscured by a wall of leaves, but if I stand on my toe's tips, I can just glimpse the garden on our right – it looks like a plant haven, bird feeder included.

I go back inside and upstairs to pee; the toilet lid doesn't sit exactly on the base, so I have to be careful. When I reach for toilet tissue, I notice a basket filled with spare rolls. We'll split this cost, I assume. I won't have to stand in the supermarket's queue every week wondering if we have enough left.

Jo's left her bedroom door wide open and I poke my head around the corner. Her room is marginally bigger than mine; it faces the garden and comes with two different desks and a lava lamp I'm tempted to switch on, but don't (what if it won't turn off again?!). A tower of books sit on the floor beside her bed and in the corner is a clothing rack of colourful dresses.

I think of my own meagre wardrobe. What if we go out and Jo comes out of her room in one of these dresses and I leave mine in jeans and a faded black jumper?

I online-shop for the rest of the morning, picking things I'd never wear and spending money I usually wouldn't because I can reinvent myself here. Jo and Cam don't know me and I can be whoever I want to be.

So . . . who do I want to be?

Someone cooler, more confident. Sophisticated, even? Effortless and kind of like, I don't go to things, they come to me, you know?

I land on a page of pantsuits; surely nothing screams confidence more than a woman in a sunshine-yellow suit. But where would I wear a bright suit to?

Don't overthink it, Maddie – manifest it.

If you have the suit in your wardrobe, an opportunity to wear it will present itself. I'm certain that's how manifestation works.

Q **Google** – Where do you wear a yellow suit to?

To work
On a date
To a wedding
The theatre
Around the house, like the bad, boss bitch that you are

Right. Add to basket then.

Okay, dresses. I already own a few, all loose and below the knee, but I remember what Shu once said when I arrived to her birthday party in a polo neck and jeans, 'Can you whore it up a bit, Mads?' I think back to what Shu and her girlfriends were wearing that night and add some tight dresses and short skirts to my basket. It's like they say, one man's whore is another woman's inspiration. Before I check out, I baulk at the three-figure total but key in my card details anyway.

I turn away from the wicker desk. If I wanted, I could put a wall of fairy lights behind my bed, get plants for the window ledge, a large bookshelf, which I'll assemble myself (once I've bought a screwdriver and one of those spirit level things), in the corner, and maybe even a bean bag chair – bright pink. I've never had so much space to fill. Looking into the mirror, I see that I'm smiling. I pull out my phone and in Notes type:

86

The New Maddie
Drinks alcohol when offered
Always says yes to social events
Wears new clothes
Cooks new food
Has different experiences (Travel? Brunch?)
Tries weed or cigarettes at least once
(but don't get addicted!)
Wears make-up
Goes on dates
Is not a virgin

I don't know what will happen when Mum returns to Ghana, but I have a year at least, a year to find out what all the fuss is about.

I look at the last two items on my list.

Ben and I are still texting what I imagine are normal getting-to-know you texts. He works in investment banking and it's a family affair with his dad on the executive board (I told him I work as an editorial assistant, which isn't a lie, it's manifesting). He lives in South London, his job is exhausting and his passion is food.

We 'talk' almost every day so is it weird he hasn't asked me out on a date yet?

Q **Google** – How long do guys wait before
asking a girl out on a date?

I don't really have a time frame I abide by, but I like to
befriend a girl before I ask her out. Sometimes finding

out if you have a connection with someone takes a
while, but it's worth waiting to find out, I think. So about
two or three weeks?
I spent four months getting to know my now-girlfriend
before I asked her out on a date.
One hour.

The Orange Tree Publishing interview is in their Farringdon offices. There are books everywhere and the non-fiction department's layout is open-plan, spacious but small enough so that you can stand, call out a name and have that person hear you loud and clear. Again, not a pair of jeans in sight, but I spot stripy tops and casual trousers.

I'm the only Black person in the room when I walk in but I don't know for sure that there are no other Black staff members. Someone could be off sick or on annual leave. Should I ask?

No, of course you can't ask. How would that sound? Do you have any questions for me, Maddie? Yes, would I be the only Black person you've hired? And if so, why is that?

No, I need this job and, to be honest, it looks likely I'll get it. They need *me*. They need me here to appear at least semi-decent to the outside world. It's easier to talk to others about how important diversity and inclusion is if you can wave a hand vaguely around the office and have me sat in the middle of it.

No, don't think like that – you'll get the job because you're qualified.

Penny Reaser is in her mid-forties, tanned, with brown eyes enhanced by blue eyeshadow. Her blonde hair is cropped short and appears to be in no particular style. She offers me a seat, and I think of Katherine's office at CGT, its clutter-free space and neat stacks of paper. Penny's bookcases are heaving and each smooth surface is covered in colourful books. Her desk is piled high with book catalogues, stationery bits and loose sheets of paper despite there being a tall filing cabinet in the corner. I think the cabinet is probably full. Katherine had a shredder under her desk. I might suggest Penny get a shredder.

We talk about OTP's list (a variety of non-fiction, but my main focus will be on food and drink) and my experience, before going on to my role here.

'The role will start off admin-heavy with my diary, minute taking, meeting prep, online orders – very much things you'll have already done and are proficient at,' Penny says. When she reaches for a sip of her tea, I notice her plain wedding band and that her nails are painted Barbie pink by someone who has difficulty colouring within lines. I wonder if she has any children. 'You'll be trained in our database MDX where all our data is stored,' she continues, 'and there's a lot you'll learn on the job. We pair all our assistants with a senior editor so you gain invaluable insight into what it means to be an editor from the very beginning.'

This sounds promising. Not so much the admin portion, especially since I know 'meeting prep' is industry talk for making tea and coffee, but if I can get through that period, I'll get to learn the realities of the publishing trade. Maybe move to a fiction department in a year or two. Look at that – I have a career plan.

Next I have to complete two fifteen-minute tasks: mark up a printout of Penny's calendar with any changes I'd make or concerns I might have. Then read through a short story and correct any errors.

I start with the short story, and spot all the to/too/two and they're/their/there errors, as well as inconsistencies (the little girl's been called three different names within the first paragraph) and mark up the relentless use of commas.

I move onto Penny's diary and this task is easy; I've been managing diaries of the overworked for years now. I already know you can't have back-to-back meetings in two different buildings and that an hour for lunch should always be set aside, even if that's not what it's used for. I move clashes, but without access to other diaries, I can only suggest changes. On paper I query if some of these meetings are in her diary for information's sake and which ones she'll be chairing and may need to bring material to. I spot some repeated meetings and make a note of them. Her days seem to start and end at different times, so I mention core hours, and I question her lack of desk time.

I'm looking over the short story again when Penny walks in. 'How was that?' she asks.

'Good, I think.'

Remaining on her feet, she takes up the two pieces of papers and lowers her glasses to read through them.

'These look good, especially the diary one.' She smiles; her mouth is closed but it reaches her eyes. 'Thank you for coming in, Maddie.' As I shake her hand, Penny says, 'You should hear back very soon.'

I'm back home an hour before Cam is and by then I've unpacked my kitchen and bathroom things and half of my bedroom. I linger upstairs because Cam's gone straight to her room and her door is shut. I wonder if I should make myself known, but maybe she wants to be alone and decompress after a day filled with schoolchildren.

Demi: No let me come 2 you. You don't know what kind of
day I've had and maybe I want to be left alone

Margaret: Bedrooms are off limits so only knock if you
need something. Keep socialising restricted to commu-
nal areas like the kitchen

Tally: OMG of course! If you want to chat that's so nice!

Chris: Don't bother me. I'm here to get away from family/
be closer to work, not to make new friends

I decide to leave Cam to it and continue unpacking until Jo
is home two hours later.

'Hi, girls!' she shouts from downstairs.

Cam's door opens and they both end up in the kitchen.

I've waited too long to shout 'Hi!' so I go down. My pulse
jumps as I do. I live with these people and they're technically strangers. I should have googled: How to get flatmates
to like you. I don't know how to make new friends.

'I was thinking maybe that new pizza place,' I hear Jo say.
'The one in – oh, here she comes, I think. Maddie?' Jo has
a bright smile when I enter the kitchen. 'Welcome!'

Cam rolls her eyes and says, 'Please don't mistake my
failure to match her enthusiasm as a comment on you
moving in. You'll find Jo and I are slightly different people.'

'Whatever,' Jo sings. You couldn't dampen this girl's
mood if you tried. 'So!' she says. 'We were thinking the new
pizza place in Clapham Common for dinner. You got our
message about not eating, right?'

'Yes.' *For goodness' sake, say something else. How was your day, maybe?*

'Good.' Jo claps. 'It's not far, but Cam said she'd drive us.'

Say literally anything. 'You drive, Cam?'

'Yeah,' she says. 'Parking's shit round here, so my car's on the other side of the road.'

'Thirty minutes and then we'll go?' Jo says. 'Let me just freshen up and get the stench of capitalism off me.' *Doesn't she work in the charity sector?* 'Which reminds me, Maddie, did an Amazon package arrive for me by any chance?'

Dinner out with my flatmates, with the girls . . .

On my way home from CGT, I used to walk past the West End restaurants and see tables of girls laughing, talking, eating and drinking. An hour from now, that will be me!

Tone down the excitement, Maddie.

'I'm not wearing heels!' Cam throws upstairs.

'That's fine!' Jo calls. 'I'll let you off today – it's just pizza!'

I'm grateful for the brief exchange. I put my only pair of heeled boots aside and replace them with trainers. Jeans and a loose red jumper later, I'm sat in the passenger seat of Cam's car.

There's something about cars that encapsulates freedom. I have this fantasy of driving my own car at night under infinite stars with my favourite, feel-good music playing. Maybe I'm on my way to meet a friend or just to get ice cream from a place that does gelato like nowhere else; sometimes I'm on my way to a date and when he asks what I'm drinking, I say, 'Nothing strong for me, I'm driving.'

'So how was your first day in the house?' Jo asks from the back seat.

'It was fine,' I answer. 'I mainly unpacked.'

'Was it hard leaving home for the first time or did you go to uni?'

'I went to uni but in London,' I answer, 'so I'd take the train in and back.'

Silence. *Keep going, then.*

'It was sad to leave this morning, but the house isn't going anywhere. I can visit whenever.'

'Exactly,' Jo says. 'You can always pop back when you miss the fam.'

A song I've not heard before starts to play on the radio and Jo, scrolling through her Instagram Stories, sings along with powerful lungs. I can't quite tell if she's good or just really loud.

Cam laughs at her and says to me, 'You'll get used to her doing that.'

There are a lot of people out for a random Thursday, but maybe the warm, dry evening needs to be utilised. Clapham Common is filled with bars, pubs and restaurants, one building after another, like a line of dominos. Some people are casually dressed, holding pints in beer gardens, and others look ready for what's clearly going to be a long night out.

Walking out of the car park, we step aside for three girls linked by the arms, in sequin dresses and heels; they even leave clouds of perfume in their wake. 'Thank you, lovelies!' one says, whilst another blows us a kiss. They teeter and giggle down the street and their mood is infectious.

Joe Public is a small restaurant and only bar-stool seats are available inside, but they have a strip of the street

93

enclosed within white picket fences for benches and tables. Jo picks the one in the middle.

'Maddie, look.' She points to a chalkboard on the other side of our table. 'They're doing two-for-one on frozen cocktails. Cam's driving, so should you and I get one?'

I'm about to say I don't really drink (more down to lack of opportunity than a personal stance), but then I remember my list, the New Maddie list. 'Sounds good,' I tell her.

It's pizza by the slice or twenty-inch and because we can't all agree on which toppings, we get it by the slice. I first go for the pepperoni and onion, Jo picks mushroom and truffle whilst Cam goes for the 'Meat Lover'.

'Appropriate,' she says, and Jo laughs. I join in, although I'm not sure what the joke is. It could be that she's an infamous carnivore. It could also be a reference to . . . penis. Obviously, vocally assuming one over the other could be detrimental.

When our drinks arrive (Diet Coke for Cam), they're pink, served in a tumbler with a straw and a halved strawberry on the rim. I take a sip. It's sweet and goes down like semi-frozen honey. I can taste the alcohol but not very much. I take a longer sip.

'Oh my God,' Cam suddenly says. 'Okay, don't look but—'

Jo begins to swivel in her seat. 'Where? Don't look where?'

Cam sighs. 'Fine, *Maddie*, don't look yet. Jo, on our right, second seat down, brown hair.'

'Guy in the grey jumper?'

'Yeah. Now, Maddie, you look.'

I act as if I'm scanning the area and look at the bench on our right. The man in the grey jumper looks our age and he's sat in a group of six but has his hand in the red hair of the girl on his left.

'What about him?' Jo asks.

'His name's Callum and he ghosted a friend of mine after three dates,' Cam says. 'Now we know why.'

Jo pretends to be sick as I look at the girl with her back to me. 'Men,' Jo says. 'Were they sleeping together?'

'They did once, after their third date.'

Jo looks up at the sky and says, 'Typical.'

'Apparently he pulled out all the stops, too,' Cam says. 'Picked Kirsten up in his car, bought her flowers, they went to dinner, he paid, et cetera. She invited him to hers, they do it, and the next morning he says he'll call her, he's running late for work or some bullshit, and then nothing. She thought he was dead until he had the "decency" to text her saying it wasn't going to work out. She was a mess.'

Jo takes a bite of her pizza. 'Unbelievable.'

'What a dick!' I throw in.

Jo coughs, 'Dick!' loudly, but thankfully Callum and his table don't hear her.

I've read many internet tales of ghosting, but it's usually after the first date or a couple of days texting, so disappearing after the third date is new. My first thought is: what did she do wrong? Then I shake my head and call myself a bad feminist.

'I can't believe people really don't call you back after you've slept with them,' I say.

'Men don't,' Cam says.

'Not even a bedside note?' I ask.

Cam laughs at this.

'He's not even that good-looking,' Jo says. 'Not to say the good-looking ones are excused, but he's . . . so plain!'

'Those kind of men always have the most audacity,' Cam remarks.

'Are you going to say something?' Jo asks.

'No,' Cam replies. 'Kirsten wouldn't thank me for it. She's talking to someone new now, anyway.'

'Where is she finding all these eligible – although questionable – men?' Jo asks. 'I have a friend who's been looking with no luck.'

I should probably contribute something meaningful to this conversation; it's like doing a group presentation and the two alphas dominate, but soon the teacher is going to look my way, say, 'You've been quiet, Maddie' and stick me with a question I have no hope of answering.

Cam pulls a face. 'Online.'

'You're not a fan?' I say, curious.

'I don't know how you could be,' she replies. 'With shit algorithms that present you with profiles proudly displaying DTF? It's hard to get excited.'

I nod supportively whilst making a mental note to google DTF. I think it means Down To Fuck, but I'd like to make sure.

'Cam is a little old-fashioned,' Jo mock-whispers. 'I'm less so.'

This surprises me as I assumed it would be the other way around. Cam gives the impression that she eats time-wasters alive, whilst Jo looks like she'd expect flowers and a heart-shaped box of chocolates on a first date.

'You can afford to be,' Cam says. 'You have Sam.'

'I don't *have* Sam,' Jo corrects.

'Who's Sam?'

'Just a guy I'm seeing,' Jo says, running a finger around the rim of her glass. 'It's not serious.'

If I ask why, is that intrusive?

'They're just sleeping together,' Cam explains.

Jo nods and it's a very nonchalant, you-get-it nod. But I don't.

'Is he not boyfriend material?' I ask.

Jo gets a faraway look in her eye. 'Don't get me wrong – he's gorgeous. Tall, dark and handsome.'

'Literally,' Cam adds. 'He's six-two, Black and very good-looking.'

'He's also an artist,' Jo continues. 'We're part of this big group of friends from uni so we've always hung out and one night about . . . two months ago? It just happened. Sometimes he comes by the flat, so you'll meet him eventually.' Jo clasps her hands under her chin and smiles to herself. 'He's great, but we both don't want anything serious, you know? I'm not ready to be accountable for someone else. And I've started messaging this guy from work – Conrad.'

'Sam is better,' Cam says and Jo rolls her eyes. 'I've only met him twice to be fair, but he gives great energy.'

'I'm young,' Jo says, waving her hand. 'Gotta keep my options open before it's too late. Seriously, one day you'll think, okay, let's just be boyfriend and girlfriend for a bit, it won't last, then it does because you're so used to each other, and dating is a hassle, and you don't want to have to go out when it's cold. Then suddenly you're married with two kids, a dog and a house outside London. So I'm keeping things casual for now.'

Casual sex. Friends with benefits? Is that still a thing? No feelings allowed or some feelings allowed? Is detached sex possible? Well, I'd need to have sex first to find out.

'What about you, Maddie?' Jo asks. 'Cam is a traditionalist from the fifties and I'm very much not. Where do you fit when it comes to dating?'

I think. 'Maybe somewhere in between? I don't date much
– it was a hard thing to do when living at home.' *And the
thought alone is anxiety-inducing.*

'But you'll start dating soon?'

'I am talking to someone, Ben, who I met at the theatre.'

'*That's* how you meet someone new,' Cam says.

'We're just texting, though. He hasn't asked me out or
anything.'

'Why not ask him out?' Jo says.

'*Or*,' Cam offers, 'she could drag her vagina across a bed
of nails.'

'Such a Leo,' Jo says. 'Drama queen. It's the twenty-first
century! It's all about equality between the sexes.'

'Then why aren't tampons free yet?' Cam turns to me.
'No, wait for *him* to ask *you*.'

Chapter Eleven

I was offered the job at OTP the next day, and started the following Monday.

My first few days are nothing but admin. Now I know why they needed someone so soon. My predecessor left months ago and the work's been piling up since. Meetings need organising rather than the grab-and-go system they've been temporarily operating under. Minutes need taking, Penny's emails need sorting, titles set up and royalties need inputting (if you thought you could escape maths by pursuing a career in books, think a-fucking-gain). I did wonder when I'd be able to attend meetings, discuss submissions and work on photographic interiors, but I can't expect too much so soon. Maybe it's something I've got to earn.

I'm only Penny's PA, but my line manager and mentor is Kristina Dorval (shoulder-length hair, flipped at the ends nineties style, reminiscent of Avi; mid-thirties with dark, green eyes). It's her Food and Drinks list I'm assisting on and her method of mentoring is very admin-focused, but I like her. She insists I call her Kris and our first catch-up lasts much longer than the allotted thirty minutes because it doesn't take much for her to turn away from her computer and talk to me about life.

She has a partner called Bruce and a cat called Alfred. No children, and I get the impression that it's a choice. She attends salsa classes every Thursday evening and goes to the theatre at least twice a month. She loves to eat but hates to cook.

'On Thursdays we have Creative,' Kris says, 'and you'll need to prioritise that in Penny's diary because that's where we discuss submissions we want to share with the wider team and our upcoming titles.'

'Do I go to that?' I ask hopefully.

'No, that's just for assistant and commissioning editors,' she says, 'but every Tuesday, the entire department meet for NFPM – Non-Fiction Publishing Meeting – where we discuss proposals/new projects, prospective authors and illustrators/photographers, our back and front list, the like. You'll take the minutes.'

A catch-up with Penny follows straight after. I was naive enough to assume the PA aspect of this job would be minimal, given that at the theatre it was a full-time job in and of itself, and it paid me a grand more than this one.

'I need to add three new meetings to my calendar this week,' Penny says. 'One with Thom, Gabby and Sabrina and then a follow-up meeting later on in the week – though not Friday afternoon – with just Thom and Gabby, and then I need a separate meeting with Marie, Levi and Chrissy from the US office – watch out for the time difference.' Penny doesn't pause for breath or look up from her computer screen as I scrawl notes at her office table. 'The follow-up meeting can be half an hour, but the other two a full hour. If no conference rooms are available, we can have the UK meetings in my office, coffee, tea, biscuits, et cetera.'

I look down at the printout of her calendar. It's alarmingly full. I wonder if she genuinely has time to pee or whether she runs on chronic dehydration.

'I know,' she says, catching me. 'I'm very full at the moment, but I do need these meetings scheduled in.'

'Right.' I nod emphatically. 'Sure.'

Something I learned my third day in? To suggest a lunch-time meeting is the equivalent of spitting in the eye of the king's firstborn son.

For the next ninety minutes, I go through Penny's diary to see if any one of her catch-ups are out of office this week. Great, Laura's on holiday, so I can cancel her thirty minutes. I ask Gabby's assistant if she can be free for that time and she agrees to move things around to accommodate. I thank her as profusely as one can over email without exhausting the exclamation mark tab, however I know there'll come a time where I must reciprocate similar generosity or risk losing any future favour.

I notice Thom and Penny have two meetings scheduled in this week and request the hour be reduced to thirty, leaving thirty minutes free at 11 a.m., but Sabrina is busy. 11.30? Yes, Sabrina can make that, but Penny's meant to be in a cafe in Leicester Square at 12:30, so I'll need to reschedule Bridgette's catch-up. I reach out to her PA, who responds with 'Maybe . . . can you check if that's all right with Susanna?' Thankfully it is, and by the end, all three meetings are in.

I push out from under my desk to use the bathroom when—

'Maddie?' Penny steps out of her office. 'Can you run me the total sales figures for Morgan Taylor's titles with us and then a separate report with his figures for other publishers? I also need our pub schedule for the next two years printed out on A3 and please categorise by month to include author, illustrator, ISBN, price, product type and editor. I've also just sent you an email with a letter, can you put that letter on headed paper – it should be somewhere on the server, have a look – and print me nine copies ahead of tomorrow's ten a.m. meeting. I'll also need its standing agenda and previous minutes.' She smiles knowingly. 'Do I need to repeat anything?'

I look down at my notepad and it's like I've drawn spider's legs across the page. 'No, I've got it.'

'Thank you.' She walks out.

I look around and the girl in front of me smiles, lopsidedly, and widens her eyes. I know her name is Eliza. She chuckles and it could be disingenuous, but her face suggests otherwise. It's round with permanently pink cheeks and she has brown Raphaelite hair that reaches the tail of her back. I smile and she mirrors it before dropping behind her computer again.

~~MT's sales figures at OTP~~
~~Letter on OTP headed paper x9~~
~~Pub schedules on A3~~

I have jollof rice and salad for lunch. I'm glad to eat at two because the dining room's emptying after the one o'clock rush. Back at CGT, I once made the mistake of sitting with my colleagues for lunch.

'Oh, what do you have there, Maddie?' Claire asked. 'Is that African rice?'

I explained jollof rice as best I could whilst looking at their lunches. Jacket potato. Soup. Jacket potato. Sandwich. Sandwich.

'I bet it's good.' She smiled. 'Smells spicy.'

I tried to laugh (because what other response was available?), but it came out as just an exhale of air through my nose.

*　　*　　*

After my lunchtime walk, I spot a missed call from Dawoud. He doesn't usually call me and my heart skips a beat. No, if something were wrong with Dad, I would have heard from Mum as well. When I call Dawoud back, it's only to ask me to order more catheters.

He could ask Mum to do that, but instead I say, 'Sure, of course. I'll do it now.' Just because I've moved out doesn't mean I shouldn't do anything for Dad. It only takes me two minutes to log onto the website and place an order.

I'm about to let Mum know I've done this, but a message from her is already sitting in our chat. Oh, she's sent me a voice note. She never does that. I didn't think she knew how. I press play.

'MADELEINE!'

Of course she's shouting. I lower the volume on my earphones.

'MADELEINE! I HAVE JUST DISCOVERED VOICE ACTIVATION MESSAGES ON THE WHATSAPP. LOOK AT HOW YOUR MOTHER IS—'

The message ends there.

I return to my desk and prioritise Penny's list. I only suffer a few hiccups, mainly with the printer because they're all bastards and will likely lead the technological charge in the eventual war against humans, but I've finished everything before Penny returns from her last meeting of the day. She walks into her office, picks up the stack of papers I left on her desk and leafs through them.

'This is everything,' she says.

I wait in case it's a question.

She looks surprised. 'Thank you, Maddie.'

'You're welcome.'

She closes her door and Eliza pops up again.

'Well done,' she mouths with a thumbs up.

I mock wipe my brow and mouth, 'Thanks!'

The following weeks pretty much follow a similar pattern. I try to see if I can help with any actual books, but Penny and office admin takes up so much of my day. Just trying to get to grips with the database can take me hours at a time. I'm electronically filing some records when the assistant and commissioning editors head into Penny's office for an impromptu Creative meeting. I wonder what they're discussing in there . . . maybe the reissue of *Free Eating*.

Free Eating is a plant-based cookbook first released when being a vegetarian was too much of an ask for people. Now we're hoping a new jacket, bonus material and the writer's expanding social media presence will give it a new lease of life. The author's brand is that he was a vegan before it became a trend (his words, not mine), and the man (judging by his correspondence) sounds a bit of a dick to be honest. He signs off every email with:

Blessings,

Jim Carper

OG Vegan

Penny's door opens. 'Maddie?'

I pop out of my seat. *Is she going to ask me to join?*

'Can you make me and Thea a tea, please, and bring it in?'

'Oh, sure.'

I used to hate making other people tea until Avi once said, 'If someone asks you to make them a cup of tea with no further information, they deserve whatever they get

– especially since they're not even paying for it' and it's been a whole new world for me since then.

I enter Penny's office and notice her table is splashed with food photography. I crane my neck to look before placing the two cups of tea on her table. I turn to leave when Penny says, 'Thea, do you need more milk?'

Thea, a petite brunette, says, 'No, thanks. It's fine.'

I nod and reach for the door again.

'Maddie,' Penny says. 'I could use more milk.' I look at her mug and wonder if she's saying this for future reference. 'Is there any left?'

'Yes, I'll grab some.'

I think I should have taken her mug with me, but since I don't know the correct amount of milk, I take the carton to her. I plan to put it on the table and leave, but Penny holds her mug out to me.

'I'll say stop,' she says.

Thea momentarily stares at her, whilst the others busy themselves with the photographs. My throat tightens at her reaction.

I unscrew the milk top, feeling strange, and pour milk into Penny's mug for her.

'Stop,' she says. 'Thank you so much, Maddie.'

I can't look at her so nod and leave the room. I feel my eyes burning, but I can't figure out why. One part of my brain is saying it's no big deal, just milk in a mug, but another part, Thea's reaction, tells me Penny shouldn't have asked me to do that.

Chapter Twelve

Ben calls when I'm back at my desk.

I answer without thinking and then pause. 'Shit,' I mouth.

Eliza looks over at me; I point to the phone and whisper 'Emergency.' I leave the room and step into the corridor.

'Hello.'

'Hi, Maddie. It's Ben.'

'Hi, Ben.'

'Why are you whispering?'

'Oh, I'm at work.'

'Right, okay,' he matches my whisper. 'Just wondered if you'd like to have dinner Saturday night at my place.'

'Dinner? On Saturday?'

An actual date? Just the two of you? Non-stop conversation for at least two hours? Do you think he'll kiss you at the end?

My mind runs a list of excuses I.could give Ben.

Period pains? Too personal.

Already have plans? Makes rescheduling an option (also, a lie).

Mercury is in retrograde? I don't actually know what that means, but everyone is saying it.

I went out yesterday night and I'm still a little hungover? Signs of a possible alcoholic.

I don't want to go not because I don't like you but because I haven't been on a date in almost a decade and the thought makes me want to be sick? Nonsensical to everyone but me.

'Yes, tomorrow,' he says.

'Ben, why are *you* whispering?'

'I don't know,' he says. 'It's weird talking aloud with someone who's whispering on the other line.'

I smile. From the office, I hear Penny ask, 'Where's Maddie?'

'Okay, dinner Saturday night at your place. Sounds good.'

'Great. I'll text you the address. See you tomorrow, Maddie.'

'Bye, Ben.'

He laughs, probably because I'm still whispering, before hanging up.

As soon as I'm out of the office doors, I pull my phone out. Farringdon during rush hour is not a street you want to walk across with downcast eyes, but these are desperate times. I won't have signal once I'm on the underground.

 Google – How to prepare for a first date

**My top four first-date tips –
article written by Lisa Fiener**
I have been on so many first dates, I've lost count.

My head jerks back at this.

So if you've found this article, you're in safe hands. Follow my top tips to ensure success on your first date.

I scroll down to see if Lisa Fiener has embedded any links to articles she's written about second dates. She has not.

Nerves: if this is your first date in a long time or even just a first date with someone you really like, you're probably working up a sweat just thinking about it. Kick those nerves to the kerb by keeping yourself preoccupied in the run up to D-day. How about fitting in an intense workout at the gym or even book in some time for a spray tan to give you that extra boost of confidence? Distract yourself to avoid overthinking; my distraction of choice is a pre-booked massage so I'm relaxed and soothed right before my big date.

These pre-date rituals are somewhat non-applicable. I don't have a gym membership or need a tan . . .

They also sound expensive. Is this why men are expected to pay for dates? We've spent all our money just getting ready . . .

Location: this is pretty obvious, but you want to pick somewhere familiar and public just to give you that secure footing. You know how much the food will cost, in case chivalry is dead, you know the dress code and the ambiance of the place. And, for extra measure, make sure you tell at least one friend or family member who you're meeting, where you're going and what time you expect to return – you know, just in case!

'Watch it!' A man and his briefcase push into me and give me a dirty look (the man, not the briefcase) before walking on. My fault for stopping in a stream of pedestrian traffic, but in my defence – if anyone cared to ask – I'd just discovered that Ben could be a potential serial killer and I his next victim.

I move aside and stand in the entrance way of a closed bank.

Q **Google** – Is a first date at his house normal?

Nicole91: So I met this guy at a coffee shop and we really hit it off. After we exchanged numbers he sends me a text asking if I'd like to have dinner with him at his place. I've only met him once and we got on well but I don't really know him. I like him though and he seems like a genuinely good guy. Should I go to his house for dinner?

SarahTK: Ted Bundy seemed like a genuinely good guy too.

Kathy78: I think it's okay to go to a man's house on a 1st date but only if you trust him.

Anon: Trusting him doesn't mean anything. We've all been duped before. What if people who know him are like, yeah he has first dates at his place all the time, it's completely normal for him, and you just happen to be unlucky girl no.8 and that's when he murders you? But everyone will back him up because, first of all, he's a man, secondly, what idiot woman goes to someone's house on the first date, it's not his fault she gave him the opportunity to murder her right? And third, the other dates he's been on will be like, yeah I met him at his place and he was a gentleman and I'm still alive.

    If I was a murdering sociopath, that's how I'd do it. #justsaying #savethewhales #seriouslyguysourplanetisdying

Simone_G: I think a first date at his house is a sign of maturity because he's not afraid to show you where he lives. It means he wants something long-term. Just let him know that your friends know where you are.

Leela: Run girl. Run far and run fast.

Helpful. Back to Lisa Fiener.

Conversation: being caught off guard or stuck in awkward silence is the bane of every first date. It's bound to happen if you don't know each other very well, or even if you've exhausted all your get-to-know-you questions beforehand. To combat this, you'll want a list of things you can talk about to keep the conversation flowing. Here are my top three conversation starters:

1. Given the choice of four people in the world, dead or alive, who would you invite to a dinner party?
2. What's your most treasured memory?
3. What would constitute a perfect day for you?

But these sound almost like interview questions? Are dates basically interviews now?

You also want to keep the conversation light. Avoid ex-girl-friends, crazy family members and politics on a first date. You want to have fun! If you feel you might struggle to do this, read my other article here on how to be an interesting date.

Fucking hell. Lisa's been through the wringer.

> Body language: underrated yet so crucial! Eye contact can be a great way of showing interest, but also disconcerting and intense on a first date, especially if you're not much of a blinker. Tread carefully, is what I'm saying. Mirroring, fronting and leaning in are clear signs of interest but make sure to employ with care.

Q **Google** – Is pre-date exhaustion a thing?

I have a date with a man tomorrow night. This will be my first date in *eight* years and I imagine the rules of courtship have changed dramatically since then.

Back then, when a boy said, 'Hey, wanna go out?' and you said 'Yeah', that meant you were officially in a relationship, but with adult dating comes the word: exclusive. One date does not mean you're exclusive and just because I've agreed to the date doesn't mean he's my boyfriend. I might not even be Ben's only date this week.

When I let myself into the flat, my head is buzzing with information and survival tips.

'Maddie?'

I'd almost walked past the kitchen without noticing Jo was in there . . . and she's an interesting sight. She's wearing a chunky, red, bejewelled headband, a floor-length, white-fringed powder-blue dress, an assortment of bracelets and *reindeer* slippers.

'Hi, sorry. My head's somewhere else.'

'I could tell,' she says. 'You looked a little dazed.'

She's using the frying pan I brought with me, which is a little annoying because it's the only non-stick one in the cupboard and she never washes it straight after. I was planning to fry some fish for dinner, but that's not going to happen now.

Jo turns away from the carrots she's cutting. 'Before I forget, I'm having a few friends round tomorrow night for drinks. Want to join?'

'Oh, I can't. I . . . I have a date.'

Jo throws her hands up and squeals with excitement. It's just unfortunate I've caught her mid-chopping session and she's yet to put the knife down because she now straddles the thin line between encouraging and threatening.

Cam's door opens. 'I heard screaming,' she says, rounding the corner in baggy shorts and a plain T-shirt. 'Who's getting murdered and can they keep it down?' She clocks Jo's knife and stops dead. 'Oh, shit. *Is* someone getting murdered?'

'No! Maddie's got a date!'

'Oh, cool,' Cam says, reaching for the kettle. 'The Ben guy?'

I nod. 'He called me this afternoon and invited me to dinner at his.' I decide to swap out the faceless mask of Google for actual three-dimensional people and ask, 'Is that weird?'

'Yes,' Cam says.

'Not at all,' Jo says.

Cam raises her mug. 'It was nice knowing you, Maddie.'

Jo swipes at Cam with her knife-free hand. 'Shut up. Maddie, don't listen to her. It's impressive he's given you his address!' she tells me. 'What if he had plans to suddenly drop you? If you wanted answers, you could just show up at his house and he knows that.' She narrows her eyes at Cam and says, 'Maturity.'

Cam narrows her eyes back. 'Murderer.'

'You've said murder three times since stepping into this kitchen,' Jo remarks. 'So you're done. Maddie, just send me the address if you're concerned and let him know that your flatmates know where you are.'

'But don't tell him where we live,' Cam adds. 'In case he comes here to finish the job.'

Jo tuts. 'What's his address?'

I forward it onto her via WhatsApp.

'SW-five,' she says. 'Fancy!'

'It is?' I ask.

'Uh-huh. That's a rich area for sure.'

'He works in investment banking and his dad is executive something and his grandad founded the company.'

'Don't sign a prenup,' Cam says.

'Oh God.' I'm suddenly very hot in my jacket and peel it off. 'I'm an editorial assistant who makes under sixteen hundred a month.'

'That's probably a third of his rent.'

I bite my lip. 'Maybe I shouldn't go.'

'Maddie, don't listen to Cam!' Jo says. 'She's just playing with you.'

'So you don't think his rent exceeds my salary?'

Jo looks at Cam and then back at me. She puts the knife down. 'Show us what you're going to wear!'

Jo ends up picking my outfit. She isn't too impressed with my wardrobe's offerings, even when I show her my online-shopping section.

'Why do you cover up so much?' she asks. 'Is it a religious thing?'

'No,' I answer, but then I think about it. 'Maybe. I guess I did grow up being taught good girls don't—'

'Have any fun,' Jo finishes.

'Said the serpent to Eve,' Cam says.

'Only support and encouragement in this room, please!'

Cam holds her hands up in surrender and throws herself on my bed. I've never had friends in my room before. I hope it smells okay and isn't too messy.

Jo has me try on four different outfits (both she and Cam roll their eyes when I ask them to look away as I change into each one) before finally settling on a long-sleeved, black and khaki green skater dress that just about covers my bum. I bought it a year ago from a website that labelled it 'The Sweet Mistress Dress' and it lives in my wardrobe only because I missed the returns date.

'Don't you think it's a bit short?' I ask.

'Yes,' Jo says, holding up my black boots. 'So?'

'In the dress's defence,' Cam says, 'if your bum were smaller, it would be an inch longer.'

'I'm not a fan of these boots with the dress.' Jo holds the two together. 'Are they really the only heels you have?'

I nod. 'Maybe I should change the dress?'

Jo's eyes light up. 'Or . . .' She checks the soles of my boots. 'Size six, yes! I have just the pair of boots!'

'You just said no to boots.'

'I said no to *your* boots. Wait here.'

Jo returns from her room with black suede thigh-high boots.

Cam whistles. 'Make sure he pays you up front, Maddie.'

'That's strike two,' Jo warns.

'I can't wear those *and* this dress, Jo.'

'Why not?'

'Together . . . it's . . .' I motion to the boots. '*Sexy.*'

Jo considers me. 'You're going on a date with a rich man,' she says. 'Isn't sexy what you want to go for?'

At seventeen, I lived in trainers, jeans and plain tops for summer then layered one of James's jumpers on for winter. My make-up routine extended as far as cheap mascara and lip gloss too pink for my skin tone.

I take the boots from Jo. Maybe sexy would be a nice change.

But only under a long black coat, I decide, before heading out on Saturday night.

When I'm out of the train station (because Uber had the audacity to charge me thirty-five pounds for the one-way trip) and on Ben's road, I pull my coat closed.

'This is how the other half live,' I whisper. *And it's very different*.

I walk under tall lamp posts and pass men with jumpers around their necks and women on runs. Ben lives on a row of houses with actual stone pillars, polished door knockers and sleek cars parked outside. When I reach his stone steps, I trip on my heel – on Jo's fucking heel – and stand at his large black door. I can hear soft jazz music coming from behind it.

'Okay, Maddie,' I say under my breath. 'Just be cool. Remember what you practised. Hi, Ben. Hi, Maddie. You ask how he is, then he'll ask you and you tell him you had a chilled afternoon watching TV because both your flatmates were out. That'll lead nicely onto, "Oh, tell me about your flatmates" and—'

On second thoughts, is that a bit sad? Then Ben will know that if it weren't for this date, I'd have no Saturday plans. Should I lie? What else can I say I was up to? Brunch? Yes, I went out to brunch with Cam and Jo.

I knock on his front door.

*Actually, no, say you had brunch with Nia and Shu —
widen your social circle.*

When Ben opens the door, I freeze. I'd almost forgotten
what he looks like and that night at the theatre comes rushing back. In this lighting, his hair, brushed back by his
fingers, interchanges between brown and black and his blue
eyes intensify with the latter. And, yup, there are those
stretched dimples.

'Maddie, I'm so glad you could make it.'

My mind blanks when I step inside and Ben turns me
around by the waist to take off my coat. He's dressed in
grey trousers and a navy blue shirt with the sleeves rolled
up. I tug on my dress because it really is short.

'You look amazing,' he says.

Say something about brunch. 'Someone knows I'm here!'
Fuck.

Thankfully, Ben laughs. 'Maddie, I assure you, my intentions are not of an indecent kind. I promise I'm just making
you dinner. Here,' and he offers me his arm, 'let me take
you to the kitchen.'

Tonight I discover that it doesn't take much to placate me
– I make a mental note to work on that.

Ben's house is as fancy as his postcode. It's on two floors
and stretches far enough for me to see into his garden at the
other end. His hallway floor is silver-grey wood and on the
wall beside the staircase is a gold-framed mirror beside a
dark oak coat stand. He leads me into a large open-plan
space where two-thirds make up a kitchen of marble countertops with padded bar stools and navy-blue-painted
cupboards. The remaining third is a dining area where,
under hanging lights, is a table covered in linen and topped
with place mats, cutlery and glasses.

'Dinner's almost ready,' he says. 'Come and sit with me as I cook. You can be my taster.' He pulls a bar stool from the other side of the counter so I'm sat inches away as he attends to various pans. There is something vulnerable about sitting on a bar stool and I think it's down to the lack of armrests. If you're not entirely centred, you can catch yourself mid-swivel. I try not to shuffle too much since Ben is so poised over his pots and pans and oven trays.

The music playing – I can't see from where – travels enough to allow comfortable silence and I watch Ben as he cooks. Dating is a weird concept, isn't it? I hardly know this man, he barely knows me, yet here I am, in his house, sat on his bar stool watching him make dinner. But that's fine because it's a date?

He's buttoned his shirt high enough that I didn't think anything of it when I first saw him, but now, when he stretches forward, I can see the hair on his chest. I suffer from an overwhelming need to touch him, somewhere or anywhere. It's so sudden, I have to breathe out slowly.

'Oh,' he says and I lean back. When had I moved closer? 'Let me get you something to drink,' he says. He briefly touches my thigh. My dress is definitely too short because I think he meant to go for my knee. 'White or red?'

I stare at him; I think he's freshly shaven. *Maddie, pick a wine.* 'Red, please.' *You hate red wine.*

'Good choice,' he says. 'I know the exact red to go for.' He pulls out a bottle from a well-stocked wine rack and pours two glasses. He hands me one, then holds his up to clink against mine. He doesn't break eye contact. I forget the wine when the tightness in my stomach returns. He smiles and says, 'You're quiet this evening.'

I remember my wine and drink. 'Hmmm.' *Actual words, maybe?*

'Shall I tell you what's for dinner?'

I nod, slowly swallowing the bitter wine, and wave towards the cooker. 'It looks extensive.'

'As you already know, I love to cook,' he says. *Is his voice deeper than before?* 'So devising this three-course menu has been a pleasure.'

Three courses? Shit. I've never had a three-course meal before. I've eaten three different things in a row, but I don't think that's the same thing.

'For starters we have roasted aubergine, feta and tabbouleh.'

'Sounds delicious.' *What's tabbouleh?*

'Then for mains we have a mushroom risotto.'

At least you know that's rice.

'And finally, for dessert we have . . .' He looks away, suddenly shy. 'You might think it's childish.'

Can I get away with touching his cheek or is that too much, too weird and too soon? I keep my hand around my wine glass. 'Try me.'

'For dessert, ice-cream sundaes.' He shrugs as if to say, *so there's my secret.* I smile with him, but really I'd like to make him laugh.

'Ben?'

'Yes, Maddie?'

'Why are you single?'

When I laugh loudly, my instinct is to cover my mouth in case I'm showing too much gum or tongue. Whereas Ben laughs with confidence, perhaps because he knows he can.

'I could ask you the same question.'

118

I don't answer because I wouldn't know where to begin. 'Your three-course meal sounds impressive. You're a real grown-up.'

'Well, I am thirty-four.'

I sit straight. 'Really?'

'Really.' Ben looks at me. 'Too old?'

Yes?

'No.' When I'd first seen him, I'd guessed late twenties, so this is quite the age gap. How should I feel about this? Would Mum approve or would she want someone closer to my age? *It's not just that.* Thirty-four means experience, and so far, Ben is proving to have a lot of it. I realise I'm nervous not just because I like Ben and want him to like me, but because he's so calm, to the point where he can stir risotto with one hand and drink from his wine glass with the other, whilst I'm furiously trying not to swivel or slouch on my bar stool.

I'm nervous because I'm out of my depth. I'm trying to remember Lisa's four rules but instead I look around and take in Ben's silver, double-door fridge and *pantry*. I've never been in a kitchen like this, I've never been handed a glass of wine specifically selected for tonight, and the last person to cook for me was my mother.

'So how old are you?' Ben asks.

'I'm twenty-five.'

'Oh, great,' he says. 'Would you mind stirring this for just a second?'

'Sure.' I put down my wine and lean over to take the wooden spoon for the risotto.

'Thanks.' He then cradles his face with his hands. 'Fuck.'

I laugh but keep stirring. 'Too young?'

He takes the spoon back and I can see his cheeks are pink. 'Nine years' difference is . . . You're very young and potentially have more wild oats to sow.'

I never considered this. Ben is my first proper date in my adult life; do I expect many more to follow him? How many men is too many men when you factor in my mother, God's wrath and my reluctance to contract an STI?

'How old did you think I was when we met?'

'I knew you were young,' he answers, 'but I couldn't help myself when I saw you, so I'd hoped to push at twenty-seven, maybe twenty-eight.'

I blink. 'You couldn't help yourself?'

He considers me. 'Please don't tell me you're one of those women who are obviously beautiful but pretend not to be.'

I drop my head. *Obviously beautiful.* No one has ever called me 'obviously beautiful'. Does he mean it? How can I be so beautiful he *had* to stop and talk to me?

I've been silent for so long that Ben uses his finger to lift my chin. I wish I could look him in the eye, maybe shrug and say, 'I've heard it a few times,' but that would be a lie.

'Has no one said that to you before?' he asks quietly. 'I find that hard to believe.' He gently strokes my cheek with his thumb and I finally look at him. I'm breathing heavily and my chest makes it visible. He smiles slowly and takes my face with both hands and the warmth of his skin makes me close my eyes.

His lips are soft on mine and my skin tingles. He inhales as I lean deeper in. When we pull away, I tell him, 'That was nice, Ben.'

'I'm glad it wasn't just me.' He squeezes my thigh. 'Let's have dinner.'

At the table, he tops up my wine and pours me a glass of water before putting our starters on top of what I already thought was my plate. (I later google it to find it's what's called a charger plate, intended to 'add to the visual effect of your table'. Again, *fancy*.) The tabbouleh tastes like rice but lighter and fresher.

'Ben, this is delicious!'

He smiles. 'You think so?'

I pile on another forkful. 'I really do.' *Slow down, Maddie. Try not to go from smooth kiss to grains falling out of your mouth.* 'I haven't had anything like it.'

'Do you cook much?'

'When I lived at home with my dad, I'd batch-cook on the weekend. Meals that weren't too complicated but varied enough so we weren't eating the same thing all week.'

'You cooked for your dad?'

Careful, Maddie. I put my wine glass down.

'You must be the best daughter ever.'

I try to smile, but there's a sudden burning in my chest because I haven't thought much about Dad this week. I should call, just to check in.

'Now I've moved out, I'd maybe like to experiment a bit more. Especially if this starter is a possible outcome!' I hope I don't sound too manic and like someone desperate to change the subject.

'In that case . . .' Ben leaves the table and pulls out a drawer next to the fridge. Inside are rows of cookery books featuring the likes of Yotam Ottolenghi, Tom Kerridge, Sabrina Ghayour and Jamie Oliver. He pulls one out titled *Simple Dinners* and hands it to me before retaking his seat.

I start flicking through its modest layout, short ingredients lists and bright photographs. It's neat, undemanding and my kind of cookbook.

'That one's great,' Ben says. 'It's not OTP, but I won't tell if you don't. All the recipes are simple but delicious. My gift to you.'

'You're giving this to me?'

'Yes.' He looks up. 'Maybe one day you'll cook me something from it.'

I smile. 'Deal.' I flip through the book again. 'You know what the ideal cookbook would be?' I say. 'One that focused on flavour pairings.'

'Lots of books do that.'

'No, I mean, just on flavour pairings, maybe some recipes but mainly . . . I don't know. Like, an index page and I follow the section on tomatoes and that chapter tells me what to pair it with and what best brings out its natural flavours. Like, why do fresh tomatoes and mozzarella work so well? Or it tells you to pair tinned tomatoes and bay leaves to make great pasta sauce. Simple pairings you might not think of but which make great flavour combinations.'

Ben considers this. 'You'd need to work on your pitch, but that's not a bad idea.'

'Pitch?' I repeat. 'No, I can't pitch the idea – I'm not at that stage. I make tea.'

'Maybe that's how you stop making tea.' He winks. 'What harm could it do to put together a paragraph and email it over? Just a hey, I am doing the work you asked me to do but had this idea, just an idea, it's probably nothing but thought I'd mention it. Managers love the self-deprecating thing.'

I shake my head, but I'm already thinking about it. Ben's right. What harm could it really do? I could even alliterate the title, something like *Finding Flavours* or *Cooking Combinations*. Hmm . . . It's definitely a work in progress.

We move onto our mains and the risotto is equally delicious and so delicately flavoured I just want more and more. Ben serves white wine because 'this one specifically pairs wonderfully'. As true as that may be (I really wouldn't know), the wine is going straight through me and I ask to use his bathroom. He puts a hand on my back when he points upstairs and says, 'First door on your right.'

I try not to take any detours, even though I'm desperate to, and when I step into his bathroom, I consider not peeing at all. 'Oh my . . .'

Ben's bathroom is larger than the living room back at the flat. My heels click on the marble floor, a caramel colour that the walls have copied. There's a large circular mirror above the sink, of which a six-month old baby could bathe in, and columns of neatly folded towels underneath the counter (why does he have eight towels?). His shower door is framed in chrome and its walls, floor and bench (yes, *bench*) are the same marble as the rest of the bathroom.

Will he be able to tell if I've opened his bathroom cabinet?

I open it anyway and it's meticulously organised. He puts me to shame because all of my bathroom products are thrown into a plastic basket under the sink. In neat rows, Ben has different aftershaves, face creams, eye creams, hair products and, oh, *condoms*. I fight the urge to giggle like a seven-year-old hearing the word 'willy'. I close the cabinet doors shut.

I shuffle over to the toilet and pee while staring at the built-in shelving housing hand towels, plants and expensive-looking toiletries. Some of which don't even have labels.

'Fuck,' I breathe. 'This is generational wealth, huh?'

I pull up my drab-in-comparison cotton underwear and look for the flush handle. Of course there isn't one because it's motion-sensored. I wash my hands with soap from a perfume bottle and dry them on a towel.

When I walk back into the kitchen, Ben says, 'Ta-da' and proudly holds up two ice-cream sundaes, tall glasses and spoons included. 'Banoffee pie ice-cream sundae,' he announces. 'You've got caramelised bananas, crumbled cookies and shortbread, salted caramel sauce and the ever humble vanilla ice-cream.'

I smile at his enthusiasm. 'You know, Ben, as the night proceeds, the less I believe you're really single.' I take the sundae he offers me. 'Somewhere upstairs, behind one of your many doors, is a thriving harem.'

'You couldn't be further from the truth,' he says. 'Can you imagine me having to make this dinner five or six more times?'

This time when he sits at the table, he pulls out the chair next to him. When I'm seated, he uses his leg to drag the chair closer to him, but I stick my spoon in my sundae. I think of Cam's friend being ghosted by the man who brought her flowers and then shortly after had his hand in someone else's hair.

I have to ask. 'Are you single, Ben?'

He doesn't waver. 'I am. Are you?'

'Of course I am. I wouldn't be here if I wasn't.'

Ben tilts his head. 'You have this real . . . innocent thing about you.'

I don't know whether that's a good thing or not; I don't know whether I want him to think I am or not. So I sit and eat my ice cream.

'I think the opposite of you,' I finally admit. 'Not that you're not-innocent, but rather . . . experienced.' I twirl a finger around the kitchen. 'You've done this before. It's been such a smooth night, there's no doubt you've done this before.'

'I don't deny it,' he says. I have to wait for him to swallow his ice cream before he continues. 'Last year, I came out of a four-year relationship.'

Four years? 'What happened? If you don't mind me asking.'

'We grew apart,' he says. 'It took me a while to accept that, sometimes, nothing is wrong.' He looks calm as he says it, maybe a little sad even. 'Growing up and apart – it can happen.'

'Growing up' catches me off guard because he's thirty-four. He's already grown up, but then I realise how naive that sounds. I don't think you turn thirty and become immune to mistake-making or lesson-learning. You grow wiser (supposedly) but never omniscient. There's always something you need to be taught, and so you keep learning and you keep growing up – until you're dead.

But I don't know that feeling and I'm having difficulty imagining it. Ben has experienced real love, having a partner, another half. He's grown older with someone, experienced life with them, years, milestones, celebrations as well as lamentations. It's a mature response to the end of all of that, to the end of four years with someone you no longer see.

'Do you date much, Maddie?'

I don't want to tell him my last date was eight years ago at Nando's and that my ex had brought his friends along so we could all share the platter. But his response was so honest I can't find it in me to lie.

'No, not much at all,' I admit. 'I am ... *or was* a homebody.'

Ben puts down his spoon to listen to me; I feel quite trapped by how warm his stare is.

'I spent a lot of time with my dad. My mum travels . . .'

I hear her voice before I say anything else. *Our matters are private, remember? You tell one person, they tell another and the next thing you know, important people are asking all sorts of questions.*

'My mum travels a lot, so it was just Dad and me for a while,' I say slowly. 'She's back now and so I moved out and . . .' I shrug, not sure of where I'm going with this, if I *should* be going anywhere with this. 'I guess I'm finally living a little.'

Ben smiles softly, firstly to himself and then at me. He holds up his sundae glass. 'Cheers to living a little,' he says.

I clink mine against his and whisper, 'Cheers.'

Ben kisses me again at the end of the night. He orders me a cab home and kisses me on his doorstep until it arrives. He uses his tongue and because he's slow and gentle, it gives me time to learn how to use mine. I can tell when I'm doing it right because Ben will sigh deeply, and I can feel his heartbeat; it moves hard and fast and I like that I'm the reason for it.

When I get home, Cam's door is shut and she's playing music. She rarely plays music. I tiptoe past and up the stairs but pause on the landing when I hear voices coming from Jo's room, of which the door is not completely closed.

When I ascertain Jo's 'Oh, fuck, Sam . . . fuuuuck' isn't her response to being murdered on a bed that isn't structurally sound, I attribute the noises to her having sex with Casual Sam.

Jo's moans make my ears burn and I don't know if I can move without being heard. Somehow if I'm discovered, the embarrassment will definitely be mine to bear.

I take another step and the landing creaks, but they don't stop. I take the opportunity to run to my room and close the door behind me.

Great.

I need to use the toilet.

Chapter Thirteen

I'm nervously tapping my foot on Tuesday when, during our catch-up, I ask Kris, 'How was last week's Creative?'

'It was all right.' She shoves her hair back with a headband. 'It was shit, actually.'

'What happened?'

'I think we're all in a bit of a creative funk,' she says. 'We don't have any fresh ideas and all the new stuff we keep losing.'

'Ideas?' I repeat. 'So the team can come up with ideas instead of waiting for agents to bring us their titles?'

'It's something Penny started when we were really struggling,' Kris answers. 'Instead of continuously trying to outbid other publishers, we'd focus on food writers already on our list and come up with exciting things for them to write about. For example, getting Carmen to write about her stay in Italy was Penny's idea.'

Wow. Carmen Loremo's *Sardinia* is one of OTP's bestsellers.

'I didn't know that was an option.' I write down: *What do we want and which of our writers can do it?* 'It's a good idea.'

'It's a good idea when we have good ideas,' Kris says. 'It's not easy getting a book about foreign cuisine from our list of writers who are . . . well, limited in foreign experience.'

In other words, homogenous in culture.

I nod. 'Of course.'

'It only worked for Carmen because her husband is from Sardinia so they travel there a lot. We'll think of something.' She closes her notebook. 'Did you manage to get that list of titles up on MDX?'

'Yes, but, actually, I've had an idea about something.' I pitch her my practised paragraph on *Cooking Combos*, a book focused on classic and unique pairings, what you can do with them and why. It would discuss the science behind the flavour combination, as text-heavy, informative cookbooks are popular now, and how to cook classic or unexpected dishes with what you've got at home.

Kris listens patiently and at the end says she'll think about it but well done me for bringing ideas to the table already.

I smile at this and, after, print out a list of our authors going back a decade. Like Kris hinted, we have a lot of white, middle-aged men writing about pies, potatoes and bread. The majority of our female authors specialise in comfort cooking and family meals. I try not to pull a face.

On the train ride home, I think about that list. We need something different, a quiet, undiscussed cuisine; we need recipes we wouldn't have thought to try or even search for, but no one on our list seems qualified.

I get home and, whilst my pasta boils, I google the rest of OTP's food writers. On one man's Instagram is a picture of a colourful food spread; nothing like the images of food found in his books. The caption thanks his wife Afra, whose page I click on. Her account is full of bright dishes: rice topped with seeds, breads bursting with add-ins and platters of roasted meats. There aren't any recipes written in the captions and I know not to judge a plate of food based on its appearance, but the titles of her dishes sound promising because I've not heard of most of them. I'm bookmarking her page when Jo rushes into the kitchen.

'Where's Cam?'

'I'm here,' she says, emerging from her bedroom. 'What's up?'

'You two are going to love me,' she says. 'Cam, I know your school will be on summer holidays, so, Maddie, can you take a week off work in August?'

'An entire week? I'm not sure – it'll only be my second month.'

'Why, anyway?' Cam asks.

Jo removes her jacket and stands in the middle of the kitchen. 'Picture this.' She stares into the distance. 'The warm sun on your skin, afternoon cocktails, summer night barbeques. I'm talking pizza, pasta, gelato, holiday sex and Italian culture – yes, in that order.' She waves a hand in the air. 'Florence,' she breathes.

'Italy?'

'Yes, Maddie! Italy! For an entire week!' She takes a deep breath. 'A friend of mine, Emma, her parents have a holiday home there and say she can have friends over to stay since they'll be in Greece for the summer.' Jo holds a hand up. 'I know. Yes, she is an incredibly spoilt friend, but that incredibly spoilt friend has said I can bring you both with me! We just have to pay for the flights.'

I've always wanted to go to Italy and travel *is* on my New Maddie list (I didn't think I'd get to that one before brunch). Rome has been on my bucket list for years. The Colosseum, St. Peter's Basilica, the Pantheon. I imagine Florence will be just as incredible. But even with a free stay, I can't technically afford it. Clothes shopping, takeaways, travelling to and from Zone One and going from four hundred and fifty pounds rent to almost double means I've had nothing to save this month.

But can you really turn down your first partially free trip to Italy?

Cam narrows her eyes at Jo. 'So you get to bring two people with you for a free stay in Italy and we were your first choice?'

Jo shrugs. 'Em and I have mutual friends she's already invited.'

'And?'

Jo sighs. 'And my other friends already have summer holidays booked.'

'There it is.'

'But so what?' Jo says. 'You weren't my *last* choice, and it's *seven* nights' free stay in Florence! First of August to the eighth! I thought I'd get more excitement out of the two of you.'

'The first? The flight out is on my Dad's birthday,' I tell them. 'I can't miss it.'

'What about joining after?' Jo says. 'Come a couple of days later, especially if you're nervous about taking that much holiday from work so soon?'

I suppose I could use my savings – just a bit of it.

I mean, what else is it there for?

'Fuck it,' Cam says. 'I'm in.'

Pre-scream, Jo turns to me.

I suddenly nod. 'Me too!'

'Yes!' Jo pulls her MacBook out from her bag, sits at the table and looks up seats available on Emma's flight.

'Maddie, we can book yours tomorrow when you've checked in with work, in case they say no, but they won't. They can't.'

> **Ben**
> Florence? Now I HAVE to make us pasta for dinner
> Second date sorted

> **Maddie**
> Are you sure you don't mind cooking again?
> Wouldn't you rather we go out for dinner, maybe?

> **Ben**
> But . . . my pasta machine

I smile at my phone screen. Ben's been very excited by his recently purchased pasta machine. He's been sending me pictures of pasta he's made and the meals he's turned them into for the past three days.

> **Maddie**
> I'm starting to think you might like this pasta machine
> more than you like me

> **Ben**
> Maddie, please don't make me choose
> Did I tell you it has TEN thickness settings?

Maddie

Yes. You also happened to mention that it came with a table clamp, a drying function and that it can make 700g of fresh pasta in minutes

Ben
750g!

Maddie
Fine, but this had better be the best pasta I've ever tasted

Ben
Challenge accepted
See you tomorrow?

I sigh. Not because I don't want to see Ben again, I really do, but – and I know you're going to think, *Maddie, I don't get what the problem is* – I need to wash my hair.

I was going to wait until Saturday, but what if Ben decides to kiss the top of my head and all he smells is the sweat and dust collected from running around the OTP offices and my scalp stewing on the underground?

I call it Wash *Day* because it really is a twenty-four hour process that I've now got to shrink into twelve hours and counting.

I finish dinner and get started. There's a method to washing my 4C hair in the least detrimental way. It's a science. Detangling my hair alone takes almost an hour and I could stop after step five and blow-dry my hair, but I prefer to minimise heat damage, and I'm sure that's one of the reasons why, when stretched, my hair rests at bra-strap length.

Everyone has their own wash-day method, but here's a simplified version of mine:

1. Shampoo hair until water runs clear
2. Apply conditioner, detangle with wide-tooth comb and leave under a shower cap for twenty minutes
3. Wash conditioner out and lightly dry hair with microfiber towel
4. Section hair, typically into ten sections, and oil the scalp
5. Spray a section with a moisturising spray, coat in a sulphate-free cream of choice, then apply a natural oil blend (currently castor oil mixed with jojoba oil). Plait the section and repeat nine more times
6. When all the hair is plaited, leave to air-dry overnight
7. Undo plaits when dry and style as desired

I know. Even for me, a doer of this exact routine for five years, it's exhausting. I'm a little way into section five when I go down to the kitchen for a snack. Jo's still in there and smiles when she sees me. 'Woah,' she says. 'Are you putting weave in?'

I frown into the fridge. 'No, just washing my hair.'

'Half your hair is long and the other is short. Did you cut it like that?'

'It's shrinkage.'

She narrows her eyes. 'What?'

I point to the shorter side of my hair. 'When my hair is wet, it shrinks.' I point to the other side of my head, 'and when it's plaited, it stretches.'

'Oh,' she reaches out and pulls a damp coil. '*Boing*,' she

says. She reaches out to do it again but Cam comes out of nowhere and gently slaps Jo's hand away. In her TA's voice, she says, 'You don't touch a Black woman's hair, Jo. Not without permission.'

I would argue you shouldn't touch anyone's hair without their permission, just like you wouldn't, or at least shouldn't, just reach out and grab someone's boob, but Jo laughs at Cam. 'Maddie doesn't mind. We're flatmates.'

I force a smile and grab a packet of crisps instead of making a sandwich.

Back upstairs, I undo my plaits and blow-dry my hair instead.

Chapter Fourteen

Begrudgingly, I admit it is the best pasta I've ever had, mostly because instead of tomato, Ben's made a smooth butternut and sage butter sauce. As I clean my bowl, he looks on smugly until I say, 'I've only ever had dried pasta from a packet, so the bar was very low.'

He gently grabs my chin and kisses me.

When he pulls away, I ask, 'No dessert?'

'Afraid not. Dinner took me hours.'

'Oh! What happened to seven hundred grams in minutes?'

'Seven hundred and *fifty* grams. The additional fifty grams is what really does it for me.' He kisses me again. 'But if you insist, let me find you something,' and he gets up from the table to pour us two glasses of wine.

'Far be it from me to judge, but I don't think that dessert has set.'

He snorts. 'Dessert wine.' He hands me a glass. 'A compromise.'

'Is it though?'

'What if you pick what we watch? I have all the subscriptions, so the film and TV world is at your disposal.'

'Can we watch David Attenborough's *New Worlds* documentary? I think it's meant to be on at eight.'

Ben smiles and squeezes my shoulder. 'I've been looking

forward to that since the BBC announced it. You're a David Attenborough fan?'

'Everyone's a David Attenborough fan,' I say. 'He's the Earth's grandpa.'

We take the wine into the living room and I make a conscious effort not to spill any onto the carpet. This room is decorated in a soft grey-black with accents of chrome and teal. A giant Jackson Pollock-esque painting hangs on the back wall, and a large TV on the opposite. There's a built-in bookcase beside the piano ('Ornamentation at this point, I rarely play') and a fireplace in the wall.

Ben closes the curtains, takes a blanket from the armchair and drapes it over us when we settle on the sofa.

The wine is very sweet, unlike the red from our first date, and I soon leave an empty glass on the table (atop a coaster, of course).

Tonight's documentary is on big cats and their increasingly difficult search for food. I'm so absorbed that I don't notice Ben coming closer until his hand is resting on my thigh. These things happen. It's quite grown-up to have a man's hand on your thigh and I *am* a grown-up, so it's fine. Now he's stroking the inside of my thigh with his thumb. My pulse spikes when he's further up my dress and I wonder if I should touch him too. Where would be similarly appropriate to touch him?

I turn to look at Ben and his eyes catch mine. I mean to smile and look away, but he leans forward and kisses me, pulling me onto his lap. I make a conscious effort to kiss him back and it feels like a game of who can apply the most pressure on the other's lips.

'I am, quite frankly, obsessed with you,' and he kisses me again. It's a nice thing for him to say and it's even nicer to hear.

Suddenly it turns into a different kiss than the others before. All I can taste is his tongue and I can feel the pressure of his hands, pressing into my thighs, squeezing my hips, rubbing my back, but always returning to my thighs. He pulls me in closer and I jump when I feel he's erect.

'You okay?' he asks.

Fuck. 'Mm-hmm.'

Ben has a boner.

Well, of course he does. He's thinking about sex. That's how it works.

Behind me, the documentary is still playing: 'With ferocious speed, the hungry lion closes in on its prey.'

Against every instinct in my body, I look down and this time I can't hold it in.

'Maddie, are you giggling?'

'Sorry, I'm sorry! I'm not laughing at you,' I rush to add. 'It's just nervous energy, I swear.'

'You're nervous?' he asks.

'Just a little.'

'That's very sweet.'

'It's just . . . I'm . . . It's nothing.'

When I press my lips together, he hardens – well, the rest of him does.

'Maddie, are you a virgin?'

'I believe that's what the kids are calling it these days. Oh, God, sorry.' I cover my face. 'That was meant to be funny, but I'm not sure it even made sense. Yes, I'm a virgin. No sex. No! I don't mean, like, never. It's not a chastity-belt thing. I . . . It's just never happened.'

I lower my hands and Ben is smiling and rubbing my arms. 'How is that *possible*? Look at you.'

I want to ask if he really means that, but end up burying my face in my hands again.

'Stop that.' He gently encircles my wrists. I still keep my eyes closed and he sighs. 'So, I take it tonight's not the night.'

Behind me, bones are crunching and I assume the lion has won.

'Granted, not the best setting,' he adds.

'Sorry.'

'Don't apologise.' He lifts me off his lap but lies back and pulls me on top of him. I rest my head under his chin, grateful that yesterday was hair wash day.

After a while, I say, 'Is it bad that I was rooting for the lion?'

'Instead of *Bambi*?'

'Lions have to eat.'

'What about Bambi's future plans?'

'Bambi *had* future plans. Not anymore.'

Ben pauses. 'So you have a dark side?' He finds my bum and squeezes. 'Good to know.'

Chapter Fifteen

OTP are going with my idea, only, no one knows it was my idea.

Kris is getting the credit because, according to the minutes of the last Creative meeting, instead of *Cooking Combos*, she proposed *Flavour Pairings*. Which is more refined, I suppose, but swapping words for synonyms doesn't make it her idea! Does it?

At our catch-up, I say, 'Good news about *Flavour Pairings*.'

'Yes,' Kris says, looking directly at me. 'Penny loved the idea, so well done, but we've got a lot to do to turn the concept into an actual book. We've yet to whittle down which of our food writers we want to approach.'

I brighten up. She said 'we've' – twice. I'm still in. 'I've got a lot of ideas,' I say, opening my notebook. 'Even some "pair" ideas for the cover.'

Kris tilts her head at my inverted comma gesture.

'I thought it might be funny,' I explain, 'to have a pear on the cover with one of its classic flavour combos, like chocolate, a bar of chocolate, I mean. Or chocolate chips, but they might look like droppings, so maybe the bar . . .'

'Ah, well, design are in charge of covers, but I can certainly mention your idea this afternoon.'

'I can take the minutes for the meeting,' I offer.

'Their assistant Kelsey takes minutes for all design-led meetings, but don't worry,' Kris says, 'there's lots of important bits to get stuck into and I can tell you want to be involved. Here.'

She hands me a list of admin tasks, some of which have nothing to do with *Flavour Pairings*.

'Great.' I smile tightly. 'I'll get started.'

They went with my pear idea!

Not pear and chocolate, but pear and cinnamon. I hear cinnamon was Georgina's (one of the senior designers) idea, so naturally the pear/pair motif was hers too. Clearly, my ideas are good and there's solace in that, but only a little when no one knows or acknowledges that they're mine. I still don't even get to join Creative, of which there are now two meetings a week. This would have been the perfect opportunity to learn so much about the process, witnessing first-hand the stages from conception to completion, but I can't seem to get in.

Maybe I don't deserve to get in. It's a bit like retelling someone else's anecdote and getting the credit – I wouldn't have pitched the idea if it weren't for Ben. But I do have an idea that is completely my own, my Afra discovery, and I'm going straight to the top with that one.

'Okay, I need meetings with . . .' And Penny lists the names of colleagues as she taps away at her keyboard. 'Right, anything else? How's it all going?' She continues to stare at her computer screen; her eyeshadow is bright purple today and she's pushed her glasses up to keep the growing strands of her hair out of her eyes. 'Kris tells me she's happy with how hard you're working.'

Now or never.

'Yes, all fine,' I answer. 'Speaking of Kris, I wanted to tell her about this proposal I have, but she's out this afternoon.'

'Oh,' Penny says.

Shit, she's looking directly at me now, her fingers hovering above her keyboard.

'Kris mentioned we needed new ideas, preferably from our own writers, and I was looking through . . . doing research . . . well, I was on Google, actually, no, on Instagram . . .'

Wrap it up, Maddie.

'I found Afra Yazden-Blake – she's the wife of baker Stephen Blake,' I say. 'She has a food blog she doesn't update much – I printed out a few of her recipes – but her Instagram is full of delicious, home-cooked Middle Eastern meals. I know she's not on our list, but she is affiliated via her husband and might be open if *we* approach her, rather than asking her to submit. She doesn't have an agent or any professional cooking experience, I don't think, but she might be worth looking into.'

Penny walks over to the table and looks at the recipes and screenshots of Afra's Instagram I've laid out on the table. 'Hmm,' she says. 'Perhaps.' She gives me a friendly smile, then leaves the papers and returns to her desk. She's back to tapping away in no time.

Ouch. Maybe I should have gone to Kris; some management don't take ideas seriously if it doesn't come from a peer.

I stand up and start gathering the papers.

'No, you can leave them there, Maddie,' Penny says. 'I'll take a look later.'

I look at her in consternation. 'Oh, okay, great.'

I leave the room triumphant.

Chapter Sixteen

> **Ben**
> Still on for Friday night?

> **Maddie**
> Of course!

> **Ben**
> Look at us. You went from taking a week to reply to under a minute and now we're going on our third date

> **Maddie**
>

But something about his message jars me. It's the mention of our third date.

> $\mathbb{Q}$ **Google** – Does a third date mean sex?

That Dating Life

The three-date rule is more of an American invention, so does it apply to those of us across the pond? Well, if it's a rule you want to follow, it really means that if you don't want to be considered a whore/slut/fuck buddy, then you need to wait at least three *paid* dates (so a walk in the park doesn't count) before having sex. Of course, this rule applies strictly to women.

The Girl Next Door

There's only a wrong way to have sex when dating and that's being pressured into it. The only 'rule' you need to stick to is having sex when you *want* to.

Q **Google** – How do I know if I'm ready to have sex?

Carmen: You just know

Tiffany: Unfortunately you tend to find out after you have sex

I think I'm ready to have sex. I'm officially closer to thirty than twenty, so I should be ready. I must be almost a decade behind most women. But we're going to the cinema; we won't have sex in the cinema. Maybe I should casually suggest going back to his place after. What's the code word: nightcap?

Is it weird that there's a part of me that wants this over with? Probably, but best to save further ruminations on that for when I can afford a therapist.

Maybe it's not that weird. Maybe that time in my life – the rose petals on the bed and lit candles on the floor – is over, or just not me. Will I regret it, though? Ben knows I'm a virgin, so if it is going to happen on our third date, does he have something *special* planned? How will I feel if he doesn't?

Ben

So sorry. I'm running late. Work's been chaos. I've already brought the tickets to collect so I'll meet you inside. Order number is 37715. Don't buy a thing. All the snacks are on me. X

Maddie

Okay, see you soon xx

I back away from the line gratefully as the prices are eye-watering. We're – or rather I'm – on Portobello Road in Electric Cinema. I've never been here before and after a quick google search I find out why.

Boasting rows of armchairs, footstools, side tables, double beds, cashmere blankets and a giant screen, the Electric Cinema promises a one-of-a-kind cinematic experience. Ultimate comfort combined with a unique movie-dining experience, available from the cinema's own fully licensed bar serving a selection of cocktails, wine, beer and champagne, with an extensive food menu to match.

With red and cream décor, decorative arches and old-fashioned lamps, the Electric Cinema is sure to give you ultimate 1920's vibes. There's truly no movie experience like it. However, you get what you pay for, with tickets alone ranging from £22 and up.

Should I only sleep with Ben if he's my boyfriend? Is Ben my boyfriend? How does one acquire this information? Will he ask me to be his girlfriend or does sex have to come first for compatibility reasons?

145

I find our seats: a velvet sofa bed with blankets and a long table at the end. I settle in and sigh in comfort.

Sex is painful the first time – I know that much. What else do I know? Well, let's consider my three main sources of sex education – ironically enough, school didn't make the list.

Church (We didn't have the birds and the bees chat at home. More the fire and brimstone lecture in church. All I definitely learned about sex was that doing it outside of marriage was to be avoided at all costs because it held the weightiest of consequences if not.)

Avi (less basics, more advanced, anal-based stuff).

The media (books and TV unhelpfully depicting a couple intrinsically knowing what to do in order to highlight their compatibility to the audience).

Should I ask Jo? Or is it a weird thing to text someone: how do I do sex?

How do I do *it*? Can I just lie there? Should I have watched porn? Can I watch porn and step into church without bursting into flames?

Don't be so childish, Maddie. Everyone watches porn.

Or do they?

Q **Google** – How to lose your virginity?

Note to self: delete search history in case I suddenly die a mysterious death and the police go through my phone for clues.

Things to know about sex before you lose your virginity

There's no denying that many of us girls have been failed by our parents and school classes when it comes to learning the realities of sex. Because is so much we haven't been told, some of us (looks in the mirror) have had to learn the hard way. Here's a list of things I wish I'd known before I starting 'doing it'.

1. So those hilarious anecdotes about men climaxing within minutes aren't just a cliché. It's actually common for a man to ejaculate faster than you – or they – expected.

2. Here's one I really wish someone had told me. Even if he does/can take his time, you probably won't climax the first time you have sex. Great if you do (!), but reasons why you might not range from legit medical conditions, endometriosis for example (at which point you should consult a doctor), to your mental state on the night.

Can I remember all of this? Should I be taking notes?

How is your mental state, Maddie? The word 'questionable' comes to mind.

3. It's completely normal to feel physical discomfort the first time you have sex. It will have a lot to do with our old science pal Friction. The ease of penetration is dependent on lubrication. Vaginas tend to produce natural lube by getting 'wet', but if this isn't enough, using lube will help and is absolutely necessary for anal play as the anus—

That's enough of that.

**Reddit: When did you lose your
V-çard and what happened?**

I was 16 and my boyfriend lied about not being a virgin.
He didn't know what he was doing and I bled all over
his bed. I had to help him do the laundry because he
didn't know how to do that either — Davina

I was 15 and it was horrible. We'd only been going out for
a few weeks but I thought I loved him. Sex lasted 10
seconds – I counted. He said sorry, then cried for half an
hour — Poppy

This is brutal.

I was 16 and it was great. He played the Lord of the Rings
soundtrack which really got me in the mood — Hallie

It was summer, and I was 16. My parents were away for the
weekend so I was home alone and my beautiful next-
door neighbour, straight 10/10, had just broken up with
her boyfriend and needed a shoulder to cry on, so I
invited her round to watch a movie.

What in the Wattpad is this?

I was 15 and with my boyfriend of six months. We did stuff

before that like me giving him handjobs blowjobs and him fingering me sometimes.

Fifteen? What was I doing at fifteen? Did I still have a Tamagotchi? Whatever happened to those things?

It was towards the end of the school year, spring, and I remember the sun being out. It was warmer than usual. I'd just gotten out of detention

Oh, fuck off.

'Sorry I'm late.'

'Ben!' I drop my phone and thankfully it lands screen down.

'You look guilty,' he says, passing me my phone without looking at it. He looks too harried to have been paying any proper attention. I notice subtle dark shadows under his eyes, and I wonder if he'd rather be home with a glass of wine and an early night, but he's chosen to see me instead.

'Oh. Ha. No, I was just looking at the reviews for the film.'

'And?'

'They're good!'

'Flustered, much?' He pinches my thigh. 'You were expecting me, right? And not some other guy you're seeing.'

'Am I? No, I'm not expecting anyone else!'

He kisses me. 'Glad to hear it,' then briefly rests his chin on my shoulder. 'You smell good.'

'Oh, well, I showered today, so you're welcome.'

You could call me a little skittish for almost getting caught, but Ben laughs. 'Classy,' he says. 'I do appreciate a showered woman. Food should be here soon.' He's whispering even though the lights haven't fully dimmed, others are still filtering in and those already seated are having audible conversations. The woman behind me asks her friend if polygamy is the one to do with sex or maths because 'Darren keeps bringing it up', and when I reach forward for my blanket, the lady seated in front of me is on her phone typing LOOOL with a straight face whilst maintaining a conversation about scrimping on toilet paper with her date/housemate. Apparently, 'it's just not on, Connor. Two-ply is the minimum. I'll not tell you again.'

'You've ordered?' I ask.

'Pretty much everything on the menu,' Ben replies. 'My way of apologising for leaving you on your own for so long.' He pulls me closer until I'm under his arm, then rests his head back.

'Things at work are manic?' I ask quietly in case he'd rather silence.

'As always,' he says. 'But lately, I don't know what's going on. It's always "one more email" before it's two hours later.' He kisses the top of my head. 'It won't happen again.'

'I don't mind.'

A man arrives with our food and places it all on our table: mini burgers, nachos and popcorn. Even pick 'n' mix in striped paper bags that remind me of nicking singular sweets from the canisters in *Woolworths* and then believing my sticky fingers were the reason they went out of business. (They really shouldn't have made them so easy to steal; if they were relying on the ethical morality of teenagers, they could only expect to be sorely disappointed.)

He next arrives with two glasses of champagne. Ben squeezes my arm and says, 'Help yourself,' just as the film title screens.

The World War One film is one I picked: during Operation

Alberich, two young soldiers have to cross enemy lines in order to deliver a message to the British on the other side and failure to do so will mean the innumerable loss of British lives. I was hooked as soon as I saw the trailer.

'It's starting,' two-ply-or-nothing says. 'We'll talk about this later.'

Halfway through the film, I sneak a glance at Ben and he's completely absorbed. I notice how long his eyelashes are and how defined his jaw is. He is handsome and I'm attracted to him, but do I want him inside of me? Do I want to forever refer to him as the man that took my virginity?

Do you remember that early noughties show *Lizzie McGuire* and how her subconscious was a small, animated version of herself? Well, I have that too. A mini-me living, breathing and moving in my head, always with waist-length twisted braids and so much more attitude. At times, she's actually quite rude. I ask her if we want to sleep with Ben and she shrugs.

I mean . . . We don't mind, do we? You read those how I lost my virginity stories and some of them were fucking grim. She lies back on a velvet chaise longue. *Here's Ben, good job, very well-paid and experienced. Yes, maybe we should care a bit more, but you know . . .* She taps her watch. *It took us this long to get here – let's not wait another eight years.* She stands to twirl on her platform sandals. *You're the New Maddie now. We're meant to be having fun, remember?*

The credits roll and I squint when the lights come on; I feel light-headed from the champagne when I lift my neck. 'Do you think it's a Marvel-kind-of-thing and there's something after the credits?'

Ben stops unwrapping himself from our blanket. 'You're into Marvel?'

'Yes, them and DC? Love those guys. Mainly the films however.'

Ben considers me. 'Favourite superhero?'

'Black Panther or Spiderman.'

'You continue to surprise me,' he says. 'I didn't think you'd choose this film for us to watch. I didn't have you down as a history buff.'

'I'm not really, but I'd heard so much about this one I thought, why not try something new, you know?'

'Yes, I do.' He smiles. 'Dear Maddie, can I interest you in a nightcap?'

A red alarm goes off in Subconscious Maddie's room. *CODE WORD ALERT.*

I try to keep my eyes steady on his. 'At your place?'

'Yes.' He holds my gaze and gently squeezes my hand. *Go for it.*

I take a small breath. 'That would be nice.'

'You have an actual bar?' I ask as Ben opens a cupboard in his kitchen. My heart is tapping and my legs feel weak. The lock of his front door clicking shut was resounding. *Just keep talking.* 'How did I not notice that before?'

'There's a reason I had this kitchen designed to include a lot of cupboards,' he says. 'What drink would you like?'

'Well, it is a Friday night, so I'll have a virgin mojito, please.'

Ben snorts. 'Sure,' he says, pouring dark liquor into the bottom of a tumbler and sliding it to me. 'One virgin mojito.'

I look at him. 'Believe me when I say, I know what a virgin mojito looks like and this is not it.' I lift the glass. 'There's hardly anything in here for a start.' I take a gulp and it instantly dries my throat. 'Ben,' I gasp. 'What the fuck?'

He laughs. 'Welcome to the wonderful world of whisky. You'll want to sip it.'

'Too late, I've finished it now. Oh, my eyes are watering.'

He leaves the bar to kiss me and hold my face in his hands. 'You're wonderful,' he says. 'So . . . *new*.'

'Thank you.' *Just keep talking.* 'The film was . . .'

He continues to hold me until I'm looking him in the eyes; I rarely do this with anyone because lengthy eye contact is too much for me. Others value it highly, but I can't – or don't want to – imagine what they're seeing (or what I'm revealing) when they stare so intently.

Ben's forehead is large and perhaps a third of the reason why his face seems long, and his hair is swept back today. His eyebrows are groomed and his eyes crease at the corners when he smiles, like he's doing now. His nose cuts right through the middle; his lips are thinner than mine, but his bottom is fuller than the one above. He hasn't shaved for a few days, or maybe he has but not too closely. I follow the lines of hair and imagine him stood between my legs whilst I'm sat on the counter, trimmer in hand, shaving his beard. We're laughing because I'm doing a terrible job.

I now have my hands on Ben's face and he's kissing my fingers and then my palm, my neck, cheek and lips. It feels nice and *manageable*.

He lifts me so that I straddle him. I'm nervous, but it must be those first-time nerves that never go away, no matter how old you are, no matter how much you know you should have done this by now. But why are the nerves only growing;

153

why has my stomach skipped the calm and gone straight for the storm? I'm not sure if I . . .

We're upstairs now, so focus on that.

Ben does feel nice, the kisses and his urgency.

His bed is really soft, so focus on that.

I feel cold when my clothes leave my skin and transparent when my underwear is off. It's all happening so fast. I cross my legs – *no, just relax* – and Ben pulls them gently apart.

His hands are warm, so focus on that.

He's heavier than I imagined. He knocks the air out of me.

I think we should stop, but I can't say it and then he enters me and I bite my tongue. He gasps as I begin to shake.

Fuck, fuck, fuck, no, oh God, ouch, ouch. Too much. I want this to be over. I want this to be over.

It's not the pleasure I've heard through thin walls or read about in books; it's not even 'not bad', it's a sharp pain that clamps my jaw shut, but in pain there is always a point of relief, and I wait for it, the point where I'm broken in or apart, but tears steep my eyes and my jaw aches. I tense when he stills and comes and leaves me.

I can breathe now, so focus on that.

Ben pants beside me, his cheeks red and his eyes closed.

I curl my toes and dig my nails into my palms. I stare at the ceiling, thinking of how I can dry my eyes without drawing attention. Can I lie and attribute the tears to great sex? Do people ever cry from pleasure? I decide on running to the toilet to pee when Ben takes my hand. He doesn't say anything.

I lay there until he's asleep. I should use the toilet anyway – I read that somewhere years ago.

I don't switch on the light in case it's anything like ours and makes a humming sound – I can't remember if it did when I first used it. My chest aches and I whimper then choke but cover my mouth with my hand. I don't know what's wrong with me.

I almost slip on the toilet lid when I find Ben dribbling down my thigh.

'He didn't use a condom,' I whisper.

I wipe my eyes. Do I feel like a grown-up, now? Do I feel like a woman of the world with a story I can share with other woman; a tale that will serve as a bonding experience? I immediately know I don't want to tell anyone about this, which doesn't make any sense. What is the point of losing your virginity if not to fit in? It's meant to *go*, like how puberty is meant to pass, like how you're supposed to age. It *has* to happen, doesn't it?

I poke at my body, waiting for something to feel different. I thought I would feel more evolved, more in control, my body a lone thinker, but instead I feel small and uneven, like I could tilt over at any point. This was the last piece of my body puzzle. My boobs have stopped growing and I will be this height for the foreseeable. I am both under and overwhelmed.

Am I okay if I'm on the pill? Will tampons be easier to use now? My mum's going to be furious if I get pregnant – what does God think of me now?

You're being ridiculous.

Is Ben religious? Does he know that I am, what I call, a modern-day Christian, a Christian who wants to get into Heaven without doing any of the dutiful stuff because surely believing in Him is enough of an entry requirement and it's really hard to go to church every Sunday and then read the Bible every day too and not drink, smoke, have tattoos, gossip, lie, and watch TV and listen to music with none of the aforementioned. 'Modern-day', in this context, is also my own synonym for 'shit'.

I should google if I'm going to get pregnant, but my phone is . . . I wore a dress with no pockets so . . . in my bag. Downstairs – in the kitchen, but I'm naked. I look down and my stomach's formed rolls. *Shit*. But it's flat when I'm on my back, right?

Who cares? Be a feminist, Maddie!

Can one be a feminist twenty-four/seven?

I wrap a towel around myself and tiptoe downstairs for my phone. Without the lights on I bump into the sharp corner of the counter and cradle my bruising rib. I suddenly think, *you're in a stranger's house.*

I grab my phone and return to the bathroom.

Q **Google** – can you get pregnant if you're on
the pill

- If taken correctly, at the same time every day, you're 97% protected against pregnancy
- Approx. 7 in 100 women a year get pregnant despite using the pill
- Factors such as your estrogen and progesterone levels must be considered, alongside any medication you may be taking and any bouts of vomiting and/or diarrhoea
- The contraceptive pill is 99.6% effective

Okay, I think I'm safe. What are the chances I'd be part of the 0.4%? *Well, getting pregnant the day you lose your virginity does sound like something that would happen to you.*

Can I . . . pee his come out? Is that why you're meant to urinate after? No, Google says that's to prevent UTIs.

Sex is currently presenting more cons than it is pros.

I eventually get back into bed and Ben stirs before pulling me onto his chest, kissing the top of my head. 'Fuck, I didn't use a condom, did I?'

'That's okay. I'm on the pill.'

'How long have you been on?'

'Since I was sixteen.'

'Gotcha,' he whispers, and I can feel him smile against my temple.

'What?'

'Never mind.' He kisses me again and falls back to sleep.

The next morning, there's a dull ache between my thighs as I walk to the kitchen.

Ben, dressed in sweats, has his back to me and is on the phone.

'Do we all have to go?' he asks whoever. 'You'd better tell me the date again, then. Yes, I'll be there, put me down with a plus-one. Yeah, she'll want to come. Thanks, Mike. Bye.'

'Hi.'

He turns around and smiles. 'Morning, Maddie.' With the heaviness of last night's sleep weighing down his eyes and his hair untidy, he looks softer than the night before. 'Come here.'

'That sounded important,' I say, walking over.

'The call? No, not really.' He kisses the top of my head and I take a seat on one of the bar stools. Ben returns to the coffee he's making and says, 'I wasn't sure whether to subject you to it. The CEO of my company's birthday is coming up and he's decided to throw a thing at the office.'

That sounds awful. 'That sounds great.'

'It won't be. It'll be lavish and overstated and he's denied two pay rise requests this month alone.' He pulls me close. 'I've got you a plus-one, but I won't be offended if you decide not to use it. If you don't, maybe I'll start coughing two days before and suddenly be too ill to attend.'

'No, I'd like to come.' I wouldn't, but attending work events is a relationship thing, isn't it? *And this is a relationship now, right?* 'It'll be fun.'

Ben smiles. 'On your own head be it. I was just leaving for a run but wanted to give you something before.'

He hands me a pink rectangular box wrapped in a black ribbon. I suddenly wish I was wearing something other than his T-shirt.

'What is it?' I ask.

'Open it.'

Inside the box, nestled spaciously on pink tissue paper are three macaroons – one pale pink, one violet and one green.

'Macaroons?'

'These are London's best macaroons,' he says. 'I saw them and thought of you.' He pulls my thighs apart and stands between them. 'Try one?'

'What? Now?'

'I did intend to give it to you last night, but we got distracted.' He leans in to bite my bottom lip. He smells different today and I wonder if it's me he smells of. 'Have one,' he says.

I look up at him. 'Ben, it's eight in the morning.'

'So?' He kisses me.

If this were all happening on screen, I'd ask if the macaroons were poisoned. Ben stares at me and I can't decide if his eyes have darkened or if I'm seeing things.

'Okay then.' I really don't want one but it doesn't feel like enough of a big deal.

Ben begins stroking my thighs and says, 'The pink one.'

I move my fingers away from the violet and lift the pink macaroon from its place. I take a bite. The shell is crisp and crunches noisily between my teeth. Its sweetness stings.

Ben taps my thighs and I look at him. He smiles, then watches me chew.

'What do you think?' he asks.

I'm hearing a tone that isn't there. Ben's voice is, as always, gentle and conversational.

I nod and swallow. I only briefly consider placing the other half of the macaroon back into the box before Ben's thigh tapping begins again. My chest feels weak and I want to cry. *What is wrong with you?* I eat the other half. This half is dry and I have difficulty swallowing it. His tapping doesn't stop until I look at him again. I almost whisper, 'Sorry.'

'Decadent breakfast,' I say.

He kisses my shoulder through his shirt and I quickly close the box.

Chapter Seventeen

> **Nia**
> I'm baaaaccckkkkk

> **Maddie**
> YAAAY! When can I see you?

> **Nia**
> Any time next week

> **Maddie**
> After I see my dad?

> **Nia**
> Sounds good. Let him know I said happy birthday

I'm thinking tonight might be the night for a bath when in the kitchen Jo says, 'I'm meeting some friends at a bar at eight and I'm dragging you both with me.'

I've noticed Jo's constant need to include us in things, to not be alone. At first, I thought her endless invitations were just friendly, but now I wonder if she always needs to feel a part of big groups.

'No way,' Cam says. 'We've got our flight to Florence tomorrow afternoon.'

'I'm baking a cake for my dad's birthday tonight, remember,' I say, pointing to the ingredients I've already left out on the counter. I haven't seen Dad since I moved out so, even though I'm no baker, I thought I'd make him a cake, then go home in the morning and spend the day with him there.

'Come on, you two,' and Jo's shoulders slump. 'You know I could use a night out. This Sam thing is getting to me.'

Yesterday, Jo told us that she and Sam had an argument and that he no longer wanted to see her. I'd googled what to do when your flatmate is dumped by someone they're casually seeing, but Google seemed very confused with at least two parts of that sentence.

'I thought you said you were fine this morning?' Cam says. 'Since you're still seeing Conrad.'

'He's nice and everything, but being with Sam was different. We have history, and maybe I . . .' She shakes her head. 'I don't want to think about that. I want to think about nothing.'

I almost ask if such a thing is possible.

Jo catches Cam wavering and adds, 'I can't believe I'm having to convince two women in their *twenties* to have a good time. Cam, I won't get drunk, especially if you're there to stop me, and Maddie, bake the cake now and decorate tomorrow. Done!'

I'd rather not, but then Jo convinces Cam and I don't want to miss out on even more; they're already going to have a two-day head start in Florence without me. Jo's right; I can bake the cake now and it'll be perfectly cooled by tomorrow morning.

*   *   *

For my first official 'Night Out', I pull a mid-length ribbed black dress out of my wardrobe. I turn this way and that. It's flattering, so I leave it on. I add studs to my ears and a small bag that can barely fit my phone and keys. I sit on the floor in front of the mirror and recreate the soft look I went for on my first date with Ben, and put my hair in its now-regulatory low bun.

I'm relieved to find my efforts rank midway between the two girls. Jo has gone all out; she's curled her dark-blond hair, smoothed on silver glitter eyeshadow, and her lips and cheeks are the same shade of pink. Although her silver dress isn't as tight as mine, it's shorter and her heels higher. She gasps when she sees me. 'You look so good!'

Even though she looks great, I don't know how to respond with the same level of enthusiasm without sounding insincere and purely reciprocal. I'm thinking of saying it back and then adding something about her dangly earrings to make the compliment more tailored, when Jo groans. Cam comes out in a shirt, dark skinny jeans and—

'Doc Martens?' Jo asks. 'Really?'

'You said dress up,' Cam says. 'This *is* me dressed up. My socks even match.'

'You haven't got any make-up on.'

Cam points to her eyes. 'Mascara.' She folds her arms. 'Take me or leave me.'

I think the word 'bar' was misleading. The space Jo opens the door to is two storeys tall with very high ceilings. There's a colourful print of a woman dancing on one wall and on the landing of the second floor is a neon sign that says ON AIR. The floor is dark on either side but right in the middle it's patterned with zigzags.

162

'Hi!' Jo waves to the other side of the room and takes us to meet four people sitting in a blue velvet booth around a paint-splattered table. Jo introduces Cam and me and I miss two names because the music's loud. One Black girl (Jennifer), maybe my age, has blond box braids and a septum piercing, whilst the white girl sat beside her (Cariad) has a sharp black bob, dark eyeliner and an Irish accent. The two boys, whose names I missed (one might be Daniel), are brown-haired and -eyed and are sat on either side of the girls. They make space for us when Jo demands it and I end up between Jo and Maybe-Daniel.

I watch Jo drop her bag, then contort her way through the mass of people to get to the bar. She returns with a pitcher of margaritas and three glasses and pours one for Cam and me before taking a seat again. She immediately launches into a conversation with Cariad about a work client they've tellingly nicknamed Cruella, and I'm happy to sip my drink and listen in. I'm glad Cam is also new here, so the attention isn't on me.

'So what do you do, Maddie?' Jennifer asks.

Spoke too soon.

'I recently started working at Orange Tree Publishing.'

They all stare until Jo says, 'It's a publishing company.'

'Oh,' Cariad says. 'What do you do there?'

'I just started, so it's mainly admin.' I pause to take a drink in the hopes that that was enough information, but their silence lasts longer than my sip does. 'I'm an editorial assistant,' and I try to make my job sound as interesting as possible by stealing bits from other skill sets. Thankfully, the mention of photo briefs takes us back to Cruella and her impossible-to-execute-on-her-budget advertisement ideas.

163

The margaritas Jo brought must be strong because after a glass and a half it feels like I've stepped out into the sun and I'm watching the goosebumps on my arms fade.

'It's about time!' Jo suddenly announces. 'I love this song! Come dance with me,' and she grabs *my* hand.

'Oh, I can't dance,' I tell her as she drags me from out behind our table and into the middle of the room.

'What? Of course you can dance! You're Black!'

'She's got you there,' Jennifer says, shuffling past us with Cariad behind her.

We're now in the middle of the dance floor (the zigzag space) encircled by strangers. Someone's come up behind me and it might be Maybe-Daniel, but it's quite dark; the way the lights bounce across the rooms affords only sudden glimpses of those nearby.

This must be a breeding ground for predators.

I shake my head. 'It's fine.' I know no one can hear me above the music and their own singing, so I say louder, 'Maddie, it's fine! Just go with it!'

I don't dance in public. I think I dance well when I'm alone, but that's maybe because I can't see what I'm doing. However, I must be really good because two songs in and I feel eternal. Everyone sings along. I can only join in on the chorus, but I use those four or five lines to shine, and I mean, solo-concert-in-the-shower shine. I don't know if I'm in time with the music, but I'm enjoying myself. The girls grow more animated as I do or maybe it's the other way around. One of us is feeding from the other and I like to think it's me giving them energy.

When the fourth song ends, I push my way to the bar for another drink because alcohol is the secret to the fun I'm having. I order another pitcher for the table, but then ask the bartender to surprise me with something.

I missed the name of it, but when my drink comes out it's got orange and yellow layers. I take a sip and it hits the back of my throat before leaving a warming sensation behind. I'm a third in when Maybe-Daniel appears next to me.

'You're new at this, aren't you?'

'I'm sorry?'

'You were having such a good time – so I can tell.'

I look at him; my vision's slightly off and I realise I've shut my right eye. 'Is your name Daniel?' I ask. I might be shouting in his face but he doesn't seem to mind.

He nods. 'Call me Danny. Can I buy you another drink?'

'I'm actually buying one for the table.' *Ask to buy him a drink. That's a bold and memorable move, isn't it?* 'Can I buy you a drink?'

Excuse me – Ben! Should you really be buying other men drinks?

I'm about to rescind my offer when Definitely-Danny blows out and smiles. 'Fuck yeah,' he says. 'Thank you, Equal Rights Act.'

I inwardly scoff and think *Hardly* but pay for his beer because what are saving accounts for if not for pitchers of margaritas and beers for strangers?

Jo comes over to the bar and waves her phone in my face. 'A friend just messaged me. Let's go.'

'Go?' I hurry to finish my drink. 'We just got here!'

'I know somewhere better,' Jo says. 'You guys staying?' she asks Definitely-Danny.

'Yeah,' he says. 'Tom's coming down, so text us and we might join you later.'

'Cool.' Jo makes her way to the door, grabbing Cam on the way and, reluctantly leaving the pitcher for Definitely-Danny, I follow.

Once we're outside and cool air hits me like smelling salts. 'Actually,' I say, 'Maybe I should go home. I was thinking if I leave the cake decorating to the morning, I'll have to wait for it to set in the fridge before I go and I really want to get home early in the day.'

'If you promise to stay,' Jo says with pleading eyes, 'I'll help you decorate the cake. I'll even get up earlier than you to start it.'

I tilt my head at Jo. Wow, she really wants me to stay; she must really like having me around. Maybe my best friend count will go from two to three before the end of the night . . .

I look at Cam who's nodding emphatically. *From two best friends to four then?*

But something tells me to go home, that I should choose my dad over Jo and that I'm not a very good daughter if I automatically don't. I suddenly think of myself back at university, walking past groups of friends to sit on my own, closest to the door.

It's just a cake, Maddie. Worst comes to worst, I'll buy one. What matters most is actually being home on Dad's birthday, right? And I will be.

'Fine!' I say and all the girls cheer. 'Where to next?'

We (Cariad in tow) walk less than half a mile to a club located in the basement of a bakery; the steps lead to a smoke-filled cave emitting an unmistakable chocolate smell. It's dark but I can see people sat at tables, a dulcet buzz in the air as they drink and smoke shisha.

When sat in a booth, Jo comes up behind us and says, 'Brownies, anyone?'

I look down at the plate she's offering. 'Are you a witch?' I ask, grabbing two before they all go. 'Where did you get brownies from?'

'The bakery upstairs.' She winks and, for whatever reason, I wink back and take a bite. They taste a little off, but maybe they were made this morning and have been left out a while. Plus, I'm starving, so I get started on the second one.

Jo laughs. 'Slow down, Maddie.'

I frown at her. 'It's chocolate, Jo. I know what I'm doing.'

Dear reader – I in fact had no idea what I was doing. Cam informs me shortly after that they're weed brownies.

I look around the table and recognise that everyone's done this before. That's why they come *here*. I slowly finish the second brownie – putting it down would scream 'novice' – whilst Cariad tells us (and three more of Jo's friends sat at the table) about a couple she's seeing.

'Couple?' I question. 'Both of them?'

'Yeah, I'm not into any of that traditional stuff,' she says, taking a drag from the table's pipe, blowing fragrant smoke into the air. 'It's all constructed so we can neatly tick boxes on forms.'

Wow. That was deep.

'I need to pee,' I suddenly announce.

I stumble a little manoeuvring out of the booth, but I'm upright in no time. In the bathroom, I start laughing as soon as I'm urinating; I try smothering it and snort instead. I go to wash my hands and see in the mirror above that I have a manic smile spread across my face. I try to straighten it out, but I can't. I tap the mirror. 'Silly, you.' My reflection laughs and makes me laugh with her. A woman comes in and I keep laughing, pointing to the mirror, trying to get her to join in, but she's not interested. 'Some people have no sense of humour,' I tell my reflection.

'Fuck off,' she says from inside the cubicle.

I return to our table.

'You okay?' Cam asks. When I nod, she eyes me up and says, 'Bit quick for these to work.'

'Maybe it hits different on newbies,' Jo says.

'Awh, have we corrupted a purist?' Cariad asks. 'Virgin, too?'

I gasp. 'Your mouth,' I tell her, 'needs soap.' I then laugh hysterically and they all laugh with me.

This is the mood now, to sit and smoke and drink and talk until we see the sun. We share secrets. I tell them about Ben and that sex is painful. 'Maybe he's shit and you're not wet,' Cariad says and I can't quite grasp what she means.

I don't know what happens to time, but the pulses of energy leak out of me, leaving me loose and serene. I'm happy to just sit here amongst distorted conversation and colourful, perfumed fog. When it's not my turn to speak, I think of old memories, things I haven't thought about in years. Like when I first came on my period and Mum was in Ghana so had to send someone I didn't know very well to help me. Or sneaking into James's room when he called to say he was staying over at a friend's house, and staring out of his bedroom window. Dad nodding to teachers at parents' evenings in a crowd filled with mothers. Watching Serena Williams play Wimbledon, Dad looking up from his newspaper and asking, 'Do you like tennis, Maddie?' I think of the lemon cake Nia made me for my fifteenth birthday; it'd looked like she'd dropped it but it tasted incredible.

Then there's blurred lights and the cool touch of glass on my forehead. We're in a cab, just Jo, Cam and me, driving out of Trafalgar Square. The world is slow tonight but shimmers brightly.

'I get what everyone's talking about now,' I say quietly. '*Move out, Maddie. Live a little, Maddie.* I never wanted to admit it, but I'm so glad to be out of the house and living my life. I hope that doesn't make me a bad person. I almost can't blame James for abandoning me, because there's just so much out there, you know? I have a boyfriend, a better job and I'm going on holiday with new friends. I don't cry at night anymore.' I hold my arms out. 'I'm free.'

'It's a good life,' Jo slurs. Cam snores from the other side of the cab.

I close my eyes and hum a song I've just made up.

Chapter Eighteen

I can't lift my head the following morning.

My phone buzzes and my temples pulse. My mouth is too dry to open. I reach for my phone and realise my eyes are still closed. The daylight is blinding and I curse the sun.

It's just hit noon and I should be at home for Dad's birthday right now.

I sit up with an unintelligible groan and think I might be sick. I stumble across my room in last night's dress to take two paracetamol tablets dry and then gag. My throat hurts and my stomach burns. I'd google **hangover symptoms** because I feel like I only have five minutes left to live, but I can't see straight – my head is *so* heavy.

I'm not that late and Dad's not going anywhere.

I won't even tempt myself by getting back into bed completely. No, I'll just rest my head on my pillow . . . only for a minute . . . ten minutes maybe.

Half an hour at the most.

I wake up to a persistent buzzing.

My phone is ringing. **Mum LONDON** and, underneath, the time: 14:47.

Fuck. I jump out of bed and answer the phone. It's fine; I'll just take the cake home and decorate it there.

'Hi, Mum. Sorry I'm later than I said I was going to be.

I'm leaving the flat in ten minutes.' I sniff my armpits. 'Twenty minutes.' I grab a towel and reach for my shower cap. 'I went to bed late,' I explain when Mum doesn't say anything back. 'So that's why I'm—'

'Maddie?'

I stop because Mum's voice is thick and heavy and she's crying enough to force two more syllables into my name.

'Mum, what's wrong?'

'Maddie, your father, he . . . he is dead. He's dead.'

I freeze on the spot, half out of last night's dress. *What did she say?*

'Your father's dead,' she repeats, then begins to choke and cry.

I frown because I can clearly picture my dad sitting in front of the TV, smiling. I shake my head. 'But it's his birthday,' I tell her.

'I know!' she says. 'Oh, God. Oh, God. To take him on his birthday. And just now too, not thirty minutes long. I've been trying to call you. But he is dead. Maddie, he is dead.'

My body finally hears her and it happens all at once, the punching of my heart, the loosening of my stomach, the burning in my chest. My belly heaves in and out.

'Maddie, your father is—'

'Stop saying that!' I snap. 'I heard you the first time.' I pull my phone away and stare at the red end call button.

'I'm sorry, Maddie.' She continues to cry down the line.

I want to tell her not to be so dramatic. It's not what it seems. It can't be today that he's died. No one dies on their birthday. My dad is not dead. There's been some mistake.

'You need to check again,' I tell her.

'The paramedics have announced it, Maddie,' she says. 'I am so sorry.'

I hang up the phone and hold it to my chest. The only thing I can think about is Mum saying he died thirty minutes before, meaning I'd have been there if I'd woken up when I was meant to. I would have seen him one last time, said happy birthday and kissed his forehead.

I stand, gently swaying on the spot until I trust my hands to pull my dress back on. I'm on autopilot when I walk out of my room and down the stairs.

I can hear suitcase wheels and pockets of conversation. They're talking about Florence. Missing the last step, I trip and end up on the floor on my hands and knees. They both rush in and Jo laughs. 'Still hung-over, huh?'

I get up slowly.

'It was a bad idea to go out last night,' Cam says. 'We need to leave in fifteen minutes. You're so lucky you don't have to catch this flight with— Maddie?'

'My dad's just died.'

For a few seconds, no one says anything.

'Shit,' Jo breathes.

Cam gently takes my arm and walks me into the kitchen. She sits me at the table. My eyes are blurry, but I hear the kettle being switched on. She makes me a cup of tea.

'Fuck, Maddie,' Jo says, shaking her head. 'What happened?'

When I repeat some of my mother's words, they stand above me and they are sorry and coo until Jo says, 'Shit, I can't believe we have to leave soon.'

'We can't go now.'

'What?' Jo turns to Cam so fast her hair whips across her face. 'Tickets are non-refundable,' she whispers.

I look at Jo, rearranging the features of her face until she's unrecognisable, and my chest fills with air. I'm trying to expel it as quickly as possible because it's not that she's callous and it's not that I'd rather they stay, it's—

I stand up. 'You asked me . . . you made me stay out.'

Jo stiffens. 'What?'

'After the first bar, I said I should go home.' I don't know why I'm saying this, but I can't bear the weight of this guilt I'm feeling, it's as if I might drown under it. I tried to do the right thing, to come home. And for a brief moment, it's not my fault anymore. 'I didn't even want to go out last night. If I'd stayed home, I'd have spent the night baking, gone to bed on time and woken up early with a clear head. Jo, if it wasn't for you, I'd have seen my dad today, before he died.'

'Maddie.' She breathes slowly, eyes locked on mine – and they're suddenly no longer the blue of cornflowers, but the blue of a storm at sea. 'I'm really sorry you lost your dad, but I didn't *make* you do anything. You decide what you do and you decided to stay out with us.'

'That's not true!' I shout because the guilt is on a round trip, returning to its rightful place and somehow the tea slips from my hand or I throw it, because the mug ends up shattering against the wall. When I blink, Jo is backed up against the sink and Cam is using half her body to shield her. I don't remember walking from the table to stand in the middle of the kitchen. I must look like I'm inches away from the edge. 'Don't worry about your non-refundable tickets,' I say quietly. 'I'd rather you were both gone. I won't be in the flat much anyway, will I? Not with a funeral to plan.'

I run upstairs, sit in the corner of my room and wait for them to leave. I listen to Jo trudging around the house. 'Still going . . . can't be here with her like this . . . We need distance . . . she said it was my fault . . . really shit of her to put something like that on me . . . don't even know her dad.'

I block my ears until the front door slams shut. I return to the kitchen to clean up my mess, but it's already been done. *Probably Cam.* What am I supposed to do now? Go home . . . but if I stay away for a little longer, I won't have to deal with any of it. The 'process' won't start until I step foot into that house. Then I spot the undecorated sponge cakes and the icing sugar and treacle and butter and my chest fills again. I punch the cakes until they burst and splatter. I throw huge chunks into the bin. Then the sugar, the vanilla, the butter. I throw them into the bin one by one with such force the bin rattles each time.

'What are you doing?'

I turn and Jo is standing in the doorway. 'Not decorating a cake,' I answer. 'Why are you here?'

Jo's head jerks back and I know I should apologise now before it's too late, because it's not her fault my dad's dead and it's not her fault I missed his final hours. The all-consuming anger starts to dissolve and makes me unsteady on my feet.

'Jo,' I start.

'I just forgot my purse.' She unhooks her shoulder bag from the back of the door. 'I'm sorry for what happened to your dad, obviously,' and her lips twitch before she says, 'but it's really harsh of you to blame me. I didn't force you to go out. Nobody did, and if you really wanted to spend your Friday night decorating a cake, you would have stayed and done that. Right?'

She doesn't wait for an answer but spins on her heels and slams the front door behind her. I just stand there, ignoring the tears streaming down my face and the sticky mess pouring from my nose.

*   *   *

Mum calls me again and I answer from the floor. She tells me how it happened in between breathless sobs. She'd been out and Dawoud found him in his chair with vomit all down his front. They tried to call her, but she didn't pick up. She walked in the door ten minutes later. 'I swear only ten minutes later; I didn't hear my phone ringing. My bag is so deep.' The ambulance arrived and he was pronounced dead. Just like that. 'Don't be heartbroken, Maame,' Mum says. 'He is with God now.'

'He was alone on his birthday?' I ask quietly. 'He was alone when he died?'

Mum begins to cry again. I end the call.

I get off the floor, slowly walk to the freezer and pull out a tub of ice cream. I sit and eat it in one go. The lower right of my stomach begins to sting and cramp. I have a chocolate bar next, biting through layers of biscuit and caramel.

Sometimes, in my secondary-school days, Dad would bring home a chocolate bar for me. It was always so arbitrary but I'd be so excited when *that* day came. I used to wonder if he walked into the shop for something else and just suddenly thought of me. Once, he got me a fruit and nut bar, even though I have an intolerance to nuts. I told him he was the best, and upstairs in my room, I ate around them.

My teeth ache from all the sugar and I lie on the living-room floor to stretch the pain in my stomach out.

James calls next and his voice is deeper than usual. 'I'm so sorry, Mads.'

My cheek is flat against the floor when I say, 'I'm sorry, too.'

'I know Dad loved you very much.'

'Thank you,' seems the most appropriate response.

'Are you okay?' he asks. I tell him I'm fine because there's no other answer to give.

'Are your flatmates gone?'

I try to keep my eyes from closing. 'Yes.'

'You don't wanna come home?'

'No, I don't.'

'I get that, but you shouldn't be alone,' he says. 'Do you have a friend who can stay with you?'

I immediately think of Nia. 'Yes, but she might be busy.'

'Call her and see if she can stay with you. Please. For me, yeah?'

'Okay.'

'Cool. I'll see you maybe tomorrow then.'

'Love you,' I say.

He pauses. 'Love you, too, sis.'

A few hours go by and the cramps subside, but the ache is still there. I'm staring at Nia's number when a message comes through.

Ben
I know we said we'd see each other tomorrow, but can I come over? Work was rough

Maddie
Yes

I get off the floor, clean the bathroom, wash my face and wait. I think about how to tell Ben, whether I even should tell him, or if I can pretend for a little while longer that my dad is still alive.

When Ben knocks on the door, I still haven't decided, but I've barely got the latch off when he bursts through, loosening his tie.

'They had to call me in on a Sunday – can you imagine? Incompetence will be that company's ruin, mark my words,' he says.

I immediately want to shrink his presence. To package him up and send him home.

'I'm so glad to see you.' He kisses me, slamming the door shut, and presses me up against the wall. He's heavy and I can't feel enough of myself to pull away. He's had a rough day and he's glad to see me. Just like on our cinema date. He's always glad to see me.

I close my eyes and try to sink into his attention, and although rough and hard, there's a bite to him that I enjoy, or at least need.

It's painful and Ben is sharp and quick with his pleasure. There's a thin crack in the hallway ceiling that I never noticed before. I briefly wonder if it will suddenly stretch open and bury us both in rubble.

I suck in my breath whilst Ben's escapes in guttural grunts.

I'm sore, again.

I use the toilet, again.

I sit on the bathroom floor, feeling nauseous but enjoying the cold tiles on my skin. Ben must hear me because he knocks and walks in to find me naked with my knees under my chin and my eyes wet, rocking gently with an empty head on tight shoulders, a weightless stomach and a pressure building in my chest.

On the floor of my bathroom in a rented flat is where I tell Ben that my father is gone and he won't ever come back, and he says the expected: the exclamation to a God he probably doesn't believe in (I still haven't found out) and a subtle shift of accountability – he really wishes I'd told him earlier (maybe I should have). Still, I suppose the news was surprising to him, too. But he's sorry. He's so, so sorry, Maddie.

Ben is very sweet, kind and delicate when he needs to be and they're qualities I should be grateful for. He holds me on the bathroom floor for what feels like hours as I explain that although Dad was ill, it was unexpected. Ben kisses my forehead and says, 'It will always be unexpected.' He wraps me in his shirt and stays with me until I'm ready to peel myself off the floor and get into bed. I lay awake on his chest as he sleeps.

The next morning, he orders breakfast to the house – croissants, Danish pastries, fresh fruit and tea. He adds a sandwich and a slice of cake for me to have at lunch. We sit quietly at the table and eat. Everything tastes like cardboard in my mouth. I chew and force myself to swallow.

I tell him I don't want to go home yet and he says he can understand why. I eat and eat until my stomach is full and I fantasise about excusing myself from the table, placing my head over the toilet bowl and sticking two fingers into my mouth.

'Do you want to come and stay with me?'

I shake my head. 'That's okay. Nia's coming to stay whilst Jo and Cam are away and I'll be between here and home for . . . the admin.'

Ben leaves in the afternoon because he has to go to work. I ignore the relief I feel at being alone in the house.

'I need to email Kris,' I say to the empty kitchen. 'They'll wonder where I am.'

I spend a few more hours sitting at the table staring at an almost transparent croissant flake clinging to the cloth's edge.

From: Mad.Wright@gmail.com
To: Kristina@orangetreepublishing.com
Subject: My absence

Hello Kris,

Unfortunately my father passed away yesterday. I'm not sure what the work protocol is; I'm not even sure what to write right now.
My father has been ill with Parkinson's and a range of related health issues for years, but the news still came as a shock. I won't be in the office this week, maybe not for the first half of the following week. I'm sorry, I honestly don't know. I just wanted to make you aware.
Best,
Maddie

I press *send* and close my laptop. A text from Cam comes in.

Cam
Hi Maddie. We arrived last night but Jo and I just want to check you're okay
As okay as you can be ofc
You don't need to message back
Just thinking of you x

I wrap myself in a blanket and sit on the sofa, staring out into the garden.

'What an ordinary day. The least you could do is rain.' I search for a cloud in the sky but don't find a single white wisp. 'How thoughtless.'

I finally call Nia to tell her and ask if she can stay over. I expect her to say she'll do her best to get here tomorrow since she hasn't seen her family for almost a year, but instead she tells me she's going to grab some food for me and get the next bus down.

'You're really coming?'

'Are you joking? Of course I am.'

I scrunch up my face when the bridge of my nose starts to sting. 'Thank you.'

'Don't be silly. You know I'd do anything for you.'

She says the last bit not in order to sound supportive or like a good friend should, but as if it's obvious. It's like how I end most of my conversations with 'love you' – she says it not because it's a reflex, but because it's true.

When Nia walks through the door, I feel a lightness enter with her; she manages to push the darkness an inch away with every step forward she takes. I think about how lucky I am that she returned to London this week.

'You look nice,' I tell her. She's redone her locs at the front and has on a shade of red lipstick that warms her brown skin.

'Really?' She shrugs. 'I was just at my grandma's. It's good to see you, Maddie. I'm really sorry about your dad.'

It takes Nia an entire minute to say those four short sentences, but that's the way she speaks, slowly and carefully, incapable of rushing sentences, of getting thoughts out before she loses them. It's my favourite thing about her.

She gives me a long hug and she smells light and fresh and of secondary school. We leave it there. She doesn't ask why or how; she unpacks the food she bought, container after container, and puts them in my fridge. Then we watch films for the rest of the day.

When Nia's in the shower, I kneel by my bed and face the window so that God can see me. I recite my usual nightly prayer where I ask God to take care of my mum, brother and . . .

'This is the part where I would say Dad,' I tell Him, 'but what do I say now? Please rest his soul? Do I still pray for him or is he taken care of? How long have I been praying this prayer? Over ten years – the same words. You could probably do without the repeat.'

I climb into bed and, after Nia gets in too, I switch off the light.

I haven't cried today and I remain awake for hours, wondering if this foreshadows oncoming sociopathic tendencies.

Chapter Nineteen

From: Kristina@orangetreepublishing.com
To: Mad.Wright@gmail.com
Subject: RE: My absence

Oh my goodness, Maddie, how awful. I am so sorry. Please put your out of office on and don't worry about work. I lost a parent only last year, so make sure to let me know how you're doing and if there's anything you want us to help with.
To be clear, we don't expect you to be at work at all this week (or next – just keep in touch).
Sending love to you and your family.
Kris x

On Tuesday morning, after Nia's helped cancel my Florence flights, I ask her, 'Is it weird that I haven't cried since Sunday?'

'Not really. Everyone's different.'

We're on the sofa together, watching the sun edge higher into the sky. It's going to be another beautiful day.

'I know but it feels weird. I just . . . can't seem to cry anymore.'

'Are you sad?'

'Constantly.'

There must be something I miss in my own voice because Nia turns to me and says, 'Don't feel like you have to hold it in. You do that a lot.'

'Do what?'

'Pretend to feel the opposite of what you're really feeling so others won't feel the same. You can cry in front of me.'

'I don't like to cry in front of people.'

'Yeah, I've noticed.' She sits back and says, 'Tell me about your dad.'

I shrug. 'I don't know what to say.' *What are you allowed to say?* 'My dad's undoubtedly a product of his generation and upbringing. He doesn't talk much; he's . . . I mean, he was, just naturally reserved and private, even with his children. We weren't really a close family; we each did our own thing; in a way, we were all just housemates.' I look at Nia and suddenly say, 'We had a lot of trouble with money when I was growing up. Before we sold the house.'

Nia tilts her head. 'You did? You always had money though!'

'No, I just always looked after my money. My mum first went to Ghana when I was twelve and after a while I would tell you guys at school that she was coming back and forth regularly, but she'd be there for up to a year.' Nia's face doesn't hint at judgement or surprise. She's just listening. 'I used to wish she'd return in winter, for Christmas and my birthday, but it was rare that she'd make it back in time. My mum's not good with the cold, you know?'

Nia nods.

'It's not even that I minded her not being home,' I continue. 'I liked doing my own thing and I was used to it, but I would think, *Miss my birthday again, fine, but*

183

Christmas? Let's at least pretend.' I don't know where I'm going with these disjointed confessions, but there's so much to tell Nia, so much that no one outside my family knows and I want to get through it all, to finally share this piece of myself. As I do, I realise a part of me has always wanted to tell Nia these things. 'My parents were together, but not. My dad wasn't very good at looking after us, so my brother relied on his friends and I sort of looked after myself. Mum would send me money to live on when Dad could only cope with paying the bills, and I'd buy cheap ingredients, pads instead of tampons, clothes from charity shops, and saved where I could, just in case.'

'In case of what?'

I shrug. 'Once, I was in a lecture at uni and Mum called me in tears because bailiffs were at the door threatening to take the TV. We had arrears of just under a grand. I'd gotten paid that day – from my bookseller job – and had to hand it all over with a bit more from my student loan. I remember the relief in my mum's voice when I gave my card details over the phone to the collector.'

Nia frowns and leans forward. 'Mads, are you serious?'

I nod. 'Mum left bills to my dad and he wasn't very good at paying them. That's why we had to sell the house in Battersea and move, not because my mum "wanted a change of scene" – sorry for lying about that, by the way.'

Nia takes my hand and squeezes.

'Then Dad got sick,' I tell her. 'But . . . you know, the worse he got, the happier he was to see me.' I sniff. 'I know that sounds weird, but he'd just always smile at me. Even if he saw me two minutes ago, he'd smile again! The first time I remember Dad saying he loved me was when I was about fourteen and he was a little drunk. The second time was before I moved out. I said, "You do?" and it was so strange because the look on his face ... he looked at me like, Maddie, of course I do.' I copy the confused frown he wore at that moment. 'Now I think, maybe he just couldn't get it out before,' I say, 'before the drugs made him forget old habits. Whenever I'd say it to him, he'd say "thank you", but I watched his internal struggle; it was like he didn't *know* those three words or like he was trying to say it in a language he hadn't mastered or maybe didn't understand. I wonder if his dad ever said it to him.' I look at Nia. 'I just . . .' I clear my throat. 'I just really don't want my dad to be dead. That's all.'

She rubs my arm before handing me a tissue.

'What for?' I ask.

She smiles sadly and when I sniff again, my cheeks are wet and my nose is running. I stare at the tissue and my hand is shaking.

'I can't . . .' My voice cracks. 'I just . . .' I close my eyes and tears spill out. 'Why didn't I get to see him one last time?'

I cry on Nia's shoulder for the rest of the morning.

I finally go home in the afternoon. My chest is uncomfortably tight and there doesn't seem to be enough air in the world.

On the train, I put on headphones that inhale and swallow any outside noise and I count the stops until I reach Thornton Heath station.

James is home. He gives me a hug and my face squashes against his chest. James is tall and well set, thanks to weights at the gym and protein powders in his shakes. His hair is still in plaits, but he has a cap on. He asks how I'm doing. I experience a flicker of annoyance and it's nice to feel another emotion for a moment. When was the last time I saw James in person? When was the last time he came to this house? I pull away and say, 'I'm fine.'

Upstairs, Mum immediately hugs me and starts to cry and I begin to cry because she smells like my mum and the last time I smelt her my dad was downstairs in his chair.

I remain upstairs; I don't go into the living room or his bedroom once. Mum tells me again what happened. I lie on her bed and stare at the ceiling as she gets phone calls from well-wishers and tertiary grievers and I have to listen to her tell the story over and over again.

When Mum was in Ghana, I thought about moving into this room; it's much bigger than mine, but it didn't feel right. I could have used the space, though.

Mum's shouting now because one of her friends said that she should stop crying; I think it came from a sympathetic place, but Mum hangs up on her.

'How can she say stop crying?' Mum looks at me, wiping away her tears. 'How can she say that? I was the one who saw him. I remember the body bag they put him in! So how can I stop, eh?'

Most daughters – I'd bet at least ninety per cent of them – would react to their mother crying, hold her, comfort her, but the sight of mine in this state puts me on edge. I sit in the corner and watch the small TV. Whenever Mum leaves the room, I whisper, 'I'm not really here. I'm not really here. Everything is fine because I'm not really here.'

Mum's Pentecostal pastor calls her and asks to speak to me. I wonder if he holds a grudge against me for choosing another church or if all pastors are happy so long as you attend one. He asks how I'm doing. Fine. He's here if I need anything. Thanks. God is with me. Sure.

Mum only takes calls on loudspeaker so when it's her turn, she cries again and, like the friend she hung up on, I wish she'd give it a rest. Pastor tells her to stay strong because her children need her.

When has that ever meant anything to Mum?

What a cruel thing to think, Maddie.

'You need to eat,' he says to her, 'even if you're not hungry. Please eat something, make sure you do.' He prays over the line and says he'll call again later. I wonder how supportive he'd be if he knew of the man in Mum's phone whose unsaved number begins with +233.

Mum goes downstairs to make lunch; I hear her and James talking in the kitchen. It's not a civilised conversation, but you can assume by now that it rarely is. It's funny, really, because what my mum dislikes in my brother is what my brother dislikes in my mum, but neither of them can see they're arguing with themselves.

I put my head around Mum's door.

'Dad was fine when Maddie was here,' James says. 'No problems until you came back. Then Maddie had to leave and Dad got sicker.'

'And where were you, eh?' Mum asks, clapping her hands. 'Gallivanting across the globe with money your mother desperately needs. When were you last here, looking after your father? You are both his children and Maddie did everything alone.'

'Last time I was here, you were in Ghana and Dad was alive,' he responds. 'So don't ask about me.'

'His sister never speaks to me this way,' Mum says. Her voice trembles and I know she's looking at the ceiling, talking to God. 'At least I have one child who loves me.'

'Maddie doesn't know you, that's why,' James says. 'You think I don't know he came to London with you this time? He tried to follow me on Facebook. Kwaku, yeah? That's why you wanted Maddie outta the house, so she wouldn't catch you. If I see that man put one foot in here, I'm gonna—'

I close the bedroom door and turn the TV volume up.

Kwaku. He must be the one behind the unsaved number. He was in London. He came with Mum, so he's been here since she has.

Where was Mum when Dad died?

Dad was fine when Maddie was here.

I remain upstairs, wondering how long I have to stay. My dad's not here anymore and I hate this house because of it. The house that I left him alone in.

I'm not really here. I'm not really here. Everything is fine because I'm not really here.

The sun bursts in through the window and I have to shield my eyes before closing the curtains.

Chapter Twenty

Ben
I'm here if you need me xx

It's an ordinary week within the most extraordinary circumstances because apparently – and this is what everyone fails to mention about the grieving process – I still have to live.

Nia has a few assignments to turn in still, which she can do online, so during the day she sets herself up in the living room.

On Wednesday she makes me pancakes and we watch TV. She opens her laptop to complete a project and I say I need the toilet but end up closing the door of my bedroom. I get into bed and watch TV on my phone. By the afternoon, I don't know how many episodes I've watched. Nia calls me down for lunch, but I say I'm still full from breakfast.

Mum calls. 'The funeral home says we need to go there and fill out some forms.'

'Oh, okay.'

'No, I'm going to get your father's brother to do that when he arrives, since Mabel is still in Ghana trying to change her return date,' she says. 'You're too young. Only twenty-five and burying your father, it shouldn't be on you. I'm going to make sure Freddie does it. I don't want that on your shoulders.'

'Thank you, Mum.'

'That's why I'm here, darling.'

'I love you.'

'I love you too, Maame.'

Nia and I go for a walk across Battersea Riverside whilst Nia tells me about one of her professors – long story short, Nia is not a fan. We then talk about school; we agree we feel nostalgic but would never go back.

Nia returns to her laptop and I try to read but the words swim on the page and the attempt itself is exhausting so I get into bed until dinner, which is sweet potato and roasted vegetables. We eat together and start a thriller series called *The Cabin Plan*. We watch four episodes before bed.

On Thursday, Nia sleeps in and I sit on the sofa, staring into the garden. I search my phone for the latest picture of Dad. When I can't find it, I panic because it's the only one I have.

'Oh God, oh God, please no.'

I scroll through picture after picture of pretty buildings and food. Finally, I find and favourite it so it's easier to reach next time. In the picture, James has dragged a chair to the front door so that Dad could sit outside. He hadn't been outside in a very long time; I'd guess months, but if I force myself to think, it could have been years. It's a horrifying thought, which even the most dedicated of introverts would baulk at the prospect of.

'Poor man.'

A tear slips onto my screen and slides right off. Dad's smiling in the photo though – a really wide smile. He's skinny, however, nearing gaunt.

'All the drugs,' I whisper.

But he's smiling. His tracksuit bottoms were stained, but he's smiling. His nails needed cutting, but he's smiling.

I wonder what he's thinking and if he's in any pain.

I triple-check the photo is under *Favourites*.

I tell Nia I've already had breakfast. I read whilst she studies, but nothing's going through, so every so often, I turn a page until it sounds like I've read a few chapters.

Then it's time for lunch and I think, already? *Did you eat this regularly before?* I can't remember.

When Nia goes home to pick up a textbook she needs, I go upstairs to pee and end up crying on the toilet, asking the floor and the empty space around me for my dad back.

A voice returns, 'Why? It's not like you were around.'

Shu visits in the afternoon. When I open the door, she stares at me with dark eyes, gives me a hug, then holds up an Asda carrier bag.

'I got you some shit for your sadness,' she says.

'You should write poetry.'

'Flatmates still gone?'

I nod.

'Where's Nia?'

'Getting some books from her house.'

She takes her shoes off once she's in. 'You're alone? You didn't go with?'

I shake my head. 'I didn't want to. I don't want to . . . talk to people.'

'Same,' Shu says, heading into the kitchen. 'Every day.'

From the bag, she takes out a giant container of soup, a 1kg jar of Nutella, two bags of popcorn, a bunch of colourful flowers, three 'share' chocolate bars, and two bottles of fruit cider. 'I also found . . . this.' Finally, she pulls out two bottles of Supermalt.

I smile, say, 'Thank you, Shu,' and search for a bottle opener, putting the other things in my section of the cupboard.

'How are you doing, Mads?'

'Well, I feel like shit,' I say. 'I look like shittier shit and I smell like the shittiest of shits. How are you?'

She smiles. 'So you're what that smell is?' Her shoulders suddenly drop. 'I'm really fucking sorry, Maddie.'

Mum LONDON
Maame I have not heard from you today. What are you doing?

Maddie
Sat in my garden with Shu

Mum LONDON
Who is that?

Maddie
Friend from uni. Meixiang-Shu.

Mum LONDON
Is she Asian?

Maddie
Yes

Mum LONDON

I've not heard of her before have I? It's not good for you to have friends who are faceless to your mother. I need to know who they are and what their intentions are so I can pray and ask God if they're the right friends for you. Where does she live?

I need her number. Thanks.

Maddie

No, you don't

'Who's that?' Shu asks, pointing at my phone.

'My mum.'

'She okay?'

'She's fine.' I throw my phone onto the garden table, careful not to knock over our Supermalt. 'She always is.'

Shu begins throwing some very questionable gang signs. 'I almost forgot, I also brought what you asked for.' She takes two joints out of her pocket and passes me one. 'Was kinda surprised, I'm not gonna lie. Didn't know this was your thing.'

'It's not really,' I admit, 'but I tried it once and I just remember feeling . . .' I think of the brownies from that night. 'It was nice.'

Shu lights our joints and I inhale. I cough twice, but it settles quicker than the brownies did, delivering a loosening, an ease I've been in desperate need of.

I lean back into my chair, inhale again and show the sun my face. 'Did you know compassionate leave is only one to two days long?' I tell her. 'Companies aren't obligated to give you any more time than that.'

Shu pulls the sunglasses from her hair. They're Ray-Bans. I remember she's on a fifty-thousand annual salary. Sometimes I forget because Shu doesn't like to spend a lot of money now that she's saving for a mortgage.

Fifty thousand a year.

Shu is five months younger than me but earns more than twice as much. But she has a business degree. So? I have one in English Literature. Reading and analysing *Middlemarch* and *Ulysses* was no walk in the park. Shu works hard. I hardly recline on a beach sipping Mai Tais. What's even in a Mai Tai?

'Only two days?' Shu repeats. 'I think the fuck not.'

'Right? Can you imagine a mother losing a child and then going back to work on Tuesday to listen to Steve ramble on about commuter traffic?'

'Fucking Steve. How much time did OTP give you?'

'Two weeks,' I answer. 'Then I can slowly reintroduce myself part-time and then full-time again when things start to feel normal.'

'It doesn't ever feel normal, Mads. It's just less shit on some days.'

I lower my unbranded sunglasses to look at her.

'Don't,' she warns.

'You never talk about your grandmother,' I say quietly. 'But I know you loved her more than anyone.'

'It's not my style,' she says. 'I get that some people like to talk; my sister still won't shut up about her and it was three years ago, but that's not me.'

I let it go. 'I'm going to change that law,' I announce. 'The compassionate leave thing. Is it a law? Whatever it is. I'm going to change it.'

'How?'

'Become Prime Minister? Although I am a Black woman with immigrant parents from a working-class background who went to state school, so it's unlikely I'll ever get voted in. But maybe I could marry a rich man who went to Eton, then poison him and garner the sympathy of voters before taking over?'

'Wasn't that the series finale to *Politician, Corrupted*?'

'Oh yeah, it was.' I shrug. 'The wife's lawyer managed to get her off the murder charges though, so it's still worth considering as a plan B.'

'Mads, the wife was sentenced to life and then suffered a heart attack in her prison cell.'

'Plan C then.' I rest my head on the back of my chair, inhale again. 'You're Christian, Shu. Do you always believe in God?'

'Yeah, course. Got to.'

'Why?'

'Because,' she says, 'I can't carry on living believing human beings are as good as it gets.' She looks at me. 'We're the worst.'

It's really quiet when Shu leaves. I'm sat in the living room staring at the TV and think about texting Nia to hurry up. The silence begins to make a ringing noise. I pull my jumper over my mouth and scream.

When Nia returns hours later, she asks, 'How were you?'

'Yeah, fine,' I answer.

She looks at me. 'You sure?'

I nod and try to put some authenticity behind my smile. 'Yes, I'm sure.'

We take a short walk to the local shop. Nia and I rank chocolate bars whilst we're there; we disagree on many but both hold white chocolate in high regard. We make omelettes for dinner and finish season one of *The Cabin Plan*.

> **Penny**
> Dear Maddie,
> I'm so sorry to hear about your father. We're thinking of you and your family at this difficult time.
> Lots of love to you and we're here for you if you need anything. Xx

Friday is cereal for breakfast and then I sleep until lunch, then decide I'm not hungry yet and skip it. I've only cried two . . . three . . . four times since my dad died? That's not enough. Only yesterday Nia made me laugh; this morning, I looked out of the window to another blue cloudless sky and thought, *What a beautiful day*.

Nia pokes her head into my room. 'Come on, let's go to Sainsbury's, the big one.'

I lift my head off my pillow. 'Too far.'

'The weather's nice though,' she says as if that decreases the distance, 'and I'm craving Twisters.'

'The ice cream?'

'Yeah. Let's get a box.'

'Okay, I'll check the bus time.'

'It's only a twenty-minute walk.'

The thought alone makes my bones heavy. 'I'm really tired, Nia, can't you go alone?'

She smiles plainly. 'I want you to come with me.'

'Are you afraid to return and find me swinging from the ceiling?'

'I am *now*.'

'Not to worry. I don't have the energy.'

'Good to know,' she says.

'I'd just take the overdose route.'

Nia claps her hands twice. 'Enough. Let's go.'

I pull my hair back and put on a bra. My socks are odd, but the world has bigger problems. I have to shield my eyes when we're outside and we begin to walk.

'Please feel like you can talk about your dad if you want to,' Nia suddenly says. 'But also don't feel like you have to.'

'Those two options essentially cancel each other out, leaving the compromise to be . . . silence?'

'I'm just saying, feel free to say what you feel *when* you feel it. I've only just been able to start talking about my dad without feeling some kind of way.'

'But it's been ten years!'

She laughs. 'Don't look like that, everyone's different.'

'You know, only recently I've been thinking that it was because I never asked.'

She shrugs and says, 'If you had, I would have shut it down quick.'

'I wish I'd called my dad or gone to see him sooner before he died,' I confess. The street's quite empty today and we stop at a red light. 'I was meant to be there that morning, but I went out drinking the night before, and I don't even drink. I didn't want to go out that night either, but I made both of those decisions and the regret is eating at me. I've never suffered such an irreversible regret before, a regret with no silver lining, and it makes me want to block out any noise or thoughts and it pulls me down until I'm heavy and tired from doing nothing other than attempting to avoid how I feel.'

We cross when it's clear, instead of waiting for the green man.

'I get that,' Nia says. 'Couple days before my dad died he sent me and my sister this soppy message. Talking about how much he loved his girls. It was so random, I remember just rolling my eyes and not even replying. I still don't know why I did that. I guess I thought I'd see him soon or whatever. There's always going to be something we regret or feel guilty about because no one is the perfect child.'

'And perfection is subjective.'

'Exactly. So you might not think you were perfect, but maybe your dad did.' Nia hooks her arm through mine. 'And I know for sure you loved him and did all you could for him when you were at home. That's not going to make you instantly feel better obviously, but you'll start to believe it, over time. Basket or trolley?'

'What?' I look up and we've reached the supermarket. 'Trolley,' I choose and search for a pound coin. 'Let's get some orange juice, too,' I say. 'Oh, don't forget the Twisters.'

Chapter Twenty-One

Late afternoon, I wave goodbye to Nia at the door.

'You know I'm—'

'Only a phone call away,' I finish. 'I know. I'll be fine.'

I wave and watch her walk down the path and turn the corner. When I close the door behind me, I take a deep breath. The hallway, narrow to begin with, seems to stretch forever. The weighted pressure of silence builds in my ears.

I put on the TV and select a slapstick comedy with a laugh track. I turn the volume up. I pick up my phone and scroll. When I check the time, only an hour has gone by when I'd hoped for at least several. The afternoon feels endless and I can only fill it with TV.

When my eyes can't stand the screen any longer, I pick up my book, but despite trying, and I swear to God I am trying, either I can't focus or this page is made up of first lines. The evening eventually approaches and my heart twitches in anticipation.

My phone flashes with a birthday reminder for Ben's CEO. *Ben*. My finger hovers over the delete button. *But you could go*. No one there, except for Ben, will know what happened. It'll be like going to a different city where the only impression anyone has of you is the one you choose to give them. I can be fun and free tonight. I call Ben, but he doesn't answer. That's fine because he saved the address in the calendar invite.

I get off the floor.

The celebration is being held in one of the many high-rise glass buildings on Liverpool Street. Outside, it's guarded by decorative stone pillars, and inside, I'm confronted with an expansive waiting area made up of flowers, sofas and cushions, ID scanners and a reception desk with a wall aquarium full of live fish behind it.

'Wow,' I breathe.

The receptionist smiles; she's very pretty and I wonder if I could pull off that lipstick shade with my skin tone. 'Beautiful, isn't it?' she says. 'Seventy thousand litres and almost a thousand fish.'

'Maintenance must be a nightmare.'

She laughs and the end of it lingers. 'Are you here for the party, Miss . . .?'

'Oh, Miss Wright – Madeleine Wright? Maybe just Maddie?'

She focuses on her screen. 'I'm afraid I can't see— Ah, yes, here you are. Please use the last turnstile on the right, just push through, very good. Down the hall and to the left. You should be able to hear them.'

'Thank you.'

'Enjoy your evening, Miss.'

I follow her instructions and walk into a large room not that full of people. Trying to find Ben is very much like the suit and tie version of Where's Wally, only Wally is also wearing a suit, so maybe it's nothing like Where's Wally. I'm the only Black person bar a few waiting staff. I'm not the only non-white person but . . . I crane my neck around the room . . . yep, definitely the only Black one. At first, I think, *Still? In this day and age?* Then I think, *Well, it's not my first time.* I did this at CGT. I do this nine to five at work. I know what to do, how not to bring attention to myself. I'm skilled in assimilation, though my subconscious is quick to remind me that it's nothing to be proud of. I have spent the entirety of my professional life in predominantly white spaces. As a bookseller, a receptionist, at the theatre, and now a publishing house. Over the years, my instinct has been to shrink myself, to make sure I'm not too loud, to talk only about subjects I feel well-versed in. Being a big reader has helped. Having been to university has helped too.

There's so much wrong with that thinking, Maddie.

Everyone talks about the importance of standing out but never the benefits of fitting in.

But you don't fit in.

I spot Ben and my fingers tingle; I *have* missed him. When he meets my eyes, his face drops; he looks at the woman standing beside him and then hurries over.

'Maddie, what are you doing here?'

'You invited me, remember?' I nod until he does. 'Sorry I'm so late.'

'Maddie, I didn't think you'd come. Your dad—'

There's a clinking sound and someone calls for Ben: a man standing atop a podium at the far end of the room.

'Ben,' he hollers. 'Speech!'

Ben's eyes are frantic when he looks back at me. 'Okay, Maddie, stay here, promise me. Just stay here.'

He walks onto the stage and straightens his suit jacket. I was supposed to tell him how handsome he looked and then he was meant to say I looked beautiful. He was meant to be happy to see me. My brain is working slower than usual and I can tell there's something I'm not quite grasping despite it being right in front of me; I suddenly think of my dad's fingers . . . *trying*.

'What can I say about the man that is Eric Harrold?' Ben gestures to a grey-haired man who turns to the crowd and smiles. People cheer, which seems a bit much for a birthday party. From what I understood from Ben, not many people actually like him.

'I remember first meeting Eric when I was only eight,' Ben continues. 'He and my father . . .'

As his speech continues and Ben takes his eyes off me, the woman who previously stood beside him slides closer. Her brunette hair is down to her waist and her eyes are a disconcerting blue under a dark cluster of eyelashes. She has lip fillers; you can tell by the shape of them.

'Hello, I'm Sophie,' she says quietly.

'Maddie,' I say just as quietly. I don't want to risk being heard over Ben's speech, but I also want to ask why her name is so familiar.

'How do you know Ben?' she asks.

Her voice makes me shiver and the word *saccharine* comes to mind.

'Oh, erm, he's my boyfriend. We've been dating for a while.'

She coughs in surprise, placing a hand to her chest. 'Are you sure?' she asks.

I turn to her and frown. 'That would be an odd thing to be uncertain about.'

She smiles and I don't like it. It triggers something in my brain and I ask, 'How do you know Ben?'

'I'm also dating him.'

My mouth opens but no words comes out.

She smiles again. 'Well, I suppose we haven't yet had the *exclusive* conversation,' she says, 'but I assumed we were, seeing as I met his parents last weekend.'

'Last weekend?' I pause. 'So the . . . the Saturday?'

She nods, frowning.

'So he slept with me on Sunday . . .' I'm blinking a lot and my throat feels tight '. . . after having introduced you to his parents the previous day?'

'You're joking.' She rounds on me and I notice by way of her tight dress that she has an exaggerated hourglass figure. I wonder how much pasta and ice cream sundaes she eats, if any. 'Or is that your deal then?' she asks me. 'Were you actually dating?'

'*Were?*'

'Or were you just fucking him?'

I don't know what to say and I feel very small. I should own a second, taller pair of heels.

I step back. 'No . . . I mean we are dating; we do date, we eat dinner. He makes me pasta.'

She scrunches her face and it creases her make-up.

'We went to the cinema once.'

'Once? Oh.'

My chest burns when I realise she's downgraded me from threat to mere obstacle.

'I'm guessing the two of you . . . have done more than that?'

There's a deafening silence. The speech has stopped mid-sentence. Everyone looks at Ben, but he only looks at the two of us.

'Ahem, Ben,' says Eric.

He blinks. 'Sorry, where was I? Yes, the foundation of this company . . .' He continues, but his eyes remain on us.

'Yes,' Sophie says. 'But apart from meeting his family for dinner, nothing serious. A few gatherings with his friends, dinners out, midnight walks. Oh, God. Did he take you on that canal boat ride too?'

I just blink and she rolls her eyes.

'Here was me thinking I was special,' she says.

She knows she is.

'Now I'm furious I gave in and slept with him last night.' She doesn't look furious. 'My own fault. My friends kept saying you can't trust a man who wants to "wait until we know each other a bit better". I hope you're going to give him hell for this.' She straightens her shoulders and tilts back her head. 'I certainly am. No offence, Maggie, but I don't share.'

'Excuse me.'

I leave the room with a familiar ringing in my ears. My vision's blurred so I can't see the way I came in and instead keep walking down a long corridor. My stomach hurts and my chest is shrinking; I need to lie down. There's a dark section between two doors that I melt into. There's not much space, so I sit on the floor with my knees to my chest and my eyes shut.

I hear Ben walk past, quietly calling my name, then, 'Soph, what did you say to her?'

'You were dating the two of us?' *Now* she sounds furious. 'Tell me it wasn't serious. I didn't think that was your type.'

'Not now,' Ben says. 'I need to find her.'

'Why?' Sophie asks. 'She's obviously gone home. You can go and see her tomorrow, to tell her it's over, but everyone in that room is going to start asking questions if we don't get back in there.' She clicks her fingers and holds out her hand. She has on fake nails so long they curl at the end. Ben hesitates, but eventually takes it. Hand in hand, they walk away.

I hear Ben say, 'Sorry about that,' before the doors close. He may have been addressing the room or talking to Sophie. I'll never know.

I wait in the dark for a bit longer before crawling out.

The receptionist is still there.

'Miss Wright, are you leaving already? Is everything okay?'

At least *she* remembers my name.

I nod, even though mascara has dried on my cheeks and I'm holding my heels. The bottom of my feet will be caked with dirt, but worse things have happened this week. I exit through the glass doors and watch the hordes entering and leaving the train station before calling for an Uber.

Thankfully, the driver's not a talker, which explains why he's rated so highly on the app. He takes one look at me, says, 'Rough night, huh?' then puts the music on a little louder.

I sit with my head against the window watching the city's lights and the road's cars and London's people, and silently cry.

Chapter Twenty-Two

Dear Maddie,
Flowers and a small card to let you know how much we are
all thinking of you and your family as you endure this sad
and difficult time. I was so sorry to hear your news and
wish you much love as you remember your dad and learn to
live with this loss.
Penny and the OTP team x

Ben didn't text that night. Just as well. I got into bed and replayed everything that had happened between us in my head. If I were watching our relationship on screen, I would have rolled my eyes at TV-Maddie, called her a sucker and claimed to have known better, that it was so obvious. But I didn't know any better. And was it really so obvious?

I chalk it up to yet another thing schools fail to teach us: how to do your taxes, how to buy a property, and how to tell when you're being taken for a fool.

The following morning, a plethora of flowers and treats are delivered. They gather on the dining-room table, propagating until they mimic afternoon tea in an overgrown garden, but I stay out of the kitchen as much as possible to avoid looking at them.

I've always wanted to be given flowers and it turns out that all I needed was for my dad to die and my apparently-not-boyfriend to get caught sleeping with someone else.

To get caught being in love with someone else?

I tell Shu and Nia what happened and they both come over. It's weird seeing the two of them together because they're not exactly friends. They only know of each other through me.

'Shower, please.'

I do as Shu says; I brush my teeth, scrub my face and pull my hair up, and when I'm done, Nia's changed my bedding and loaded the washing machine. Shu has taken the overflowing bins out and picks at the chocolates Ben had delivered. She mops the kitchen floor and I watch her. She's had a haircut; it's to her collarbone now and is so shiny that individual strands streak silver when they hit the light. She has on her multiple necklaces and she's added another ear piercing to her collection. She wears an oversized jumper and bike shorts. Her eyelash extensions mean if I look close enough, they're either resting on her cheeks or reaching for her eyebrows.

I love Shu very much.

Nia's bought more food and lots of salad and fruit. We sit in the living room and eat on the floor.

Shu kisses her teeth. 'I never liked him, you know.'

'You met?' Nia asks.

'No, but I looked him up on Facebook and he was still active on it, so that was a red flag,' Shu explains. 'Facebook is now solely for stalking purposes, distant foreign relatives excused. He's not even good-looking,' she adds, popping a grape into her mouth. 'Small eyes and stretched lips. I knew you'd end up having funky taste in men.'

'Maybe Maddie's more focused on personality?' Nia helps.

'I doubt it,' Shu says. 'His was clearly shit.' She turns to me. 'Were you with him because he was rich?'

I lift my head from Nia's shoulder. 'Thank you for essentially calling me a gold-digger, Shu.'

She frowns. 'I don't know why you're offended. Gold-diggers are our nation's hardest grafters; do you know how much effort goes into pretending to give a shit about some guy for his money? A lot. Hoes are Britain's unsung heroes.'

'Let's not further that thread. How are you feeling?' Nia asks me. 'All this Ben stuff isn't great timing.'

'I didn't love him,' I admit, 'not the way I was supposed to and I know that, but I loved feeling loved and . . . wanted. I just don't understand why this happened.'

'This isn't your fault, Mads,' Shu says, looking closer at her phone. 'I think I found her. This bitch?' She turns her phone to me and on it is a picture of Sophie with pouted lips in another figure-hugging dress. In the caption she thanks 'babe' for the sparkling bracelet encircling her wrist. The picture was posted two days ago.

'Yes, that's her.' I stare at the photo and try to pick faults, but it doesn't matter if I find any. He still chose her. *Maybe if you'd worn tighter dresses* . . . 'How did you find her?'

'She's tagged on his Instagram,' Shu says, widening the image. 'Oh, look at that. Big lips and wide hips.'

Nia tuts. 'Typical.'

I look between the two of them. 'What am I missing?'

Nia continues to stroke my hair. 'Ben may be a certain type of man,' she says gently.

'He likes your features, just not on you,' Shu finishes bluntly. 'Now that I look at him closely, he does give off that racist vibe.'

I jerk back. 'Racist? That's a bit strong. Ben's not . . . He doesn't *hate* me.'

'Maddie.' Nia looks at me with pity. 'A white person can date a Black person and still be racist.'

'Because there's levels to that shit. Like a lasagne.' I frown but Shu says, 'Stay with me. So, on the top, that cheesy layer, that's what you can see clearly. Hate speech, mad looks and violence. Obvious stuff you can't ignore. But all them layers underneath, the ones that are harder to see, microaggression and unconscious bias? Giving your white girlfriend jewellery, boat rides and meet-and-greets with the family, but your Black girlfriend pasta in your house? Racism, hun.'

I'm still not entirely convinced – maybe Ben is a bad person to every woman – but then Nia says, 'I know it might seem too small an action to fit under such a big word, but the simple idea that the white girl he's seeing as the one to invest in suggests your level of worth to be less than hers, and it isn't. You are worth everything she is, do you hear me? You are not the problem.'

I look at her and quietly ask, 'I'm not?'

'You're not,' she says resolutely. 'Maddie, what you'll come to learn is that not everyone is capable of dating a Black woman. Not that—'

Shu coughs.

'Or an Asian woman,' Nia adds and Shu nods. 'Not that men who do are somehow superior, but there's a level of learning and understanding that goes into it. You don't just date her but her history too. Too much is going on and revealing itself for you to think love will conquer all. Does he educate himself, follow the news, raise his voice in uncomfortable conversations? Does he ever question the system that works very well for him but does the opposite for you? He doesn't have to do it with a megaphone but he does have to do it. You don't want a boyfriend who isn't racist, Maddie. You need a boyfriend who is actively anti-racist.

'Ben probably isn't even aware he's projecting these micro aggressions,' Nia continues. 'Hey, I'm sleeping with a Black girl and like it, I can't be racist! In his head, he's chosen Sophie because he's known her longer or maybe they work in similar fields, whatever, but really, a man like that clearly exists in a certain environment and maybe telling his parents, or "explaining" you to his friends, is just too much hassle.'

Too much hassle. Even the idea that this could be true makes my heart break. Why didn't I get dinners out or a boat ride? Why didn't he introduce me to anyone? Was I ever really his plus-one or was it always going to be Sophie? I want to make excuses. Maybe she's a big Marvel fan, maybe she loves eating pasta and watching wildlife documentaries; I only met her once so maybe ninety-nine per cent of the time she's really, really nice. But then I'm also all of those things and these excuses don't explain the blatant preferential treatment.

I think about the macaroons and the thigh pinching and the eye contact and my submissiveness. I can't picture Sophie in the same situation. Again, I don't know her, but I assume she'd have said something like 'Macaroons at eight a.m.? Fuck off, Ben.'

He wouldn't have even made the attempt, but he knew he could with me.

I realise I only want to make excuses because I really tried with Ben and not much hurts worse than being deemed not worth the effort after.

'I hated sex with him,' I confess, 'but I still did it.'

Nia freezes and Shu says, 'I'm gonna kill him.'

'Maddie,' Nia says. 'Did he *make* you?'

'No!' I move away. 'I . . . I didn't really want to, but I didn't say no either. It was more that I liked that he wanted to. I thought it meant something, that . . . that he loved me. Maybe.'

'Using you "for now" isn't love, Maddie,' Nia says gently. 'Enduring sex isn't what being loved feels like either.'

I feel silly for asking, but here goes: 'What does love feel like?'

'Sunshine and rainbows?' Nia offers.

'She's not seven,' Shu says. 'It's not always about what it feels like, Mads, because sometimes it feels pointless. It's about what love *is*. Which is trust, commitment, empathy and respect. It means really giving a shit about the other person.'

Nia nods in agreement.

'How do you both know all of this?'

Nia and Shu look at each other, then simultaneously answer, 'Practice.'

'I wish I'd known this before I met Ben.'

'Some things you're not meant to be saved from,' Nia says. 'Some things have to be lessons.'

'And you don't share much,' Shu says, 'about anything. You kinda keep things to yourself. But now that's going to change, so let's talk next steps. I think you should buy the book *The Alchemist*.'

'I've already read—'

'It's not for you to read,' Shu says. 'We're going to use it to set Ben's house on fire.' She pauses for effect. 'Irony.'

'I think you mispronounced arson-ry,' I tell her. 'Which happens to be a crime.'

'Only if you get caught.' She turns back to me. 'You still got his address, right?'

Before I answer, the doorbell rings and when Shu goes to answer it, Nia holds out a forkful of spinach.

I turn my head away. 'Salad for breakfast is unnatural.'

She laughs, says, 'Grow up' and shoves the fork into my mouth.

'Hey, Mads,' Shu shouts from the corridor. 'It's the guy who fucked you but didn't want to date you. Should I get rid of him?'

I run to the door, which happens to be wide open. 'Shu, my neighbours.'

'The dickhead's here,' she says.

'Please, call me Ben.' He tries to smile, but he'd have had better luck with Nia. Shu grimaces. He looks at me. 'Oh, your hair is different.'

'Yeah, she's Black,' says Shu. 'Her hair changes all the time. What do you want?'

He winces. 'Can we talk, Maddie?'

I think about what Shu said about Ben's lips and eyes and, suddenly, I can't quite spot what I found attractive in him to begin with. His face is unnaturally long, even ghoul-like in the wrong light.

'Her name is Madeleine,' Shu tells him. 'You've been demoted.'

'Shu, it's okay.' I nod at Ben. We go into the kitchen and he closes the door.

'She's very scary,' he says. 'I didn't get that impression when you told me about her.'

'She's only rude to people she doesn't like.'

He looks sadly at the table, at the unopened boxes and his drying flowers. The ones Penny sent are thriving, their stems in water by the window. 'At least you liked the chocolates?'

'Shu did.'

'Oh.'

I fold my arms. 'What could you possibly have to say to me, Ben?'

'I know there's no coming back from this,' he says, 'but I have to apologise for . . .'

'Getting caught?'

He winces again. 'I am sorry, Maddie. I care about you so much, you have no idea.'

'Ben, are you here to apologise and leave or apologise and ask for a second chance?'

He looks away. 'I don't expect you to forgive me, obviously.'

'Because we were always short-term, weren't we?' I ask him. 'You and Sophie – that was the end goal.'

'Short-term is . . . Maddie, I've loved spending time with you—'

'Having sex and eating?'

'But we're very diff—'

'I found sex with you very unpleasant.'

His shoulders sag. 'Fuck, Maddie, that's a low blow.'

'Sorry. Well, no, I'm not sorry, but maybe I could have phrased that better. Sex was very painful for me, and I should have told you, but also, you should have known and maybe you would have if you'd put as much effort into satisfying me as you did sneaking around with Sophie.' I pause before adding, 'I also would have liked dinners out and boat rides and I've learned you're a dick for deeming one girl worthy of that and not the other, although it's pretty obvious what influenced your decision to do so.'

He throws his hands in the air. 'Come on, Maddie! Don't play that card. How can you think that of me?'

'Pretty easily, because if I'm so great and you *loved* spending time with me, how has this happened? Why are you getting rid of me and not Sophie? She doesn't even eat pasta, does she? I bet she hates ice cream, too.'

'She has very sensitive teeth.' He quickly realises how stupid a response that is and begins massaging his forehead.

'Ben, it's only a "card" to people who think it's a game.' I lift my chin. 'Now, please, get the fuck out of my house.'

He hesitates. 'For what it's worth, I *am* sorry.'

When he turns to leave, I say, 'Did you know I starting taking the pill at sixteen because of bad period pain?'

'What?'

'I've been thinking a lot about our time together, and when I told you I started taking the pill at sixteen, why did you think that was?'

'I thought what anyone would think, Maddie. I thought . . .' He doesn't finish and I nod.

'That's why you said "Gotcha", after our first time,' I say. 'You thought I was lying about being a virgin.'

He sighs. 'Maddie, I'm sorry. I don't know what else to say.'

I nod again. 'Just leave.'

'What a dickhead,' Shu says when he's gone.

'You heard us?'

She shakes her head. 'Just stating facts.'

'It *is* a fact. He's also a . . . a complete . . .'

'Go on, say how you feel,' Nia encourages.

'Such a . . .'

'Say it with your chest, Mads.'

214

'Blackguard!'

'What?'

'It means scoundrel,' I explain. 'A dishonourable man.'

Shu rolls her eyes. 'In what century?'

Nia steps forward. 'Do you want me to stay again?'

'Would you mind? Jo and Cam are back tomorrow, so it's just for tonight.'

'Of course I don't mind,' she says.

I have a dentist appointment in the afternoon which, considering current circumstances, feels ridiculously trivial. When I get the reminder, I think it's a joke, but it's not and cancelling only hours before will land me with a fee I can't afford this month.

I'm thinking of what train will get me to the dentist on time when my heart starts beating really fast, nausea blocks my throat and, suddenly, I'm dizzy. I pull my top off to cool down. I end up on all fours breathing heavily. I might pass out. I think I'm going to die. I don't want Nia to find me dead and topless. What are people going to say about a father and daughter dying within a week of one another? They'll think we had some kind of twisted pact.

I try to stand, but I'm still shaking, so I stay on all fours for a little longer. My heart is beating so fast – short, hard, endless beats. Sweat drips down my back and my stomach loosens and I have to run to the toilet and as I sit and poo, my breath comes out in shallow puffs.

I can hear Nia on the phone downstairs. 'Is that Jem in the corner?' she says. She must be on FaceTime.

'Yeah, he's come over after his shift.' With her mum.

In the background, Nia's stepdad says, 'Put that down, Zach.' Zach is Nia's nephew. General family hubbub.

215

They're planning on having a barbeque since the weather's been so nice.

I close my eyes and, a few minutes later, I've come back to myself.

Was that a panic attack?

I shake my head. I don't suffer from panic attacks.

I get dressed and wait for the next train.

Shu
A panic attack before the dentist
Are you scared of the dentist?

Maddie
I don't *love* the dentist but I'm only getting a check-up. I once went in for root canal surgery and didn't have a panic attack

Shu
Sometimes panic attacks come for no reason
Or maybe it's because of your dad

Maddie
I'm sure it's nothing.
But when did dentist bills get so expensive!

The next day, Nia says, 'Let's go for a bike ride.'

'I just got in.'

'You did?'

'You saw me taking the bins out.'

She rolls her eyes. 'Is the bike under the stairs yours or one of your flatmates'?'

'Cam's, but she once said she's happy for me to use it.'

'Okay, you take that one and I'll get one of the city bikes; there's some round the corner. Come on.'

It's thirty-two degrees, but it feels like thirty-eight in the sun. I change into a vest top and we head out. I haven't ridden a bike in months and Cam's is heavy and my arms ache, but I enjoy pulling it out from its corner and persuading it through the narrow hallway.

We ride along the river with no destination in mind. At each road break or turn, we wordlessly decide to keep going. The path is surprisingly clear, but Battersea Park is full of people listening to music, having picnics, walking their dogs, and we pass food stalls and outdoor bars, keeping to the river and boathouses until we can't any longer and there's only road left.

At the start, I'm not very steady and have to concentrate on not riding into people and on manoeuvring tight spaces and sudden turns and downward slopes, but there's something freeing about the required concentration followed by the lack of it on smooth surfaces and straight paths. When we decide to turn back after an hour, Nia points to a local shop. 'Should we get ice cream?'

'But we have some at home.'

She laughs. 'Okay, Mum.'

We ride home; she's sunburnt and I feel sticky. She cuts us slices of watermelon and we eat them over the sink.

I'm exhausted after; my muscles ache and I can't help but lean forward when I walk, as if fighting gravity. At dinner I look for whatever's already cooked: macaroni cheese and a piece of chicken, followed by ice cream. We sit and resume *The Cabin Plan*.

My bones feel heavy when I drag them to the shower and when I'm out, my room is really warm. I remember my panic attack.

> Q **Google** – Symptoms of a panic attack

The Medical Community

CindyKO: Hi guys. So a couple of hours ago, out of nowhere, I just fell down. I didn't faint but I couldn't breathe and I was sweating buckets and my chest hurt a lot. It was over in a couple of minutes and it hasn't happened again, but since then I've been feeling really tired. Has this happened to anyone? Is it serious or no big deal?

Jonah91: The same thing happened to me and after a good night's sleep I was fine. It's probably something you ate. Drink some water and take some paracetamol and go to bed. You'll be fine in the morning!

Genevieve Mac: I also once displayed similar symptoms, 24 hours later I was in A&E and the doctor tells me I almost died.

So, 'roll the dice' is what I'm reading.

Before I get into bed, I kneel by my bedside and close my eyes.

'Dear God,' I say. 'Please don't let me die. I don't think my mother could handle it. Please remember all the times I went to church even when I didn't want to go. Amen.'

Chapter Twenty-Three

Jo and Cam are back.

I need to apologise for what I said to Jo, and the words have to actually leave my mouth this time. Yet a part of me hoped that they would return and Jo would act as if nothing happened, but when I hear the door open, I already know it's too much to ask. I take a deep breath. The sooner you do it, the sooner it's over.

I walk into the kitchen and they stop talking. A lot has happened to me since they left, but all that's changed for them is the tan of their skin.

'Hey,' I say. 'Welcome back.'

Jo busies herself with her bags, but Cam gives me a hug and asks, 'How are you?'

'Good,' I answer. 'Better than I was when . . . you know.'

Cam nods.

Jo says, 'Hmmm.'

'I want to apologise, Jo.'

She looks up, surprised.

'What I said to you,' I continue, 'was uncalled for and obviously not true. I didn't mean it and I'm sorry.'

Jo lifts her chin. 'You were in shock, so let's just forget about it and move on.'

'Great,' I say. 'Thanks.'

*   *   *

I wouldn't say we've moved on. Jo and I don't talk much and instead make the other uncomfortable. We talk, if we have to, mainly via group chat and give each other tense smiles if we meet in the kitchen. Cam and Jo sit in the living room together almost every night. Cam invited me to watch a film with them one evening and I said yes, thinking it would help. The atmosphere was stiff the entire time. They'd been talking about Florence before they heard me on the stairs and all conversation ceased from then. Now I camp out in my bedroom and listen out so I can avoid them in the kitchen or on the way to the bathroom. Jo must do the same because we rarely cross paths now, but it means I spend a lot of my time alone in my room. It's not that bad.

I'm lonely, but it's not that bad.

In the afternoon, I'm on the way home for a traditional Ghanaian ceremony Mum told me about last night and I'd never heard of before then.

Within the first two weeks of someone passing away, surviving relatives visit the house of the deceased to perform a libation. Apparently, we believe that during this time the spirit of the deceased is still around, calling to the spirits of family members who have already died, in this case, my dad's parents and his older sister. We pour a glass of strong liquor on the ground outside the house as a way of inviting them here, so we can let them know that Dad is joining them.

I vaguely remember my dad's sister, Aunt Rebecca; I must have met her in Ghana because I associate her with earthy ground and red dust. She had deep, healed tribal marks on her right cheek or on both. She wore a Kente head wrap and a matching cloth tied around her waist to form a skirt. For me, that is Aunt Rebecca in her entirety.

That's the thing about distant relatives you hardly know; they're like Schrodinger's cat – the relative in question might either be dead or alive, but often your reaction doesn't differ dramatically when you find out which.

James is here along with Dad's brother Freddie and his wife Aunt Felicity – they flew in only yesterday, but Auntie Mabel's still in Ghana. She left London right before Dad died and has been trying to move her return date forward. Her son, David, who is dark, lean and carries himself awkwardly, is here on her behalf; he looks vaguely familiar even though he definitely hasn't visited Dad since he became ill. The remaining attendees include Mum's pastor, along with a couple from her church whose names I don't catch.

Uncle Freddie pours the alcohol onto the ground and then water on top of it. I'm late, arriving halfway through, and he's speaking Fante, which when spoken quickly is like trying to catch bubbles before they pop. My brain needs a second to translate a word, but he'll have already moved onto the next one.

Heading back into the house, he comes over and shakes my hand gently. I can't remember the last time I saw him. Maybe six years ago? He doesn't like to leave home and Ghana will forever be his home. He has to lean forward when he walks, so we end up the same height; he wears a crackled leather flat cap on his head.

I briefly wonder if it's harder to lose a father or a brother.

In Fante, he says, 'I'm so sorry you've lost your father.'

In English, I respond, 'Thank you. I'm sorry you lost your brother.'

'Hmmm,' he says, but I notice something different in my uncle's sadness. Its existence seems to have already been accepted. The downcast of his eyes, the heaviness in his back, the sorrow in his smile, and something says to me: *This is your Uncle Freddie now*. Grief has already set in and changed him, not drastically but markedly. Have Nia, Shu, Jo or Cam noticed anything like this in me?

I am still Maddie. Just a little emptier.

'There you go.' Uncle Freddie lets go of my hand. 'Get yourself a treat.' He leaves a one-pound coin in my palm and smiles.

'Wow.' I grin. 'Thank you. I can finally afford to quit my job as a chimney sweep.'

He chuckles indulgently; I don't think he understands the joke and I love him for it. 'Don't spend it all at once.'

I look down at the coin and suddenly remember myself back in my primary-school uniform. There was a day when I stole ten pounds out of my dad's wallet whilst he was in the shower. I'd bought myself and my friends so much chocolate from the corner shop – it was cheap back then. The cashier gave me only a single pound change in exchange for a heavy blue and white striped bag. I remember being impressed that, in the days of 39p chocolate bars and 45p drink cans, I'd managed to reach a whole number.

Somehow Dad knew it was me who had taken the money and when he got home from work that evening, he didn't say anything, just . . . looked around me when I was there. Things were back to normal the next morning and neither of us brought it up, but every now and again, I think about it. I realise only now that I never asked Dad for money after that, but rather waited for him to offer some instead.

In the hallway, Mum greets me with a hug. The procession is leading into the living room, but I pause before the doorway, letting Mum walk into me.

'Maddie?' she questions.

I don't answer and just carry on into the living room. Dad's special chair is already gone. The dining table in the corner, previously used to house papers, stray carrier bags and Dad's medication, has been cleared. On top lie an assortment of snacks; Mum's made rock buns and bofrot and tied them in individual bags: to-go. There are canned drinks, bottled water and a crate of Carlsberg beer.

I remember that beer from our first house, in Battersea.

I was eleven, maybe twelve, and I opened the fridge for something to drink. I noticed Dad's opened beer beside the milk and lifted it out. Dad, standing at the stove, looked over his shoulder, as I took a sip. He was going to tell me off, but before he could, I was spitting it out into the sink. Dad chuckled. 'Now you know. Don't waste my beer again, eh?'

I rub my eyes hard because I'd never recalled that memory until today.

Once we're all gathered in the living room we go around the circle retelling the story of how we found out Dad had died. James and Auntie Mabel (who's joining us via video call) had both called Dad in the morning to wish him happy birthday, knowing they wouldn't be visiting. They bond over that and my own jealousy is tinged with anger. Auntie Mabel I can understand, but why was James given the opportunity to speak to Dad before he died and I wasn't?

'He sounded fine,' Auntie Mabel says, her lips turned down. 'A little off, just a little slow and tired, but sometimes that is how he would sound. How were we to know? How did he sound to you, Baaba?'

My heart sinks and I open my mouth until my tongue dries. It's an innocent question, I know it is, because of course I should have been there with Dad on his birthday. If we had put money on who would have been by his side when he died, even I would have bet on me. My eyes sting and Mum puts her hand on my knee.

'Maddie was on her way over when I told her the news,' she says. 'Her plans were to be with her father on his birthday.'

Auntie Mabel clucks with affectionate pity that I don't deserve. 'Indeed, it was a sad day,' she concludes.

They should have known something was wrong with him. I blink hard at this accusatory thought. But no one sounds fine and then dies hours later. *You would have been able to tell, right?* I pinch my arm until a dent forms. *He would have sounded off to you and you would have called the doctor, like you always do.*

I bow my head and silently cry.

We next discuss the financial aspect of the funeral but run short of reaching a conclusion. Dad's brother tells us how he'd had money set aside in Ghana but somehow, due to either the economy or dubious family members – my grasp on Fante is looser than I thought – it's now gone. I look over at James and he appears to be following the conversation better than I am. Maybe the three years before me gave him the space to learn. The bottom line (and every-one agrees) is that we need money, but no one has any. They all promise to do their best but what this means is left open to interpretation.

When everyone begins to filter out of the house, I tidy away what's left in the living room and take it to the kitchen sink. A man (the husband of the couple whose names are still a mystery) pops his head round. I smile politely, hoping he's taken a wrong turn to the bathroom.

'You don't remember me, do you?'

He's quite a circular man, with a round stomach and a head reminiscent of a football.

'Sorry, no.'

'I'm your uncle Kojo,' he says. 'I used to know your father, years ago.'

And where have you been since?

'The last time I saw you, you were small-small,' he says. 'Young. Maybe ten years old?'

'Oh.' I don't know how to react to this revelation. It's been a long time since I was small-small. 'Well, it's nice to see you again then.'

'You really don't remember me?'

'Fifteen years is a long time.'

He nods. 'Of course it is. My condolences to you.'

My hands drip soapy water as I say, 'Thank you.'

He stands and nods.

I turn back to the sink.

'I am sorry for your loss, but it's not the last time you will see him, you know?'

I sigh. 'Yes.'

'Don't cry too hard, yes?'

'Yes.'

'Lamentation is just an opportunity to renew your trust and faith in God, you see?'

I look at him. The corners of his eyes crease without aid and silver-grey threads hide within his nose. I don't know this man. He hasn't kept in touch, so of course I don't know him. It strikes me that the dedications 'auntie' and 'uncle' have lost all meaning. Anyone can wander off the street, tell me they're my aunt/uncle from years ago, drive it home with a creased brow, a disappointed frown and a 'You really don't remember me?' and I would nod and welcome them in.

'I'll leave you now,' he says.

'Okay. Nice to see you.'

Uncle Kojo. I likely won't see him again.

However, a familiar face I also wasn't sure I'd see again presents itself ten minutes later.

'Madeleine-y!'

I turn from the washing machine and there's Dawoud, all six-foot-something of him, blocking the doorway. He's in black trousers, a T-shirt and a caramel windbreaker. I'd almost forgotten about Dawoud, which is cruel of me. Mum must have invited him. I'm so glad that she did.

'How are you?' He pulls me into a quick hug, which he's never done before, a big palm slapping my back. My instinct is to tense up – should older men I don't really know hug me? But the smell of him, faint cigarette smoke and cleaning soap briefly makes me think my dad is still alive. 'Sorry I have not appeared,' he says, letting me go. 'I go to other patients, you understand.'

'Of course.'

He nods and suddenly says, 'I miss your father.'

This surprises me, and I almost ask if he even knew Dad.

'My other patients,' Dawoud continues, 'they don't like to talk with me.'

I frown, thinking of Dad, tired and reserved in his armchair. 'Talk?'

'Yes. Your father, he always talk to me.'

I clutch my shirt at the navel, where the pang starts. 'He did?'

'Oh, yes,' and Dawoud smiles brightly. 'I always start talking and his brain warm up, then we talk together. I tell him about my day, family at home, my home-home, you understand.'

I nod eagerly. I want to hear more. I need to hear proof that the man he's talking about really is Dad.

'I tell him about my job,' Dawoud continues, 'I read him newspaper, and then he tells me things about his home-home. Kumasi.'

Oh my—

'His family, his sister, erm, Becca?'

'Rebecca, yes.'

'And you!'

'Me?'

'Ha! Of course. You Madeleine-y! Always you,' he says. 'You at school, getting good scores, you come home and read. No trouble for him. Easy child. Good, good daughter. Yes, he will always talk about you. Oh, why are you crying?' He frowns and rips off a piece of kitchen towel to hand to me. He's frowning because he thinks I know all of this, but I don't. He thinks Dad and I always spoke, but we rarely did. He thinks I sat down and waited for Dad's brain to warm up, but I didn't, because Dad had always been so quiet and aloof before he was sick that it never even occurred to me that aspect might have changed. I didn't think to check. I thought Dad was like me, that we didn't need anyone. James and Mum were the social ones, and we were the introverts.

What if all this time I'd been wrong?

Chapter Twenty-Four

When a message comes in from Mum the next day, my anxiety spikes. I try to read the first line to glean whether I should open it or not. It looks harmless. However –

Mum LONDON

Maddie how are you today? You and your brother need to gather some funds quickly because it's the children who bury their father.

Once the body is released you will have only two weeks to put him to his final rest.

You can get a bank loan if you don't have the money.

Thx.

Maddie

What does this tradition say about the wife?

Mum LONDON

Surely I have a part to play in the financial and planning and if I had the money I would have done everything for my children but the children taking responsibility is tradition.

As I stare at her message, all those symptoms return: a hit of dizziness, shortness of breath, a tight chest, the illusion that my bedroom is shrinking. However, it's not fear I feel this time, but anger.

> **Maddie**
> Considering the children are not financially stable, it isn't a very good tradition and it won't be one I force onto my children.
> You're very quick to suggest I get a loan, considering me going to university with loans was also your idea.
> When I'm a mother, my job won't be to sit around and watch my children grow in debt.

> **Mum LONDON**
> Of course I don't want to see you in debt but you are young with a degree you will get through debt better than me. This is a very challenging time for us all and we have to unite. Please show your mother some kindness because I need it now more than ever.

I turn my phone off. On my laptop, I search for whether we qualify for any funeral expense help.

We don't.

James calls me to the house the next day. I stand in the corner of the kitchen as they argue.

'Call him "your father" one more time,' he says to Mum. 'He was your husband before our father and you're the only one living in his house right now, so you'd best gather some funds too.'

'How?' Mum asks. 'I don't have any money here! It's all tied up in Ghana!'

'You could get a bank loan,' I suddenly say.

She looks at me. 'Maame, what bank will give me money? I'm not living here half the time.'

'Whose fault is that?' James asks. 'You run an entire business – how are you always broke? It shouldn't be only on us when you've been chilling in Ghana and we've been here with Dad.'

I round on James and feel that flicker of anger yet again. Shu once said that brothers have a level of audacity sisters couldn't possibly reach – or get away with – even if they tried. James has done very little to prove her wrong. He hasn't taken his jacket off, but it's unzipped and he's well-dressed, as usual. 'Always gotta look fresh, Mads,' he'd say. 'You never know who might catch me on the streets.' James has always played the part of a life he wants rather than the one he has, the rest of our needs be damned.

'I'll be expecting money from you, too.'

James looks at me and frowns. 'Yeah, course. Some.'

'Some?' I repeat. 'You should pay the most since you hardly helped in any other way. You're the eldest and, supposedly, the head of the household now. And I'm pretty sure you make more than me.'

'Yes,' Mum says, nodding at him. 'Look at you.'

'But let me guess,' I continue, 'I'm expected to use my savings because you're low on funds, again? Where did you spend all your money this time? Brazil? Russia? Italy?'

His face drops. 'Mads.'

'What?' I ask him. 'Mads, what?'

'You know I did the best I could.'

I look at his shiny black puffer jacket and spotless train-ers. 'No,' I tell him. 'No, you didn't. But it's too late now, isn't it? I needed you both – desperately, at times. Dad and I both did.' *You would have been able to tell he was off, right?* 'Now it's too late.'

I walk out of the kitchen and then the house, slamming the front door behind me.

> **Mum LONDON**
> How much savings have you got and how much will you use for your dad?
> I am sorry but your brother and I don't have much so most will come from you. Thanks.

> **Maddie**
> Stop adding "thanks" to the end of your messages. It's annoying.

> **Mum LONDON**
> Your mother is annoying?
> Madeleine your mother is annoying?

I type out a reply but hesitate.

In secondary school, I once heard a friend tell her mum to shut up over the phone. I couldn't imagine the trouble she'd get into at home and told her as much.

'I tell her to shut up all the time,' she assured me. 'She doesn't take it seriously.'

I couldn't believe children told their parents to shut up and survived to tell the tale. It wasn't – and still isn't – the way my family worked. Even aged twenty-five, I wouldn't dare. It's not like I'm scared of Mum, because I know I can outrun her now, but I just don't have the attitude in me.

Or I didn't.

I press *send*.

Maddie
Yes. Very annoying.

Chapter Twenty-Five

I'm eating lunch in my room when my phone rings with a private number.

I've been looking forward to this stew and I'm really hungry, so I think about just letting it ring out, but decide last minute to answer it.

'Hello?'

'Hello, is this Madeleine Wright?'

I clench and my heart drops. The woman on the phone has a tone that is slow and sad; it's to do with Dad.

'Yes, it's me.'

'Hello, dear. I'm just calling to give you your father's post-mortem results. Your number is on the contact sheet and we can't reach your brother. Is now a good time?'

She tells me Dad died of twisted intestines, medically known as distal large bowel obstruction, which is a complication that can occur when suffering from Parkinson's. For some reason, she tells me that Dad would have been in pain, only briefly, but still, I feel a knot in my own stomach. She tells me we'll need to register my father's death next and I almost ask her if this process will be over soon. I instead end the call in a more socially acceptable manner.

I ring Mum to tell her, but it goes to voicemail, so I try James. No answer. I text them both instead.

I put on a comedy show and when James calls back, I ignore it. I go to bed, leaving the stew on my desk.

Q **Google** – When do you start feeling better after losing a loved one?

- It can take up to five years
- There is no one-size-fits-all timeline for grief; it will vary from person to person
- Rather than it getting better, it gets easier
- So long as the memory of the person lives on, will you ever stop grieving?
- Grieving doesn't always mean crying your eyes out and yelling 'why, God, why?' so long as you still miss them, you're still grieving, but that doesn't mean you're not getting better. There are no rules to this process.

Mum eventually calls to say that Auntie Mabel's finally changed her return date so the funeral planning needs to start moving forward.

'You and I both need to go to the funeral home.'

'I thought you were going to get Uncle Freddie to fill out the forms?'

'I tried, darling, but the funeral home wants the person who is making the deposit to be the one to sign. When can you do? Two days from now? Don't forget, we need to register the death tomorrow.'

I feel sick from the moment I wake up and it happens again; my body freaks out and my brain turns soft. I wait it out on my bedroom floor. I can't tell if this panic attack is longer or shorter than the ones before. As I shower to wash away the sweat, I consider the possibility that this is my life now. Even thirty minutes later, the pressure on my chest lingers.

The call to register the death is scheduled for half one and then we'll need to call the funeral home after.

I arrive home ten minutes ahead of time. Mum did offer to come to my place, but she'd probably stay longer than I'd have liked, and I don't want to deal with introducing her to Jo and Cam.

I don't go into the living room and head straight upstairs to Mum's room instead.

'Hello, darling.' She gives me a long hug and rubs my back, which she hasn't done in years. I find it soothing.

The Register Office calls and I already want to be back at my flat. I don't understand this aversion to being at the house; maybe I just hate having to be in the same place where my dad died, but Mum and James don't seem to have that problem. I'm tapping my foot on the floor when I notice the *pressure* again in my chest. It feels like smoke slowly filling a stoppered bottle.

The woman on the phone gets her fatuous pleasantries out of the way and then the form-filling, on her end, begins. She asks for my dad's name, gets it wrong when we tell her, then asks us to spell it out. When Mum spells over the phone, she makes things twice as long by using the NATO alphabet. I try to calm the sudden storm brewing in my head by silently coming up with my own. G for ginger. E for elephant. O for opioid. R for reality. G for . . . Gandalf. E for Earth. Then W for water . . .

'Did he have any middle names?' she asks.

'No,' Mum says.

'Was he known by any other name?'

The simple answer to this is also 'No', it's also a very stupid question because what does it matter, but of course Mum wants to ruminate on this.

'Well . . . no, I don't think. I mean, his friends would call him Fiifi. No, there are no E's. It is pronounced Fee-Fee but spelt with I's. Yes, Fiifi, that's his name day, but only his close friends and myself called him that, so does that count?'

Why tell her all of this? Why risk confusing the slowest secretary in the world?

'Okay, that's fine,' she says. 'Bear with me.'

The longer she's gone, the hotter my chest burns and my patience is reaching its limit. I'm picturing the sands of time when she finally returns.

'Right, so that's George Wright,' she says. 'Where did he die?'

'At home.'

'What's the address?'

'Thirty-seven Cornisham Grove.'

'One moment.' *Tap. Tap. Tap.* 'Is that Cornisham Avenue?'

'No, Grove. Grove.'

'Dear God,' I say under my breath.

'Bear with me,' the lady repeats. Two minutes and a massage of my temples later, she's back to ask, 'He died of a large distal bowel obstruction, is that correct?'

'Yes.'

'Okay.'

'Don't you have the coroner's report?'

'Mum!' I snap. 'Let her finish!'

Mum pauses and stares at me, stunned.

'Just one minute,' the lady says.

'What?' But she's already gone.

'Okay, sorry about that. What was George's occupation?'

'He did many jobs,' Mum says. She eyes me and I lock my jaw. 'Security guard,' she adds quickly. 'Just put that.'

'In death?'

Tick. Tick. Tick.

'No, he was retired due to medical reasons.'

'Okay, one minute, please.'

'Another one?'

Tick.

'I'm sorry?' she says.

'You need another minute?' I clarify. *Tick.* 'We've been on this call for twenty minutes and you've hardly taken any information. What the fuck is this?' *Tick.* 'You register the death of loved ones – of all things to be inefficient in, this is not the fucking one!'

Boom!

'Maddie!'

I didn't realise I was yelling or that I'm now on my feet.

'I'm sorry,' the woman on the phone says. 'I understand this is a difficult time for—'

'Oh, my condolences.' I tell her. 'Is your dad dead, too?'

'Well, no.'

'So where the fuck is your *understanding* coming from?' I ask. 'You don't get to say you understand in a poor attempt to shut me up. What's taking so long on your side to fucking do this? Is it technical difficulties? Do you want to call us back when you have your shit together?'

'Maddie! That's enough!'

I turn back to Mum and blink. I wipe my eyes but they won't dry. 'I can't do this,' I tell them both. 'Get James to help you finish. It'll be the first thing either of you've done for Dad in months. Posthumous – just your style.'

Mum's face falls.

I flee the house. As I speed-walk, ignoring the sweat dampening my shirt, I look up the train departure times; mine is due in four minutes and it usually takes me seven to get there. So I start to run. The one after is in half an hour and I can't wait around for that long. I need the train to get me away from here *now*.

I run until my lungs sting and my legs cramp, but I make it, jumping into the nearest carriage only a second before the doors slide shut. I let out a breath of relief that happens to be a suppressed sob.

Thankfully no one's in the flat when I get back. I run up the stairs and scream into my pillow. After, I go into the bathroom and place a damp towel onto my face; I press it down until it's heavy and smothers. It's not easy to breathe and I wonder if the reduced air will eventually suffocate me. Death by hot-pink face cloth. Some latent survival instinct is what has me remove my hand and lift the cloth.

Mum LONDON

I'm here for you Maame
I know you are sad and angry. But don't be angry with me please. We have to stick together during this terrible time

Chapter Twenty-Six

It's quickly agreed that of the six thousand pound funeral bill, I'll put in three, leaving my savings account completely empty. Mum and James say they can only pull together one thousand each and Uncle Freddie and Auntie Mabel one thousand combined.

It's hard to see the money go, to no longer have a financial safety net, and I cry about it. Then I wipe my face and get on with folding my laundry because he's my dad and I have the money, so there's nothing else to be done. James called to apologise, to say he was sorry he couldn't give more and that it was up to me again. He said he thought he'd have more time to help with Dad. I cut the conversation off there because the way I see it, apologies only benefit the beggar. They get a clear conscience and I get a sequence of hollow words incapable of changing anything.

Someone knocks on the door and I discover I'm home alone when it goes unanswered. I ask who it is and a man says, 'Oh, it's Sam?'

'You don't sound sure.'

He laughs. 'It's Sam. I promise.'

I open the door and there stands a tall Black man with an incredible smile.

'Sorry about that,' he says. 'You must be Maddie.'

'You're Sam? Jo's Sam?'

He lifts his mouth to the side.

'Sorry,' I rush. 'Jo's ex-Sam. Ex-boyfriend. Casually.'

Shit.

'Yes, that's me. She didn't tell you I was coming?'

We're not really on speaking terms. 'She must have forgotten.'

He holds up his phone. 'She says she's on her way. Mind if I come in?'

That's when I remember he's been here before. I heard him with Jo in her bedroom only weeks ago. They used to be just friends, but then became friends who have sex. I wonder how you get there – what's the uncertain in between?

No, you can't ask him.

'Of course.' I move out of the way and nod. 'Want to wait in her room – no, that's probably a bad idea. All the memories. Of conversations you shared, I mean!'

He presses his lips together before saying, 'Living room's fine.'

He takes a seat on the sofa and when he leans forward to tighten the laces on his trainers his knees are almost the height of his chest.

'Okay, well, I'll leave—'

'You work for OTP, right?' he suddenly says. 'Jo mentioned.'

'Oh, yes, I do.' I play with my neck because I haven't got a bra on.

'How are you finding the place?'

'It's . . . good. Sorry, how do you know about OTP? People outside of publishing tend to blank when I mention it. Wait, Jo did say you're an artist?'

He smiles. 'I prefer the term illustrator.'

I don't know what that preference says about him, but he continues to look at me, so I sit on the other side of the sofa. 'Have you submitted samples to OTP?'

'Not yet, but my agent alerted me to the fact that someone there has been asking after my schedule. Thea?'

'I know her!' I then think of the milk jug. 'Kind of, but I know she only approaches people she's really interested in.'

'That's good to know.'

We sit in silence and I wonder if I should excuse myself and how. He's still looking at me and there's a slight dip between his eyebrows. I don't get the impression he's frowning.

'Jo also mentioned you lost your dad recently.' He says this quietly and his eyes have changed. He looks genuinely sorry for me, which I find odd because he doesn't even know me. 'I'm so sorry.'

I mentally pull out my short list of acceptable Google-provided responses, but before I can pick one, his phone vibrates.

'Probably Jo.' He reads the message, but then rolls his eyes, laughing to himself.

'She's running late?' I ask.

'What? No, that was a text from my mum.'

'Your mum texts you, too?' I realise quickly how weird a thing that is to say. All mums text their children.

'Yeah, my mum's . . .' He frowns and shakes his head. 'You don't want to hear about my mum texting me.'

'No, I do!' I say before I can help myself. 'My mum . . .'

Is this a weird conversation to have with someone I've never met before today? But he's listening with his head tilted and his eyebrows raised.

'My mum sends me texts that make me roll my eyes. Lovingly. Sometimes. Not often.' I wave a hand dismissively. 'All mums do, I guess.'

Sam considers me. 'My mum isn't like other mums,' he says slowly. 'I told her I was coming here today and she asked if I'd prayed for guidance. She's not Jo's biggest fan. I know!' he says, clocking my expression. 'I'm almost thirty.' He puts his phone away. 'My mum's . . . my mum.'

Then there's a key in the door. 'Sam?' Jo is back. Her cheeks are flushed pink and she's fixing her hair. 'Oh, Maddie.' It's both a question and a statement.

I excuse myself and the living-room door closes when I'm halfway up the stairs.

I don't know what it is in me that vigorously hopes they don't get back together.

It's not a very nice thought, but I think it nonetheless.

An hour later, they're still in there and I decide to hire a bike out to the river. Getting ready to leave the flat takes three times as long as it did before and each time I forget something or check my phone or need the toilet, I think of staying. Then I tell myself all I have to do is slap sunscreen on, close the front door and let my stubbornness take care of the rest.

The familiar route encourages me to keep going, so I put my headphones on and listen to music. I don't realise I'm nodding my head to the beat until a roller skater doing the same smiles as she passes. I look back at her and laugh. I sing random bits quietly until suddenly I'm belting them out. I focus on the path ahead and people either ignore me or smile as I ride past. I feel swaddled in my headphones and whenever I stare out at the river, I have a sudden pull, a brief thought of what it would be like at the very bottom.

I bounce my head to the music, attempt high notes, shake my shoulders and consider the possibility that people will think I'm weird. I revel in the fact that I don't care if they do – secretly, they wish they were as free as I am! I wonder if I'm actually happy or just momentarily distracted.

Maybe the latter is what happiness looks like for me now.

Chapter Twenty-Seven

There's nothing but silence in my ears on the way to the funeral directors and when Mum and I enter the small room, the lady goes through a form, slowly – why always so slowly?

If this weren't about my dad's death, I'd probably like her – Ros. She's short with blond hair pulled into a limp ponytail and looks in her early forties. I can tell outside of the office she loves the colour pink. She wears rectangular glasses and has a French manicure she may have done herself. Her voice is gentle, but her words stretch unnecessarily, thinning my patience.

'Okay,' she says, and for a word that is often spelt with only two letters, she makes each syllable work hard. I slightly hate her. She's reached a large box on the form and turns to me. 'Can you tell me a little bit about Dad?'

I look at her. 'Why?'

'Don't worry, sweetie. This is just for us here at the funeral home, so we know him a bit better.'

I want to shake my head and tell her how nonsensical that is. *It's a bit late to get to know him now, don't you think?*

Ros prompts an answer by asking, 'Just, you know, what he liked to do; what football team he supported, things like that.'

I recall the evening I told Dad I'd be moving out; there was a football match playing, but I don't remember which teams so I can't answer this question. Dad didn't do much because that's Parkinson's for you and I didn't have much access to his life before.

'He liked to watch TV,' I say slowly. Although that may not be true. Dawoud and I just always put it on for him because I couldn't stand the thought of him sitting in silence all day. 'Mainly football,' I say, 'and the news and some cooking channels. He supported . . . erm, sorry, I'm not sure which team. I think he used to like reading? He read newspapers – he would always buy them on Sundays.'

Ros writes this all down and I hope that's enough because my mind is blank and I must look like a selfish daughter who never took any interest in her dad. She doesn't know that he preferred not to share. She doesn't know that was Dad.

'Sorry, my memory isn't great.'

'That's okay, sweetie,' Ros says. 'Did he like to cook? Did he have a favourite dish?'

I falter; I think he liked my lasagne, but then Mum says, 'When he was able, he liked to make soup, traditional pepper soup.'

Of course. Pepper soup – how could you forget that?

'And he did love to read,' Mum continues. 'He was once a librarian, before Maddie was born, until he was offered a better-paying job at a private school. His love of reading is where Maddie gets it from.'

I frown at Mum's revelation, only stopping when Ros looks at me and smiles, creasing her pink lipstick in the process. 'Oh, that's so lovely, isn't it?'

I try to smile and hope it works because I don't think a love of reading is genetic, otherwise how do you explain James who once said, 'I don't read for shit'?

I didn't know Dad had been a librarian, though. I think of him, much younger, wearing glasses and a thick jumper, stacking books onto shelves. I used to spend my weekends in libraries, bringing home as many books as my library card would allow. The local librarians used to love me and openly said they didn't know any other child in the area reading as much as I was.

I start bouncing my leg and breathing deeply as Mum and Ros talk endlessly; the conversation has moved onto flowers now. But who gives a shit about flowers? Ros gets out a tape measure; did Mum ask how large their flowers are?

'You just pick,' I tell her when she asks for my preference.

Mum nods, then says to Ros, 'Before I forget, we need clippings of his toenails and fingernails.'

What?

Ros nods sagely. 'I've heard of this tradition,' she says. 'Are you Ghanaian? Yes, I thought so. We've done this before.'

'Yes, his brother and sister will scatter them back home in Ghana,' Mum explains.

'Of course,' says Ros. 'I'll make sure to include that.'

I look at Ros; how does she know that and I don't? She must learn about all sorts of traditions here. I think about her job. All the professionals I've had to interact with since my dad died have left me internally asking, *Why is this your job? What led you here? Surely you didn't choose this?*

'Maddie, would you like your father's fingerprint?'

I blink at Ros. 'That's possible?' *There's still a piece of Dad left.* 'Please! Sorry, yes, of course I would.'

Ros adds my answer to the form and I have to fill out another section asking for my name, address, relation to Dad and bank details.

These processes really should be quicker.

Welcome to FuneralCare, Maddie. We have two services for you to choose from today. We have the fast-track option carried out in a perfunctory yet expeditious manner, featuring minimal conversation and a desultory delivery. Or we have the compassionate snail trail which, even though we've never met you and we go through this process multiple times with other people literally every day, features intermittent coos and spontaneous moments of silence allowing you to linger in melancholy. A little more costly, but this service lasts three times longer than necessary in order to show how much we care. So, which would you like to go for?

Ros eventually goes to call the cemetery for a date. I'm still bouncing my leg and have started pinching my skin. I can't wait to leave.

When she returns, she says that Saturday the twenty-first of August is the earliest availability.

Ten days away! 'That long?'

'Darling, I am sorry about that,' Ros says. 'I understand the wait can be awful, but we only have certain days available.'

I never imagined we'd have to take the schedules of random members of the public into account. I thought these people were on standby every day waiting for people to die.

'Fine. Fine,' I say because I just want to get out of here. I push my seat away from the table.

'Okay,' Ros says, 'now, finally, we need to take a list of the clothes he'll be wearing when buried and anything you'd like to put in the casket.'

In an alternate universe, I flip the table and Ros's coffee goes everywhere. But in this reality I sit back down and watch her pull out a rectangular notebook; she stops to blink slowly and stare at Mum and I in turn.

She eventually asks, 'Is that okay?'

A monster begins tapping on my chest and my jaw is clenched so tight, I worry about cracking a tooth. Mum and Ros go through the things Mum's brought. It turns out she's brought too many clothes because she wasn't sure of what's needed.

'I'll have to call a friend of mine later and come back to you,' Mum says. 'I want to do this right. If you do things wrong for the dead, they can come back and haunt you.'

There's a brief moment of respite where the monster and I roll our eyes.

'So, let me just check I'm doing everything right and I'll return tomorrow . . .' Mum looks at me '. . . alone.'

On the train home I can finally breathe. I look around and there's a man digging for gold in his left nostril, a woman with two lines of black thread for eyebrows, and another woman reading a prayer booklet. At the sight of it, I want to shout DON'T BELIEVE ANYTHING IT TELLS YOU, but I don't know why. I don't even know exactly what it is that I no longer believe.

Chapter Twenty-Eight

I can't sleep the night before I'm due to see Dad.

When Mum asked if I wanted to see Dad one last time, it took me two tries to answer her. 'How can we see him – oh, you mean his body before he's buried? I can choose? Yes, I should. I mean, I will, yes. When?'

I meet Mum at the bus stop, my body aching and my throat sore from continuously having to swallow my nausea. We get the 450 bus, just the two of us. James will be going to see Dad with Auntie Mabel.

I can't stop tapping my feet and when Mum takes my hand and squeezes tight, I think that someday, I'll have to do all of this again for her. When the time comes, I might be on the bus by myself.

At the funeral home, Ros is dressed in black.

She takes Mum and me into a small room with dimmed lights and candles in the corner.

My hands start to shake and I don't know where to look. Then I see him and a helpless cry escapes before Ros even manages to close the door behind her.

No. 'Oh, Dad.'

The coffin lid is propped up, resting against the wall. Waiting.

That's it. He really is gone.

'No.' I shake my head. 'No.'

Mum rubs my back. 'It's okay, Maame.'

'No! It's not okay!'

Mum pulls me to her and I cry into her jumper until my throat is tight. I step away and roughly dry my eyes because I need to see him. This will be my last chance to see him.

I turn my head and notice he looks . . . the same, except maybe his lips have thinned a little. He could be sleeping. I stare until I realise I'm waiting for his eyes to open.

There's no look of frustration or uncertainty on his face, the expressions I'd grown used to seeing. His forehead is smooth, and his hands, placed on his stomach, are still. He's not in pain anymore.

He has on his grey wedding suit, a white shirt underneath, and I press a hand to my mouth when I see he also wears his chunky silver bracelet, the bracelet he has on in the photograph I have of him, the bracelet that has been on his wrist through sickness and in health.

Mum speaks to him in Twi. 'May God bless you, Fiifi. Go with him, okay? Go with God; see your parents again; they're calling you and waiting for you. Have peace and have rest.' She's crying harder than I've ever seen before. Tears are streaming from her eyes and she punctuates her sentences with hiccups. 'You have suffered so much,' she says to him, 'trapped, but now you are finally free. See? Look at you already? Your swollen foot is no more. You're already free. Go with God and be free.'

It's comforting to hear, not so much the words, but my mother tongue. The language of my parents – they rarely spoke to one another in English.

You really should learn to speak Twi.

Before we leave, I look at his face one last time and say, 'I love you, Dad. Very much, *okay?*'

An intense peace settles on me when I board the train, almost like I'll never cry again. I know that isn't true, but I'm happy to believe it for now.

It was Nia's idea to do something after so that I didn't have to go straight home. She knew that before seeing Dad, I wouldn't be able to stomach breakfast, so she suggested lunch. I said, sure, but so long as it was somewhere I haven't tried before. Somewhere new.

Nia picked a spot in London Bridge called *Casa de Maria*. A Portuguese restaurant she went to years ago with an old boyfriend. It's lowly lit and the tables and chairs are wooden. There are plants in the corners and posters on the wall. Each table has a glass bottle of water and an unlit candle.

We order mushroom and caramelised onion empanadas, green rice, batatas fritas and half a chicken to share. Nia chooses a beetroot smoothie to drink.

'What? Sounds interesting,' she says. 'So does the spinach and orange. Want to get one each and then we can share?'

I order a Diet Coke.

'So, how was it?' Nia asks.

'It was good,' I answer. 'Considering the circumstances, and what I mean by that is, no one else died. He looked the same, kind of like he was sleeping. I wanted to reach out and shake his arm, like a kind of "wake up, Dad" thing.'

'Ah, Maddie.' She rests her hand on top of mine.

'No, it really was good to see him.'

The waitress drops off my Coke. There's ice in my glass and I swirl the cubes around with my straw.

'I'm glad he looked the same.'

'Didn't they put make-up on him?'

'Not that I could tell.'

'They did with my dad.'

I leave my straw alone and watch Nia stretch her arms behind her back.

'His lips were blue,' she says, 'so they put make-up on him, and to try to hide that his eyes had sunken a bit.' She rests her elbows on the table. 'My uncle made me touch him and I was resisting and he was pulling my hand, saying, "Go on, you have to touch him! It's your last chance!" until I did and my dad was block-hard and cold. After, I was like, yeah, thanks for that, Uncle.'

'This is the first time you've really spoken to me about your dad dying.'

'Like I said before,' and she shrugs, 'I didn't want to talk about it.'

I remember when Nia came into school to tell us that her dad had suffered a heart attack in his sleep. She was wearing one of his jumpers – it swamped her, and I just stood there, silent. I almost didn't believe her. Dying in your sleep sounded too fantastical, something that happens only on TV to sweet, old grandmas. I didn't know what to say or what Nia might need, so I hoped, if anything, she'd just tell me – she was that kind of person. Open. Honest.

That's what I told myself anyway, but really—

'I pretended it didn't happen,' I confess. 'I thought the less I asked, the less it would be true and you would still be the Nia you were before you lost your dad. I'd never suffered a loss like that before so just assumed you'd rather not talk about it. I thought, why would you want to be reminded?

But now I know, you don't actually forget. I'm sorry I never rode the bus over at night or brought you containers of food or made you go outside.'

'It's all right, Mads,' Nia says. 'And you know what? I liked that when we did talk during that time, it was about different things. I've got a big family and they were over all the time, just talking about my dad being dead. I needed those breaks.'

'But I didn't do that on purpose. I didn't know it was helping.'

'Doesn't matter,' she says. 'The fact that it did help is what matters.' She pushes her mouth to one side. 'We all grieve in different ways, you know?' she adds. 'Losing someone is universal, but I think that's about it, really. The rest is our own thing.'

If I were Nia, would I have held a slight grudge? What would have happened to me if Nia hadn't gotten me eating, talking, walking and cycling in the sun? I couldn't have gotten to this stage alone.

Our food arrives and I try Nia's beetroot juice.

'Is it good?' she asks.

I push the glass back to her. 'It's . . . refreshing. Has a unique earthy note to it.'

Nia laughs. 'All right, Nigel Slater.' When she tries it, she moves her head side to side to say *so-so*.

It's almost thirty degrees out, so after lunch, we walk from London Bridge to the West End. I marvel at how much has changed in my life since I was unceremoniously fired from CGT. I still haven't heard back from HR.

Near Embankment we choose a park to sit in for a few hours, not really talking about anything but passing words between us. A woman sits one bench over, eating red pepper hummus with a spoon.

Eventually I say, 'I'm exhausted,' and Nia nods.

She takes the bus home whilst I opt for the train.

Jo has friends over in the garden when I get back – Cam is with them; they're all laughing and drinking in the early evening sun. I stand by the stairs and introduce myself. They ask if I want to join them but I politely decline and go up to my room, but because Jo's bedroom is on top of the garden and she keeps her window and door open during the day, I can still hear them.

'Times like this you've got to leave her alone, I think,' says one of Jo's friends. 'Especially after the whole it's-your-fault thing.'

'Yeah, I kind of leave her to it,' Jo says. 'I'm not fussed and I don't hold grudges.'

'How's it been living with her in general?'

'Fine,' Jo replies. 'She's clean, quiet. Although, I always have to pull the showerhead up. Whenever I get into the bath after her it's at nose-level, which is funny because she's at least an inch or two taller than me.'

I frown because I always have to pull the showerhead down when I get in the bath after Jo. I never questioned it; it's been a reflex ever since I moved in. But now I realise it's because I don't wash my hair every day and she pretty much does.

'That's weird,' her friend says flippantly.

'Yeah, but it's fine,' Jo adds. 'We don't really talk. Well, we did before, but she doesn't really talk at all now. Most of the time, she's alone upstairs or just sits in the living room watching TV.'

'Aw, bless, that's sad.'

'I know.' The doorbell rings. 'That's our pizza!'

I wipe my eyes dry.

A little later, I go down to cook some pasta.

From the kitchen, I can hear them even clearer than I did upstairs.

'So, how did your talk with Sam the stallion go?' one of them asks. 'Back together yet?'

I sneak closer to the door. 'Almost,' Jo responds. I picture her with her head thrown back, her mouth open and the cooling sun on her face, surrounded by friends who look and sound just like her. 'When he came by, we had a good long chat. He said he was sorry for ending things so abruptly and explained that it was because he wasn't in the best headspace at the time.'

'Yeah, his friend, right?'

'Yeah,' Jo confirms. 'Anyway, he was talking about how it was less complicated when we were friends and I thought that too, but . . . I didn't tell him this, but now I think I want more from him?'

The girls all squeal with delight.

'What about that Conrad guy from work?'

Jo sighs and I imagine her swiping at the air dismissively. 'It wasn't the same, you know?'

'If we go out for your birthday, I'm definitely inviting Sam,' someone says.

'Yes!' Jo says. 'You have to!' And I can tell she's smiling.

I suddenly hate that she's smiling, because that's all she does. Laugh and smile and talk to her friends about boys who really like her. Does Sam really like her? Of course, he does – people like Jo. Men must be attracted to fun, to simplicity, to a lack of baggage. Or at least to someone who can hide their baggage well. My problem is that I'm not simple; I'm not a good time, unless I'm lying or pretending to be okay.

More laughter spills from the garden. I move away to boil the kettle and I think about Sam. Sam and his easy smile. Sam and his mum, who sounds a lot like my own. Sam and his friend – it sounded like something had happened, maybe he had a fight with a close friend of his. But he seemed fine when he came over that time, so perhaps they'd made amends? Then I'm thinking about what Jo said. How since they got back from Florence, I've just been sitting in the living room and watching TV or existing alone upstairs.

'I'm sure there was a time when I was happy,' I say to the boiling pot of pasta. 'But how do you measure that? How do you know if you're genuinely happy or if you're just mostly *all right*, with sprinkles of laughter and occasional shit storms of sadness? Maybe I've only ever been *all right*.'

I was a happy baby, Mum once told me. I laughed so much I'd get the hiccups. My pre-teenage years were uneventful and maybe that's happiness: a lack of tragedy. Maybe when Mum started staying away for longer and the responsibility grew? Definitely when Dad became ill and every single day was marred with moments of worry and concern and guilt.

Which means I actually haven't been okay for a while and it's scary having to think so far back. It means I've been slowly falling apart for a very long time and it might take even longer to piece me back together.

Yet another burst of laughter escapes the garden and I wonder what I've missed.

'But yeah,' Jo says, 'on Sunday, Em and I are trying that new brunch place in Highbury and Islington you told us about, Liv. On Saturday, I'll go and see Dad, then in the afternoon Claudia's mum's having a barbeque, so that should be fun. Which reminds me, I can't show up empty-handed; you know what her mum's like. I'll need to do a bit of a shop tomorrow. Any of you know a good cheesecake recipe?'

I eat my pasta in my room, but keep replaying Jo's words, and feel lonely in a way that hollows out my chest and stomach.

I log into church online and load the latest message. I realise I haven't been since Dad died. I'm sure God understands I'm on annual leave from everything.

It begins to play, but I can't give it my full attention, so I tidy my room at the same time. They play a song with a catchy refrain and I'm humming along as I rearrange my bookshelf. The pastor welcomes everyone to church, those in the building and those of us watching at home. I know it's a recording and no one can see me, but I still move out of the camera's sight line.

I zone out, catching words and scriptures, but something snaps me back to attention right before the group prayer starts.

He says, 'We want to encourage you all to pray right now, those of you here today and those of you watching at home. If there is anyone out there suffering from loss, financial insecurity, anxiety, illness, trouble with employment, family and/or friends, we want to pray for and with you, right now.'

This is a staple of the Sunday service; it's an ending as

guaranteed as death. I have heard these words on so many Sundays that I could recite them if I wanted to, but today they feel new and tailored. I've never been one of those people in a crowd of hundreds who believe someone on a stage is talking directly to them, but today I feel maybe that his words are meant for me.

He sounds so sincere when he looks directly into the camera and says, 'We just want to pray for you.'

I could exit the browser; I could just shut my laptop, but instead I listen, captivated, as he prays to God on our behalf. We are His children and there is nothing God wouldn't do for us. We are loved and we are blessed.

I cry, not because I agree, but because it hurts that I don't. Because I wish that I did. Instead, I wake up every day and I smile when I need to and talk when I have to, but I am in constant pain, and I have been for too long.

One song closes and another is sung. We're encouraged to go to God not only for our material requests but all things. I recall my prayers over the years; I remember that I have not asked for a car or money I didn't earn. In varying degrees of desperation, I have asked to be fixed.

I wipe my nose and tell the empty space around me that all I want is to be less sad.

After the service, my phone buzzes with a reminder: *Carrow Writers deadline*. It's the writing opportunity I found in the library.

I click onto the website and, sure enough, the deadline is midnight. I look through my WIP folder, and without opening the document, select the nine-hundred-and-something-word passage I wrote about leaving Dad. I submit it without rereading. It's a terrible submission; I can't imagine the number of spelling mistakes it has or if it's even coherent, but at least I've done something with it.

I close my laptop, get into bed and lie there wide awake until midnight.

Q **Google** – Why can't I sleep?

Insomnia – Help guide

Depression is one of the most common causes of insomnia and difficulty sleeping can cause symptoms to worsen. Other common emotional and psychological causes include anger, grief, bipolar disorder and trauma.

Q **Google** – What to do when you can't sleep

7 reasons why you're not sleeping – Mogg Health
Beat stress and feel more relaxed
What should I do if I can't sleep – forum
Why can't you sleep – here's the answer
How to fall asleep in 60 seconds
Sleep disorders and problems: 10 types and causes
Tired but can't sleep – take this quiz to find out why
Try our app – the number-one app for sleep and meditation
The ten most popular apps today
Join our dating app today

It's past midnight and Jo's bedroom is still open. A cork is popped. Laughing. Bottle neck clinking against glass.

PROFILE NAME: Maddie Wright

AGE: 25

AREA: Wandsworth, South West London

UNIVERSITY: Birkbeck University

OCCUPATION: Editorial Assistant

I IDENTIFY AS A:

Woman ↓

Man

Not Listed

ARE YOU LOOKING FOR:

Women

Men ↓

Everyone

BIO:

What to say about myself . . .

I turn over and stare at the ceiling.

Q **Google** – Dating app bio examples female

Kim, 28

When Harry Met Sally is my favourite movie and I once drove from London to Brighton with an ex-boyfriend and a chicken.

Delal, 32
I just want a guy who says bless you after I sneeze.

Mira, 25
'She's all right. I like her' – my best friend Sarah
'Flosses regularly and never needs fillings' – Dr Reid, my dentist
'Not as crazy as she looks' – my ex Jeremy (the last words he ever said to me before he mysteriously disappeared)

Okay, so keeping it short, funny and inoffensive seems to be the trick.

> **BIO:** I love food, I read for fun and I did *not* spend an hour attempting to draft this bio

Is that last bit charming or sad? I imagine it will depend on who's reading it.

'I'd chuckle,' I say quietly, 'but then again, you're a little weird, Maddie.'

The bio doesn't sound exactly like me, but I think that might not be the worst thing.

ADD PROFILE PICTURE

I scroll through my gallery. I don't like taking pictures of myself; what I look like in the mirror and what I look like through a camera somehow seem to be two different people, so there aren't many images to choose from. There's one of me from two years ago; I have twisted braids in my hair, but other than that, nothing else has changed. I think I still have that top somewhere . . .

Instead, I click *next* and I'm suddenly presented with a man's image, a tick and cross under him. Decidedly savage, yet undeniably time-efficient.

Will they know if I press the cross? No, surely not.

I scroll and scroll, tick and cross, trying not to judge on appearance (but obviously judging on appearance at least somewhat) and mollifying my moral compass with my firm, personal belief that anyone can be handsome, really. Remember Ben?

A message from **Alex** comes through mid-scroll. I scream and throw my phone across the room. I somehow failed to take into consideration the social aspect of this early-morning, pity-fuelled venture.

'Maddie?'

Of course the exact moment my phone hits the wall is when Cam uses the bathroom.

'I'm fine! Just a spider, but it's gone now!'

She closes the bathroom door. I wait until she's back downstairs before picking up my phone and not making eye contact with it until I'm back in bed.

ALEX Hi. You work in publishing? My sister's writing a book – can you publish her? Lol

MADDIE Ha! No, that's a common misconception; she'd need a literary agent first and sadly I don't have acquisition power.

ALEX There's something attractive about a person who knows how to correctly use a semicolon. I guess that comes with the job.

I smile and tap into his profile. Alex is white, brown-haired and -eyed with a slight dip in his chin. He's easily attractive, like many men are – you could even overlook him.

Alex, 27

BIO: I recently read *The Imaginary People* and it floored me. I work as a Senior Sales Executive for a tech company but my passion is photography. Born in Michigan but raised in London. I'm bisexual so try not to stereotype.

Bisexual? Does that mean he's only dating women right now? What happens when he prefers men again? Is that how it works? Can I ask him? Probably not.

MADDIE You work in sales but love photography? They're so different, aren't they?

ALEX Yeah, I know my way around an extensive Excel spreadsheet and needed to put that to some use but I love taking photos. It's going to sound cheesy but there's something special about immortalising memories and having the sight of a thing change through the view of a lens.

MADDIE I don't think that's cheesy at all.

ALEX Do you have a project or a thing that gives you that feeling?

MADDIE I used to write a lot . . . but ran out of things to say.

ALEX I like how you type. It's like you're actually talking.

MADDIE I've been told that before, well, once before: 'It's like you're in the room, Mads.' Jury's still out on whether she meant that to be a good thing.

MICHAEL Want to see a picture of my cat?

MADDIE I'm more of a dog person but sure!

MICHAEL *Image*

MADDIE Sir, why are you naked in this photo?

EZRA Don't freak out but I'm really into Race Play. It's not a racism thing just a preference thing

MADDIE *Is typing . . .*

EZRA Hello?

DARREN Fun fact about me is I never dated a Black woman before but I always wanted to try it. See more of whats out there

I don't fall asleep until three. I spent the first few hours of the morning talking to Alex. Even Jo went to bed before I did.

Alex lives in Putney, prefers green tea to coffee and has a rescue Labrador called Rufus. I was the last to message and he hasn't sent a reply yet.

Maybe because it's a weekday and regular people are on their way to work?

I remember why I'm not on my way to work.

I get out of bed and the house is empty. I decide I'm going to try to look at my emails today. I wrap a cardigan around me and sit out in the garden with a tall glass of water. There's almost two hundred emails in my work inbox, which is less than I expected considering a good portion of them will be threads and emails I didn't need to be cc'd into in the first place. I imagine Penny told relevant parties not to bother me.

I skip through all the condolence emails, opening but not really reading them. There's one I spend twenty minutes drafting a reply for but, in the end, choose to delete it. Then I see the repetition of the words *Love Stories*.

Love Stories? What's that?

Via a thread of emails, I discover they've followed up with Afra Yazden-Blake and signed her on, with Kris acting as head editor. I'm not usually cc'd into Creative emails, but I think Penny's been adding me in when the rest forget to. I go through them all and gather that Afra's book will be called *Love Stories from the Middle East* and when published it will be a three- to four-hundred page book on food, drink and dessert from the Middle East.

A synopsis has even been drafted:

When Afra came to London from Iran twelve years ago, alone and severely homesick, she began to cook and bake food from her mother's sparse notes as a way of expressing what she could not yet vocalise. She started meeting men and women via social media and various community organisations before holding, what she called, 'home parties' in her studio flat. Her dinners started off with just three people bi-monthly; each guest would bring a dish from their home to share and they would sit, eat, drink and reminisce. Soon, friends invited friends and the number of dishes arriving through her studio's doors grew until her dining table was full and people were sitting on the floor, the kitchen counter, beside the sink. Afra looked forward to these dinners because her evenings would smell like home and of cities she hadn't seen. The 'home parties' were disorganised but she loved this chaotic expression of love and friendship. Eventually she began storing her recipes and collecting guest recipes to create an Instagram account full of Middle Eastern cuisine.

I go through every single email in my inbox and not once am I mentioned for bringing Afra forward. Maybe they said it out loud in the office, but I doubt it. I unclench my jaw. *No way. No fucking way.* Not again and not this fucking time. I hit Reply All to an email thread about how to best present the fact that not all the recipes in the book are Afra's but also from her dinner guests.

Subject: **RE:** Love Stories

How about **Love Stories from the Middle East** by Afra Yazden-Blake et al? When I first found Afra on Instagram, she was quick to credit any recipes that weren't hers, so I think she'd like that.

Best,
Maddie

It's not the best idea I've had, since cookbooks don't ever feature the words *et al*, but I needed to write something that would allow me to mention that I was the one who found Afra.

I hit Send.

Q **Google** – Does your line manager steal your publishing ideas?

I find an editorial assistant forum discussing all kinds of things, from pay differences to appropriate work banter. Last year, someone asked: Does your boss pretend your ideas are his?

Kieran: No. I'm credited for all my ideas. I might not have the experience to follow it up, but my line manager always lets the team know who came up with what idea, even if it's tiny.

Lia: Same here. I can't always follow up because I don't have that training, but I always get a 'Lia came up with this great suggestion/congrats' from the team.

Georgie: It's a question of intellectual property belonging to the company you work for. I'm sure you were credited somehow, but don't expect your name in the Acknowledgments.

Steph: They do this because they want to keep you an assistant for longer. It's better for them to pay you an assistant-level salary rather than acknowledge the position you really should have.

An email from Kris pops up.

From: Kristina@orangetreepublishing.com
To: Maddie@orangetreeepublishing.com
Subject: RE: Love Stories

It's so good to hear from you, Maddie, but know there's no pressure to return to work. If you feel you need to, do only bits of what you can, but we have plenty of breathing space on the schedule for this. Selecting your favourite photographers for *Love Stories* might be a fun task – see email below.
K x

I don't ever get to do anything creative such as choose photographers – I assumed the Design team would do that

– but this task must have been given solely to placate me. Still, I click the links to various portfolios and spend the rest of the afternoon going through food websites and photographs, keeping the book's synopsis in mind.

His style is more focused and appealing – the red of tomatoes, the drip of olive oil.

Her photos are more ranging; she tells me an entire story in only a few shots.

She's very clean and neat, maybe too much so? Afra uses the words 'chaotic expression' and I don't see that here.

He's very bright and colourful. He'd be great for the summer section but for winter too?

Is this too sparse or is it minimalist?

Ooh, I like him. Incredible with close-ups. I know it's an autumnal recipe from that photo alone . . . Pumpkin tagine – I knew it. Henry the Eighth royal banquet vibes.

She's good at incorporating people into her photos. Can I pull off that pale pink nail colour?

I whittle my top eight down to three and send those to Kris, cc'ing in Penny. By three in the afternoon, I have no other responses to my 'et al' email and close my laptop.

Jo's sent a group message to say she's got a date and will be back late. I immediately wonder if it's with Sam, and then decide she'd have said if it was. I shouldn't care if it is, but I do.

It's still warm, so I stay outside with a bottle of cider and respond to more app notifications. I hope there's one from Alex.

NATE Have you dated a white man before?
MADDIE Yes, I have

NATE Bet he's not like me

MADDIE That would be in your best interest

NATE Sounds like you're still mad at your ex. I'm out

MADDIE You were never in!

ZACK You look so innocent but I bet you're not. I bet you
only date good boys that's why you're still single.

MADDIE Then what's your excuse?

ZACK Who said I was single?

MADDIE Bleugh.

ZACK Lol

DAVID Can you twerk

MADDIE Can you waltz?

Nothing from Alex. Fine, I'll message first; twenty-first century, feminism and everything. I take a gulp of cider for courage before I remember that this brand is non-alcoholic.

I open our chat to realise the reason he hasn't messaged back is because it was my turn to, so I ask him what his weekend looks like.

ALEX I'm over at my mum's in Richmond on Sunday; it's my
sister's baby shower so the family is slowly descending
upon her poor house

MADDIE Oh that's nice. Is she having a boy or girl? Nice use
of a semicolon, by the way.

ALEX I put it in there for you. ;)

See what I did there?

Yeah it should be good. I've guessed girl, but we'll find out
the sex on Sunday.

The fam have made a real game of it now. Bets were just for fun at first, winners get bragging rights, that kind of thing, but now there's a pool going and I'm £20 in so far!
Typical.
Are you and your family close?
MADDIE . . .

I take another gulp of non-alcoholic cider.

MADDIE Very. I moved out a couple months ago (quite late, I know!) but keep going back. I don't usually beat my brother to it though. He's three years older than me but he and I are really close too.
ALEX That's good to hear. Your parents are still together? Isn't it weird that that's a rarity these days?
MADDIE Yes, they're still together. Happily married, last time I checked! We're just your average family, really. Talk on the phone, Sunday lunches at home, my brother brings his laundry over, walks in the park, etc. Boring, I know.
ALEX Sounds ideal actually. Normality used to be considered boring and now it's incredibly underrated. My parents divorced years ago and now have their own partners. They're cool but I'm closer to my mum. Family are everything aren't they.
MADDIE . . .
They really are.

HORNY-ZA You local?
MADDIE I'm not a free-range chicken
HORNY-ZA I just want to f*ck your big as* with my big di*k.
MADDIE I'd rather you didn't

ALEX Would you like to have coffee (umbrella term to also include tea and other beverages) with me, tomorrow if you're free?

A date? Something outside this app? Something . . . real? I don't know why I didn't consider this being an outcome.

I shouldn't be dating right now. But I like talking to Alex. I forget that I'm sad. I like who I've chosen to be with him, my mythical family dynamic and all.

MADDIE Yes, I would.

Chapter Twenty-Nine

Alex is bisexual.

Now that he's asked me on a date, it's another thing I have to think about. The first is that he is another white man. Now I know I shouldn't tar every white man with the same Ben-shaped brush, but what did Nia say? If I want to save myself any more pain (and it's been a pretty busy time in the heartbreak department this year), I can't date just *any* white man. Alex has read *Imaginary People*, which I know is a non-fiction book about Britain's tendency to erase the contributions of non-white people throughout history and into the modern day. Does that mean he's an anti-racist? It's not exactly a book you read for laughs. I guess I won't know without more information.

Circling back to the fact that he's bisexual. What does it really mean? He finds men attractive too, so could both of us find the same man attractive? Does that matter? If he were straight, he'd still find other women attractive, so what's the difference?

The difference is, it's hard enough competing with just women, now I've got to compete with men, too. What if he wants man-like qualities, like testosterone-fuelled strength? What if he likes specific sexual-related things that I can't perform properly *because* I don't have a penis?

I click onto a chat room and the starting question is: Should I go official with a bisexual man or am I asking for trouble?

LucyS: As long as he's monogamous why does it matter if he's bi? Let's be real. We're all a little bi.

ReginaP: My honest opinion is that he's on the road to gay so your a beard hun.

JennyFlen: Go for it! I'm dating someone who identifies as pansexual and it's been great. I used to think, does he really want me or is he waiting until he finds the right man blah blah blah but I wish I hadn't wasted all that time. He's my soulmate. People are going to talk but just follow your heart.

TinaDewer: I agree with every1 here because I've had mixed experiences. It helped 2 talk 2 some 1 who is bisexual.

I pick up my phone and call Shu.

'Shu, why are you a lesbian and not bisexual?'

'Hello, Maddie,' she says. 'How are you? I'm fine, thanks. It's a lovely day outside.'

I might be in my garden again, but Shu must be close to an active road because I can hear streams of pedestrian traffic, snippets of different conversations and the beeping horns of impatient drivers.

'Sorry, Shu. You're right,' I say. 'Let me start again. How are you, and do you miss men at all?'

She laughs. 'You're fucking weird, but there's usually a reason for it, so let's make this quick. No, I don't miss men – they're still fucking everywhere. I'm a lesbian because women are more sexually attractive.'

'Do you find me attractive?'

'No.'

I frown. 'Don't you want to take a minute to think about it?'

'No need. You're not my type.'

'Because you don't think I'm pretty? I knew it.'

'Because you start a phone call by asking why people are lesbians,' she counters. 'Where is this coming from?'

'Just curious.'

'Look, I'm a lesbian because women are better, okay?' she says. 'We're incredible but we're the only ones willing to admit it. I honestly think people should give me money and presents because I'm able to bleed for five days every month, from my *vagina*, and— What are you looking at?'

I look around my garden. 'Shu, who are you yelling at?'

'Some guy on the street. Staring like he's never heard the words *bleed* and *vagina* before.'

'Where are you right now?'

'Outside work.'

'So, the middle of Liverpool Street?'

'Yeah,' she says. 'Anyway, we bleed for five days every month and don't die. Statistically, we outlive men, too. Do you know how much blood I've lost since puberty? I'm on my period today and went for a run this morning. A *run*, when my uterus is ripping itself to pieces. Then I came into work. Maddie, if a man came into work with blood running down his leg or out of his dick, the boss would say "A&E or home? Which do you want?" I'm fucking superhuman.'

'It's hard to argue with that, Shu.'

'Plus, we look and smell better.'

Who does Alex think smells better? Or is it like having cake and eating it too (a phrase I've never understood because what else would you do with cake?) and he gets to be with nice-smelling women *and* handy-with-tools men?

If you were a real feminist, you'd be good with tools, too.

Or are these all stereotypes and not only am I not a feminist, I'm sexist?

'Were you ever bi, then?' I ask. 'Was there maybe an intersection, a space of time, right before you became a full-time lesbian?'

'I kind of went right there, to be honest. Being bi just wasn't my vibe, no shade. Love who you want and all of that. What is this, a research project? Mads, are you bi?'

'We're all a little bi, Shu.'

'Fuck off.'

'Okay, I'm not. Women are nicer to look at, but I don't think I'd want to deal with two vaginas when one requires such maintenance as it is, you know?'

'No,' she says. 'Your time's up. Bye, Mads.'

She ends the call.

On Saturday I spend two hours getting ready before accepting that jeans (the second pair I tried on since the first don't fit me anymore) and a red jumper are as good as it's going to get.

When I arrive at the Scandinavian-style coffee shop that smells of warm butter, sugar and cinnamon, Alex is at a table by the window. He stands when he sees me and smiles. Thankfully, he looks like he took his profile picture this morning. Exactly as advertised. His brown hair is swept back and he has on Converse, jeans and a plain white tee.

'Hello, Maddie. Glad you could make it,' he says – deep and friendly with the slightest American lilt.

We sit and on his table is a pot of tea, two cups, a Danish pastry for him and a brownie for me.

I point to the brownie. 'How did you know I wouldn't stand you up?'

'I only hoped you wouldn't and told myself that if you did, I would eat your brownie as consolation.' He smiles again. Or maybe he hasn't stopped smiling? 'It's nice to properly meet you. You're very pretty.'

'Oh, thank you.' I try not to look away. 'You're also very . . . the male version of pretty.'

He laughs. 'I think that's handsome,' he says, 'but I'll take pretty. Can I get you a coffee or anything?'

'I don't mind some of your tea.'

'This is green tea,' he says, pouring himself a cup. 'Have you had it before?'

'No, but happy to try it.' As he pours me a cup, I say, 'You didn't bring your dog?'

'I should have, but I thought I'd save him in case I needed help securing a second date.'

I smile at him and try green tea for the first time. It's a little bitter but instantly warming.

'So, how have you been?' he asks.

My face falls and I brace myself before remembering that Alex doesn't actually know how I should be feeling.

'Pretty good,' I answer. I tell him about *Love Stories* and make up a spontaneous evening bike ride for last night. He asks what I've got planned for the rest of my weekend. I offer him half of my brownie while I think of

276

something interesting to say. I come up short so end up sharing a lie.

'Tomorrow my friend Em and I are going for brunch in Highbury,' I tell him, 'but today I'm just going to pop home to say hi to the parents, then my friend's having a barbeque at her place. Which reminds me, I don't want to turn up empty-handed, so I should remember to go to the shops and pick up a few bits. What about you?'

'Well, it's my sister's baby shower tomorrow, but tonight I might foist myself on my flatmates – they're going to catch a movie.'

If I'd been honest about not doing much, would he have asked to extend this date?

'I haven't been to the cinema since . . .' *Ben.* 'In a long time,' I finish.

'Is this your first time online dating?' Alex asks.

'Ouch. Is it that obvious?'

'I promise it's not. I've just heard the cinema tends to be a good online-to-real-world date option.'

'It is my first time,' I admit. 'I've always been hesitant, but one night I decided to just go for it. You?'

'I'm a couple of weeks old now.'

'Any success stories?'

'Besides you?'

I roll my eyes. 'Smooth.' I drink my tea to hide the smile.

'Let me think . . .' he says. 'I've been on two dates before this one. I met a girl for an hour in the park, but it didn't work out. We didn't have a lot to talk about. Last week's date we just went to lunch, but yeah, he was nice.'

I jerk back at the "he" but collect myself. *Yes, Alex is bi. You knew that.*

'Did me saying "he" throw you?'

Shit, he can read minds? ABORT. ABORT.

'No.'

He laughs. 'It did! That's okay. If you've never dated someone who's bi, it can be jarring, like a sudden car brake.'

That's exactly how it felt.

'What is it like being bi?' I ask. 'Oh. Sorry, I didn't . . .'

'Don't be sorry,' he says. 'You can ask *me* because I'm happy to answer. It was tough at first because I asked myself all the questions: does a sex dream prove anything? Is it a phase? Who will I marry? I also had to challenge a lot of the normative constructs around being a man since I am "outside the norm".'

'Do you meet a lot of bisexual people on the app?'

'Not really, no,' he says. 'Which is a shame. Right now, I get asked about my sex life *a lot*. The word threesome has entered multiple chats. Some gay men don't take me seriously and some women doubt my motives. To the uneducated, bi-erasure is prevalent and bisexuality is just a pit stop. Gay is the green light and I've stopped at yellow.' *Note to self: Google bi-erasure.* 'To them it's kind of like, I can't be both; depending on who I marry, I'm either straight or gay. I used to just put "queer" on my profile, but I felt I was hiding myself a bit.'

I think of the messages I've gotten from men. They all started off innocuously enough, questions about my job and hobbies, but eventually the topic of conversation would land on my skin tone, my body shape and my perceived sexual prowess.

If only they knew the truth regarding the latter.

'I'm guessing online dating hasn't been easy for you?'

'Yeah, it's been . . . interesting,' he says.

Neither of us say it, but we're both thinking about me now. Dating as a Black woman.

'I can imagine,' I finally say.

He nods. 'Even so, I still have to ask, is me being bi a problem for you?'

'No.' I shake my head. 'No, I don't think it is.'

After almost two hours, we leave the coffee shop and stop outside my station.

Alex asks, 'Is it all right if I kiss you?'

It's a soft kiss that makes my stomach pleasantly churn. We say goodbye and I smile all the way to the supermarket. Then I remember that I don't actually have a barbeque to go to and head back to the flat.

Chapter Thirty

I sigh and flop back onto my bed.

I've been avoiding having to write this tribute, but I'm running out of time.

I love my dad and spent most of my time with him, so I expected the words to pour out of me, to effortlessly flow, but my notebook is still blank. This is an impossible thing to put into words. To some, it will look like we didn't have much of a relationship, even at the end. What is a relationship if there's hardly any conversation; if I don't know what he's thinking and he doesn't understand what I'm saying? The thought that Dawoud might find writing this easier than I do stings a little.

Q **Google** – How do you write a eulogy for your dad?

How to write your dad's eulogy

It's never easy at the beginning, but you want to start off by brainstorming. Put your dad's name in the middle of the page and around it, write down treasured memories and anecdotes. You'll find words start to flow after that. Essentially, you want to tell the audience about him. Was he funny? Did he have any dad jokes? What were his hobbies?

I shake my head. 'No, this isn't my dad,' I tell my phone. 'Anecdotes, jokes, hobbies? Dad was different. He was complicated.' I shake my head again. 'You wouldn't understand.'

A father's eulogy from a daughter

At the end of the day, a eulogy is all about memories. Daughters tend to be more 'Daddy's girl' than 'Mummy's girl' so you just have to talk about him: the times you shared together and the things he did to make you smile. Why are you a 'Daddy's girl'?

The words 'Daddy's girl' make me cringe.

What did he do to make me smile?

~~Whenever my dad came home with a chocolate bar for me, I~~

No, a singular chocolate bar isn't impressive if other dads are buying their daughters cars.

But the chocolate bars meant a lot to me. Other people just won't get why.

~~My dad was the light of my life~~

Then why did you leave?

~~My dad grew up as one of four siblings~~

And now there's only two left.

~~My dad enjoyed watching TV and~~
~~Before my father was diagnosed with Parkinson's, he liked~~
~~to~~
~~He spent most of his time~~
~~He used to be a librarian~~

I rub the bridge of my nose.
  I'll try again tomorrow.

Chapter Thirty-One

I'm returning to the office today after two weeks away. Already I'm looking forward to getting home this evening and telling myself I'll never have a first day back at the office after my dad died, again.

My hands shake as I button my cardigan and the heat I've come to know so well creeps up my throat.

When Jo is gone, I have ten minutes of silence, in which I use the toilet twice. I stand facing the front door. 'Please, God,' I whisper. 'Just let me get through the day.'

Like always, I hear no answer and will have to wait to find out whether He's heard me.

Mum LONDON
God is with you Maame. Have a good day and call me if work is too much

It strikes me that my mother would not be who I called in the event of a bad day because, chances are, I'd end up feeling worse or, at the very least, dramatic and ungrateful. But perhaps I shouldn't assume. Everyone has the element of surprise within them.

*　　*　　*

The train ride isn't long enough and my heart beats hard and fast at the looming sight of the OTP building. I enter with my fob key alongside Tina in Sales. We know *of* each other; she says hello and I parrot a reply, then she turns the corner to her department.

I'm relatively early, so not many people are in yet.

Kathy says, 'Hi, Maddie, how are you?'

I smile and pretend not to notice the head tilt and answer a quiet, 'Fine, thank you.'

Thea, who's sitting beside her, nods and smiles, and I take that as two birds with one stone.

I walk to my desk, exhaling. If that is what I can expect, maybe—

Kris opens her door. 'Maddie! Welcome back! Come in a sec.'

The conversation is less painful than I feared and in a sentence, I'm free to go home at any time if things feel too overwhelming.

The only thing I want today is no attention and it comes at me from everyone. My palms are soon dented with half-moons and the inside of my bottom lip is bleeding. I've used the toilet six times and it's only past lunch, which I haven't eaten. Instead I forget my container in the fridge and leave the building.

When I'm back, Penny invites me into her office to repeat what Kris said. I nod and smile convincingly.

For the rest of the afternoon, I barely use my voice because I don't want to invite conversation. I just want to exist. I keep my head down and work.

At the end of the day, my to-do list looks like this:

Check prelims and endmatter of HVT
~~Reschedule TR meeting~~
Change pub date for RPS and add royalties
~~Email David about contracts~~
Anglicise text for DF
~~Organise review copies to be sent out~~
~~Draft letter for above~~
Unanswered emails
Add *Hungry* to MDX
~~Type out pre-order pack notes~~
~~Penny's expenses~~
~~Find missing £5.72 receipt~~
~~Invoices x3~~
~~Excel spreadsheet of MTS editorial and design costs~~
~~Public enquiries~~
~~Add amends to publishing schedule then upload on database~~
~~Order milk jug for the office~~
~~Send out foreign rights deals for approval~~

I write down my to-do list for tomorrow so I can keep busy, same as today. Then I look up and realise I'm the last person in the office.

I shut down my computer, pack my bag and slip on my jacket. I remain seated, staring at the quiet office. The only noise is the hum of the dishwasher – not sure who turned it on as the task typically falls to me. Well, it could have been me.

Am I hungry at all? I could probably go without dinner.

I turn off the office lights and go home.

Chapter Thirty-Two

> **Alex**
> How do you feel about bowling tonight?

> **Maddie**
> On a school night? Sounds like a second date.

It turns out I'm rather skilled at bowling. It wouldn't have been my preferred hidden talent of choice, but right now, it's serving me well.

'How was the barbeque?' Alex asks.

'Barbeque?' *Yes, your fake weekend plans.* 'Oh, right, it was great.' I recall what I overheard Jo saying to Cam. 'Dad burnt more than he should have but called it caramelised. Classic.'

'So it was your barbeque and not your friend's?'

'What? Oh.' I look at the scoreboard to buy time. 'No, the barbeque was at her place, but our families are really close. We've known each other since we were babies and our dads are best friends. So naturally they had a cook-off.' I smile as I say this, at the thought of a big, warm extended family bonded together by decades of memories and charcoaled burgers. 'How was the film?'

'It was fine.' He bowls and knocks down five pins. 'But I don't love sitting in the dark for hours during the day. It's like my body itches to go outside and do something physical.'

'Like lose at bowling?'

Alex raises his eyebrows. 'I'm not that far behind! Be warned, all great comebacks start like this, with a cocky opponent.'

'You're right. I should be more graceful.' I watch as he approaches the alley, ball in hand. I shout, 'You suck, Alex!' just as he stands at the line.

He laughs, 'Mature!' and rolls his ball into the gutter.

After the fifth round, we sit in a booth with a milkshake each, watching a couple bowl. They look to be in their forties and she's winning but we think he's letting her.

'So, senior sales executive but photography?' I ask. 'Tell me more.'

Alex rests his arm behind me – he has one of those smiles where his sharp incisors manage to amplify it to twice its worth. 'Yeah, so sales is my to-live job and photography is my dream job. I used to have big dreams when I was a kid, or maybe they just seemed big because I was so small. Typically, as I got older, I just wanted to make a lot of money; I thought if I could buy everything I wanted when I wanted it, then I'd be happy. So I got a job with a great salary, et cetera, but it just doesn't . . .' His inability to verbalise this specific feeling has him settle for a gesture instead. He taps his chest, right above his heart. 'It just doesn't live in here,' he says. 'I'm a late subscriber to the theory of being responsible for your own happiness and only realised recently that your job has a huge part to play in that. I think a lot of us prioritise money and appearances and instant gratification. And in the process, genuine happiness became undervalued. Does that make sense?'

I nod. 'It does. I had a theatre job that made me miserable, but I needed a steady salary.. Then I was fired.'

He straightens up. 'What happened?'

I tell him the whole story; I pause for him to laugh at Avi and roll his eyes at Katherine; I tell him about the lack of fulfilment and the alienation. 'I cried almost every day. I thought I was depressed.'

Woah, that's a big word to use on a second date. I don't think Lisa Fiener would approve.

Subconscious Maddie removes the sleeping mask from her face and rubs her eyes. *Hey, at least you're telling him the truth now.* She stretches excessively. *See how good it feels? Telling him all about CGT. You didn't even tell your own mother the truth about that.*

I turn to Alex, who only considers me. *Why* did I tell him so much?

To negate the lies. Yes, maybe.

To give him at least some authentic piece of yourself. He's been nothing but honest with me; I owe him some truth.

Doesn't make the preceding lies forgivable and, wow, have there been many. I've become so good at lying. *Yes, you have.* At inventing an alternate Maddie, a happy, carefree Maddie. A Maddie that's effortless to love. A Maddie I wish I was.

Maybe you want to tell him the truth now, though? Do I? Why would I want that when the truth is so sad? I like Alex, but the person he thinks I am isn't real and I'm not ready for my reality and this fantasy to clash in an irreparable way.

Alex puts a soft hand on mine. 'Were you depressed?'

I wipe at an imaginary stain on my jeans when my pulse starts hissing. 'No, no. Depression is . . . it's so big, and I didn't have a reason, you know? A reason that stands out. I wasn't stressed or overworked or under pressure like Katherine. *That* was depression.'

'Maddie,' he says softly, 'you were stuck in a micro aggressive, passive-aggressive, emotionally trying job, and then were unceremoniously fired. There's a reason.'

The woman screams with joy at having bowled a strike.

I shake my head. 'I don't know. People go through worse every day.'

'Comparison is no friend of mental health,' Alex says. He leans forward so I can spot the lighter specks in his eyes. 'What you go through and how it affects you is just as valid as someone dealing with their own situation. What did your parents say when you told them? They sound the supportive type.'

I blink and remember which Maddie I'm supposed to be right now.

Losing track already?

I rest my palms flat on either side of my hips, feeling them prickle with sweat. I focus my attention on watching my legs swing back and forth. 'I didn't tell them,' I say. 'I didn't want them to worry.'

'Maddie.'

'I know! I know, but it's okay.' *Not to mention, it's now impossible to tell half of your parents because one of them is dead, and when you told the other, her response was: pray harder.* 'Really,' I add, 'I'm so much better now.'

289

You're the worst you've ever been.

'Since leaving the theatre job?'

Well, OTP could be the new CGT – it's TBC: to be confirmed.

I look at Alex and try to brighten my face with a smile. 'Exactly!'

I've little doubt in my mind that there's some kind of ethical code I'm breaking by withholding a life-altering truth such as a death in my family. But there are only three responses someone you've just started dating can give to: my father died last month.

Oh, Maddie, my condolences/sorry for your loss. Tell me about it/him. How did it happen? Why? How are you doing? – i.e. questions I don't want to give a practical stranger the answers to.

Not even three weeks ago? Should you be *out*? Should you be dating? Do you want me to take you home? – i.e. questions which in turn will make me feel like shit, a terrible daughter and a rotten, irremovable stain upon humanity's cloth.

Oh ... wow. That's heavy. (Insert awkward silence, unsubtle glances towards the door and fidgeting here.)

Lies it is.

$\boxed{\text{Q \quad \textbf{Google} – Symptoms of depression}}$

Unhappiness

Hopelessness

Crying

Anxiety

Exhaustion yet difficulty sleeping
Suicidal thoughts
Appetite changes
Most people can feel all of the above when going through
a hard time or a major life change and these feelings tend
to improve once the storm has passed rather than being
signs of depression.

See? I knew it. There's no greater life change or hard time
than your dad dying as soon as you leave him. The panic
attacks, insomnia and loss of appetite didn't start until
after he passed away.

But everything else occurred before.

That's only because I was unhappy at work – another
hard time.

Comments:

Dinah: It's scary how many of these symptoms I've been
displaying lately.

Joel: This wasn't helpful. Everyone feels all of these things
some time or other.

Frances: I have to say these symptoms are all very vague
and the last note misleading and detrimental. To attribute the symptoms of depression solely to 'hard times'
may have you feeling like you should wait it out instead
of seeking professional help. What if you're going
through a series of 'hard times'? You'll be waiting for the
storm to pass until you're dead. Depression varies from
person to person. For example, I had extreme mood
swings, which isn't mentioned above and is rarely talked
about regarding depression. I was on cloud nine one
day and being tormented in hell the next, and things

did not change until I got help. So you need to ask yourself (and answer truthfully): do you think you're depressed? The answer is obviously yes, otherwise you wouldn't be reading this page. Do yourself a favour and seek help.

Chapter Thirty-Three

On Wednesday, I join Penny in her office. She looks at me and smiles. She has on the same blue eyeshadow she wore during my interview. Her blond hair is even shorter now and it sticks up in corners she maybe can't see.

'Maddie,' she says. 'I don't know if you're aware, but we have a counsellor who comes into the building twice a month. I'd like you to see her, just to keep on top of things.'

I frown. 'Am I doing something wrong?'

'Not at all,' she says. 'You're flying through your admin; I've just noticed you've been arriving early and staying late since your return. Allan in Facilities said he saw you leave at 9.30 Monday night. You're very quiet in the office and sometimes, well, morose may be a little too far, but you're certainly not yourself – understandably. You did seem perkier this morning, but I imagine your feelings during a time like this alternate in waves.'

I'm burning with embarrassment at the idea of being The Girl Who Clearly Can't Cope. I briefly put myself in Penny's shoes. She must hate having this conversation as much as I hate hearing it. She shouldn't have to deal with second-hand grief. I already know Kris and Eliza have lost someone and they didn't mention needing a counsellor brought in.

'I'm fine,' I insist. 'I can get my work done, same as every—' I cut myself off thinking of Katherine, crying in the toilets, working when her mental health was at risk, pretending everything was okay. I asked Claire if it mattered people thought her weak, so long as she got help. I'd no idea I'd struggle to take my own advice.

Depression can do that to a person.

I shake my head and say nothing.

'We want to help you, Maddie,' Penny says. 'Career longevity is our goal with you here at OTP – hence our counsellor. We thought it best to pair you with a Black woman specialising in bereavement. So, every other Friday at three in the HR room. You don't need to tell anyone what you're doing and you're of course excused from whatever meetings may fall into that hour slot. In fact, the counsellor is here today and free for the next half-hour if you'd like to pop down and introduce yourself before lunch. How does that sound?' Penny nods and smiles until I mirror.

I've never been to the HR room, so it takes me a couple of wrong turns to find it. I can't help but feel like I'm in trouble, that I am doing something wrong. You go to therapy if you have serious problems, if you're a threat to yourself. People lose relatives every day but they're not all in therapy, so why me?

I can't tell Mum about this. Unless God works for the HR department, she'll find this unacceptable.

I knock on the door and enter a small room with only a sofa, chair (where a Black woman sits) and wooden table in between. The floor is grey carpet and the walls are cream, with only one small window and a clock. It's warmer in here than it is upstairs and I wonder if there's an intentional reason for that.

'Hello, Madeleine? Penny mentioned you might pop in. Please take a seat,' the woman says. Her hair stands out in an Afro and her lips are well-defined with a sharp Cupid's bow. I think, it must be easy to apply lipstick.

'Oh, that's okay. I'm only here to introduce myself,' I tell her. 'But I'll see you on Friday.'

'You're here now and I'm available, so why don't you take a seat?' She gestures to the chair opposite; her tone is gentle but no-nonsense.

I put my bag down and do as she says.

'Madeleine or Maddie?' she asks.

'Maddie is fine, thanks.'

'Good. You can call me Angelina.' She crosses one leg over the other. She's wearing a navy pantsuit with a white blouse underneath and high heels on her feet. I want to ask if she has suits in brighter colours. A yellow, maybe. 'How are you today?'

'Fine, thank you. You know, as I can be.'

Angelina nods and waits , her mouth closed as she smiles. I outwait her. 'And returning to work? This is day three?'

I nod. 'Fine, too.'

She waits and I start pinching my palms.

'I just wish . . .'

'Yes?'

'I think you'll judge me.'

'It's not my job to judge.'

'That doesn't mean you won't.'

'That's fine to think so,' Angelina says, although I notice she doesn't deny it. 'What were you going to say? You just wish . . .'

'I wish people would stop asking how I am.'

'That's natural.'

'Yes, but I'd also be offended if they didn't. Like, how dare you not care enough to ask? Even if you think I'd rather be left alone, it's social convention that you ask.'

'Go on.'

'I wish everyone would ask me how I am at once,' I say, 'so I can give them all one answer simultaneously because now I'm just repeating myself, which feels like a disservice to my dad, and then sometimes, the person asking just waits, stares, and I think, do they want me to break down and cry, are they judging me and wondering why I'm not? Or are they giving me space to talk and that's not actually what I want right now, but maybe they know better and it's what I need? I don't know. I got really angry because Melanie wasn't in on Monday, which meant I'd have to start all over again the next day and the next day with someone new and so on. It's just tiring. I'm tired.'

'You are entitled to feel tired.'

'That's it?'

'Yes.'

'You have nothing else to say to all of that?'

She uncrosses her legs. 'Were you hoping for a solution today, Maddie? I'm afraid there isn't one. I'm just here for you to talk to.'

'But then couldn't I speak to anyone? Why are you different?'

'Perhaps there's some advice or reassurance I can provide you that others maybe haven't.'

'Right.'

'You sound sceptical? Has well-meaning advice or words of reassurance proved fruitless so far?'

'You could say that,' I answer. On my first day back, my

mum said: God is with you, Maame. Have a good day and call me if work is too much. It was too much, but I didn't call her; I just skipped lunch and walked around Farringdon.'

'Your mother calls you Maame?'

'Yes. Maame means—'

'I know what it means.' Angelina smiles – a bit sadly, if I'm not mistaken. 'I'm the eldest of three sisters and it's what my mother called me.'

'You're Ghanaian?'

'I am indeed. Which means I'm well aware of the importance of names in our culture. In many ways, they're given to us in an attempt to speak to our future. Growing up, I had many friends named Glory, Patience, Wisdom, Comfort. It seems there is a link between our names and our supposed destiny. We could apply that thinking to the name Maame: the responsible one. The woman. The mother. Often before her time.' Angelina closes her notebook. 'How do you feel about that name, Maddie?'

I shift. This question has suddenly made me very uncomfortable. 'Why are we talking about my nickname?'

'Because I'd like to get to know you,' she answers simply. 'I mainly provide counselling services to companies with a mental-health initiative and it's been a while since I've seen someone so young with such heavy shoulders.'

'I can't be the worst person you've met.'

'*Worst* would imply there's something wrong with you – and there's not. A person's troubles are not measured by the size of those troubles, but by how much they weigh on the individual carrying them. I've noticed already you're very concerned about how others feel rather than focusing on how *you* feel. I asked about your first days back and all you've spoken about is whether you're reacting in a way that your colleagues will find appropriate, or easy to process. It's not your job to make your colleagues feel comfortable all of the time. That in itself is a burden too heavy to carry when grieving. I imagine your instinct to put others first, even if detrimental to yourself, also plays a part in your personal life.' She fixes her gaze on me. 'But I believe I asked you how you felt about the name Maame.'

Seconds tick by before I hear myself say, 'I used to love it.'

'And now?'

'Now? Now, I might hate it.' I give my brain time to process. 'I think I hate what it means and what it's done to me.'

'What has it done to you?'

'It made me grow up,' I answer. 'It made me grow up when I should have had more time. It made my dad overlook me when I was a child, my mum leave me behind, and my brother get away with doing the bare minimum. It made me lonely and it made me sad. It made me responsible and guilty. It made me someone, if given the choice, I wouldn't want to be.'

After I leave the HR room, I head straight for the exit.

The last thing Angelina said to me was that maybe Maddie and Maame could use some distance, as if it would be easy to separate the two. They're the same person – always have been.

I start walking until I realise I've gone from Farringdon to Tottenham Court Road. I make it to the traffic lights just after the station and when I turn back, I spot Mum through the glass window of a coffee shop.

What's Mum doing here? Is she looking for me? She rarely comes to central London because, and I quote: 'It's too noisy and busy for no reason.' But there she is, sat at a table by the window, and if she'd only look to her left, she'd notice me. I think she's about to before she's joined by a man in jeans and a white T-shirt. Immediately, instinctively, I know this man is Kwaku, my mum's . . . boyfriend.

The green man signals we can cross the street, but I let people push past me and tut until I'm jostled to the edge. I can't take my eyes off the coffee-shop window. Through the glass, I can see Kwaku must be in his fifties, like Mum, but he's very well built and he sits with his back straight and his hands now holding my married mother's.

Widowed mother's.

I creep closer and crouch behind a letter box like the world's shittiest spy, and stare. Kwaku gently rubs the back of Mum's hand and my first thought is, how does he manage to do something so gently with hands as big as his? My second thought is, he looks nothing like my dad.

Maybe that's the point.

Mum looks down at their entwined hands and I notice her head is slightly bowed and her shoulders loose. Then when he moves to sit next to her, his arm around her shoulders, she turns miniature. She rests her head on his shoulder and only then, with her head upturned, do I see the tears running down her cheeks.

I straighten my back because I've never seen my mum so soft and taken care of. Kwaku wipes her eyes with his thumb, kisses the top of her head and she closes her eyes. He loves her and, worst of all, she loves him, too. Suddenly, this is unforgivable.

I walk up to the window, not taking my eyes off them until Kwaku clocks me and frowns. Realisation hits him between the eyes, assisted by Mum sitting upright with a face slack with horror. In that moment, I wonder if it's too late to pretend I didn't see anything because this version of my mum unnerves me. There's no confidence or assuredness; she's stuck with no way out. But I'm down the rabbit hole. People sat at surrounding tables are staring too, at the young woman with her nose inches away from the glass.

Then I'm running, running across the road and into Tottenham Court Road station, down the escalators and into the next train arriving on the platform, but sat in an almost-empty carriage, I realise this is not a spontaneous journey to who knows where. I'm going to Thornton Heath via Balham. Then I'll take the 250 bus home.

And I'll wait for Mum there.

Chapter Thirty-Four

But Mum isn't the first person through the door.

Whilst I'm pacing in the kitchen, clenching and unclenching my fists, trying to make sense of the words and scenes running in my head, James walks in.

'What are you doing here?'

He scratches his head. 'Mum told me you saw her.'

A car's engine dies down outside. 'Oh, good to know you two can band together in times of a crisis. I'll have to keep that in mind.'

Mum runs in and I start to clap.

'Here she is! James, look! Here. She. Is. God's number-one spokesperson!'

James's eyes widen. 'Mads, are you all right?'

I'm shivering and sweating and I eye the sink in case I need to vomit. 'No. No, I'm not.' They both try to say something, but all I can hear is my own voice. 'So, Mum, adultery's the one you went for, huh?'

'Madeleine!'

'I mean, out of all the rules from the Big Boss Upstairs, what is adultery? Top ten? Coming in hot, right under murder!' My voice alternates in pitch whilst it familiarises itself with my rage. 'Where were you when my dad died?'

Mum doesn't answer, she doesn't need to. She was with *him*. Her face is pale, her eyes are pink and she's shaking too. This is the first time I've made my mum cry, but my own tears today won't even crack her top fifty.

I step towards her. 'You tell me how to live, how to pray and who to see, but who's telling *you* these things?'

'Maame, please—'

'DON'T CALL ME MAAME!'

Mum's head jerks back and even James tilts his. Like me, they both don't know where that came from.

'I am so tired of everyone in this family acting the way they do because *Maame* is always there to pick up the pieces, to sort out your mess, to look after you. You are both supposed to be looking after me! You.' I point at Mum. 'With your condescending "adages" and "your mother knows these things", your nitpicking and nothing I do ever being *enough*. There is always something else *Maame* can do for you.'

James claps. 'That's what I've been saying! Mum needs to—'

'James, fuck off.'

Subconscious Maddie, like everyone in the room, stands with her mouth gaping open.

'What?' I ask him. 'Why do you look so surprised when *useless*, thy name is James! When have you ever put me first? Huh, when? Exactly! I am the youngest one in this fucking family but no one takes care of me. No one gives a shit! Sometimes I think I could get by just fine without the two of you, but I can't help but wonder, where would you both be without me? Now that Dad's no longer here, one day you're going to find out the answer to that question. One day, sweet, little dependable, pushover, spineless, pathetic Maddie is going to leave you two to pick each other apart!'

'Maame, you must—'

'*I said*, don't call me Maame!'

We all stare at each other for a time.

I wipe the spit from my chin and ignore the sweat under my nose and running down my back. My throat is dry and a headache is building at my temples. Subconscious Maddie is sat in the corner crying. I walk towards the door but turn back only to say, 'My name is Maddie.'

And this new Maddie feels great. I mean, *really* great. She's cool, audacious and carefree. She's finally everything she's always wanted to be.

After leaving the house, I sent an email to Kris telling her I felt sick after counselling and went straight home. Whatever. Then I got back to the flat and made myself comfortable in the living room. Threw my feet up on the sofa and turned the TV on. When Jo walked in hours later, she stopped short and said, 'Oh.' I looked her in the eyes with raised brows and said: 'Everything okay?' She gave me a tight smile, nodded and went straight to her room. I ordered a takeaway, ignored the calls from Mum and James until my phone battery died, and fell asleep on the sofa.

Yes, the new Maddie felt great, but it's a shame she didn't bother to stay for very long.

I wake up at 8 a.m. feeling sick, foggy and anxious.

How will I convincingly lie at work today?

Please, you're a pro now.

What am I going to say when I finally do have to talk to Mum?

Cross that bridge when you get to it.

Did I really swear so many times?

Yes, yes you fucking did.

Chapter Thirty-Five

Two hours into work, I realise I should have taken today off too.

I'm monosyllabic and on the verge of tears all day. Everyone gives me *the* look, the one where they glance my way, then at someone else, before nodding in my direction. I ignore them all because I don't want to be called into Penny's office. Thankfully, her day is too full of meetings for her to pay any attention to me.

I work through lunch and leave at four. Only outside does it feel like I can finally breathe and the relief has me burst into tears on the street. People walk by, throwing me looks but continuing with their day. I understand. They might have plans which talking to me might delay.

I walk back into the OTP building to use the toilet and wipe my face.

> **Alex**
> Still on to meet at 6?

I really miss the new Maddie but I don't have time to lament her recent departure. It was already time for me to be someone else, time to be yet another Maddie. Alex's Maddie.

*   *   *

I'm so glad to see Alex that when I spot him exiting the station, I run up and hug him. So quickly has he become my safety net, my *break*.

'You know what, Maddie?' he says into my neck. 'I've missed you, too.'

The plan is to walk through the park to his flat and watch a film. He asks me about my day and I make it up with ease, with pleasure.

I should google if lying to this degree is a skill performed deftly only by the criminally insane. My lies are stretching so far from the truth that I can no longer see them. I shiver at the thought of my current family affairs.

No, that didn't happen in this world. Alex's Maddie simply came home from work last night, had dinner with her flatmates, and went to bed.

As he tells me about his day, Subconscious Maddie sits, looking far from impressed. She folds her arms and pushes the twisted braids from her eyes. *He thinks Dad is alive!*

I ignore her and she adds, *Ben lied to you. How did that make you feel?*

I lose my footing, tripping over loose rocks. Alex reaches out in time to grab my hand. 'You okay?'

I nod, wiping my forehead before looking at him. He's smiling, using one hand to shield his eyes from the evening sun whilst the other still holds onto mine. What if I did tell him? Just came out and said it. I lied about going to a barbeque. My best friend's name is Nia, not Emma. Our dads aren't best friends. Our dads are dead. Hers died ten years ago, mine just under a month ago. I'm so, so sorry I lied.

There's no way he'd stay; honestly, I'd judge him if he did, because it's a crazy thing to lie about. But to lose Alex now would be unbearable. I'd have nothing but grief left. We're not serious; I know this won't last, but I need him to stick around until the days don't seem as long, until the funeral's over and I'm better, more stable in this new reality of mine.

So you're using him? No!

Like Ben used you? Shut up!

What happens to Alex and fantasy Maddie when you're "better"?

'Ouch – Maddie?'

I look up at Alex. 'What?'

He holds up our hands. 'Tight grip,' he says. 'You sure you're okay?'

'Sorry!' I let go of his hand.

Subconscious Maddie looks smug and I internally remind her she's meant to be on my side.

I am on the side of truth!

I look at Alex again and smile hard. 'I'm fine, just a little clumsy.'

But my thoughts follow me through the park and up to his flat.

It's halfway through the film when Alex kisses me. I know where he wants things to go and for one brief, inexcusable moment, I tell myself sex will make up for my lies. It has to because I need him. I need a pause from my life and the emotional turmoil determined to come with it. I get that respite when I'm not being me. I get that respite with Alex.

My cardigan comes off and goosebumps cover my skin. It's okay. I like Alex. I like him a lot. He's kind and thoughtful and easy. *That's why you're having sex with him. That is the only reason why.* But I can't connect his lips to my skin. I stare at his living-room ceiling and think maybe I'm not a fan of foreplay.

'Is this okay?' he asks, positioning himself above me.

I nod and he doesn't read my mind. When he enters me, it's less painful than it was with Ben, but it isn't comfortable; I shift under him because I feel like he's in the wrong place, even though he can't be. I accept what it is, but no matter how closely I hold him, if I shut my eyes it feels like we're miles apart. The inability to connect, the stifling, undeniable dissociation with first my mind and body, and then my body and his, somehow feels worse than the acute physical pain I experienced with Ben. *That* I at least managed to place; it was temporary, and promised the gift of relief if I gave it a few hours. With Alex, the sofa's cushion rubs and pulls at my back. I feel my body is being used, but I can't understand why when this is something I told myself I wanted.

There's silence between us after. I ignore it, but it follows us to the kitchen. I watch Alex as he watches the kettle. I don't want to speak into the silence because I'm scared of what it will give back. Alex taps the counter; I feel him gearing up. He pours hot water into a mug with a green teabag at the bottom and places it in front of me. Then he takes a seat at the dining table.

'There's something you're not telling me,' he says quietly.

I want to hold it in, to lie again. I'm just so good at it. For something so universally condemned, lying truly appeals to me; it often seems like the only way to maintain peace and comfortable continuity. But another part of me is tired – tired of pretending and keeping track, tired of being worn out after sex, like I've spent the entire time running away from my own shadow.

'I don't particularly like sex,' I tell him. 'It's painful and always has been.'

'Oh.'

I watch him consider all the paths this conversation might take him down, but he doesn't need to tell me something so clearly printed on his face.

'That's a deal-breaker, isn't it?'

'No,' he says quickly.

I smile sadly. 'Please be honest.'

Alex drops his head into his hands and something sharp hits me in the chest: a burning swell of rejection. Yet again.

'I'm sorry, Maddie,' he says. 'I'm going to sound like such a dick, but sex is important to me; I need that physical connection and intimacy. I wish I could pretend otherwise, but I know myself and I don't want to promise you – especially you – one thing and secretly want another.'

I look down at my cup of green tea. The water's completely taken up the teabag's colour and the smell is partially medicinal, but it's soothing, like that of eucalyptus.

'Maybe we can try again?' I offer.

Alex has already sat back in his chair, pulled away from the table and from me, but I'm desperate. 'Maybe it will get better and I just have to keep trying?'

'I can't know you're in pain and still . . .' He looks up at least. 'I really am sorry.'

It's that easy to get rid of me. To erase me from his life and whatever slot I may have filled in his future. He doesn't need to think on me a little longer. Short-term.

Just like you wanted, right?

I nod my head because this is what I deserve, and he does the same.

One thing I can appreciate is his honesty, because God knows he received none of that from me.

Chapter Thirty-Six

Friday afternoon, Penny reminds me of my first official appointment with Angelina. I nod. 'I'm going now.'

Penny never reminds me of anything because it's my job to do that for her, but I know it's because I look like the bird the cat dragged in and I can only imagine what people told her once I'd left the office yesterday.

I put my computer on sleep mode and head downstairs.

Today Angelina's hair is straight and tucked behind her ears and her wooden earrings almost rest on her collarbone. Her lips, like her nails, are painted a burnt orange – *how bold*.

'Maddie, you look . . . Are you all right?'

'Of course,' I answer. Last time, the HR room was hot, but I'm shivering today. 'My dad's funeral is tomorrow, so I've not had much sleep. I'm fine though. I've been meaning to ask, do you have a yellow pantsuit?'

Her face remains unreadable. 'I do.'

'Me too, but I still haven't worn it.' I look at the clock. Only two minutes have passed. 'I talk to myself a lot. In my head and out loud,' I tell her. 'Is that weird?'

'Why do you talk to yourself out loud?'

I shrug. 'Sometimes my head is too full and it makes what I'm thinking clearer. I know not to do it in public.'

'So you're often alone, I take it?' she asks. 'If you talk to yourself a lot, but not in public, you must be by yourself quite a bit.'

'I like my own company.'

'Have you always?'

'What do you mean?'

'I believe in two dominant introvert types. Those who have always enjoyed their own company and those who have grown to prefer it because they weren't given much of a choice. Which do you think you fit into?'

I think about how small my room back home is and how I used to tell myself I loved it because its purpose was to house only one and I fit comfortably inside. James had a life I wasn't cool or old enough to fit into, Mum had a life on another continent, and my dad had his slowly taken away.

'Maybe the second,' I answer.

'Do you talk much to other people?'

'Of course.'

'About more significant things?' Angelina clarifies. 'Not just every day pleasantries but private matters. How you are and what you're thinking, for example.'

'Why?'

'Maybe you talk to yourself because then you don't have to factor in another person's reaction. Or even, you enjoy engaging in conversations where you can be completely open and honest, but maybe you feel the only way to do this safely is when alone. Do you tend to keep how you're feeling bottled up?'

She steadies me with a look that informs me she already knows the answer.

Our matters are private, remember? You tell one person,

they tell another, and the next thing you know, important people are asking all sorts of questions.

Saliva is building in my mouth and I hope I'm not going to be sick. 'Maybe,' I answer. 'I'll have to think about that one.' I look up again and five more minutes have passed. This isn't going by fast enough. 'I also say I love you a lot. Is *that* weird?'

Angelina tilts her head. 'What constitutes a lot?'

'People might think I use it too frequently and it's starting to lose meaning, but I do mean it every time I say it. At the end of a conversation, or when I'm saying goodbye to someone. I always make sure I say it.'

'Who do you say it to?'

'Oh, not *everyone*. Friends and family. People I love.'

'And maybe people you want to love you back?'

I don't answer.

'Do they verbally reciprocate?' she asks. 'Actually, do they ever say it first?'

'I'm sure they do. I just remember it always being a response.'

'What about your parents?' Angelina asks. 'Did they say it often?'

'I never heard them say it to each other. Is that weird?'

Angelina slowly closes her notebook and gently says, 'There is no weird, Maddie. Every individual's experience is unique. Did they ever say it to you?'

I shift in my seat. 'Say what? That they love me?' I nod. 'Of course. Well, my dad did twice. Once when he was drunk and another when he was . . . unwell. I think his brain had forgotten itself. A little loose and addled with medication at the time, you know? But I know he loved me; you can't not love your children, especially the unproblematic ones.'

'And your mother?'

'Yes, she must have.' I think of all the compliments Mum's given me; she calls me darling, her baby and a blessing. They're all the same thing as love. 'I tend to end our phone calls with I love you.'

'So, again, you initiate?'

I begin tapping my foot because my stomach feels like it has no lining. 'I'm sure she has said it first on multiple occasions, I just can't remember. She's not a bad mother.'

'I didn't say she was.'

I close my eyes and shake my head. 'I'm sorry. I thought these sessions were going to be about my dad passing away and the grieving process.'

'They are,' Angelina says. 'But you cannot hope to understand an end without starting at the beginning.'

'My mum does love me.'

'I didn't say she did not,' Angelina replies. 'I'm saying the opposite, rather.'

Bringing my hands together I feel my pulse jump.

'I think you know your mother loves you,' Angelina begins, 'but your uncertainty may stem from a lack of convention, of the typical. How someone shows you they love you has less to do with you and all to do with them. There are healthy and unhealthy expressions of love and not all of them should be accepted.'

This is meant to be about my mum, but I think about Dad and how I used to believe that if someone loved you, they had to *say* it, otherwise it wasn't real, it wasn't *known*, but I understand now that's not the case. My dad rarely said those three special words, whether due to his upbringing, his stoic generation, whatever, but I always knew, inexplicably, that he did.

'Many assume love is straightforward,' Angelina continues,

'when really it is the most complicated of things. There is a right way, a preferred way, for each individual, to love and be loved by someone – but there isn't only one way. I believe the difficulty of life has much to do with understanding and then navigating how the people you love both express and receive love themselves. It cannot be your responsibility, your burden, to reshape people into someone you'd like them to be. Ultimately, you must either accept a person for who they are, how they behave, how they express themselves emotionally, and find a healthy way to live with them, or let them go entirely. Either way, you must release yourself from that responsibility.' She pauses. 'What don't you want to talk about, Maddie?'

'I don't understand.'

'These questions of yours, whilst insightful, I think are intended to waste time.'

'Are they?'

'Maddie. You are splitting at the seam.'

My eyes are watering. My chest is tightening and my fingers are twitching. 'I just don't want to think too hard or too much today.'

'Why?'

I breathe out. 'It's exhausting, everything is exhausting. Talking, moving, feeling, thinking, living. I could use a break.' I catch her frown. 'That's not what I . . . I don't need an eternal break. I just . . . I'm fine.'

'Are you?'

'Yes! I know everyone must think I'm depressed—'

'You are suffering from depression, Maddie,' Angelina says. 'That much is simple to see.'

I look up from my lap and Angelina's face is still, but her eyebrows are joining in the middle. I hear my heart beat and want to stick my fingers in my ears.

'Why? Because my dad died? By that reasoning, almost everyone should be depressed. So many people have lost someone.'

'Comparing yourself to others and deeming yourself better off is no remedy for mental illness. The remedy is internal work – lots of it. But acknowledging the issue at hand must come first. You are suffering from depression, Maddie.'

I push my bottom lip into the top one and tears pool in the corners. 'But I'm carrying on, so I'm also fine.'

'You cannot be both.'

'I disagree.'

'All right,' she says calmly. 'For argument's sake, in what ways are you both fine and depressed?'

'I'm fine because I'm still living, I'm still going to work, returning home and waking up the next morning. I'm not so fine because my dad died right after I moved out, my mum is too difficult to comprehend and attempting to manage her drains me of everything but tears. I don't know what the fuck my brother is doing. The person keeping me momentarily sane broke up with me, but in his defence, I was lying to him – about everything. I think my flatmate hates me, so I stay in my room most of the time. I think I now hate that room, because I gave up my dad for that room.'

'Maddie—'

'I think my ideas are being stolen by my colleagues, but I honestly can't tell. I don't understand what intellectual property means. I want to ask Nia and Shu to drop everything and look after me again, but they have their own lives and maybe they're tired of feeling like babysitters and . . . it's hot in here!' I stand up, pulling at my jumper. 'Sorry, I . . . I just . . . When did it get so hot in here?'

'Maddie?'

Angelina's suddenly very blurry. Is she melting?

'Oh, it's happening again,' I say, stretching my collar. 'Panic attack. Anxiety. Something, I don't know, but I—'

There's a blinding light in my eye.

So it's true what they say about following the light when you die.

'Maddie?'

'God, is that you?'

'No, it's Doctor Rusher.'

'What?'

The light disappears and someone hoists me up and into a chair. My vision is still fuzzy when someone hands me a cup of water.

I fainted apparently, induced by a panic attack. Luckily, the doctor who visits the company a couple of times a month, a doctor who can only be seen by way of an appointment booked a week prior, is in the house. He decides I don't need to be taken to A&E, but I do need to go home and rest, and that I should book some time in with a GP just to be safe. Ask for something to help with anxiety. 'A beta blocker, perhaps,' he says.

I notice Penny standing in the corner; I wonder if she regrets hiring me.

'I can work from home.'

'No, you heard the doctor,' she says gently. 'You need to take today off. I'll call you in the morning to see how you are. Kris gave your mother a call and she's on her way.'

I almost frown, wishing she'd called Nia or Shu, but fix my face in time. 'Thank you.'

Penny tuts at my sincerity. 'Don't be silly.'

*　　*　　*

315

Mum was very quiet when she came to pick me up. She asked if I was okay, felt my head, held onto my arm as we left the building, but said nothing else in the cab ride to the flat.

I was planning on going straight to bed when we got back, but Mum steers me until she finds the kitchen and sits me at the table before filling a glass with water and placing it in front of me.

'You didn't have to come,' I tell her when it's been quiet for too long.

'Of course I came,' Mum says, incredulously. 'I'm your mother.' She fidgets as we sit at the kitchen table and I slowly drink my water. 'Not your boss Penelope, but your smaller boss – what's her name? Krissy?'

'Kris.'

'Yes, her. She . . .' Mum sighs. 'She gave me attitude over the phone. All I asked is why you fainted and she said "maybe because her dad died!" As if I don't know that! They made it sound as if you've been unwell and I've been ignoring it, but grief happens to everyone.' She shakes herself off. 'Anyway. You're my daughter. I know when you're fine and she—'

'I'm not fine.'

'What?'

'I said I'm not fine!' Thankfully, my glass is empty when it topples over, which Mum simply catches and refills. 'Mum, for goodness' sake, why would I be fine? My dad is dead.'

'Maddie, I know that,' she says, 'and I know it has been difficult for you, but you need to pray for the strength and rely on God for—'

'Prayer doesn't always work.'

Mum slams the glass down. 'Then you are not doing it right!'

We stare at each other until she sits down.

'I don't know what else to tell you,' she says. I don't know how else to comfort you. I used to understand you when you were younger. You just loved your books and your school friends and—'

'And then you left,' I finish quietly. 'And you kept leaving.'

'I'm here now and it's more than some children have.'

'It's also less than other children have.'

She sighs. 'Maddie, just tell me what's wrong, eh?'

I look down at the table and I'm surprised when I say, 'I feel like it's my fault Dad's dead.'

'Maddie! How can this be your fault? Because you moved out of the house? What do you think you could have done to stop it?'

'At least I should have seen him on his birthday.'

'Yes, that part is a shame, Maddie, and I am sorry for that. But you were there for all the other birthdays when James and I were not. Sometimes I didn't return from Ghana because I knew, for your father, having you there was enough.'

I look up.

'It's no excuse, I know, but try to remember, if you feel guilty,' she says quietly, 'for missing one birthday when you were there for all the others, for Christmas and all the Father's Days, then how must your brother and I feel?' I notice she's looking down and pinching her palm. 'Of course, your brother should feel more guilty because I was on the other side of the world and he was in the same city but . . . but still.'

When silence settles, I know it's time. 'Mum, about my screaming-in-the-kitchen—'

She waves her hand. 'No, no.' Then presses a finger to her lips.

I think about letting it go; I've been granted permission to pretend it never happened, but I've filled my yearly quota of lies in these last few months alone.

'Why do we never talk in this family?' I ask. 'You keep telling me not to tell others too much of our business, but it means I had no one to even talk to.'

'That was because you kept telling your friends at school that I wasn't around,' Mum says. 'Schools take it very seriously when mothers are not around.'

'What you said, that phrase: *Our matters are private, remember?* It's been following me for years. And it meant that I would never talk to anyone.'

'You don't need to talk to everyone. I'm your mother. You can talk to me.'

'Okay. Let's talk about Kwaku.'

The glass in Mum's hand slips. She wipes her hands with a towel. She sighs and the neck of her jumper billows.

'I met Kwaku at university, in Accra,' she says quietly.

'What? All those years ago?'

She swipes at me. 'I am not so old, and if I am, it is because you children have aged me. Anyway, I met him there and fell in love with him there.'

'Love? Then why did you marry Dad?'

'Because your grandfather told me to.'

I stare at her and it's like looking at someone else. Instead of looking at my mum, I'm having to look at my grandfather's daughter.

'Do you know much about bride wealth?' she asks. 'Well, of course not. I never spoke to you children about it because it's not a tradition I wish for you to consider. I told you both that I moved to London for greater opportunities, and met your father via a cousin, but that's not true. When I was much younger, I was promised to your father in return for wealth. It was an arranged marriage.'

I cover my ears.

'Oh, Maddie.' She pulls my hands away. 'Your father and I were just people with real problems, neither one of us was perfect. I loved your father in my own way and I did the best I could until I could not any longer.'

My mother has never said anything as profound as that. My parents are not special people, they're ordinary, and one of my problems is that I'm expecting perfection from ordinary people. They're not saints or masters of knowledge, just people, people who have children, which, last time I checked, required no proficiency test. People who continue to make mistakes, attempt to learn from them and repeat, until death.

'Do you still love Kwaku?'

She nods. 'I do. I left him in Ghana when I came to London to marry your father, but we reconnected on one of my many visits back. I was reminded of how much we had in common, our childhood was very similar, our parents very alike, and he is so kind. He is my best friend and in my life, there are not many. I have many friends of course, I have always been popular, but no one knows me as well as he does.'

I think of them sat in the coffee shop. 'The day I saw the two of you, why were you crying?'

Her shoulders sink. 'Guilt,' she answers simply. 'I cry about it all the time. I pray about it all the time. You were right the other day – although you are not allowed to swear at me ever again – but I preach a lot when I, too, am going against God. I don't want the same for you. It is a struggle I've been fighting every day. I was going to leave your father, do things properly, but then he got sick and I accepted that this was my punishment from God and my penance would be to look after him whilst I was here. But your grandfather's business in Ghana was my loophole, my escape.

'I know you loved your father in a way James and I failed at; I truly thought you were okay here, that you wanted to stay at home and not that you felt you needed to. Then you spoke of anxiety and hopelessness, it was like you were depressed, and after your phone call, it haunted me. I prayed and prayed and thought maybe the answer was to get you out of the house, living your life. Now look. The result is you blaming yourself for your father's death.' She nods. 'Yes, I have made many mistakes.'

When she looks away, her neck stretches, forming dips, and her head looks smaller because of it. Has she always had bags under her eyes? I haven't seen them that dark before, and that jumper, that pale blue knitted jumper, didn't it used to fit a lot tighter?

'Mum? Are you okay?'

She looks at me and sniffs her emotions away. 'Of course I am.' She gets up from the table and opens the fridge, burying her face inside. 'I'll make you something to eat and then I have to go home and get the house sorted for the funeral.' She frowns and pulls out a nearly empty vodka bottle. 'Does this belong to your flatmates?'

'Yes.'

She purses her lips. 'I don't like them very much.'

As she busies herself around the kitchen, I remember something she said about her brother. *Your uncle wants more time with the hostel, bit late to help out now but anyway.*

'Mum?'

'Yes, darling? Is the bottom shelf yours?'

'Yes. Before Grandad died, was it just the two of you a lot? You and your dad?'

'It was the two of us always,' she says. 'You know your grandma died when I was small and you know your uncle is a lazy, good-for-nothing. Which frying pan is yours? Ah, I see. So, yes, it was just your grandfather and me.'

Despite myself, I smile at the fact that Mum has yet to draw the parallel between us. I know Grandad couldn't have been in the greatest state of heath before he passed and I doubt Mum had the help of carers and a GP who could drop by the following weekday. And if my uncle is anything like James, she was very much on her own.

I have a lot to learn about this woman. At least this time I'm not too late.

'I have something to ask,' she suddenly says.

'What's that?'

She begins washing rice under the cold tap. 'At the house, you said I should not call you Maame. What did you mean by that?'

'Oh, just – I don't really like what Maame means.'

'And what does it mean to you?'

'Woman, right?' She nods. 'But you've been calling me a woman, an adult, since I was a child.'

'You've always been wise beyond your years,' she says. 'That is not a bad thing. However, Maame is only a term of endearment.'

'I don't think it—'

'Your grandfather would call me Maame from when I was a baby!' I watch as she laughs to herself. 'My brother, your uncle, would say: "What would Daddy do without his Maame?" What would your father have done without his, hmm?' She returns to the fridge. 'We grow up fast. Not by force, but because we are needed.'

'I think sometimes we're needed for the wrong reasons.'

She pretends not to hear me. 'You don't have much here,' Mum says. 'I hope you haven't been spending all your money on food from outside. I can make you a stew with what you have. Go and lie down and I will call you when it's ready.'

'Thank you.'

She nods me out of the kitchen.

Chapter Thirty-Seven

People are already outside the house when I arrive on the day of my father's funeral.

James, who gives me the longest hug ever, is already here, as well as Auntie Mabel and her son David, Uncle Freddie and his wife Felicity, Uncle Kojo from the kitchen and his wife, and members from Mum's church whose faces are recognisable to varying degrees. All are dressed in black long shirts and trousers or cotton dresses like my own.

More condolences. More hugs. More sympathetic pats on the back.

I run upstairs. Mum's in her bedroom putting make-up on in front of the mirror. She drops her powder and rushes over to hold me. 'Are you okay, Maddie?'

I nod.

'Your mother is still here.'

'I know.'

I lean against her bedroom wall as she goes to put in her earrings, then puts them back down. 'I almost forgot myself,' she says.

'What?'

'Family, especially spouses, don't wear jewellery on the burial day.'

Mum is called downstairs and I stay in her room, taking

my earrings out. My name is mentioned a few times, but I just close the bedroom door.

I look at myself in the mirror. My make-up is minimal and my hair is brushed back. I have plain, black ballet shoes on and my first ever mourning dress. The fabric is black and a little hard so that it keeps its straight corners, and has rows of small geometric shapes printed on. The neck is square and the skirt comes down to reach just below my knees. It's a little tight and difficult to walk in, but it's fine. *When are you going to wear it again, right?*

There's a photo in Mum's room of us. I remember the day that photo was taken. Fourteen years ago, Mum complained we didn't have any recent family photos so booked a professional session in a department store in Tooting. I can still picture the road it was on, even though Tooting has changed so much in the past decade. It was after church one Sunday because, 'We'll already be wearing our best, so, good timing, eh?'

I remember my mum and me in front of the bathroom mirror brushing my hair out. Dad came to church but not to the photos. He didn't want to and, at eleven years old, I already knew not to ask why – that was just Dad. So the photos are only of me, Mum and James.

I'd give anything to go back to that time. Maybe I could have convinced him to join us.

'The hearse is here,' Mum calls.

I start to sweat and I can feel my stomach melt.

I look out of the window onto the road and there he is, in a coffin surrounded by flowers; one of the arrangements spells out DAD.

The whir of the room's fan is loud and I think, what

would happen if I just left? Just ran out the door and kept hopping on trains and buses until I was far, far away?

I could go to Brighton. Everyone is happy by the sea.

'Maddie? Maddie!'

Brighton is far enough and I won't tell anyone where I've gone.

'Maddie, where are you? Your father's outside; come and pay your respects!'

I don't answer as Mum shouts through the house until she bursts into the room. She finds me crying and heaving.

'I can't do this, Mum. I can't.'

'It's okay, it's all right.' Her tone is gentle, but she's pulling my arm and fixing my hair. 'Come outside, come and cry near the coffin.'

'What?'

'It's okay, it's tradition,' she says. 'To cry near your father.'

I almost manage to laugh. I think my mother makes up many traditions just to get her way.

More people have arrived and approach me to say sorry, to give me pats of condolence. One after the other until I'm facing a woman with a rigid back, a black duku wrapped around her hair, painted eyebrows and pursed lips sat solidly in the centre of her face. She looks down at me underneath full lashes. 'Baaba, I am your Aunt Abena,' she says in Twi. 'One of your father's many cousins, and this is your uncle Osei.' She gestures to the man beside her. 'Our condolences,' she finishes.

'Thank you,' I tell them both.

She tilts her head. 'Hmm?'

'I said, thank you.'

She doesn't move and continues to hold her rectangular purse to her stomach. 'Try again,' she orders.

'I'm sorry?'

'Am I speaking to you in English, Baaba?'

I feel the sun burn my cheeks. 'No. You're speaking Twi.'

'Exactly. So why are you responding in English? Do you not know your own language?'

I look around for help, someone to interrupt us, but no one is paying any attention.

'I know some.'

'Then try.'

'Thank you – *Medaase*.'

She nods. 'Good. How have you been?'

She wants more? '*Me . . .*'

'Go on,' she pushes.

'Leave her be,' her husband says.

'No,' she responds, looking at me. 'She can do it. The day of her father's funeral is no day to be lazy, is no day to speak English. He was born surrounded by those speaking in Twi and he will be buried the same.'

If she wasn't so intimidating I'd tell her that those were strong words coming from a woman I'm sure I've not met before. I'd tell her she doesn't have the right to tell me how to act or speak at my father's funeral, but looking around, it's clear that this is my extended family in a nutshell. It doesn't matter if we talk every day or if we've never even met, she is family and that means she can drop in whenever she likes and remind me of who my father is and by default, who I am.

'Go on, Baaba.'

I almost say I don't know how to respond but then remember my mum's response to another auntie minutes ago. '*Me ho ye*,' I say slowly. '*Wo ho te sen?*'

326

My pronunciation isn't great and I've probably missed out a word or two, but she breaks into a big smile. *Approval.*

'See? She knows it,' Aunt Abena says. 'She thinks she doesn't, but it is in her.'

She passes to go into the house and I think about how the language I've mourned never learning has on some levels already been taught. A language I thought too difficult to warrant effort has already embedded itself into me. I can probably converse simply by recalling the responses of others. So I listen as we wait and it's a nice distraction. I listen to my family's chatter and translate in my head and try to store the words I might need today and maybe tomorrow.

Yefre wo sen? What do they call you/what is your name?

Me din de . . . My name is . . .

Mente asee – I don't understand.

That will come in handy.

We're not very organised. The dead is more prompt than the living, as the living are currently deciding which cars to go in. Aunt Abena is unsurprisingly taking the lead. She pushes Mum towards one car, then folds her fingers into her palms repeatedly, says '*Bra ha*' to James and he helps Auntie Mabel into his.

'Are you in this one?'

'*Nante yiye.*'

'Let's go now.'

'The address. What's the address?'

'*Kyere me kwan no.*'

Twi and English are flying in the air. Heels on the pavement, engines revving and car doors slamming. For a moment, I stand alone because if Dad were here, his would be the car I'd sit in. For years, wherever he went, by bus or by train, to the supermarket or the GP, I'd go with him, until I had to begin going instead of him.

Aunt Abena gently pulls on my arm and tells me to get into the silver car.

The man at the wheel is familiar, belonging to the group from Mum's church, but I don't know his name. He's a friend of the family, or a family friend, or family but not blood-related, whichever one, it doesn't matter. We pull away from the house and travel down the road.

We're the third car behind the procession. Every time the hearse turns a corner and I see the photograph of Dad, large and framed, sat at the end of his coffin, the tears resurface.

People on the street turn to watch us. A dog barks. One old man makes the sign of the cross. When their eyes meet mine, my chest opens and I feel exposed. I hope I remember never to stare at a funeral procession as it passes ever again.

I've never been through a graveyard before; I used to avoid cemeteries because I worried it would tempt fate. Looks like fate found me anyway.

The sun is hot and the ground is uneven. My black cotton dress feels too heavy when I watch the cemetery workers lower my dad into a burial plot. They talk amongst themselves as they work because this is their own personal brand of 'just another day at the office'.

People I didn't greet at the house come up to me, but I don't really see any of them. Hello, Uncle. How are you? *Me ho yɛ.* My condolences. *Medaase.* You're so big now. *Aane.* Do you remember me? Sure.

Then we're all stood surrounding a rectangle of hollowed-out earth. In there, at the bottom, is my dad. Aunt Abena is adjusting her headpiece and my uncle Osei swats at a fly. James is staring at the ground, Mum is pinching the bridge of her nose, Auntie Mabel has her head bowed and Uncle Freddie dabs his eyes with a white handkerchief. Suddenly I miss the noise from before: the Twi, the cars, the movement.

'Are we all here?' Mum's pastor asks. He's a tall, lean Black man who must duck to avoid a tree's swooping branches.

'Yes,' Mum says.

'Then let us pray. Lord God, we commit this day into Your hands,' he says. 'We are gathered here to celebrate the life of Mr George Wright . . .'

He finishes by telling us that Dad is in a better place and that we as Christians need not mourn, but give thanks to God that we have a place where we will reunite with loved ones someday. We are blessed as believers because death is not the end.

The tributes are read: 'George Wright was clever and studious . . . As he was a faithful man, even when physically weakened, he will be at home now, with the Lord and family already gone . . . He was a hard-working man and his discipline allowed him to travel from Ghana and make a living in London . . .'

I'm the only one who struggles to get started. I bite my lip and breathe through my nose. When words still won't come out, Mum rubs my back and whispers, 'Take your time. There is no rush.'

'I will remember my dad for the smile on his face whenever I walked into the room.' I clear my throat. 'Although he often preferred his own company, in his final years his love for his children only grew. It is, and will continue to be, strange going home and . . . and not finding my father there. Life is different without him now; I wish I could say I was at peace, but the truth is that it's difficult and I'm struggling. But I'll get there. And if it takes a while, that's fine, because if there's anything my father's smiles taught me, it's that it's not too late to start again. It's not too late to be the person you want or were always meant to be.

'I . . . Sometimes I think of love as pieces of one heart. When I love someone, I break off a piece and give it to them. There are not so many because that way each piece is substantial, but without a doubt, my dad has one of the biggest pieces I have and will ever give. It cannot be replaced. It is his forever. God bless my father and may he rest in peace.'

I don't like my eulogy because I don't feel it encapsulates everything, but how could it? How can I, in front of my family, describe that I'm not only mourning my dad but the life I lost when he became sick and the life I've lost now that's he's gone?

Dad's immediate family sprinkle earth onto his coffin, we sing hymns and Pastor prays again. I stare into the deep rectangle of earth carved into the ground, where, at the bottom, in a box, my father's body will remain forever. Auntie Mabel sings a Ghanaian burial song and then we watch the grave being filled. It takes a forklift, a truck and a man with a shovel. I rest my head on James's shoulder, my cheeks hard and dried. He pulls me into a side hug. He smells expensive, not of acrid body spray or heavy aftershave, but light and reminiscent of gummy sweets.

'Sorry I was never there, Mads.' He sniffs and when I look up, he's crying. 'After what you said the other day in the kitchen, I see what we did to you. I don't even know what to say.' He nods towards Dad. 'And there's nothing I can do for him now, either. I missed all my chances.'

I could say something soothing, but I don't have anything to offer. I've run out of lies. Dad's gone and the chance to help him has gone with him. I could say it's fine and that it no longer matters, but that won't negate how much it did matter at the time. I decide not to say anything at all.

One day we'll be orphans; one day I'll be faced with the question of: who am I without my parents? I know I will never live at home again; that home as I know it may cease to exist. Mum will likely sell the house, and in a few months, she'll go back to Ghana. James will continue to be reachable only after the second call. Then there will be me. Maddie. Madeleine Baaba Wright, twenty-five. Nothing else about me as definitive as those facts.

'What's your job, Mads?' James asks.

'Huh? I'm an editorial assistant.'

'And that's what you want to do, in life, I mean?'

'I think so. Why do you ask?'

He shrugs. 'I didn't know. I knew it was something to do with books but didn't know what exactly.'

'Oh, I should have specified.'

'Nah, I should have asked.' He speaks quietly, squeezing my shoulder. 'I never thought I needed to check up on you. I'm sorry we're not the family you deserve, Mads,' he suddenly says. 'Dad's gone and Mum's just not very maternal in that way. I know you want her to be, every kid does, but not every mum is *that* mum. When I was at school, I'd be wishing she'd act like the other mums, pick me up from school, make me dinner, help with homework, and some-times it looked like she'd changed, but it never lasted 'cause you can't pretend to be someone you're not for very long. So don't waste your time wishing for it, because it's not anything *you're* doing wrong, yeah?' James sighs. 'Mum and I really just left you from young and I think about that a lot now. The family and our house would have collapsed years ago if it weren't for you looking after Dad and paying the bills, and you did all that from the heart, cos I know we didn't act grateful. I could never; I don't have that in me, man. I'm thankful for you, Mads, and I'm sorry, for . . . for a lot of things. For everything. But Dad loved you, you know.'

'You were barely there,' I say. 'How can you be sure?'

'It's like you said – he always smiled at you. When it was just me and him, he was cool, but he'd always ask, "Is Maddie home?" and then not say a lot after. You made him feel safe, maybe – I don't know. More than I did, anyway.'

Hearing James say it like this makes me feel proud, comforted. All the years I spent at home weren't for noth-ing. I made Dad happy in a world that likely didn't make much sense to him.

'I hope I can do better for you now, when you need help,' James says.

'Help with what?'

'Anything,' he says undeterred. 'See what comes up.' There's one more pause before, 'Mum told me about you going to therapy and I think it's great, Mads. Please keep going. Especially since it's free.' One more shoulder squeeze, then he looks at his shoes. 'I . . . I love you, yeah?'

My lip wobbles and I have to swallow to keep my voice steady. 'I love you, too.'

When the grave is filled, we put our flowers on top. James lifts the heavy ones and won't leave until they're all positioned well on the uneven ground.

I'm the last in the line to leave and I turn round for one more look at the mound of flower adorned earth. 'Bye, Dad,' I say. 'I love you, *okay?*'

Auntie Mabel calls hours later in the evening when I'm lying on Mum's bed alone.

'What you have to remember, Baaba, is who looked after him when Mum was in Ghana and James was never in the house?'

I answer, 'Me'.

'That's right,' she says, 'and he was grateful. No parent wants to rely on their children, but your father was so grateful to have you. Whenever I mentioned your name, I did not even finish my sentence before he would smile. You were so true about that. It is a sad day, but never forget what I said, do you hear?'

'Thank you.'

In the living room, I trail a black bin bag alongside me, emptying plates straight into it. I can't wait to get into bed and fall asleep. The funeral was the hardest part and now that it's over, things will get better from here, I'm sure.

I walk into the kitchen and Mum's washing dishes, her wrists deep in soapy water. She turns to look at me. 'Hello, darling. How are you doing?'

'Fine,' I answer. 'What about you?'

She nods. 'Also fine.'

I'm clearing the countertops when she says, 'I overheard you and James at the cemetery. And I want to say it again – I'm sorry that I was not here more.' Her eyes seem to search the greying water. I don't think there's anything left in the sink to wash, but she keeps her hands submerged. 'Maybe things would have been different, if I were here. But I would come back and see how well you were doing without me and it was easier to stay where I had a purpose, in Ghana. I have my own life there now, and you have yours here.'

Tears race down her cheeks. 'I have made many failures in raising you children,' she says, still not meeting my eyes. 'I am better than most mothers, but I should have done better by you, at least. You, Maddie, are special. God is in you. And everything you do, you do without being hounded to do so. You have a selfless heart and sometimes James and I, well, we are not so different, that's all.'

As she sniffs in desperate attempts to control herself, my mother looks incredibly *vulnerable*, even more so than she did at my flat, or at the coffee shop. She's always been stubborn and self-assured but, right now, she looks tired and just plain human. I look around the kitchen and realise that after signing the forms at the funeral directors, I've done nothing else to prepare for today. The order of service, the invitations, the food, the house prep, even my mourning dress . . . none of it was me and I doubt it was James.

I feel an overwhelming surge of love for my imperfect mother. I place a shaking hand on her back and submerge the other into the sink. Mine rests on top of hers and we stare into the blurry water together.

'It's done now,' I whisper. 'You're right. Your life is in Ghana and mine is here. But just because it's done, doesn't mean it's over.'

'I am here, though,' Mum says. 'For you. I don't show it well and that is my failing, but I am your mother always, and I will always do my best, okay?'

I kiss her cheek. 'Okay.'

'Before, when you were asking about your grandad – I see now that I expected you to take on all that responsibility alone, without complaint, because that is what I had to do, but the lives of my children were meant to be easier than mine. I forget that. Your boss, Krissyline—'

'Kris.'

'It is the same. On the phone, she told me about the counselling – that you go regularly.'

I did wonder when this would come up. 'Yes, I do.'

'But you didn't tell me and I know why.' She sighs. 'At first, I didn't like the idea of strangers – Godless strangers most likely – directing you. I hoped you'd find your answers in God, but maybe this will help you seek Him, for answers to the bigger questions. Therapy can help the smaller things. I don't want you to struggle with . . . mental problems, so if this opportunity means you won't, then you should take it.'

'Really?'

'I will of course pray about the counsellor. What is her name?'

'Angelina.'

'Is she Black?'

I nod and this seems to mollify her instantly. 'That is good.'

'Ghanaian too. I think she's even Christian,' I add. I obviously have no idea if she is the latter, but Mum looks pleased.

'Maybe she can mentor you for your future career,' she says.

'Mum, I work in publishing.'

'And so? Can you not keep your options open? Publishing doesn't make you a lot of money, does it? How much does Kristine make?'

'*Mennim.*'

Mum raises her eyebrows and a wide smile breaks out across her face. We continue to converse in Twi and she corrects me where I go wrong until I can repeat it correctly.

'Try and find out Kristine's salary.'

'That will be difficult.'

'I bet Angelina makes more.'

'Maybe.'

'Maame,' she says after a while.

'Yes, Ma.'

'Seriously, when do you think you will marry?'

I smile and look her in the eyes. 'Not any time soon.'

When I get back to the flat, I pour myself a glass of water and sit in the kitchen, drinking it slowly.

Upstairs, I untie my hair, brush my teeth and shower, standing with my head low under a cascade of hot water. When out and dressed, I sit on the floor facing the window. I stare out to the sky with my back leaning against my bed and my legs crossed.

'Hi, Dad.'

I wait to see if the sky changes at all and when it doesn't, I continue.

'It's me, Maddie. I'm not one hundred per cent sure how heaven works, whether you can see me or if it's possible to tune out everyone else who's talking to heaven right now just to hear me, but it's worth a shot. I thought I would start doing this, if you don't mind. We didn't talk much when you were here; I always thought you didn't care, but maybe you thought I was the one who didn't care. Regardless, maybe we could get to know each other a bit better; start from the beginning almost.'

I clear my throat.

'I'm twenty-five now, twenty-six in four months. I know your memory was slipping at the end so you couldn't remember those kinds of things, but you're healthy again now, that's how heaven works, right? When Mum and I went to see you at the funeral home, your feet were no longer swollen. Can you walk on your own now, Dad? Can you run? You must feel so free. You can stretch your fingers and run laps in the clouds.

'I haven't heard you have a proper conversation in years and I know it's because your brain wouldn't let you. You must be talking people's ears off now. I wish I'd recorded your voice . . .'

I would get a tissue but I don't want to move, so I use the back of my hand to pat my face dry.

'Maybe it's not even a physical thing up there and it's just your weightless soul and that, for you, is just a feeling, so you're not actually running or stretching but you are weight-less. The soul thing would explain how everyone fits in heaven. If you could have a chat with God about some questions and doubts I'm having, then come and explain them to me, I'd appreciate that. Don't feel like you can't come and visit me, not in a spooky way – I scare easy – but you know, in like a dream or a voice in my head? Although, not in a way that will make me think I'm having a psychotic breakdown. I'll leave the technicalities up to you. Have a chat with the other souls up there and see what the preferred method of communication between the living and the dead is.

'Anyway, Dad . . .' I take a deep breath. 'I'm sorry we had to say goodbye to you today. I'm sorry I wanted to leave the house, to move out and find out who I was. Especially since it was all for nothing; I'm not entirely convinced I'm any better than I was before. Maybe, that's a bit harsh.' I think of Alex. 'I learned some things.' I think of Ben. 'I learned a lot of things.' I think of Mum and James. 'Actually, I'm going to take that back; it wasn't all for nothing. But I'm sorry that on some days the guilt melts away and I feel relieved about not having to worry about you so much. I'd have you back in a heartbeat if . . . I probably shouldn't have said any of that. Please don't hate me.'

I pause, thinking about what Angelina said about love and all its varied forms of expression. 'I do love you and you must know that, but it is a relief to not worry, to know you're no longer in pain, spending your life sat in a chair swallowing pills. I'd rather you were here, but I can't help thinking you're much happier now. You must be. Are you happier now or am I kidding myself?'

I sit in the silence with my eyes closed.

'I hope you're happier,' I whisper. I open my eyes and wipe the sticky mess from under my nose. 'Night, Dad. Talk to you tomorrow, *okay*?'

It's only when I get into bed and hear him say, 'Okay, Maddie,' that I finally smile.

Because there's no tremor in his voice when he says it.

It's raining and I can't find myself amidst the dark night, but I keep running because I have to save him. The cemetery is so large, larger than I remember it, but I spot the tree he's buried under, sprawled and wild in the wind, the mound and its familiar flowers. I drop the torch I'm holding and begin to claw at the wet dirt with my hands, mud embedding my fingernails.

'Hold on, Dad,' I shout above the storm. 'I'm coming! I'll save you!'

Lightning cracks across the sky, but still I dig and dig until my hands bleed and the rain streams down my face; I'm wet through, my clothes cling to me, the cold burying itself into my lungs. My arms shake with exhaustion, but I can't stop.

He needs me; my dad needs me. He must be terrified and all alone. I can't leave him, not again.

I drag at the dirt until suddenly two people grab either of my arms.

'Miss, you're not supposed to be here; it's midnight.'

I fight against them. 'No, you don't understand. My dad is down there. I have to save him! Please, let go of me!'

I wake up and my back is wet, my throat is dry and my arms are sore from reaching out for something in the night. I look at my phone and it's 2:07 a.m. I settle back into bed, wipe my eyes dry and fall back to sleep.

Nia
I know I already called but just wanted to check up on you. How'd you sleep last night? X

Maddie
Like a baby. You don't need to worry about me x

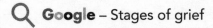

🔍 **Google** – Stages of grief

Shock – denial – anger –
bargaining – depression – acceptance

Maddie's stages of grief

Shock – denial – depression – shock again – anger – did I
skip bargaining and is it too late to start? – depression –
acceptance – depression

Chapter Thirty-Eight

Twenty minutes in, Angelina says, 'I'd like to refer back to our previous session and discuss two things in particular. Your need to end conversations with "I love you" and the name Maame. Which would you like to discuss first?'

I pick the first option, though I'm uncertain what more there is to say.

'We agreed,' Angelina begins, 'that a part of navigating life has to do with navigating people and their *isms*. We didn't dig very deep, but we briefly discussed your parents and how you were sure they loved you even though they failed to verbally express it.'

'Yes.'

'So, Maddie, would you say you're well-loved?'

'That's an odd way to phrase it.'

'But you understand what I mean?' she says. 'One of my first observations was your obvious need to be loved. Your craving of it is reflected in your tendency to people-please, even if at cost to your mental health. Would you agree?'

'It's difficult not to.'

'Even contributing to your depression?'

Although there's still so much left for me to unpack regarding my relationship with depression, I nod.

'Good. I ask if you think you're well-loved because it's easy to conflate being well-liked with being well-loved.

There's often a misconception that to be well-loved, the love has to come from multiple sources, when truthfully, one or two people can love you with the strength of ten. Do you have people in your life who love you with the strength of many?'

I immediately think of Nia and Shu. I think of how Nia has never directed one inch of resentment towards me for not being the kind of friend she's been to me when her dad died. How she can move to America and return as if she's been gone only for days instead of a year. How at the beginning she said she'd do anything for me and has wordlessly proved she meant it.

I think of Shu coming over with shit for my sadness in the middle of a weekday. She rarely takes time off work. She could have waited for the evening or the weekend but instead came as soon as she heard. Did she walk straight out of work? I remember how she came over with Nia when I found out about Ben and Sophie. What had she been doing before I called her? What had they each dropped last minute for me? Shu didn't have to talk to me in that lecture hall all those years ago just because she saw me on my own. And the time she answered her phone when I called to ask why she was a lesbian, even though I know she never touches her phone during office hours. Yet I subconsciously knew she would see my name flash on her screen and pick up.

'Yes,' I answer quietly. 'Yes, I'm very well-loved.'

'Good. It will serve you well to remember this, especially at times when certain sources of love fail to deliver.' Then Angelina says, 'Maddie, at the beginning of this session we spoke about your father's funeral, your feelings during and after; we spoke about your family, immediate and extended. You said you'd never felt closer to your culture and who you are – and more importantly, who you want to be going forward. How do you feel about the name Maame now?'

I'm about to say nothing has changed – but that would be a lie. 'It's complicated.'

'Try your best to make it simple. Say your thoughts aloud if that helps you.'

I take a breath. 'Before, I said I hated it, but I don't think I do. I like the name. It can feel heavy and it won't be what I call my children if I choose to have any, but it's really a term of endearment. Well, it's meant to be, so maybe what I didn't like was how my family turned it into an excuse. The name Maame put a lot of pressure on me, but it also made my dad feel safe when he must have felt trapped and uncertain. It made my mum's life a little easier and, ultimately, it taught my brother a lesson. It made me someone I needed to be so I could find out who I want to be.' I smile at Angelina. 'I suppose I owe Maame a great deal.'

Angelina smiles so wide I notice her dimples for the first time. 'That's a wonderful way to look at it, Maddie.'

Nia
So I'm on the hunt for a nice place to live. Any chance you are too?

Maddie
Yes please!

Chapter Thirty-Nine

From: info@CarrowBooks.com
To: Mad.Wright@gmail.com
Subject: Carrow Books Mentorship Programme

Dear Maddie Wright,

Thanks for submitting to the Carrow Books Mentorship
Programme. Your sample has been read and I am sorry to
say that we won't be taking it forward. We wish you the
very best with your writing in the future.

Sincerely,
Carrow Books

I'd forgotten all about the rough draft I submitted, which
makes the rejection no real loss. I put my phone away and
pause beneath the office's spiral staircase when I hear Penny
and Kris walking up.

'I think Maddie should be more involved with *Love Stories*
than she currently is,' Kris says. 'She did bring us Afra and picked
out great photographers – we're even contacting two of her
choices. She's been on top of her admin since she started and is
full of ideas for an assistant. I did tell you the concept of *Flavour
Pairings* and the play on the word pair were her ideas, didn't I?'

What?

'You did, and I know,' Penny says. 'I am impressed, but we were drowning in general admin before her and we can't afford to split her focus now.'

'We should give her the opportunity to do both.'

'She's just lost her father,' Penny says. 'Let's not overwhelm her.'

The door closes behind them, but I stay where I am. So it wasn't Kris 'stealing' my ideas, it was Penny refusing to acknowledge they were mine. Why would she do that? Was that person from the internet right? Is it to keep me as an assistant for longer, rather than pay for my promotion *and* for a replacement ? Should I confront her?

You can't confront your boss and accuse her of stealing.

I briefly close my eyes and accept that I don't have the energy to fight the (wo)man today.

My phone buzzes again.

> **Unknown number**
> Hi Maddie!
> I'm not sure if you remember me but it's Emma here. I got your number off Jo she thinks I'm asking you for publishing tips so if she asks play along! I don't know if you and Cam know but it's Jo's birthday on Sunday and I want to throw her a surprise party at your place in the garden. Can you both help? xx

Emma has been to the house a few times with her boyfriend, Tinka. I remember her from her very short, blonde bob and freckle-splattered cheeks.

I'm about to type out an excuse to get out of it when I think, maybe this is how I make amends for blaming Dad's death on Jo. Even though I don't plan to stay for much longer, I am rather tired of going to work and coming home only to go straight to my room when she's in the kitchen or in front of the TV. I did apologise but clearly that wasn't enough. Maybe this action will speak louder than my words.

People pleasing?

Maybe, but baby steps.

I check in with Cam before responding.

> **Maddie**
> Hi Emma,
> We'd be happy to! X

Cam and I spend the whole of Saturday together, driving around town in her car, picking up balloons, snacks, barbeque food, cups and decorations from various shops. We stopped for lunch and both ordered soup and grilled cheese sandwiches. I give her a very brief synopsis about my return to work, *Love Stories*, and Ben, but not Alex. I tell her I'll be moving out soon to live with Nia. She tells me all about teaching summer school classes and her students, who are hilarious but aren't learning as quickly as they should (she blames the rise of social media) and how she's been thinking a lot about renting out her room and going travelling.

On Sunday, my job is to set up with Cam whilst Emma is out with Jo. We move the big fold-out table into the garden and put on some music as her friends trickle in. We set up snacks and drinks in the kitchen and Olivia, the first of Jo's friends to arrive, gets started with the barbeque. Cam and I play host to Jo's friends until we hear her scream at the door. She must have seen the numbers two and eight balloons we tied to the front door's knocker. When she comes in, we yell 'Surprise!' let off party poppers and someone pops open champagne which spills on the carpet. We all choose to ignore the growing dark stain.

More of Jo's friends arrive and an hour later, I'm sat in the corner of the garden with Emma, who's finishing her Masters, Olivia who works at a literary agency, Kenny who's a junior casting agent, Tinka a dancer, Cam, Jo and . . . Sam.

'Look, I know you loved it, but it's overrated,' Kenny says. 'Yes, it is!'

I'm quickly learning that Kenny is very opinionated. He's Black, wearing a fedora hat and a brightly patterned shirt. How he pulls them both off is a mystery that I highly suspect has something to do with his attention-drawing personality.

'That doesn't mean it was bad,' he says, 'but people have shone this ridiculous light on it to blind others into thinking it's ground-breaking stuff when really? It was just okay. There I said it.'

'You're absolute garbage, Ken,' Emma says.

'Something I have in common with that book.'

We laugh and Jo throws crisps at him.

'It wasn't garbage,' he says. 'I retract that declaration. Look, I enjoyed it, it was good, but I didn't *love* it and I have difficulty believing those of a high literary standard did.'

'But didn't you love *how* it was written?' I ask, gesturing enthusiastically towards him. A pickle falls out of my burger in the process. 'It was so different from all the other bestsellers we've been reading recently. It was beautiful and raw and written so . . .'

Kenny smiles. 'Sparsely.'

'It's called economical language.'

'Aha! And who coined that phrase, dear Madeleine?' Kenny asks. 'A group of actual readers or her publicity team who couldn't think of another way to say, my writer lacks a little imagination.'

Jo boos.

'She detailed everything without saying much,' Olivia says. 'That's natural talent.'

'Says *who*?' Kenny asks. 'All I'm really asking is that we examine these "rules" of good writing.'

'The love story was beautiful,' Tinka says. 'You have to admit that.'

'Fair, that aspect I enjoyed,' Kenny says.

'Wait, what?' Olivia says, roughly pushing brown ringlets from her face. She's Emma's cousin, but the two couldn't be further apart. Emma is blonde, has an angular face and wears a tight lavender dress and knee-high boots, whereas Olivia showed up with her hair in a top knot, overalls, muddy trainers and not a scrap of make-up. '*That's* what you enjoyed? That was my one problem with it! No teenager feels love that strongly, I'm sorry. All adults agree, teenagers are shit. We didn't know who to vote for, let alone what real love is.'

'Speak for yourself!' Emma says. 'I knew to vote Conservative.'

'You did what?'

Emma holds her palm out to Tinka. 'That's a discussion for another day. Liv, you're just bitter you've never felt it: a love so poignant and true and—'

'Excessive?' Olivia offers. 'Facetious? The author's a sensationalist, no question.'

'That's why it's so popular,' Sam says and I turn to him, having mistaken his silence for disinterest. 'Because it described the love we all want but likely won't have. Love that's raw and wonderfully painful and all-consuming; intrinsically becoming a part of another person; the subtlety and quietness of their co-dependence. We won't admit it, but maybe that's what a lot of us want. Liv is right – the author plays into that, but it doesn't diminish the writing. Love is so watered down now, tied to peer pressure and proximity and self-esteem, I think readers enjoyed having it concentrated. It's a thrill imagining yourself with that capability, with the capacity to hold that almost unbearable weight of love for someone else, and the possibility of someone out there feeling exactly the same for you. It's a heady, envy-inducing thought.'

We all stare at him, until—.

'Will you marry me, Sam?'

Everyone laughs at Jo – including Sam – except me. Instead I stare at him, because what he said is exactly how I felt when I read the book, so much so that I've yet to read the last page. The story and my bookmark are stuck on page two hundred and eighty-five.

Sam. I don't know his middle name. His surname is usually *comma Jo's ex*.

I look at Jo who's considering Sam with a soft fold in her forehead. I still don't know where the two of them stand; they must be back together if he's here and Jo can publicly joke about marrying him. He instead looks behind Jo, to the tree and its canopy of branches fairy lights have been tangled between.

When he catches my eye, I look down at my half-finished burger and drink the rest of my prosecco.

As the evening goes on, our group shifts and changes; we talk about politics, about careers, friends, family, food and nights out.

'I'm going to stretch my legs,' I suddenly say and leave the garden by way of the gate. A lot of us are lingering outside the house and I walk further down to the stone steps leading to the main road and sit alone.

It's been a good night. Jo gave me a quick hug when she saw everything and spoke to me more in the first hour than she has this entire week, but it didn't fill me up as much as I thought it would. Then she barely acknowledged me for the rest of the evening.

As for Jo's friends, they seem to like me, but I know I might never speak to any of them again. At least today they know me for the better side of me – the funny, conversational, intelligent side of me. I had an opinion on every topic presented and my opinions were that of the majority, so I firmly belonged, but I'm tired now. There's an hour left of the day and I feel drained and in need of a forty-eight-hour break. I'm staring into empty space when Sam appears.

'What are you doing out here?' he asks. His voice – calm and measured – makes me think of Nia.

'Recharging.'

He nods and offers me a cigarette. I look at it and smile, recalling the list I made on the day I moved in.

The New Maddie
~~Drinks alcohol when offered~~
~~Always says yes to social events~~
~~Wears new clothes~~
~~Cooks new food~~
~~Has different experiences (Travel? Brunch?)~~
~~Tries weed or cigarettes at least once (but don't get addicted!)~~
~~Wears make-up~~
~~Goes on dates~~
~~Is not a virgin~~

'No thank you,' I answer. 'I don't smoke.'

'Neither do I.' He lights a cigarette and draws from it. 'It's a nervous habit. Do you mind?' He gestures to the step.

'Go ahead.'

He sits beside me.

'Why are you nervous?' I ask.

'I have an important meeting tomorrow.'

'It'll be fine.'

He turns to me and that easy smile I remember slides seamlessly into place. 'How do you know that?'

'I don't, but it's nice to hear, isn't it?'

He nods. 'You've done a great job with this party, by the way; Em was just telling us and Cam was quick to acknowledge how much of it was down to your execution.'

I frown. 'Eugh, Jo must think I'm such a loser. We . . . we're not really that close.'

'No, she was touched,' Sam assures. 'But if you're not that close, why do so much?'

I shrug. 'I had amends to make, plus I like making an effort for other people. Turns out, I'm a bit of a people pleaser. It's something I'm working on. But I just like the idea of people being happy because I know how great it is to feel happy, if that makes any sense.'

He draws from his cigarette. 'Are you generally sad?'

I look at him and he doesn't turn away. 'Yes,' I answer. Sometimes I'm really sad. It sounds like a childish word to use and depressed is the adult equivalent, but for me "sad" works best.'

'What causes it?'

I'm surprised by his genuine interest and once again hear those words from Mum about keeping our matters private. 'Sometimes, nothing,' I tell him. 'It's been a rough couple of months. I got fired from a job I hated, was dumped by my boyfriend after finding out he was someone else's boyfriend, and then, as you already know, my dad died.'

'Yes, I remember. Do you want to talk about it?'

'No.'

'Want to trash-talk the ex-boyfriend?' he offers. 'What was his name?'

'Ben.'

'He sounds like a dick.'

I shrug. 'It was my first real relationship, if I can call it that. I didn't love him, but it hurts knowing I got a different man than the one his actual girlfriend did. She got the better version of him; he *gave* her the better version of him. I don't see why I'm good but not good enough,' I say quietly. 'I once thought, maybe I should only date Black men who date Black women because maybe I'd never feel let down, well, in *that* area anyway. I wouldn't have to psychoanalyse their actions towards me or think thrice about something they've said or feel misunderstood or make too much effort to understand and maybe, just maybe, I could end up being *loved* – just for who I am.'

When I look at Sam, his mouth is slightly open.

'Shit,' I say. 'Sorry, that really brought the mood down. I'm experimenting with honesty. Erm, so what's tomorrow's meeting about?'

He smiles sadly. 'I'm really sorry someone made you feel that way, Maddie.'

'Life lesson, I suppose.'

'Yeah, dating gives you a lot of those.'

We both look at one another. 'Bad experience yourself?'

'You could say that.' I think he means to stop there but then continues. 'An ex of mine could talk for days about other social issues, but when it came to racial discrimination, she just didn't care enough; she'd almost shut down. Soon she was providing excuses and playing devil's advocate too often.' He looks at me. 'I'll never get that – playing devil's advocate, like we're talking pineapple on pizza. You know, she once said that to my mum? She told my deeply religious Zimbabwean-born mother that she was "only playing devil's advocate".'

I think of how my mum would react to that phrase. The mother who wouldn't let me watch Harry Potter because she didn't want me to invite witchcraft into the house. She'd probably ask how much the devil was paying me to advocate for him. 'What did your mum say?' I ask.

'Mum asked if she was an agent of darkness.'

I fight a laugh. 'Sorry things didn't work out,' I tell him.

'It's all right,' he says. 'It was a year ago, now. We were arguing a lot and I would just think, if you don't get it now, after *everything*, will you ever?' He shakes his head. 'Sometimes relationships are tricky and things happen.'

'Very well said.'

He laughs and stubs out his cigarette. 'How's life at OTP?'

I breathe out. 'I'm going to confront my boss tomorrow.'

He smiles. 'Did you just decide that now?'

'I did.'

'Good for you. What atrocities have they been up to?'

I tell Sam everything, from *Flavour Pairings*, to the incident with the milk jug, ending with *Love Stories from the Middle East*.

'You should definitely say something.'

'Easy for you to say.'

'I know, but I mean it,' he says seriously. 'I think when working in white spaces we can feel programmed to not rock the boat; like, we got a foot in the door and we should try to keep that door closed behind us. Which means you begin assigning any and all problematic issues to just being a part of the job. If someone's not treating you right, you should say so. The milk jug might be difficult to explain – understanding why that shouldn't have happened requires nuance – but the use of your creative ideas whilst excluding you is an issue that needs to be dealt with. Again, easier said than done, but so worth it in the long run.'

I wonder how things would have gone at CGT if I had given Katherine a piece of my mind? Instead I kept quiet, took her abuse and got fired anyway.

'You don't deserve to have other people's comments and actions eat away at you five days a week, fifty-two weeks a year. My dad always says: "Regardless of how you behave, a lot of things are going to be out of your control because this world was made to test you. Protect your peace in whatever and every way that you can." '

'Hey, Sam!' Kenny leans over the gate. 'Our car's here – ready to go?'

Sam gets to his feet and I'm reminded of how tall he is. 'Coming in?'

'No, I might stay here a while longer,' I say. 'Thanks for talking to me.'

'It was a good talk.' He stops at the gate and calls, 'Hey, Maddie?'

'Yes?'

'Good luck tomorrow,' he says, smiling yet again. 'I'm rooting for you.'

Chapter Forty

When I walk into the office, rough samples of *Love Stories* sits on my desk with a note: *Make sure Kris approves these today*. I pull the note aside to read the proposed cover:

Love Stories from the Middle East

Afra Yazden-Blake & Co

& Co? They took my et al suggestion seriously?

I leave the samples there and knock on Penny's door. When she says 'Come in,' I close the door behind me. I stand in front of her desk until she looks at me.

'Is everything all right, Maddie?'

'I'd like to take on more responsibility here,' I blurt out. 'I wasted a lot of time at my old job because I didn't feel I had anything to contribute, but clearly I do as an editorial assistant. I may not understand why exactly you changed Cooking Combos to *Flavour Pairings*, and paired the pear with cinnamon instead of chocolate, or changed et al to Afra and Co. but . . . those ideas did come from me.'

Penny doesn't look angry, but I wouldn't call her happy. Her jaw is locked, but at least I have her attention.

'Afra is getting a lot of attention online,' I continue, 'and I brought her here. I'm just—'

'Maddie,' Penny interrupts, 'it may have been your *ideas*, but it is us who employ you and us who put the resources behind those ideas. It isn't just you here.'

'That's not what I'm saying.' I don't know what I thought walking in here. If I could get fired from CGT for something I didn't even do, surely this could be considered grounds for dismissal.

I think about apologising and leaving her office when she asks, 'Then what are you saying, Maddie?'

'I'm saying . . . I'm asking to *learn*,' I answer. 'I think I could do more, I'm asking to do more.'

Penny suddenly takes her glasses off and pinches the bridge of her nose. Without the rim of her glasses, I spot the faint shadows resting under her eyes and I have the sudden urge to ask if everything is all right. I think again about leaving when she says, 'What is it you want, Maddie?'

'A seat at the table.'

She raises her eyebrows and a smile fights the corner of her mouth.

'Sorry,' I say. 'I was watching *Mad Men* last night and that sounded cooler in my head.'

Penny gently throws her head back and laughs. I've never seen her laugh before; it gives me enough confidence to continue.

'What I meant is, I'd like to be involved in the creative meetings. The meetings I make tea for.'

'We still need tea, Maddie.' As I'm about to respond, she holds up her hand. 'I know.' She sighs and gets up from behind her desk. 'I'm sorry.'

I breathe out. 'You are?'

'Yes,' she says. 'I am. You're right – you have good ideas, fresh ones. You're innovative and assertive. When I was an editorial assistant, I didn't have the courage to ask my manager for what I wanted and I should have. I always knew I should have.' She folds her arms. 'I consider you an asset, Maddie,' she says. 'It's not a bad thing to recognise that, so, yes, you can join the creative meetings.' She lowers herself behind her desk. 'I still expect you to get your admin tasks done, however.' She closes her eyes and places a finger and thumb to them.

Fuck it. 'Are you all right, Penny?'

She looks at me, her mouth slipping open, and for once I don't see her mind working on something else behind the scenes. It's gone and her mind is whirring again. She turns back to her computer. 'Of course I am, Maddie.'

In the afternoon, Penny exits her office and the editors gather around. The senior team, along with Sales, Marketing and Publicity, are meeting with an illustrator (I think her name is Charlotte) they've been watching for weeks in one of the conference rooms. From what I understand, Charlotte blew up overnight because of a set of illustrations she did for a restaurant's website and now so many food writers want her drawings in their books instead of photographs.

'Now, as I said,' Penny continues, 'we found out from the agent that the primary reason we're being considered is because they found out we pay our illustrators of colour the same standard rate as our white illustrators.' She holds her hands up. 'Apparently that's not the case elsewhere. Now, Maddie, bearing in mind you will be one of only two people of colour in this meeting of eleven and I have no intention of parading you around to prove some kind of point, do you want to attend? It's up to you.'

I think there's a contradiction somewhere in what she's said, but I don't really have time to think it through when half the office is staring at me.

Penny smiles and asks, 'In other words, would you like to sit at the table?'

'Yes.'

The Griffiths Room is the largest meeting room in the building, with shelves of books and large bay windows, and is often reserved for the most important meetings. I straighten my trousers and pull my top from where it's sticking. At least at Creative I'd know everyone there, but what if Charlotte starts asking me questions? Thinking on my feet is not an area in which I thrive.

We walk in and Penny says, 'Charlotte, Sam, it's lovely to finally meet you.'

I look around and it's my Sam. I mean, Jo's Sam!

He's not as surprised as I am. 'Hello, Maddie.'

'Sam?' I step towards him. '*This* is your important meeting?'

Penny looks at us. 'The two of you know each other?'

'We've met once or twice before,' Sam says.

I just nod.

'Well, Maddie, since you already know Sam, this is Charlotte, his agent,' Penny says. 'Please take a seat, everyone. Rosie will take our drink requests if you have any.'

I'm usually the one who makes the tea and coffee.

'Maddie, sit beside me, please.'

I never sit beside Penny. She's usually flanked by other senior members of staff, of which there are many present today. I take the seat she gestures towards and diligently take notes as Rob from Marketing and Sadie from Sales lead the meeting. I sneak glances at Sam and my pen slips on the page whenever he catches me. He's very good-looking, but then I think of what Shu said concerning my 'funky taste in men'. Sam's face is made up of hard, straight lines, but his brown eyes soften him. Maybe he's only good-looking to me? I catch both Sadie and Thea staring at Sam's lips whilst he talks.

Maybe not.

It's an impressive pitch and Sam says as much at the end of the hour, along with, 'I'm afraid I have to leave now.'

'Meeting with another publisher?' Penny asks.

Sam laughs. 'No, I promise, and to prove it, Charlotte's going to stay behind and catch me up later.'

Penny says, 'In that case, Maddie will show you out.'

I nod – that's fine. I usually do that, too.

Sam says goodbye to everyone and we've reached the building's entrance door before he says, 'You didn't say much.'

'I tend to just take the minutes in meetings like that.'

He folds his arms. 'Did you manage to talk to your boss in the end?'

'Penny, yes. That's why I was even sat in your meeting. I think things are going to change, but only time will tell.'

'Good for you.' He seems to genuinely mean it.

'You didn't seem that surprised to see me.'

'Well, I wasn't sure I would. I knew I'd be seeing members of Marketing, Sales, Publicity and Editorial, but I assumed only Penny and Thea from the latter.' He looks at the door briefly. 'Maddie, will you have dinner with me? How do you feel about burgers?'

'It's one of my favourite food groups but . . . you're asking me on a date? Can we do that?'

'How do you mean?'

'What about Jo?'

'Is me having . . .' He presses his lips together and thinks of a better way to define their relationship. 'Is the two of us having been involved a problem for you?'

'Shouldn't it be?'

He smiles. 'Are you asking me, Maddie?'

'Right.' I shake my head. 'I should make that decision.'

'For what it's worth,' he says, briefly holding out his hand as if to physically offer me his thoughts, 'I really hope it isn't a problem.' I think about how both of mine could fit into one of his. 'Jo's great, as you know . . .'

Debatable.

'But we didn't make much sense outside of . . . well.'

I nod, only eighty per cent sure he's referring to their physical relationship.

He gestures to the notebook and pen I have pressed to my chest. Inside the cover, he writes down a number and hands it back to me. 'Ball's officially in your court. Just think about it. If it is too uncomfortable a thought, "no, thank you, Sam" is a viable message to send me.' He smiles again and I judge him, wondering if he's ever really heard those four words from a woman before.

'Okay.'

'And if you do decide to message me,' he says, 'will you mind if I don't pick OTP to work with?'

'Of course not, but I think you should pick us.'

'Why's that?' He leans forward and whispers, 'I thought they were stealing your ideas.'

Shit. 'First of all, everything I told you was strictly confidential and cannot be used against us. Second of all, your editor would be Thea and you shouldn't tar every editor with the same brush.'

'Fair point.'

'And third of all, I could give you the usual speech that every publisher in this auction has given you, about how hard they work, how much they love you and your art and their promise to do big things and make you the next XYZ, but I think you noticed we didn't say too much of that. We tell you what we know we can do, which is impressive in and of itself, then when you sign our contract, we go away and figure out how we're going to do better. That's what we do here. We do more and we do . . . better.' I lift my chin. 'It's also worth mentioning that I might be part of your editorial team and I've recently been told I have very good ideas. *Fresh* ideas.'

'Wow, I'll keep that in mind,' he says, smiling. '*Fresh* ideas, you say. Well, it would be foolish to turn that down.'

Chapter Forty-One

How do I feel about Sam?

That's a good question. What I know is that he's hand-some, tall, softly spoken and creative. He might also be funny and kind, but I've realised these things must prove themselves in time in order to be true. I know he and Jo have history, casual history, but history nonetheless.

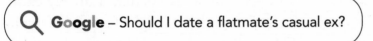

Q **Google** – Should I date a flatmate's casual ex?

The nuance of my request proves too much for Google to comprehend and instead throws up responses for: can I date my friend's ex? I briefly consider the fact that my first descriptor for Jo is not *friend* but the more ambiguous *flatmate*.

Grace: Absolutely not

Erin: Is he tall?

Olu: Depends how close you are. If she's your best friend then no but if you just know her like if you saw her on the street you might not even wave, then it's fine

Megan: Were they official or was it some kind of 2 week thing

Debs: How did they end things? If he cheated on her that means you don't care about her feelings or how the relationship affected her. If it was amicable then I don't see why not

Maddie
Jo's ex (casual sex, no relationship I think) asked me out to dinner. Should I go?

Shu
Who's Jo?

Nia
Is he nice?

Maddie
Jo's my flatmate
I think so

Nia
You could use some nice

Shu
The one we don't like? Go for it.
You and her ain't even close so why not?

Maddie
Well, if we look at Dante's Inferno, the ninth circle of Hell is reserved for women who betray other women.

Shu
Who the fuck is Dante Inferno?

Nia

If you want to feel less guilty maybe you should talk to

Jo

See how she feels

But you know you don't have to say yes

when a guy asks you out Right?

Maddie

I know

Shu

I have to get back to work. I'll check in later

Maddie

Sorry, Shu. I forget you don't like group chats

Nia

You don't have to date if you don't want to. If it were me, after the couple of months you've had, I'd move to the woods

Maddie

It has been pretty full on, huh?

Nia

Talk to Jo

Update us

Shu

If she tries to swing at you lemme know

After work I find Jo in the garden sat in a chair with her head back, appealing to the lowering sun.

'Mind if I sit?'

With trepidation, she responds, 'Sure.'

Her top is off-shoulder and thin blue veins trail her skin, whilst brown freckles fill in the gaps. I think about how I've only noticed how many freckles she has nearing the end of my time here.

'Firstly, I'm going to be moving out to live with my friend Nia.'

She looks at me. 'Why aren't you telling this to Cam, too?'

'She already knows.' Jo pushes her mouth down and shrugs subtly. 'Second, Sam came into OTP. We're hoping to publish his next set of illustrations. He asked me to have dinner with him and I'm going to say yes.'

Jo breathes through her nose, and rubs her left eye with the heel of her palm. 'I knew it,' she says. 'He kept looking at you.' She turns away to stare at the ground. Where Sam sat only yesterday. 'Here, in the garden for my birthday. I thought you were genuinely oblivious, then you went to "stretch your legs" and he followed.'

I hear her quote marks. 'That is what happened, at least on my end,' I tell her. 'It wasn't orchestrated.'

'You sure?'

'Why would we do that?'

Jo returns her attention to the sun. 'What you do is your business, Maddie. I suppose it's convenient you're leaving; it would piss me off having to hear you fucking him from across the landing.'

The last bit of what she says draws my head back; the flippancy and lack of emotion behind it makes it seem like that's who she thinks I am. That I'd date Sam to upset her or because I've got nothing better to do.

Because I'm tired, I say, 'Sorry.'

When she looks at me I'm reminded of the Jo I met for the first time. It's strange that she looks so much older now, tenser and a little tired. Is that my doing? My presence in the flat and in her life? I forget that people don't just affect me, but that I affect others – that I even can affect others. I assume people meet me, I leave and their world carries on like it did before I arrived. I'm suddenly curious to know how Ben is doing. How Alex is doing.

'Can I be honest?'

I hesitantly zone back to Jo. 'Of course.'

'I don't see us being friends when you leave.'

'Are we really friends now?'

Her sad smile throws me. 'No, and I guess we never were. We were always just . . . flatmates.'

We look at one another until she gets up and walks back into the house. A little lighter, I notice.

I wonder if she's right. There was a time I'd assumed we were friends – or at least, that she wanted to be my friend. I have her number saved in my phone. We had dinner out together; she picked what I wore for my first adult date; we went to a club where she asked me to stay when I said it might be time for me to leave. But maybe the prerequisites for making friends, *real* friends, aren't that simple.

I look at Jo's empty seat and accept that whilst her confession was sad, it doesn't break my heart.

An hour later, I answer Mum's call.

'Maddie, you need to come home,' she says. 'Can you come right now?'

'What's wrong?'

'Your father's solicitor is here.'

'What?' No. *There can't be more debt. I don't have any money left.* 'Why? I paid the last council tax arrears earlier this year! I wrote the date and reference number down somewhere. Tell him there are no more outstanding bills; I checked with everyone.'

'Maddie, the solicitor is here to read your father's will,' she says. 'It's not about bills. Come now, please and he says bring ID. Jump on the first train.'

Mr Ackah, Dad's solicitor, is a tall man with greying hair, oval glasses and a dark suit. I've never seen him before in my life. He offers his condolences and takes a seat on the sofa opposite where Mum sits. James is sat at the dining table.

I've chosen to remain by the door. 'I didn't even know Dad had a lawyer or had written a will.'

'You didn't?' Mr Ackah says.

'No, I . . . I don't think he has anything.'

'He invested some money a decade ago and it's been growing in interest since.'

Mum sits up straighter.

'You'll be splitting that with us,' James says quickly.

'Will I? Maddie will get a little bit, of course – she has spent a lot of money on this family, but I'll need the rest. I need financial help in Ghana,' she says. 'It's not free to live and work there and you are both financially secure enough.' James's jaw locks. 'What?' she says, looking at us in turn. 'It is only money; you both should not be so attached to this Earth's material things. Matthew six, verse nineteen.'

Un-fucking-believable.

Mum turns back to Mr Ackah. 'So, how much is there?'

He looks at me. 'Can I confirm your name is Madeleine Wright and you are the daughter of George Wright.'

My tongue feels dry. 'Yes, I am.'

'Did you bring some form of identification?'

I give him my passport.

'Good, good.'

'What's going on with the money then?' Mum asks.

Mr Ackah looks at her over the top of his oval glasses. 'He's left it all to Madeleine. Fifty thousand pounds.'

The room begins to spin and both Mum and James look at me.

'What?' Mum says. 'All of it?'

'Yes, all of it,' he answers. 'Now, Madeleine, due to the amount, you need not pay inheritance tax. If you need further help regarding what you'd like to do next, you can contact me at any time. Your father was very fond of you. I'm sorry that he is no longer with us, but I hope you know that he wanted you to be well taken care of.'

I pull my jumper away from my neck. 'But I don't under-stand,' I tell him. 'Isn't the money for everyone?'

'Your father was adamant it was left solely in your name,' he says. 'I chose not to ask any questions and I suspect you all know why he might have done this better than I do. He was well enough, according to his doctor, a Doctor . . .' He checks a piece of paper. 'Emmanuel Appong, who declared him of sound body and mind when he drafted this will. I believe it had been a year after his diagnosis when he signed it and his condition was still stable.' Mr Ackah removes his glasses. 'Madeleine, you can of course do as you please, but this money is now yours. Your father didn't have anything else.'

I stand there silent but hear James say, 'What's wrong, Mum?'

I turn and notice she looks blindsided by the news.

James however is smiling, resting his hand on her shoulder. 'You're not upset about *not* getting the money, are you?' he says, and his gold tooth glints. 'After all, you shouldn't be so attached to this Earth's material things. Matthew six, verse nineteen.'

Chapter Forty-Two

'Have you decided what you're going to spend the money on?' Nia asks.

I'm speed-walking through Shoreditch trying not to bump into anyone as I speak through my earphones and follow Google Maps at the same time.

'I thought maybe I could donate some of the money to a Parkinson's disease charity, but there are so many. I need to keep researching.'

'That's a really nice idea, Mads,' she says. 'How's James taking the news? Must be a bit of a blow.'

'I think he was upset, but he knows he wasn't around when I was dealing with a lot.'

'Good, as he should,' Nia replies. 'Are we still on for viewing the flats on Saturday? We got two in Brixton and one in Crouch End, which is kind of far but looks really nice.'

I smile, remembering Avi once suggested I move to Crouch End. 'It's not far,' I tell Nia. 'Oh, I can see the burger place and Sam is sitting at the window. He's seen me; I have to go. I'll see you on Saturday.'

'See you on Saturday.'

'Okay,' I say, swallowing a mouthful. 'This is the best burger I've ever had.'

'I told you.'

'Could you look a little less smug?'

Sam, in jeans and a knitted grey jumper, scratches where his beard is growing and says, 'This is me trying, so no?'

'Regardless, thank you for bringing me here. I had no idea this place existed.'

This burger bar tucks itself into a corner in Shoreditch. It's decorated like a cabin, with framed photos on the wall and a bar at the front. The lights are low and our window looks out onto the street and a corner section of Old Spitalfields Market.

'My pleasure,' he says. 'Are OTP happy to have me?'

'Extremely. They didn't think they'd get you, we know we didn't offer the most money.'

'You still offered a lot and I liked Thea's art direction the most.'

'Penny thinks your decision had something to do with me.'

'That would be highly unethical – let's leave it at that,' he says, smiling. 'I am still a little surprised you messaged me.'

'Really?'

'You seemed concerned about my history with Jo.'

'I managed to talk to her about it.'

'I heard.'

He talks to his ex because they're still friends. Is that a red flag?

He must see my expression because he clarifies. 'I also spoke to her about us; it should have been a conversation I had with her anyway. She suspected more was going on between us because apparently you looked very guilty.'

'That is how I felt.'

'Why?' he asks.

'I don't know. It's another thing I'm working on.'

'Do you often feel guilty for things that aren't actually your fault?'

My elbow slips from the table while he casually picks at his plate as if to defuse how big a question that is.

'Why did you ask me that?'

'I just want to know how you're doing,' he replies.

'Is it because of the whole "I'm sad" thing in the garden? Look, I know that was weird. I'm really sorry—'

'Don't apologise,' he says. 'I'm asking because when you said it, it came from somewhere deep and I felt it.'

'I was being dramatic.'

'Maybe not.'

I frown. 'Sam, why do you care?'

'Because I didn't once before. With someone I knew.'

'Right.' I put my burger down and push my plate away. 'That's why you asked me to dinner. Pity?'

His eyebrows shoot up. 'What? No.'

I don't know what happens, but my brain switches off and then coloured sparks fly. I have to blink and rub my eyes to get rid of them.

'If you must know, Sam, no, I'm not doing very well today,' I say. 'Which is so frustrating because I thought I'd be better by now. I was supposed to have done the six stages of grief thing, I was supposed to be used to the guilt, and some days I am and feel good and together, but other days I feel like I'm back at square one and I just want to know when I'm going to be fine again.' I have to grip the table to breathe out the air I didn't take in. 'So there, Sam. There you go.'

'Maddie.'

I don't want him to look at me, so I cover my face with my hands and try to calm my breathing. I started crying a while ago. I hate that people might be looking at me but the thought doesn't stop the tears from spilling.

A thumb begins stroking the back of my hand before I hear his chair pull from the table. When I look up, Sam and our food are gone. I sit, trying to wipe my face as best as I can when he returns with paper bags.

'The leftovers taste even better in the morning.' He hands me one of the bags and takes my other hand – it's warm and swallows mine. 'Come with me, Maddie.'

We step out into the warm evening and silently Sam walks me down a straight road. He still holds my hand, his fingers slotted in between mine. I don't know a lot about him but I feel as if I could close my eyes, sink into his warmth, and still arrive wherever we're going intact. We walk for ten minutes before we make a right and enter an ice-cream shop. He sits me at a table and goes to the counter, where there are rows and rows of ice-cream containers. It's bright in here and the shop's name, *Moophoria*, is in neon lights behind the counter. When Sam returns, he places a cup of ice cream in front of me.

'Thank you.' I take a spoonful and the sugar makes my eye twitch. 'This is very sweet.'

'They make it like that on purpose,' Sam says. 'It's good for shock.'

I look at him, knowing I wouldn't blame him for cutting this date short. 'Thank you, again. Sincerely.'

'You're welcome.'

'Why is yours green?' I ask.

'It's mint.'

'Eugh.'

'You don't like mint chocolate ice cream?' he asks incredulously.

'Do you like eating chocolate after you've brushed your teeth?'

'Not the same thing.' He offers me his spoon. 'Here, try some.'

I taste his and, 'Okay, it's not the same.'

'See?'

'But it's not far off.'

He smiles but puts his spoon down. 'Want to talk about what just happened?'

I clear my throat and shift in my seat. 'I don't know if I have anything else to add.'

'Then I'll just answer your question.' Sam leans across the table. 'You are.'

'What question?'

'When are you going to be fine again?' Sam clarifies. 'And I'm saying, you are fine. This is your new fine, Maddie.'

I consider this. 'That's depressing.'

He laughs without joy. 'I know it sounds it. But you're not supposed to "get over" someone dying,' he says, 'especially someone you loved, and your feelings of guilt may not be justified, but they are natural. Thing is, you don't ever go back, Maddie, to life before, and my advice is to accept that. To accept that you're not the same person you were when your dad was alive and you can't be again. Accept that your life is different now because of this monumental, irreversible change and that it's okay to feel guilt one day and indescribable happiness another. *This* is life now,' he says. 'This is how you live.'

He lifts his spoon and stirs his ice cream until it melts. *It's good for shock.*

375

'Have you lost someone?'

He pushes his ice cream to the side and wipes his hands. 'Little over a month ago, I lost a close friend of mine to suicide,' he says. And right there he turns into a different Sam, a more haunted Sam. 'He'd been secretly battling depression and drug addiction and the day before he died, he called and asked to hang out. I think he might have said he *needed* to hang out.' Sam shakes his head. 'It's funny what you don't hear when you should have been listening. I said I was too busy working on a project, the very same project that's just secured me a contract. A contract and advance that feels very tainted. Maybe if I'd agreed to meet him . . . We always think we'll see death coming and that we'll have more time, until we're reminded otherwise.'

So it wasn't a fight he'd had. His friend had killed himself. I slide my ice cream towards him. 'I'm so sorry, Sam.'

He looks up at me. 'Thank you.'

'So you asked me out because . . . we have that in common? Because we know what the other is going through?'

'No,' he says. 'Maddie, I asked you out because when I sat talking to you about my mother, I felt like we had a lot more to say to each other. I like when people speak honestly, in a way that suggests they can't help it. I'm very attracted to you. Those are my reasons. Having someone close to us die is where that common link ends. The relationship you had with your dad is different to the one I had with Connor. I don't mean to say in intensity or duration, but they just can't be compared. Having lost someone doesn't mean you understand what it's like when someone else grieves.' He sighs. 'We seem to be developing a thing where we only have serious talks when we meet – I'm sorry.'

'Don't be,' I say. 'I like it. The honesty. I don't have to overthink.'

'I'm a fun guy, really.'

'Only non-fun guys say that.'

'Well,' and he smiles, 'give me some time to prove it.'

And I think I will.

I wonder what Subconscious Maddie thinks of Sam; I've not heard from her in a while.

Dearest Maddie. Thank you for getting in touch. I'm currently out of office and on annual leave for the foreseeable because, quite frankly, I need a fucking break. If your query is urgent, please contact Your Gut. She should be able to help.

Best wishes,

Subconscious Maddie

The following morning, I text Sam.

> **Maddie**
> You were right. The burger does taste better in the morning.

As an immediate reply, he sends a picture of himself, mouth full, burger in hand, with the caption: *Great minds . . .*

Chapter Forty-Three

A few weeks later

After lunch at his local pub, we go back to Sam's place. He recently bought a one-bedroom flat in Muswell Hill, which made choosing Nia and I's flat in Crouch End much simpler.

His kitchen is small but tidy, and everything has its place. I know inside his cupboard is a box of green tea for me. I like that the window above the sink is large and looks out to an apple tree.

We drink tea and split the giant doughnut we bought at the Farmers' Market, sixty-forty to me.

As Sam washes our plates in the sink, I shuffle on the spot.

'Are you loitering, Maddie?'

'Yes.'

He smiles but carries on with the washing. 'Okay.'

'Shall we have sex then?' I ask. 'I'm not too full.'

He laughs and I watch small soap bubbles with pink edges escape the sink. 'Do you want to have sex?' he asks.

It hadn't been on my mind for a while until yesterday evening. We were at dinner with Sam's friends (maybe they're my friends now, too?), Juliette and Aiden, and it was only when Aiden took out his wallet to pay and I saw a condom in one of the slots did I remember that couples have sex.

When I don't answer, Sam turns around and says, 'That means no.'

'We've been dating for three weeks,' I say. 'We've been on ten official dates and you pay for most of them.'

He frowns. 'And sex is my reward?'

'No, of course not. I don't know why I said that.'

'Okay.'

'I do want to have sex with you,' I say. 'I just don't want to have sex.'

Sam dries his hands on a tea towel. 'Why is that?'

My instinct is to lie. The day I told Alex the truth was the last day I ever saw him. I want to keep seeing Sam and—

'Maddie, stop having conversations with yourself in your head and tell me the truth.'

Well, damn. 'Sex is painful,' I answer. 'For me. Painful and . . . distant, maybe. I just want to have the sex I've heard about, but I don't know how.'

He considers me. 'Have you tried doing it alone?'

I look away.

'Maddie?'

'It's . . . it's not really my thing.'

'That's fine. Are you always wet?'

I chew my lip and try to think. 'Maybe?'

'Have you ever been on top?' he asks.

'During sex? No, I tend to just lie there.'

He steps forward and holds out his hand. 'Would you like to try that?'

I take his hand and slot my fingers through his. 'Yes, I would.'

∗   ∗   ∗

In Sam's bedroom, my heart thumps in my ears when he closes the door. It's a large room with the bed's headboard under an alcove and a desk, covered in his artwork, situated in front of the window.

I wipe my forehead when his back is turned. We undress and he's very slow with me. He brushes his fingers against my skin and I shiver. He puts a condom on and there's no shuffle under the duvet or asking if I'm on the pill. Sam starts to kiss me and, naturally, I relax because we kiss all the time, until he's sat on his bed and gently pulls me in. I trip over my feet and fall onto him, my elbow hitting him in the cheek.

'Sam, I'm so sorry.'

'It's okay.' He smiles, amused. 'Maddie, it's okay. Let's try something else.'

Sam lies me on my back and climbs off to push a pillow under my waist. He presses a palm to each of my thighs to pull them apart; I resist at first, like an elastic band that won't pull any further.

'Is everything all right?'

I lift my head. 'Yes. Sorry.'

'That's okay. We can go slower.'

He leans over me, balancing himself on his arms, and slowly kisses my neck. His lips are warm and his kisses bury deep into my throat when he uses his tongue, bites and pulls away. He does this along my chest and my nails dig into his arms when he sucks on my nipples. I arch my back in an attempt to ease the pulsing between my thighs.

The warmth leaves my skin when Sam sinks to his knees. I know where he's going to put his head next, I've seen it happen enough times on screen, and sweat begins to drip down my back.

I hope I smell okay down there, but I don't think anyone smells like honey. Just don't think about it. I pick a spot on the ceiling and focus on it because there's something too open and vulnerable about being naked and ... there. There for anyone to see. For months, being naked has been synonymous with having a man on top of me with barely any room left to breathe—

I gasp and my instinct is to pull my knees up, but Sam has a gentle grip on both. I ball the sheets into my palms as he takes me in his mouth, sucks and pulls between tongue-heavy kisses. I swallow a cry as Sam makes his way deeper into where my heart now thuds and again he has to hold my thighs apart. His grip now firm because I can't keep still. He feels ... and this feels ... *incredible*.

I want to say this out loud, but then he presses his tongue flat and I say his name instead. I say it over and over because it's the only intelligible word on my tongue and Sam likes that, it's his incentive to go faster and heavier.

I hook my legs across his shoulders and, with greedy panic, I press him in deeper because I think it would be unbelievable if he'd take more of me and he obeys without a word. It's a soft bite that makes me climax, that makes me scream and forget my own name.

Sam stops; I'm left shaking and would really like to fall asleep.

I close my eyes and wonder if he'll kiss me and if I want him to; if I want to know what I taste like. I decide that maybe I don't and he doesn't.

He climbs on top of me and I wrap my thighs around him because I want to do that again, to feel that release again. How do I make him feel what I just did?

His skin is soft and his smell familiar; it brings to mind the comfort of borrowed jumpers and nights on his sofa in front of the TV; drinks under his arm when out with friends, and hugs hello. He enters me and the pain builds the further in he goes. I'm about to ask him to stop, then he's all the way in, my pulse triples and the pleasure from before returns. I have to grip onto the backs of his shoulders. There's an exquisite pull in my stomach and he gasps as I move with him to deepen the pull. He moans into my neck and the desperate sounds coming from him make me love him, make me want to hold him forever.

He falls back and I stretch to meet him, pushing my hips forward and then back down and repeat, repeat, repeat. I bury my face in his neck and the creaks of his mattress come closer together. He wraps his arms around my waist. I moan and he begs.

When he stills and comes he says, 'Fuck, Maddie,' and I almost cry.

From: Eloise.Forrester@simoneballad.com
To: Mad.Wright@gmail.com
Subject: Untitled Manuscript

Dear Maddie,

I hope you're well.

I understand you've now been told you weren't selected for the Carrow Books Mentorship Programme. I hope you weren't too disheartened because I was the literary agent assigned your sample and I found it to be raw, compelling and extremely emotive for such a short passage. I did wonder if you'd sent it in its earliest form because it did feel rushed and incomplete, even for that style of writing.

This was mainly why you weren't selected for the programme. However, I think there is something there. Your application stated that this was currently a Untitled Work In Progress, but Jess, your protagonist, intrigues me, as does her relationship with her father. I'd be happy for you to submit to me when this manuscript is ready.

All the best,
Eloise Forrester

Epilogue

We didn't get to choose where in the cemetery Dad was buried, but he's under the branches of the largest tree. So although I don't always recognise my path, I always recognise that tree.

I jog when I get closer and kneel when I reach him.

'Hi, Dad.' I pull out some weeds and brush away loose rubble; I'm used to the insects now. 'It's just me today. Sam says hi; he wanted to come, but he needs to finish off some artwork samples and I told him he doesn't have to come with me all the time.' It's a little windy, but the sun is out so I pull a small blanket from my bag and sit on the grass. 'He's a good egg, isn't he? That means a good person, by the way. I don't know how familiar you were with British idioms. I don't know where that phrase derives actually; I might google it later.

'Work's good,' I continue. 'Penny tells me I'm four to six months away from making assistant editor if I stay on track. I'm also . . . I'm also writing something about you.' I pull out my printed nine hundred and seventy-one words and Eloise's email. 'I don't know why I brought this with me,' I say, waving the papers. 'Just wanted to show you. Anyway, I drafted the first three chapters and Eloise wants the entire thing now, so I'm kind of . . . making us into a book. Nothing's been promised and maybe nothing will happen, but it would be nice, wouldn't it? To immortalise you here, somehow.' I shrug and return the pages to my bag. 'It's probably nothing but worth trying, right?'

Mum said I don't need to keep visiting Dad's grave except to tidy it up and lay flowers out of respect. 'If you want to speak to him,' she said, 'then you look up. You must speak to his soul, not his empty body.' This I can agree with, but if I'm here anyway, I like to sit and talk to Dad about a lot of things.

'Sam took me to a really nice restaurant the other night where I had the best risotto and apple tart I've ever had. Shu and Lydia spent the weekend with me and Nia; Nia and Shu are quite different, but they get on well enough, and it helps that Lydia is loud enough to fill any silences. James is currently in Manchester, but we spoke on the phone this morning. He likes to call even if he hasn't got much to say. Mum's flight back to Ghana is coming up and I've booked to go with her for three weeks. I'll spend two in Accra and one in Kumasi. It'll be nice to see where you both grew up.'

Mum calls at that very moment. 'I'll call her back. She also calls me a lot now; usually after I've been to therapy, to ask what I spoke about. She doesn't agree with everything: "always childhood, childhood. Is no mother safe from criticism?" But she doesn't disagree with everything either, and that's something. She's also started talking to me about grandad and her childhood. Of course, Ghana was more challenging than the UK, because she had to walk hundreds of miles to school in sandals, through jungles with tigers roaming free and snakes in the trees. Apparently.' I roll my eyes. 'But she listens and that's new. Sometimes I talk and there's silence and she'll say "Go on, I'm just listening." I can tell when she's biting her tongue and sometimes she can't help herself, but that's fine. Baby steps. Oh, now she's sent a text.' I read it out loud.

Mum LONDON
Do you think Sam will propose soon?
Does he know he needs my blessing?
I will give him my blessing but still he must ask.

After a while I say, 'Dad, I should go. Sam's mum's coming round for lunch and she prefers it when everything is home-made, so I need time to reheat and convincingly plate the food Mum made the night before.' I pull my knees to my chin and look at Dad's headstone a little longer before getting to my feet. 'See you soon, *okay?*'

The sun gleams against his marble headstone and throws a strip of light onto my face. I laugh and look up to a patch of blue sky.

'Subtle, Dad,' I tell him, squinting in the sun. 'Really subtle.'

Acknowledgements

I will *attempt* to keep this short because if I don't, I run the risk of this being pages long and you've already read an entire book. If I don't succeed, know that I tried.

Every author says this (perhaps because it's true) but I couldn't have done this without three special people. First up, we have literary agent extraordinaire Jemima Forrester who had nothing but love, laughter and I think a few tears for Maddie the moment she read my manuscript in its earliest stage and rawest form. To Sarah Cantin, my US editor, whose personal, soft spot for Maddie and her father resonated with me so deeply, I knew she was the one as soon as our call had ended. To my UK editor Olivia Barber, who loved *Maame* so much that during the submission and auction process the words 'She won't go down without a fight' were uttered more than once. I'm glad you kept fighting to win *Maame*. I'm not sure it's often an author enjoys a lengthy editing process but as I've mentioned many times, (one particularly long email I sent on the 28th of July comes to mind), I loved it. The three of you make an unrivalled team in my opinion and I love that this is only the beginning for us.

And of course, to my US agent/matchmaker Michelle Bower; thank you for introducing me to the wonder that is Sarah, and for voluntarily joining online meetings at what I imagine felt like the crack of dawn for you.

To Jo, Kimberley and everyone else on the *Maame* team, who I've met in person and have yet to meet, thank you so much for falling in love with *Maame*. I've heard only a fraction of all the magic you're doing for this book and I thank you for it because it's an incredible thing to have Olivia tell me how much of a unanimous decision it was to take me on as an author.

To my mum, who, although more thoughtful and supportive than Maddie's, is just as full of funny one-liners. To this day my favourite continues to be this Valentine's Day special:

> **Mummy Dearest**
> Darling
> Have you a valentine this year?

> Me
> No, mum

> **Mummy Dearest**
> Ok.
> Let Jesus be your valentine.

I couldn't make up your one-liners up if I tried. Although I jest, I can't describe what it's like or means to have a mother who constantly thinks of and prays for you, especially when I remember you do so because you truly believe it's the greatest thing you can do for me. I hope to never forget that. Thanks for eventually coming round to my dream of being an author after I mercilessly trampled on your dreams of me becoming a lawyer/doctor/veterinarian. To my older brother who unknowingly saved me when he refused to get off the phone until I asked a friend to come and stay with me, and to my younger brother who, whenever I'm asked to talk about him, my first response is: 'I just love him very much'.

There is a reason why Nia and Shu are undisputed favourites for readers. To Ashleigh La'Rose Wright Mitchell, my very own Nia, who *never* runs out of pride and encouragement when it comes to everything I put my mind to. I can't quite describe Ashleigh, you just have to know her and it's a downright shame some of you never will. In a world of fair weather friendships and fickle acquaintances, the greatest thing anyone can do, is have an Ashleigh in their corner. I try not to think on it too deeply, but if you hadn't dropped everything and packed a bag to come and stay with me when my dad died, I might not have written this story. I don't say how grateful I am to have you in my life enough but now that I've written this book, perhaps I won't always have to (even though I'm sure it's always nice to hear).

To Camila Bloise, my Shu, who I'm certain has no idea she kept me as 'Jess' when my dad died. I was saying to myself just the other day that for more than a decade, despite different universities, jobs, friendship groups and area codes, we always find our way back to each other. I often think about the time I sat you down in the Dishoom in King's Cross after you brought me back so much chocolate and candy from the US it warranted an extra suitcase, just to tell you how much I loved you and wished I'd appreciated you more years before. I've not stopped appreciating you since and now you can't get rid of me. Now I'm the friend who sends you eight-minute-long voice notes about coconut jelly in my bubble tea on a random Wednesday afternoon whilst you're trying to work.

To Chris Modafferi because she is the ultimate, feel-great-about-yourself hype woman and every author needs a

Chris. Nobody effervesces quite like you do and I hope you know that. To Delal Jamal, simply because I still have that card you brought me, with **the best is yet to be** on the front, when after hundreds of submission rejections, I found an agent.

Last but by no means least, to Dad – obviously. Thank you for everything even when you weren't doing much. Writing this book has reminded me of a lot and I'm so grateful for that. I'm so grateful to have been given the opportunity to immortalise you in print, our wordless memories trapped within paper and ink. Our introverted tendencies meant we have hardly any photos or videos together, and I've heard a lot about how it can get harder and harder to remember a loved one the more time passes after their death. I know it has nothing to do with how much you loved the person or how much they meant to you, and I don't see myself forgetting certain things about you on purpose, but alas, memory and age are not the greatest of partners. That combined with a lack of photographic evidence needed to illuminate a fading memory, it wasn't looking good for me. Now, I'll always have this book. So the dedication at the beginning reads: *For Dad*, but secretly, in invisible ink perhaps, it reads *For Jess* as well. This book is for days when my memory could use an extra bit of help.

Dad, I'm not sure if you're reading this as I'm unaware of what the book delivery system is like up there but just in case, I hope you like it. Just don't read the naughty bits. I love you, *okay?*

I said last but not least, but I do have a few words for readers. Thank you for taking the time out to read *Maame* when there is a literal sea of books you could have selected from. If I may, if you have a loved one in your life, write something down about them. Take a picture and record a video and keep them safe, for days when your memory could use an extra bit of help.

So, how did I do? Too long?

Jess x

Credits

There are so many people working behind the scenes to put a book into your hands, so I wanted to say a huge thank you to the whole Hodder & Stoughton team for their support for *Maame*.

Editorial
Olivia Barber

Copy editor
Jade Craddock

Proof reader
Kay Gale

Audio
Ellie Wheeldon

Contracts
Emma Mojarab
Ellen Harber

Design
Alasdair Oliver
Kate Brunt
Natalie Chen

Editorial Operations
Jei Degenhardt
Cecilia Rushton

Marketing
Vickie Boff
Katy Blott
Laura Bartholomew
Sofia Hericson

Production
Rachel Southey

Publicity
Rebecca Mundy
Oliver Martin
Maya Conway

Sales
Catherine Worsley
Isobel Smith
Richard Peters
Drew Hunt
Kerri Logan
Sinead White
Georgina Cutler